SHADOWS OF WAR

UNBROKEN FIRE

ANNE WHEELER

For Andy.

But I say to you, love your enemies and pray for those who
persecute you . . .

MATTHEW 5:44

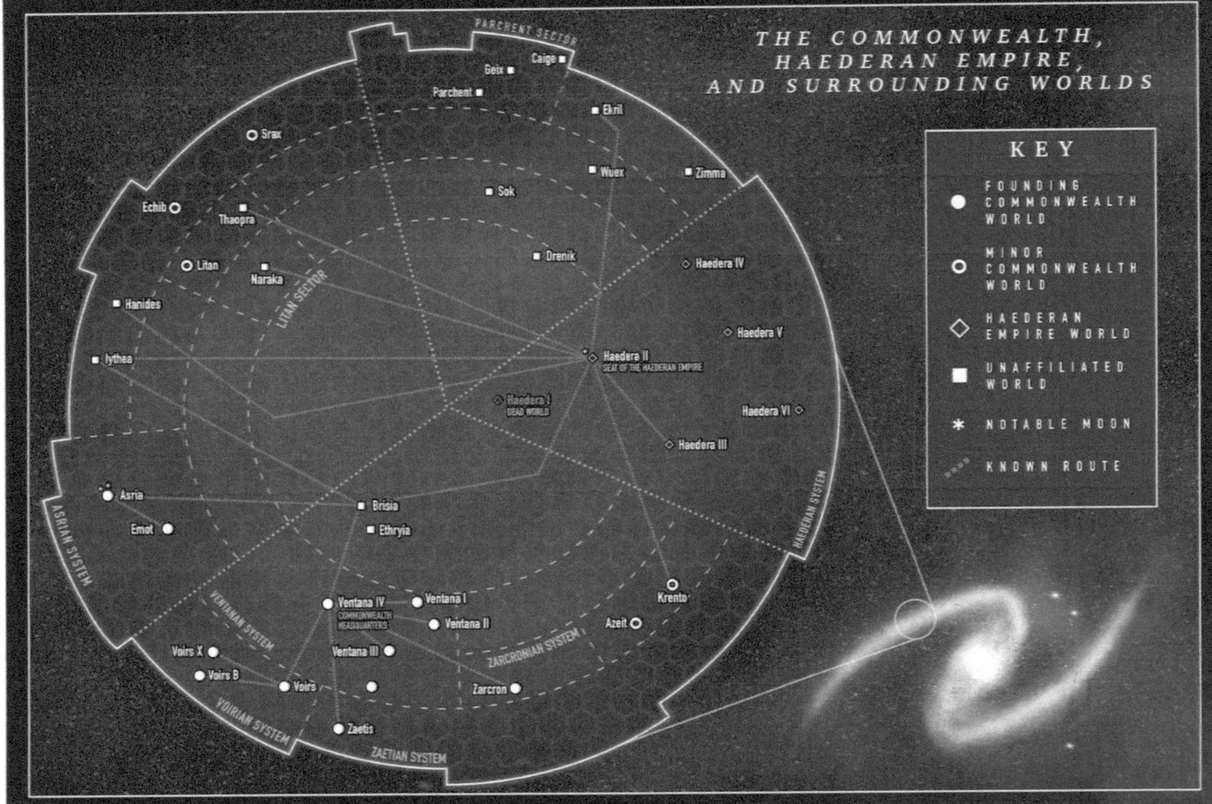

THE COMMONWEALTH, HAEDERAN EMPIRE, AND SURROUNDING WORLDS
KEY
FOUNDING COMMONWEALTH WORLD
MINOR COMMONWEALTH WORLD
HAEDERAN EMPIRE WORLD
UNAFFILIATED WORLD
NOTABLE MOON
KNOWN ROUTE
PARCHENT SECTOR
Caige
Geix
Parchent
Ekril
Srax
Wuex
Zimma
Sok
Echib
Thaopra
Drenik
Haedera IV
Litan
Naraka
LITAN SECTOR
Hanides
Haedera V
Iythea
Haedera II
SEAT OF THE HAEDERAN EMPIRE
Haedera I
DEAD WORLD
Haedera VI
Haedera III
HAEDERAN SYSTEM
Asria
Brisia
Emot
Ethryia
ASRIAN SYSTEM
Krento
Ventana IV
COMMONWEALTH HEADQUARTERS
Ventana I
Ventana II
Azeit
VENTANAN SYSTEM
Ventana III
ZARCRONIAN SYSTEM
Voirs X
Voirs B
Voirs
Zarcron
VOIRIAN SYSTEM
Zaetis
ZAETIAN SYSTEM

CHAPTER ONE

There was nothing left.

Nothing but white ash and charred wood and blackened stone.

Avery dropped another scorched book to the ground and watched as the pages floated away in the wind. Back at the Defense Forces base at Villiers, they'd told her Sabino had been destroyed, but this level of devastation was shocking. The outbuildings where she'd spent her childhood watching wine production—and sampling when the workers' backs were turned—were leveled. The stately home where she'd grown up, which had stood through countless wildfires and the occasional earthquake, had been gutted by fire. The Haederans had been thorough in their destruction.

She tried to wipe the remains of the book's pages onto her pants, but the soot clung to her, leaving marks on her arms, though it didn't show on her long, dark curls. Her seemingly clean hair was a bright spot, vain though it may be. There weren't any other bright spots today. She and Hadley had dodged Haederan patrols the whole way from Villiers—had it been worth it?

Probably not.

A low whistle sounded through one of the three vineyards

where her father had grown his most prized grapes, all of them now burned to the ground. It wouldn't have surprised her if the Haederans had tainted the soil as well, making sure nothing grew at the Sabino estate for the next two hundred years, but so far, her sensors had picked up nothing except ash.

That was promising. Perhaps she could do something with the land if Asria ever threw off their invaders. The faintest bubbles of hope welled up. She would do it with Merritt, if the Haederans ever released him.

The bubbles popped.

The Haederans would never let him go, not after the ill-fated attack on Alcaris that had resulted in his capture almost a year ago. Merritt wouldn't want her anymore, anyway. Even though she still wore his ring, it had been so long, their relationship so volatile.

She pushed Merritt to the back of her mind and hurried through the ash in search of Hadley's whistle—he must have found something that interested him. She found him crouched over a flat door in the ground that led to an underground shelter, and her lips tilted up in one of her first genuine smiles in weeks. Why hadn't she remembered the shelter? Despite the destruction surrounding them, there was hope.

Hadley popped open the hatch and looked up at her, eyebrows raised.

Still silent. Was he still so angry with her that asking a simple question was so difficult? Apparently so.

Avery shook her head in reply. "I'm not going down there."

Not after what Gareth Chase had done to her. She took a step away from the hatch, her pulse already racing. Even the small merchant ship which had brought her back to Asria had made her so anxious that she'd spent most of the trip in her cabin with her eyes closed. She wasn't going to climb down into a dark hole.

Hadley looked at her with the first sympathy she'd seen from him that day, and, to her surprise, mumbled agreement. He lowered himself into the hole; she tossed him a light and waited. The shelter led far underneath the vineyard, and it would take him at least fifteen minutes to search the whole thing. Maybe the servants had salvaged something. Photos. Mementos of her parents. A backup seed vault. Something, anything. Memories or something more tangible, it wouldn't matter. She dropped to the ground to braid her hair again while she waited.

It wasn't safe to sit here alone—or at all—but Hadley wouldn't have left her here if he thought there was another option. They would hear anyone coming from kilometers away, but they hadn't seen a patrol in hours. Haederan troops were all over the local village, to be sure, but not out here in these agrarian lands. They'd wrought so much destruction on Sabino that no one would be interested in the estate.

Ironically, it was a beautiful day despite the damage. Late spring in Sabino always was, Haederans or no Haederans. The usual oppressive heat hadn't yet descended on the valley, and a cool breeze blew through the mountains, cutting through what little warmth there was. A small lizard eyed her warily from a nearby rock. The birds were enjoying the day as well, their songs the only sound in this part of the vineyard.

Well, besides what sounded like farm equipment in the distance. Life in the valley was returning to normal after the Haederans' invasion, even if the Rendon family would never make wine here again. Still, she was happy for her former neighbors. They didn't deserve to be punished simply for living on the same part of the planet as their erstwhile king and queen.

Avery smiled at the sound. She lay back in the dirt and let the sun beat down on her face as she listened. The lizard had the right idea—because she was too pale. Everyone at Villiers was too pale. The base had artificial sunrooms, of course, but just like on the Commonwealth deep space ships she should have been serving on right now, they were far too booked for everyone to get the time they needed, and she refused to use her position for a guaranteed slot. Today would go a long way in rectifying her pallor, though, and with any luck, she wouldn't look half dead when she and Hadley returned.

The machinery grew louder as the sun beat down on her, and she scrambled to her feet. Were people farming on Rendon land now? She couldn't complain about that, but neighbors would recognize her. Even though the locals supported the royal family more than anyone else on the planet, they couldn't see her. Not here. Not now. She wouldn't put them in that precarious position.

She was debating where to hide when the source of the noise appeared on the far side of the vineyard, and her heart threatened to stop.

Today there were worse things—way worse—than nosy neighbors, and one of those things was coming straight at her.

It was an aeroflyer.

Dizziness assaulted her, and she crashed onto her knees next to the hatch. With shaking hands, she pounded on the open door, praying the sound reverberated throughout the whole shelter.

"Hadley!"

How loudly could she whisper? The aeroflyer was almost silent now, its engines reduced to idle for landing. Haederan? All commercial and military aeroflyers looked about the same to her, but with her luck, it had to be.

She squinted in the glare of the afternoon sun, heat and ice warring on her skin.

Yes, there it was—the seal of the Haederan Empire on the side of the gray ship. Those crossed swords that haunted her dreams each night.

"Hadley!" Fear choked her throat. She wasn't going to wait for the figures in green fatigues that would soon come pouring out of that flyer. How far back under the vineyards was he? "Hadley, they're coming!"

She didn't need to say anything else. Hadley darted up and pointed back down.

"No! Hadley, I—"

She couldn't go down there. He knew that. In that instant, even being taken prisoner by the Haederans was a better choice.

"Don't be stupid. Get down there, and keep that light off, too. I'll make sure they go away without searching for anything."

The anger in his voice changed her mind. Her mind blank, Avery scrambled down the shallow stairs without him, feeling for each tread in the dim light with her feet. Hadley slid the door shut above her, and the shelter went black.

Black and quiet. So quiet her breathing was the loudest thing she'd ever heard. So silent and dark that her heart thumped against her chest. She took a deep breath and coughed softly, trying to slow it, but it refused. Uncooperative, traitorous body.

Tentatively, she reached out a hand to the dirt wall and let it guide her farther away from the door in the dark, more blue than black. Hadley had been right—the shelter was empty, but that had become an advantage. She didn't need to be tripping over farm equipment and crates of wine-making supplies, not now.

She sank down against the wall and gripped her knees. How long did she need to wait? There were no sounds above her, thanks to the heavy door, and anything could be happening up there. Talking. Threats. Maybe Hadley was dead already, lying there in the ruins of her family's land. He deserved better than that. So much better, after he'd saved her life more than once. Would they be able to tell he was Voirian, not Asrian? Would his citizenship be suspicious to them?

There were too many questions to sort through. Hadley could talk his way out of any situation, anyway. But what about her? What if the Haederans searched the shelter? They'd find her, they'd recognize her immediately, and if they were Haederan Army, they'd turn her over to the Imperial Security Command.

If they *were* Imperial Security, well . . .

But there was no point in worrying about Colonel Chase, not anymore. What more could he possibly want from her? He knew what she'd discovered. He knew what she'd stolen. There was nothing he needed or wanted from her anymore. Nothing except revenge, perhaps.

Her entire body shook. Chase's vengeance, when it came to her, would be terrifying. It would not be a painless death. He would make certain of that.

The door above whooshed open. Avery blinked in the sudden light and scurried into a darker corner. But what good would hiding do? The shelter wasn't that large, and the Haederans would find her within minutes. Seconds, if they had lights, which of course they did if they were bothering to land here and search things in the place.

The thought froze her. She couldn't move, just pulled her knees up to her chin and wrapped her arms over her dirty hair. Tears? Fear made those impossible.

Until they grabbed her.

Panic exploded in her brain and in her heart. She kicked and fought and tried to strike out with her hands, but powerful arms held her close to her attacker. She landed a kick on a shin, extracting a grunt. The blow hadn't been hard enough to do any actual damage, but she couldn't manage anything stronger at this angle.

Was there any point in screaming? There had to be. Maybe Hadley had gotten away. Maybe he'd hear her and be able to do something. She opened her mouth to shriek his name, but a hand clamped over it.

"Stop! Stop. It's me. It's just me. Calm down."

Avery blinked.

Hadley.

Her arms flopped uselessly at her sides, the relief unbearable. She struggled out of his grip and forced her trembling hand to wipe damp hair from her face.

"You all right?" He peered at her, then flicked the light in her face.

Words wouldn't come through her gasps for air. She opened her mouth, then shut it and nodded.

Hadley narrowed his eyes. There wasn't any point in lying to him—he'd always been able to see right through her.

"They're gone," he said. "Just checking on reports of looting here. They slapped me on the back and told me to take what I wanted."

"Right." She swallowed. "Right."

It was no surprise the Haederans were letting people loot her parents' estate. It was no wonder that there was nothing left. Silently, she let him lead her upstairs and back through the remains of the vineyard to the car.

Hadley gave her a grim look as he draped an arm over the controls. "I really thought we would have found something. I didn't know the estate would be so ravaged, or I wouldn't have brought you here. I'm sorry. And I'm more than sorry that patrol came by."

"Are you really?" she asked sharply.

Hadley instantly retreated into the sullen silence he had treated her with since she'd returned to Asria. Avery turned away from him and resumed her attempt at ash removal. It was an hour before she spoke again, the silence too painful.

"I'm sorry for being short with you." She wiped her hands on her pants again, then gave up. "And I'm sorry for . . . well, you know. How many times do I have to apologize to you?"

His jaw tightened.

"Oh, I don't know. I think at least a dozen more times, and you might come close to making up for getting me arrested and held on treason and espionage charges for six months. The Villiers detention area isn't made for long-term imprisonment. Not that I belonged there at all." He gave her a sideways glance and raised his voice. "Those are capital charges, in case you weren't aware. What would you have done if they'd tried and convicted me?"

"They wouldn't have tried you. You know they were waiting on the Commonwealth—" *To do that*, she'd almost said. "And it's not as if they could have executed you."

"Easy for you to say."

"We don't have the death penalty on Asria. Even for treason. The Commonwealth doesn't either."

Though it wouldn't be a bad idea. There were at least a dozen Haederans running around the quadrant who deserved it, and those were just the ones she could think of off the top of her head.

Punishment.

Revenge.

It was the only thing she could think of these days. The heat of her anger kept her warm in this new, cold, raw world.

"Voirs does." She flinched at Hadley's hostility. "If you hadn't run into our scout ship, if you hadn't been able to tell them what really happened, I'd be on my way there now. That's not exactly how I wanted my first visit home in five years to go."

She resisted the impulse to remind him that his home planet hadn't executed a single person since joining the Commonwealth. Or that he'd never have been transferred to Voirs, anyway. He'd have served a life sentence on Asria—or at the Commonwealth headquarters on Ventana, if the war ever ended.

"I'm sorry. I don't know what else I can say or do to make you believe how sorry I am, but it's true."

Hadley appeared determined to punish her for the next fifty years over what she'd done anyway. He fell silent for another hour, then stopped the car in the middle of a dry wash where it was hidden by tall riparian trees and a few large boulders.

"Why did you believe him?" Hadley's rage turned to genuine anguish. "You know me. You've known me for years. How could you think I'd do that?"

Avery leaned back against the opposite window and stared at her hands. No wonder Hadley had been acting like a petulant child. He wasn't offended she hadn't trusted him—he was hurt. She shook her head, trying to clear the haze that had appeared where her brain was supposed to be. Hadley had always been emotionless, but not any longer.

But it was no wonder. She'd believed Major Elex Feye, Hadley's longtime partner, over him. She'd believed the lie that

Hadley, rather than Feye, had been working for the Haederans. It was a lie that had gotten Feye killed, Hadley arrested by the Defense Forces, and her captured by the Haederans.

"It was strange," she began, "to hear someone saying that about you. I didn't believe it at first. But he spun everything around, so much that I didn't know what to believe anymore. You pulled me out of that prison in Cadena, something I didn't think anyone could do. After everything Major Feye said, it only made sense that you'd been able to do it because you'd had inside help. I thought that maybe . . ." She hated accusing him like this, but it had haunted her for months. "I thought that maybe Colonel Chase allowed you to rescue me so I'd lead you to the chip. And Feye was so persuasive . . ."

It was a poor defense, and she knew it hadn't made a bit of difference when Hadley's eyes grew sadder.

"Do you know what happened after you left?" he asked.

She'd heard most of it from General Cevall but shook her head anyway. Hadley needed to vent, and she deserved to hear it all.

"They came for me not three hours after I saw you in the corridor. It wasn't so bad at first. They made it clear I'd be handed over to the Commonwealth as soon as possible. I'm not sure they really believed Feye's story either. They treated me well, all things considered. Then you disappeared, and that changed."

"Hadley, I don't think—"

He slammed his first against the window. "No, dammit, you're going to listen to it. All of it. You owe me that much."

Avery nodded.

"They—" His eyes fell. "Never mind. Suffice it to say, they just barely skirted the bounds of legality. If we weren't at war, and the queen of Asria hadn't just disappeared, heads would have rolled if Ventana had found out what they'd done. Do you want to see the bruises?"

Those bruises were long gone, but she'd seen pictures—as punishment for her part in the mess, she sometimes suspected. They hadn't hurt Hadley all that much, but the wounds in his pride—the accusations of treason toward a man who valued loyalty over most everything else, those were the bad ones. It was skill, not treachery, that had gotten her out of that cell.

"You trusted him too, you know," she said.

"Yeah. I did. For a really long time." He blew out a deep breath. "I shouldn't care, you know," he finally said. "You did what you thought needed to be done with the information you had at the time."

A slow smile spread across his face. Not the friendly grin she was used to, but it was a start.

"I'm surprised you listened to me rant about all this," he went on. "I'd have thought you'd have started walking back to Villiers at least an hour ago."

"Like you implied, I deserve it." That was true enough. And there were some things worse than listening to Hadley reprimand her. More painful. "And I'm not in a rush to get back underground," she admitted.

"Ah." The smile faded as he made the connection. "Then you haven't been accidentally falling asleep on that bench in the greenhouse all these nights."

Hardly.

The explanation she'd given the Defense Forces security officials couldn't be further from the truth. Even in that four-story vaulted room, she could barely sleep, but it was better than her own quarters. Each time she shut her door, panic assaulted her.

She shook her head, wondering if tonight would be the night they finally escorted her back to her own quarters.

"It's the only place," she replied, "that doesn't feel like a grave."

"Then what do you say we sit out here for a while longer, Lieutenant? Enjoy the sun and wind and freedom." Hadley checked the time and took a deep breath. "But then we need to hurry back—because I have a surprise waiting for you."

CHAPTER TWO

SHE AND HADLEY TOOK A MEANDERING ROUTE THROUGH A NARROW canyon six kilometers from Villiers, deep underground on the opposite side of the mountains from Cadena. They left the car in a rocky wash, covered in a portable force field that was supposed to hide it from an air search. From there, it was another kilometer through an underground passageway that could scarcely be called a tunnel before they arrived at the only entrance to the base, heavily guarded by both sensors and armed security.

Only safety was an illusion, and it wouldn't be long before the enemy found a way in. Claustrophobia or not, most days she wanted nothing more than to hide in her quarters behind a locked door—which also sounded like a good enough plan for the rest of the afternoon. But the activity when they arrived back at Villiers was unlike anything she'd seen in the months she'd been there. To be sure, the guards at the large blast doors were the same, as composed as ever, but inside, the undercurrent of something was undeniable.

Avery shot Hadley a questioning look as they passed through the last set of doors into the main side of the base and melted in the crush of military uniforms.

"Hadley, what's going on?" she asked under her breath. "I feel like I've missed something."

A Haederan attack nearby? Her breath grew short for the second time that day. But no, she would have seen that coming from outside—and Asrian security would have never given her and Hadley the go ahead for their visit to Sabino if they'd suspected anything. Unless there had been no warning. The Haederans' initial attack on Asria had been unexpected, after all. Whatever it was, if something was happening, she'd need to find somewhere to hide.

As if you can hide from them if they take Villiers.

She frowned at him when he didn't reply.

"Hadley?"

Hadley wasn't paying any attention to her, though—not that his dismissive behavior was anything new of late. Instead, he had cornered a young Defense Forces lieutenant who had been hurrying by, but Avery couldn't hear all of their conversation. The lieutenant looked afraid of him, but then again, being accused of treason probably gave one a sort of reputation she didn't dare guess at. Hadley probably wanted out of Villiers more than she did.

But enough was enough.

"Captain Hadley." He turned at that, and she forced a calm smile. "What's going on?"

"General Teruel wants to see you. Immediately." There was a sparkle in his eye that she hadn't seen in weeks as he looked back at the lieutenant. "Briefing room two?"

"That's not an answer," she protested as he led her down the corridor. "Don't tell me you're in on some secret as well."

"Not my place to explain what's going on," he said. "But you won't want to miss this."

Avery crinkled her nose at him as they approached the briefing room. If the entrance to the base had been active, the briefing room was a spectacle. A dozen officers were leaving as they entered, a crowd she'd seen at Villiers perhaps once. General

Teruel, General Cevall, and a few others she didn't know by sight were left, and stood when she walked in.

"Your Majesty." The head of the Royal Asrian Defense Forces greeted her formally, odd for him, and inconsistent with the cheerful look on his face.

"General Teruel." She nodded in return, noting the gray in his dark copper hair for the first time. They'd all grown old in the past year, hadn't they? "Did I miss a party?"

"No." He smiled. "Just a successful raid on the Haederan prison at Alcaris."

He might as well have punched her in the chest for as much as she could breathe.

"You didn't rescue—"

Cevall cut in with a wide smile. "All of them. And destroyed three Haederan ships in the process."

Avery's hand went to her mouth.

"You did it. I've heard people talking off and on about it for weeks, but I didn't think it was actually going to happen. I didn't realize it was a serious plan." More than that, she hadn't wanted to *hope*. "No one said anything to me."

"Grec approved it after discussing it with Baylen," Teruel said. "I'm sorry, Your Majesty, but you—you were too close to the situation to be unbiased about the decision."

Unbiased must be Teruel's polite way of saying she would have made any decision, even a bad one, to get Merritt back. That was . . . fair. And Lidia Grec made sense anyway, since the defense minister had authority over those decisions. But Baylen? It was surprising he'd been involved, especially without telling her.

Her shoulders sank at the memory. Two months ago, she'd told the prime minister of her desire to offer herself to the Haederans in exchange for Merritt's freedom. It was a spontaneous remark, but as she'd considered it more and more, it'd become a concrete plan. There was no question that the Haederans would accept the offer, and she'd have gladly sacrificed herself to save him. It was a wonder they hadn't suggested the swap themselves.

Baylen had betrayed her intentions to Teruel, and she was suddenly shadowed everywhere she went, by more security than any one person needed. When she'd cornered the general about the constant surveillance, he'd exploded in anger over her idea. There was no leaving Villiers after that. There was barely any leaving her quarters, and she'd been shocked when Hadley knocked on her door to take her to her family's estate.

Well, she'd deal with Baylen later.

"The trip to Sabino?" she asked.

Hadley chuckled. "I was supposed to get you out of here for a few days so you couldn't foul anything up. It would have been hell for you to have to sit around and wait for news, anyway. You can kill me over it later—or thank me, whichever."

And sending Hadley out of Villiers with the queen was Teruel's tacit acknowledgment that he could be trusted again . . . for no one on Asria, least of all anyone in the Defense Forces, would ever apologize to Hadley directly. Forcing her to spend time with the man she'd condemned to indefinite detention was probably more of her own punishment as well.

"I need to sit down," she said to herself. Hadley pulled out a chair from the conference table and she dropped gratefully into it. If she kept standing, she'd ask the question that wasn't appropriate yet. Business—her duty as queen—had to be finished first.

"Casualties?"

"No fatalities." Cevall sounded smug. "Seventeen injuries, two critical. They should make it. We lost an aeroflyer, though."

"I want to see them as soon as they're in the condition for it." Tears filled her eyes, and she blinked them away before the group of bystanders noticed. She wanted to see all of them, but one in particular . . . one in particular who no one had mentioned yet.

But of course they weren't. No one was mentioning Merritt because they hadn't found him. She could read between the lines. It was obvious what they weren't saying. They'd rescued everyone but him. He wasn't at Alcaris, not anymore. He was dead—or transferred by the Haederans to somewhere the

Defense Forces would never find him, which would be just as bad.

"We've already arranged visits for you."

"And the Haederans? What's their response been? Nothing against civilian targets?"

"Quiet so far. They already knew we were here," Teruel said. "The only additional thing they know now is what we're capable of. We'll all need to lie low for now."

Avery nodded and took a deep breath, even though she was certain they could all hear her heart beating. Was official business concluded enough to ask what she really wanted to know? Hadley was staring at her expectantly, so perhaps it was. Everyone involved in this mission had likely placed bets on how long it would take her to ask.

"And Merritt?"

* * *

Avery crept into the room, Hadley behind her, having evidently forgiven her enough to stick close by. Or maybe he just didn't trust the Defense Forces with her safety. In any case, she was grateful for the company and the fact he was speaking to her again, especially now, because the beeping of the machines was troubling, worse than if she'd been alone. But underneath the noise, so quiet she couldn't hear it unless she listened for it, was the sound of Merritt's breathing. The doctor was leaning over him and turned when she heard Avery.

"Is he . . ." she began.

The doctor smiled. "Lieutenant Colonel Parker is sleeping off the pain meds. The monitoring is just precautionary until they're tapered down a bit."

Thank you, Holy One.

"How is he otherwise?"

"Fine." The doctor ran a hand through her hair. "He will be fine. He told the medics he thinks he has a concussion, but he was responsive and none of the scans showed any brain trauma. I'm more worried about the breaks in his legs and left arm. He'll need surgery once a room's clear, and I'm optimistic, but there's always a chance for long-term problems. It's not likely he'll get away without at least one or two major implants."

Breaks?

That didn't make any sense.

"But Cevall said there were only two critical, and I already saw—" Avery stopped herself. Maybe the general hadn't considered a few broken bones serious enough to mention.

Hadley shifted audibly, and a chill ran down the tips of her fingers.

"The injuries preceded this mission, Your Majesty." The doctor looked past her at Hadley, and Avery couldn't ignore the fact she wasn't meeting her eyes. "Some are old. Some are new."

Her meaning was clear, and Avery's stomach dropped. "I—I see. Just him?"

The doctor looked uncomfortable but glanced away from Hadley toward her. "Yes. Just him."

The sick feeling intensified. They had hurt Merritt because of *her*. Their enemy had tortured him because she cared about him. Because she loved him, and they knew it. This was her fault.

But why?

Chase's orders. It had to have been. Revenge for her escape. For her theft of their technology. He couldn't get to her, so he was punishing her through Merritt. She would have gladly died in that prison cell in Cadena if it meant Merritt would have been spared this suffering.

Adrenaline pulsed through her, like her body remembered how that verium-enhanced fighter had shot off the Haederan cruiser all those months ago.

"I'd like to be alone with him, please. You too, Hadley. I'll be fine," she said in response to his concerned look. "But thank you."

Overcome with relief that Merritt should be fine, even as bad as he looked, she dragged a chair from the corner and collapsed in it to watch his chest rise and fall. His brown hair, short enough the last time she'd seen him, was shorn, and livid bruises covered his oddly pale skin. It gave him the look of a man twice his age, and she reached a finger toward his cheek, only to pull it away.

After five minutes of watching him, satisfied she wouldn't break him with her touch, she clutched his hand with hers and laid her head down on top of both. His steady breathing settled her heart, and she was closed to dozing off when he spoke, startling her into sitting up.

"You're still wearing it."

"I told you I would." Sudden tears fell at his words. She would never take that ring off again. "You don't know what it's like to see you again."

Merritt tried to laugh, but it was obvious he was still in too much pain for even that slight movement. His gray eyes that had never quite faded from her memories did it for him.

"I have a bit of an idea." He traced her ring with the tip of his finger, then lifted her right hand to kiss the back of it. "We need to do something about it being on the wrong hand, Your Majesty."

"Now's not exactly the right time to talk about a wedding, Mer." She wiped her tears away. He couldn't just pick up a months-old conversation like that, could he? Not the one where he'd proposed and then walked off to certain death. But then, Merritt had wanted that one thing for almost ten years. "Those must be some good pain meds."

"Too soon?" A little color returned to his cheeks. "No matter. I promised myself if I ever got out of there, I'd never let you get away again."

"I won't." A laugh broke through that time. "I couldn't even if I wanted to down here. Not trapped at Villiers."

"Do you want to?" Darkness crossed his face, just a little, at her joke. "Get away from me? You know, they . . . they might not be able to fix all of this. I might never walk again. You have so many responsibilities. So many more important things to do. Do you want the responsibility of taking care of me for the rest of my life?"

"You aren't a burden to me or anyone else, Merritt, and I don't want to hear you suggest that again." By the way his face fell, she'd hesitated just a fraction of a second too long. "That's an order, straight from the queen herself. But . . ."

She wiped the insistent tears away again.

"Everything that's happened to you has been my fault. Do you really want to be joined to someone who might get you killed? I don't want that. I told myself when this all started that I'd walk away from you to keep you safe, and I still mean that. I can't let them hurt you just so they can hurt me. I love you too much for that. Besides—what about your career?"

The career that had almost been the end of them just the day before the Haederans' invasion. Maybe it didn't matter anymore . . . one way or another, his career was likely over.

"Love, this isn't your fault. You can't blame yourself."

"It is." He was so wrong. He didn't know the entire story. "You saw Gareth Chase at Alcaris, didn't you?"

She rubbed her eyes with her free hand. Not that Chase's absence would mean anything. The Haederan Army soldiers at Alcaris would have jumped to obey an order from an Imperial Security Command officer, just as afraid of the Haederan secret police as she. More so, perhaps. Yes, Chase could have ordered Merritt's torture from anywhere.

"That Haederan Army police captain who kept following you around?" Merritt looked like he couldn't decide whether to laugh at her insanity or shake his head at such an absurd question. "Of course not. I really thought I had a little more time before the debriefings started, though."

Avery blew out a breath through clenched teeth. If Chase hadn't been involved, maybe what happened to Merritt wasn't her fault. Maybe she wasn't responsible for what they had done to him. Maybe Merritt just had bad luck . . . maybe he had pushed the Haederans too far himself.

"Though it's funny you ask, because I had a dream about him in the beginning," Merritt went on. "It was strange since I'd only met him twice, but you know how dreams are. I really thought he was there in the cell with me until I realized his uniform was all wrong."

Her stomach twisted as the room spun around her.

"Avery, what—you look like you're going to be sick." He reached for the comm on the other side of the bed with his free hand, but she grabbed that one too before he could summon the doctor—or worse, security in the form of Hadley.

"Don't call anyone in." Dizzy, she sucked in a gulp of air. It didn't help. "I'm all right. Merritt, he was dressed as an Imperial Security Command colonel, wasn't he?"

"How did you—" Fear and anger flared in his pale cheeks. "What the hell did he want with you?"

Avery reluctantly let go of his hand to rub her eyes. Merritt had processed the news faster than she had when Chase had revealed his true identity to her. He would kill her when she told him, just like Drex had wanted to, except Merritt had never sworn to protect her like her former bodyguard had. He'd have no qualms about telling her exactly what he thought of her foolishness.

"I suppose no one's told you yet." She bit her lip, but Merritt's expression told her she was only delaying things. "Just after the invasion, the Commonwealth came to me wanting my help. I spent almost ten months passing them information. Important things, Merritt. And the short version is—somehow the Haederans found out."

Except there was no somehow about it. Just before he'd murdered Drex, her own handler, Elex Feye, had told them—even though he claimed in a suicide letter that he hadn't. But that didn't matter anymore. Did it?

"Anyway, Chase isn't Haederan Army like he said. He's Imperial Security. And he was after me. He—"

She stopped. Merritt didn't need to know what Chase had

done to her after Merritt's presumed death trying to take back the Defense Forces' headquarters at Alcaris. Not yet. He didn't need to know about her imprisonment, the weeks of beatings and starvation and sleep deprivation and interrogations. He especially didn't need to know about her theft of a Haederan fighter off one of their cruisers. He would never let her out of his sight once he found out, and she wouldn't be able to tell him he was overreacting, either.

"He did this to you, didn't he?" she asked instead.

Merritt shook his head, though his sharp stare promised a long talk about her exploits later.

"No," he said slowly, as if he didn't quite want to remember anything that had happened prior to his rescue. "One day . . ."

His voiced strengthened, becoming matter-of-fact, like he just wanted the story over and done with.

"He came in one day and stared at me for what seemed like forever, but it was probably only five minutes. It was as eerie as anything you can imagine, but that's what I thought it was. Imagination. A hallucination. I was so bad off by that point—fever and all—that they took me to the infirmary the next day. Fixed me up, let me recover. They transferred me to Emot after that. Did you know the Haederans have a prisoner of war camp there now?"

She hadn't. Emot, that insignificant planet on the edge of the Asrian system where Merritt had tried to propose years ago, brought back nothing but bad memories.

"Except for missing you, things weren't all that bad out there. They treated us decently." His face went dark. "But after a month, they told me it had been a mistake and brought me back to Alcaris. They broke my legs again as soon as I arrived. I guess they had just been trying to keep me from dying. I knew I'd never see you again. I prayed every day—sometimes all day—that I'd be able to escape, but the likelihood of that got slimmer and slimmer. The physical pain—that was easy—but the thought of never seeing you again . . ."

His voice was barely a whisper now.

"Eventually I started praying I would die, figuring killing me would be easier for the Holy One than getting me out, but He wouldn't answer that prayer either."

As carefully as she could, Avery climbed into bed and curled up next him, careful not to touch anything that looked painful. There wasn't much to touch. She settled for lying her head against his side. His heart beat against her cheek, and in that second, it was the most wonderful thing she'd ever felt.

"I admit this is pretty selfish of me," she said, "but I'm glad the answer was no."

CHAPTER THREE

THERE WAS ONE DEFENSE FORCES OFFICER IN THE TINY VILLIERS chapel when Avery arrived, and he couldn't leave quickly enough as soon as he recognized the queen. That kind of isolating treatment was nothing new, even if she could understand it a bit. She'd rather be alone while she waited on Merritt to come out of surgery anyway.

As an afterthought, but a necessarily Asrian one, the room had been blasted through solid rock like the rest of Villiers but not completely finished. Someone had probably decided the rough wall added character instead of being the symbol of a cost overrun. Whatever the reason for the odd design, instead of being beautiful, to her it was just another reminder that she was trapped underground. The dark, exposed rock behind the altar and slightly musky smell of earth didn't help. The shadows lurking in the corners certainly didn't.

She'd been honest with Hadley when she'd implied how bad off she was, but she hadn't told him the whole story. He didn't know the truth of how her imprisonment had affected her, not really. It wasn't just her small quarters which made her ill. It was Villiers in general. Not being able to see stars. And the darkness was so pervasive in an underground base, enough that she never turned the lights out anymore.

She'd hidden that humiliating secret from everyone until a month after arriving. That day, she'd come home from a day-long meeting with Teruel to find her room dark—cleaning personnel had been in—and had sobbed in the corner for hours, unable to move enough to switch a light on. They'd found her curled up in a ball the next morning when she'd been late for yet another meeting. Since then, any personnel who entered her room were under strict orders to leave her quarters lit. Well, half lit, since bright rooms held almost the same terror the shadows did. Everyone in Villiers thought she was damaged beyond repair.

Avery pushed away the memory and waved the lights up halfway. The lingering feeling of peace that always hung over this place washed most of the claustrophobia away. If only it could become permanent and portable.

There was a cream-colored lace scarf laying on the table just inside the entrance, and she picked it up and let it fall through her hands. It was an odd thing to find here, not because there was a lack of women at Villiers, but because Asrian women had stopped routinely wearing head coverings during worship over two hundred years before. Her mother had resumed the custom after marrying her father, something Avery had never understood— though Carina had always had an easier time with the unwritten requirements of the royal family than she. Avery wound the scarf around her head as she approached the altar. Maybe her mother had known something she didn't.

It was strange to kneel in the presence of the Holy One, whose existence she'd questioned for most of her adult life. But Merritt was alive, something she'd given up hope of a year before, and along with that astonishing miracle, prayer and thanks came easily.

Thank you for the blessing of life and not more death. Merritt and the others. We've had enough death on Asria in the past year, haven't we?

She was hit with a twinge of guilt that she hadn't prayed for much of anything over the past year except Merritt's safety, but this new faith would have to come one step at a time. That was something else to mention.

I'm sorry I ever doubted You, Holy One. I'm sorry I've been so distant. Can You forgive me?

The answer to that question had been pounded into her head as a child, but putting the theory into practice was something different. If forgiveness was difficult for her, it must be difficult for the Holy One as well.

And forgiving others, as Drex had always said she had to? Praying for the ones who had done this to Merritt? Those who had attacked their world?

She wanted them all dead. Most nights, when she was alone in her quarters, she prayed for some apocalyptic calamity to befall Haedera. A supernova which wrapped the planet in flame, or a drought that left their children sobbing for water. She didn't care how it happened, only that it did. Sometimes she screamed it instead of quietly praying for it. Sometimes she demanded revenge from the Holy One. The hate was the only thing which helped her deal with the betrayal and loss.

Help me with my hatred. It's eating my soul. I can feel it more and more every day.

Footsteps distracted her from her rambling, and she jumped to her feet, almost tripping over the lowest step. How had she been careless enough to let someone sneak up behind her? Her security detail waiting outside shouldn't have allowed that. If they were good for one thing, it was keeping unwanted visitors away from her most of the time.

But as her eyes refocused, it was Grant Baylen who entered.

Breathe. Baylen's safe.

Baylen, to her satisfaction, said nothing about the antiquated custom or her overreaction to his entrance, only nodded his head in recognition. How much did he struggle with the same memories? She'd disliked Asria's prime minister from the day her uncle had appointed him, right up until the night Perrin had her and

Baylen arrested. The same night Perrin had claimed to have had Merritt and his men murdered. Even with the surveillance he'd ordered on her, it was impossible to hate someone who'd shared an experience like that, and she was glad Baylen had found his way to Villiers and to safety.

"Zenos Hadley said you were looking for me, Your Majesty?"

"Yes."

Mechanically, Avery unwound the scarf, folded it, and placed it back where she'd found it. he gestured outside, past the security detail. The three men and two women hung back twenty paces, and she was grateful for that. No one needed to hear her personal business—except Baylen, thanks to an ancient law no one had seen the need to change yet.

Another deep breath.

"Thank you for finding me so quickly. You know Merritt arrived at Villiers today."

"You've seen him, yes?" Worry shrouded his features.

"He's in surgery now. He'll be fine," she said, as Baylen's face creased in concern. "That's not what I wanted to talk to you about. We want to be married. Immediately."

"Ah." Baylen grinned. "And we're all tied to our history and responsibilities, aren't we?"

To say the least.

"I know the senate is in an interim status—" she began.

Or no status according to the Haederans—

"I'll save you the embarrassment our law likes to impose." The grin turned to a laugh as he read her discomfort. "Consider this the senate's permission and my personal blessing. You two deserve some happiness."

"Thank you."

Bless Baylen for understanding how awkward it was for her to ask. Any other time, she'd have been able to file a formal petition, which would have been electronically voted on in secret. There certainly wouldn't have been any need to ask the senate face-to-face. Maybe there was some way she could save her heirs from the embarrassment of any kind of petition. It was a ridiculous and outdated requirement, designed to prevent off-worlders from inheriting any stake in Asria. Like worrying about off-worlders marrying into the royal family mattered after an invasion.

"Now that that's out of the way," Baylen said, "there's one thing I need to discuss with you, but it's best discussed somewhere more private."

He gestured down the hallway toward his office, and Avery followed along beside him. What could Baylen possibly have to say that was more private than what she'd just asked him?

"You're aware," he said as soon as the door to his office shut, "that no help from the Commonwealth fleet has come in months."

She perched on the chair closest to the door. That wasn't the discussion she'd been expecting.

"Help will be here. It will," she insisted at the doubtful look on Baylen's face. "It's just a matter of time."

"I disagree. We have to assume that the Haederans' idea worked, and the Commonwealth believes we have gone along happily annexed." Baylen gave her a sad smile. "A Haederan colony. It's happened before."

Avery sat back and stared at her hands. So, Baylen believed this was about General Perrin's claim that the senate had voted to withdraw from the Commonwealth, not under duress, as was the reality, but under a legal, binding vote. Perrin had sent Senator Larris to Ventana to argue the fact, keeping his family on Asria as hostages.

Maybe he was right.

Unconsciously, she twisted Merritt's ring. "I don't think you're giving the Commonwealth enough credit."

He perched on the edge of his desk and swung a leg, feigning informality. Avery could have laughed—there wasn't much informality about Baylen. Even during an occupation, even trapped in an underground military base, he still exuded an aura of wealth and style.

"I have all the respect in the world for the Commonwealth

military," Baylen said, "and for your service to them, but the Council is something completely different. It's likely they consider the coerced Asrian vote to be an answer to a prayer. One less system to defend, especially a lightly populated one, one so far removed from the rest of the quadrant? Why would they even question the senate's vote? It's the perfect outcome for them."

He had a point, as loath as she was to agree. The bureaucracy of Commonwealth politics made the Asrian senate look positively functional on its worst day, something which was of course far from the truth. Even Baylen—especially Baylen—knew that.

And she knew what he was getting at.

"You want me to go to Ventana."

"Yes. Plead our case in person. It worked to keep them from helping us; it might work to gain their support as well. I would go myself, but your connection to the Commonwealth makes you the better choice. I doubt they could say no to your personal request. And I hate to put it this way, Your Majesty, but we'd much prefer you away from Asria for the time being." He smiled faintly. "I was glad to see you back, but some of us are less expendable than others."

She wanted to argue that Villiers was perfectly safe, but there was no point in arguing a lie. The Haederans could break through the fortified underground installation any day, and then where would they be? They might not have had weapons capable of such feats when they had first invaded, but they'd had months to bring in additional artillery from Haedera. No, Villiers wasn't as safe as any of them wanted to believe.

But she'd spent so much time and effort trying to get back to the surface . . . back home to Asria. Leaving the planet, especially with Merritt here now, would be nearly impossible.

"If we're talking expendability," she replied. "I'm not sure getting me off Asria is the safest move."

She probably sounded frightened, but Baylen couldn't possibly have a plan that would work. She'd refused Drex's similar offer of escape before, the same night Merritt had been captured, knowing it would have almost surely been futile.

Drex. It still hurt to think of him. His murder was something else she'd never forgive Elex Feye for.

"It's risky." Baylen shrugged. "But—and General Teruel can fill you in on the details—we've received word the Haederans may be close to allowing limited civilian space departures and arrivals. If that's the case, we can surely sneak you off the planet."

She frowned at his wording. Was this really about pleading their case on Ventana or was it about evacuating her to a safer planet? Maybe Baylen knew something about the Haederans' plans that she didn't.

"I want to speak to General Teruel before I agree to this."

"I can call him in right now, if you'd like."

She stood, shaking her head. "I'd like to check on Merritt now. Can you see if Teruel—no. Wait." She still had authority on Asria, as limited as it was. She wouldn't phrase her orders as suggestions any longer. "Have him write everything up and send it to me. I'll decide what I want to do after I hear his details."

Baylen nodded. "Of course, Your Majesty."

Everything official would have to wait until she saw Merritt again.

CHAPTER FOUR

AVERY RAN HER PALMS DOWN HER SILK ROBE IN UNCHARACTERISTIC shyness and lit another candle on the small table by the door. Fire, so dangerous in this kind of structure, was a temporary privilege granted to her by Villiers's emergency personnel for tonight only, and for the first time, her quarters felt like home, really and truly home.

The flickering candlelight helped, but it was Merritt's presence who made it so, she knew. This was her Merritt sitting there on the bed—the same man she'd wanted for as long as she could remember, who she'd prayed ceaselessly for over the past year, the one she'd never quite been able to walk away from. Every line on his face, every scar, even the implants in his legs . . . they were hers now, forever, no matter how far apart they were.

"We're always saying goodbye," she protested. An irrelevant complaint, but she needed to say something to dispel the heat in her cheeks.

"Try again." Merritt winked from across the room. "It's not goodbye this time. I'm never saying goodbye to you again. From now on it'll be . . . see you later. That's a promise."

"Then that's a promise I'm going to hold you to," she replied.

She lit another unnecessary candle. Ambience was a hard thing to create when the shadows of candlelight made one twitchy, but candles were a requirement tonight. She blew the match out slower than necessary, just to watch Merritt's eyes widen.

"Deal." He patted the bed next to him, and her heart skipped a beat as she sat. "And we have a whole four weeks together before you leave. Long Asrian weeks. The kind you can really enjoy, not those short Commonwealth ones they try to pass off as any kind of real time."

"It still seems too short." Anything other than forever was too short now, after believing he was dead. She hadn't been able to take her eyes off him all day, afraid he'd vanish if she did. Leaving him this time would be physically painful.

But she wouldn't focus on that now.

"Time always does." Merritt laughed. "And it's going to pass even faster if you just sit there and look at me."

His eyes ran up and down her body, which responded in turn. Avery pulled her hair down to torment him just a little while longer, and the impatient look on Merritt's face made her want to tease him even more.

"I can't help it. It's going to be such a long time away from each other." She leaned into him, reveling in his touch, imagining the weeks and months to come without it. Why did Ventana have to be so far away? Why couldn't the prime minister go in her place? "I wish you could come with us."

"I wish I could too, but I think being able to walk properly is a prerequisite for that kind of thing."

"I know."

She drew her fingers over his knee. Modern medicine and painkillers had worked wonders, but Merritt hadn't yet regained full movement in his legs. Flying? Well, they would have to wait and see about that, the chief surgeon had said. He hadn't sounded hopeful though, and she was caught between sadness for

Merritt's ruined dreams and hope he might finally slow down. Next time he might not be so lucky.

But Merritt had blown off the doctor's predictions right after his third surgery and told her he wouldn't stop trying until he was behind the controls of a spacecraft again. Teruel had argued with him, she had argued with him, the doctors had argued with him—but there was no winning with Merritt these days. Three hours after his latest surgery, he'd been drafting memos for Teruel while she and the surgeon had watched with disapproval, unable to make him stop.

"Good thing it's not a prerequisite for other things." Merritt twisted a hand through her hair and pulled her closer. She hoped he didn't see the hair on her arms standing on end, but his grin said otherwise. He leaned closer so he could whisper in her ear. "Wedding night, remember?"

There was no way she could have forgotten, even though their wedding had been an unplanned and casual affair, nothing like Uncle Victor's extravagant celebration that had taken place when he married his late wife. It was surprising the interim Asrian senate even considered her and Merritt's ceremony valid—the ceremony which had taken place in a chapel half the size of her quarters, only witnessed by General Teruel and Hadley. Instead of the elaborate parties and balls which had followed the last Asrian royal wedding, their ceremony had been followed by an extensive meeting on her trip to Ventana. War made normal events strange, and that was fine with her. She only wanted Merritt.

But if she'd forgotten they had been married that morning, the sensation that ran through her at his lips on her ear left her no choice but to remember. Merritt knew her too well, knew how to focus her racing thoughts back to him.

"I couldn't ever forget that." Not with the unrelenting heat which was working itself from her inside out. "But this wasn't how I ever planned on it happening."

"Mmm. Nothing is ever as we plan. I never planned on being encumbered with the designation of Prince Consort of Asria either, but there you have it." Merritt's longstanding uneasiness with the negligible trappings of Asrian royalty was all but legendary, and Avery would have been offended at his remark but for his grin and the desperate longing in his eyes. "If it means you're mine, I wouldn't have it any other way. And no matter where or who we are, I think tonight is salvageable."

"Oh? I do think you might be right, Your Highness."

Her eyes sparkled as she lifted his shirt over his head, but fell when they landed on the scars and bruises that still covered his chest and arms. Seeing them in the clinic was one thing, but seeing them now, when they should have been thinking about nothing but each other, was something totally different and heart-breaking.

It's your fault. What happened to him is all your fault. They only did it to hurt you.

She knelt back as far away from him as she could get on the small bed and twisted her hair into a knot, unable to touch him again. Her robe fell open, and she pulled it closed with her free hand, grateful to have an excuse not to touch him. It would kill her if she were to damage him even more. If *they* hurt him again because of who she was.

"Merritt, I don't want to hurt you. I love you so much, and I just can't—"

Irritation erased his desire, but she was almost certain it wasn't directed at her. Almost.

"Oh, no you don't. I know that look. Don't you dare cry on me, love. Not right now." Merritt grabbed her hand. Her hair fell into her face, and he pushed it behind her ear. His palm burned her cheek where their skin touched, and the tingling ran down her neck. Further, even. "It's all right. What happened to me is not your fault, and you won't break me, I promise. And we've been apart too long. This is about us now, no one else. Nothing else."

Silent, Avery let a finger trace one of the yellowing bruises that ran all the way down his chest. It wasn't as easy as he claimed.

"Here. Look here instead." Merritt lifted her chin with a finger, and she stared into his eyes, as intense as she'd ever seen them. Years ago, the intensity would have terrified her, but tonight she wanted to fall into them and never leave. "Better yet, close your eyes."

Before she could protest, his lips were on hers, warm and alive, and she forgot about everything but his touch.

CHAPTER FIVE

The shuttleport outside Jeph, a harrowing fifteen-hour aeroflyer ride from Villiers, was much more crowded than Avery had expected. She followed as closely as she could behind Hadley, head down, her heart pounded more with every step she took. It wasn't likely anyone would recognize her halfway across the planet from Cadena—even Merritt hadn't known who she was when they'd first met, after all—but the security cameras might, if they could get a good picture through the hundreds of other travelers milling about the terminal.

Colonel Chase *definitely* would.

"I thought travel was only opened to merchants and trade," she said under her breath to Hadley's back.

"It is. But some people are trying their luck to get off-planet anyway." He pushed his way past a throng of stationary people. "I don't know where they think they are all going, though. The Haederans have a strict list of who's allowed off."

Obviously Teruel had made sure she and Hadley were on it, but the Haederan military police milling about with the Asrians here gave her pause, especially knowing how the Imperial Security Command used them as a cover. She hadn't seen this many

Haederan Army police since arriving back on Asria months ago, an exploit she didn't care to repeat.

Still, Hadley would have a plan to get them through the checks. And General Teruel had claimed to have an agent in place at Jeph, but who really knew? All she knew was that they would never make it back to the relative safety of Villiers if they were spotted now.

"I have to ask." She lowered her head further as the crowd dispersed a bit. "What would you have given me for a surprise had that mission not been successful?"

Hadley laughed, and the sound reassured her. "I'd have stolen some flowers from the greenhouse and left them in your quarters. A distant second best, I know." He stopped at an empty window overlooking the departure pad and tossed his bag on the empty bench in front of it. "That's it, right there."

He pointed to a merchant ship parked just outside. It was smaller than she was comfortable with, but she'd have to give it the benefit of the doubt for now. The engines were as large as the ship was small, and speed was all that mattered today.

"Great. I assume it's guarded? How do we get to it?"

Hadley opened his mouth for what was likely a smart comment when a green-uniformed man shoved his way in between them.

Avery ducked her head away. How had Hadley not noticed this Haederan officer's approach? He'd just made a fatal mistake.

She was about to take a step away, about to take off running, when the Haederan stuck his arm out behind her, blocking her escape. Panic rose in her chest, along with intractable nausea. She looked sideways past him at Hadley, her eyes wide, but Hadley was staring at the ship out the window with rare obliviousness.

"Excuse me." The stranger's Haederan accent made her heart flutter. She could have gone the rest of her life without hearing it. "I'm looking for Hangar Bay Seven."

"That's on the other side of the station," Hadley replied, eyes focused on the ship, still unaware of who was standing next to them. There was no way she could let him know without her voice cracking. "It's at least a twenty minute walk."

"My shuttle leaves in fifteen. I'll run."

"You'll never make it. Maybe there's another option for you."

"Only if that other option is headed for Brisia."

Hadley's shoulders sank in relief as he turned around. "Commander. It's nice to meet you."

The Imperial Haederan Navy commander clapped him on the shoulder. "Better hurry. Launch window closes in less than fifteen minutes."

Was it her imagination, or had his accent become uneven?

Hadley took her by the arm and led her behind the Haederan, who was cutting through the lessening crowd with ease. Well, that was one way to hide in plain sight. Passengers simply parted for him. A polar opposite from the rest of the heavily guarded hangar bays at the shuttleport, the launch pad where their ship sat turned out to be reserved for previously cleared passengers and pilots. The commander let them out a side door, and Avery forced herself to walk at an unsuspicious pace. The door slid shut as soon as the three were inside the ship, and she got her first good look at who she prayed was their escort.

Dark hair, green eyes, patrician nose, and the accent he had affected with his last words to Hadley . . . It was like looking at a male version of herself in a mirror and hearing herself speak before she'd spent three years on Ventana. This man could never be mistaken for the Haederan officer he claimed to be. He looked just like her, just like the rest of her people who'd descended from the erstwhile Asrian nobility.

"You've got to be kidding me." The rude comment spilled out before she could stop it, but there was no way someone who looked like him could get away with the disguise for long.

"Stev Kanmar, Your Majesty." He bowed formally, a gesture made all the stranger by the abhorrent uniform he wore. "I'm sorry for the deception—and for the uniform."

"I'm surprised it fools anyone. You look exceedingly Asrian, Commander."

Hadley coughed. "Let's get moving, shall we? He can explain the rest once we're in the air."

The rest?

Kanmar nodded and led them to the small bridge, where another Haederan-uniformed officer was running through check-lists. "Commander Cayne March," he said simply. March nodded, in too much of a rush with his procedures for any formalities, which was fine with her. "Cabins—this way." He guided them through the small ship, no more than a flying cargo hold with a crew compartment attached as an afterthought. "We have a missavia harvest from the south on board, in case anyone gets suspicious enough to check on what we're carrying."

Kanmar showed them the first small cabin, and Avery was contemplating the possibility of getting through six weeks without a panic attack when the launch alarm rang. She strapped herself into one of the pull-down jump seats in the hallway of the cabin section and focused on him instead of the claustrophobia.

"I've got to know now." She nodded at his jacket, and the insignia that proclaimed him a Haederan space operations officer. "How long did you think you could get away with that?"

Kanmar looked at Hadley. "You didn't tell her the rest?"

There was that phrase again. *The rest.* Being kept in the dark was tiring—and infuriating. Had her father dealt with the same thing during his brief reign?

"Don't look at me, sir." Hadley tightened his straps. "Your queen has never heard the phrase 'don't kill the messenger.' I'm afraid you get to explain this mess to her."

His queen?

Then this man *was* Asrian.

Kanmar sighed. "I'd hoped General Teruel would have done it himself, but it appears no one wants to talk about it." He looked at Avery with no small amount of doubt, probably anxious about Hadley's warning. "It's not a disguise. Two months ago, the

Haederans decided it would be prudent on their part to assimilate any Defense Forces officers they could, as a way of limiting protests and insurrections. I'm pleased to report the reaction to their offer has not been entirely favorable for them."

He grinned. "But some of us were unlucky enough to have been recruited by our friends at Villiers. I was perfectly happy in Tarragona daydreaming of sabotage before this, but Cayne and I have been ferrying people out for over a month now. Usually, we take Haederan officers to the command ships in orbit, but sometimes . . . others. Now you. That's made this whole thing worth it for me."

The Defense Forces had agents in place in the Haederan military?

"I think I'm getting a headache," she said to Hadley. "And I can see why Teruel conveniently avoided telling me about this himself."

"It's the only way to get you past orbit. Coming back to Asria is one thing," Kanmar said, giving her a pointed look, "but only a Haederan-controlled ship would make it out, and we are officially Haederan officers. Just ones who have old loyalties. We also have the codes, the routes. And since this is it for us, the uniforms are going out the air lock as soon as we're on our way, Your Majesty," he assured her. "Our Asrian ones are aboard."

Avery rubbed her eyes, then tightened the straps on the seat as the ship lifted off. *Goodbye Asria . . . again.*

"I'm surprised they trust you," she said.

"Oh, they don't. Not much anyway. We're glorified delivery drivers and propaganda instruments." He grimaced. "I'm not sure I'll ever forgive myself for that second part. But every once in a while, the job works in our favor."

"And is it really Commander Kanmar?"

"Lieutenant colonel, ma'am. March too." His tone approached something like bitterness for the first time. "They gave us equivalent rank in their navy as a gesture of 'goodwill.'"

"I see."

She'd discuss this entire situation with Teruel later and find out how many others weren't as loyal. It had better be a short list, and she wouldn't be forgiving toward those officers who had truly taken up with the Haederans. Why was her job so unpleasant? Why was this even her job to begin with?

Right.

Because of her own family.

She closed her eyes, signaling the end of the conversation on her part. They broke orbit less than an hour later, and she passed out on the narrow bunk in her assigned cabin.

* * *

Hours later, just after she'd watched the buoys that marked the edge of the Asrian system pass out of sight, Hadley collapsed on the sofa across from her in the cramped salon.

"Marriage agrees with you," he said. "You look content. I've never actually seen that look on your face before."

She forced a smile. That was because he had only known her as an ambitious cadet at the Commonwealth's Academy on Ventana IV, determined to head her class, then a princess of an occupied planet, determined to stay alive. Or was there more to it?

"In other words," she said, "I should have done this years ago?"

Merritt had pointed that out the morning she left Villiers, and it'd caused an argument. She couldn't understand why he had needed to focus on the past. They were married now, weren't they? Nothing except death could change that. Her chest ached at the thought. Death was closer than either of them deserved.

"I should be the last one to say this, but yes. You look happy —" He waved a hand. "No, you *are* happy, and I'm glad to see it."

Avery laughed. "Well, you're right. It turns out marriage is not nearly as bad as I thought it would be ten years ago." Or eight years ago, when she'd turned down Merritt's almost-proposal and almost ended their courtship. "You should try it sometime."

It was Hadley's turn to chuckle. "I don't think so. Marriage would slow me down too much."

She was about to make a comment that was better left unsaid when Kanmar walked in. He slid onto the double sofa next to Hadley, clearly avoiding the larger one she sat on. Cramped didn't begin to describe the salon, and she hadn't yet decided if it was a good thing that everyone gave her as much space as possible. A relief sometimes, that was true, but isolating at the same time.

"So, here's the plan," Kanmar began. "We make Brisia in four more days, and there we'll meet up with my contact. She's got the new ship ready to go, or so I'm told."

He didn't sound sure enough about the status of the new ship for her comfort. They were losing almost a week stopping at Brisia, but it was too risky to continue on to Ventana in a ship that might have been marked leaving Asria.

"From there, it's only another four weeks to Ventana," Hadley added. "As long as we avoid any Haederan issues."

And that would be the real trick. The published routes between Brisia and Ventana all veered much too close to Haederan space for anyone's comfort. A new ship would help, but Avery couldn't help the lingering feeling that it wouldn't be enough. And Brisia, as a completely independent planet, one that had no loyalties but money, wasn't friendly to the Haederans or Commonwealth. One more potential snag in their plan. It was a good place to buy a clean ship, though.

"Covers?" Hadley asked.

"Erlite miners looking for work throughout the quadrant, since we can't go home to Asria. I'm Emmed Vincan, traveling with my sister Jessa and two cousins, one of whom just happens to be a pilot. The Haederans shouldn't care about a few apolitical Asrians who haven't set foot on Asrian soil in over a year." He glanced at Hadley. "That's assuming, Captain, that you can drop that Voirian accent. If not, we'll have to come up with some other explanation for your background."

"I don't think dropping the accent will be a problem, sir." Hadley's normal Voirian drawl had disappeared—he sounded more Asrian than Kanmar.

Kanmar raised an eyebrow, and Avery laughed.

"He does a Haederan one even better. It's—well, unnerving is an understatement." It had even fooled a prison full of Haederan soldiers. "But what if we run into trouble? I'm not sure Asrian cover identities will be the best protection."

"Don't take this the wrong way, Your Majesty, but have you looked in a mirror lately? It's not a perfect cover, but neither you nor I stand much of a chance of passing as anyone else. It'll be enough to buy us time if we're boarded. Which I do not expect at all." Kanmar frowned, probably picturing their route. "I probably don't need to reiterate that the goal here is avoidance."

No, he didn't need to remind anyone on board of that. And Hadley was good at avoidance, even in those situations where one thought confrontation was inevitable. Kanmar sounded certain enough, and Hadley had the skills. It would be enough.

It had to be enough.

CHAPTER SIX

Six hours out of the Brisian docks, Avery stood in the center of her new cabin with her arms out, relieved she couldn't reach any of the walls. The transport ship Kanmar purchased from his Brisian contact on behalf of the Asrian Defense Forces was almost three times the size of the cargo ship they'd departed Asria on. Their discarded ship was now parked in a temporary dock at one of Brisia's many orbital mercantile stations, with instructions to place it for auction. If luck held, she would never see it again. No more of the ship that had taken her away from home and had subjected her to weeks of near panic in her small cabin.

In the doorway, Hadley chuckled at her test. "Better now?"

"Better will be when I can have my rooms in the palace at Cadena back, but this will do for now." She smiled, hoping he wouldn't see the comment as a complaint, but as the dream it was. It was astonishing how much she wanted to go home. Not to Ventana IV, not to Villiers, not even to her family's estate in Sabino, but back to the royal palace in Cadena.

Where she belonged.

"Closer and closer to that every day, I think."

Hadley was more optimistic than she'd seen him since her time at the Academy, and it put her in a better mood as well. The stop at Brisia had been good for all of them. Avery had sent yet another message to the Commonwealth's council on Ventana—though with any luck they would be there before it arrived—and they had all soaked up the news that had been available from a free planet.

There hadn't been enough news though, and they had wanted more. More news and better news. Thaopra and Hanides, occupied by Haedera since before Avery had returned to Asria, had been liberated by Commonwealth forces in just the past month. She'd swallowed a bit of frustration and anger at that information —the two planets were not Commonwealth members, and both their populations were so limited that it almost seemed a waste of effort and firepower. At least it appeared the Commonwealth Navy was finally headed in Asria's direction. That was something encouraging, at least.

Unless it was true, as Baylen feared, and the Commonwealth wouldn't be coming to help them at all. The senate had voted almost officially to withdraw from the Commonwealth, after all—even if it had been under duress. Did the manner of the vote matter in Asrian or Commonwealth law? She hated to acknowledge she had no idea.

And was Baylen right about the other things? Was the Commonwealth relieved they had one less planet to defend? There were Asrians serving in the Commonwealth fleet that very minute, thousands of them spread throughout the quadrant. The Commonwealth's refusal to defend Asria would be an insult to them more than anyone else.

Avery shook her head at his optimism. "Do you really believe that? That we're close to winning this thing?"

"I think the Haederans will have to start running soon. They couldn't even hold mostly uninhabited planets. What makes them think they can control larger ones?"

"They controlled the habitats on the open-air uninhabitable planets through fear." Hadley knew the answer, even if his hopefulness was clouding his mind. "That's easy when you're talking only a thousand people. In Asria's case, they're controlling us with the bombers in orbit. We can't do anything to provoke them on the ground—much of anything, anyway—without reprisals that will be much greater than the few executions the smaller planets have suffered through."

A few executions on Asria would be bad enough, no—*had* been bad enough, but even worse retaliation, more widespread retaliation, had been her greatest fear for the continued existence of the underground base at Villiers. The Haederans had requested their surrender over and over, and the request had been alternately ignored and denied, depending on Teruel's mood on the day of the request.

The denials were a risky endeavor. How much longer until the Haederans punished ordinary citizens for the Defense Forces' continued defiance? Or how much longer until the Haederans broke through the not-quite-impenetrable defenses at their new headquarters? Would they bomb city after city out of existence just to punish them?

So far, they had not, and it was only an uneasy martial law that persisted in Cadena and the other large cities, but something had to give. Maybe that was another of Baylen's concerns, and another reason he had for getting her out of Villiers and off Asria. But Merritt was still down in Villiers, and she couldn't lose him again.

"But maybe you're right."

She gave Hadley a smile that was supposed to appear tired instead of anxious. Faking hopefulness was the only way to hope.

"I have to be." His look grew distant, like he was seeing straight through the ship's hull, out past it into deep space. "You know we're passing Voirs just off to our left right now?"

"Just off?" Avery tested the water faucet over the small sink in the cabin. The water had a chemical smell like it hadn't been run in several weeks, and she rubbed her nose. "More like hundreds of light-years off our left."

"It's the closest I've come in years." He looked at the running water and shook his head at the smell. "Ventana is like a second home, but it's not . . ."

"Home?"

Hadley smiled. "Right. You know, I missed my sister's wedding on Voirs three years ago. I can't even remember what sector I was in then. I'm not sure she'll ever forgive me. I'm not sure I'll ever forgive myself. Whatever I was doing couldn't have been that important if I can't even remember what it was."

"You could always resign. You must be past your obligation date by now."

"Now?" He shook his head. "There's too much going on. The guilt of abandoning the fight would eat me up until I died. Besides"—the smile was unfeigned now—"what if I hate unemployment?"

"You could start a new life on Ventana. You always seemed happy there, and they would be glad to have you at the academy full time, I think."

"Teach? Now there's an idea." Amusement was clear in his voice. "A crazy one."

"You taught me. I know you haven't already forgotten that."

He raised his eyebrows. "I didn't teach you very well."

"I am almost certain the fault lies with the student, not the teacher." It wasn't Hadley's fault she had appallingly poor espionage skills. "And a lot of other unfortunate circumstances that you had nothing to do with."

Her smile fell. Maybe Elex Feye was the reason Hadley didn't seem as happy planet-hopping as he had when Avery had known him as a cadet. Feye's betrayal ate at her some empty nights, sometimes so much that she ended up staring at the ceiling in frustrated tears for hours. It would have to be worse for Hadley, who had worked with him for longer than she'd known him.

"Well, it doesn't matter. No more unfortunate circumstances for us. Can we make that deal?" Hadley held out a hand, and she shook it, wishing they had that much control over their futures.

* * *

Even tired as she was, going right to sleep after her conversation with Hadley in the middle of the ship's day cycle hadn't been a wonderful decision. She'd struggled with long-distance space travel her whole life, and it became worse with each trip. No more, or at least very limited, long-distance space travel was one perk of her new position, it seemed—and even though she'd accepted her new life, she still needed to count its benefits.

She'd tried to contact Merritt during their brief stop on Brisia, but the communications delay had been too long to make a conversation worthwhile, so she'd recorded a message and sent it on. With any luck, one of the Commonwealth scout ships in the Asrian system could relay it to Villiers.

Wide awake, she stumbled down the corridor into the salon. She was toying with the hot-water dispenser, which was making her night worse by refusing to dispense anything, when Kanmar walked in, laid eyes on her, and promptly walked out again. Thrilled for someone else's company, and unwilling to let that company escape back to his quarters, she chased him down the hallway.

"I hope you didn't leave on my account," she called.

Kanmar looked trapped, and she almost regretted following him out the door.

"I was just going for a walk. I don't want to intrude, Your Majesty."

"You're not. Truly. Hadley is good company, but he's not Asrian, and I'm half starved for Asrian companionship." Especially the kind that would treat her as a person and not a monarch. Which ruled Kanmar out, but she wouldn't be particular when her options were so limited. "Come back and have a drink with me. Anything, as long as it doesn't require boiling water."

He looked reluctant, but followed her back to the wardroom anyway, where he made quick work of the wayward dispenser.

Not that he'd let her make him a drink—his formality was much too oppressive for that. Was it his personality, or was it her?

They sat in uncomfortable silence with their steaming tea for almost ten minutes before she spoke.

"Why did Teruel pick you for this?" she asked.

It wasn't the light conversation she preferred in the middle of the night, but it was the first question that came to mind, and she was curious about a person who would have agreed to this mission. For she doubted Teruel would have ordered someone to do this.

"He didn't pick me. I volunteered."

"Why?" It wasn't the worst job to volunteer for, but it wasn't the safest. Anymore, she didn't trust people who volunteered for jobs that weren't safe. Did Kanmar have an ulterior motive in stepping forward for this mission?

Surely not. Teruel would have made sure Kanmar and March were absolutely reliable, beyond reproach. He'd initially refused to let even Hadley go with them—*for security reasons, you must understand, Your Majesty*—and Avery, furious Teruel wouldn't acknowledge Hadley was not actually Asrian and therefore not subject to his whims, had pulled royal rank on the general for the first time that she could remember.

So yes, Kanmar had to be trustworthy. Maybe he had been bored on Asria and needed some excitement. But that uniform he'd been wearing when she'd met him gave her pause. Perhaps it wasn't as uncomfortable for him to wear as he had pretended. The idea sent a chill down her spine, a chill she hid with a smile.

"My wife and three children live in Tarragona," he said, as if that explained everything.

"Ah."

Well, that certainly explained much of his decision. Tarragona, the small town on the other side of the world from Cadena, where the Haederans were *still* mining verium for their stealth spacecraft.

Only verium didn't matter any longer, since the Commonwealth had the verium-enhanced fighter she'd stolen. It was only a matter of time until they created their own version of the stealth fuel—perhaps there were stealth Commonwealth ships out there right now, headed for Asria. One could only hope their engineers had created something similar so quickly. But that wasn't even the most pointless part of the continual mining at Tarragona.

Verium wasn't as effective as the Haederans believed—the stealth ships were traceable if you knew what you were looking for. That had been the actual information she'd risked her life to get off of Asria. That vulnerability in the Haederans' technology was what the Commonwealth had needed to know more than anything else.

And no matter what he'd done before, Elex Feye had given his life to keep that secret.

"Many people on Asria have family in places worse off than Tarragona," Avery went on, running a finger along the edge of her cup. "They didn't volunteer."

Why did that spill out of her mouth? Movement caught her eyes as Hadley walked up to the door. She made eye contact with him over Kanmar's head, hoping he could read her almost imperceptible head shake. He kept moving, and she focused her attention back on Kanmar, who was looking at her with a little more respect.

"Has anyone ever told you you're very perceptive, Majesty?"

I thought so.

"Ah, never, actually." In fact, Merritt had once told her the opposite was true, though that had been years ago. She was getting better at reading people—a necessity now. "I take it I stumbled across an incomplete explanation?"

Kanmar looked out the door of the wardroom as Hadley passed by in the opposite direction. Avery expected he'd try to make a run for it again, but he answered her with another question.

"How much do you know about why the king—about why *he* left Asria?"

Interesting. Both the question and Kanmar's unwillingness to say her uncle's name.

"I thought I knew everything. Everything General Cevall told me at least."

"Then you know about the coup."

The coup.

The group of Royal Asrian Defense Forces personnel who hadn't agreed with some of her uncle's policies regarding the Commonwealth—and who'd done something about it. They'd been found out before they could overthrow the king, but her uncle had fled Asria because of it anyway. And his decision had touched off . . . everything.

"Attempted coup, you mean," she replied.

She didn't like where this was going. It wouldn't be possible for Kanmar to have been one of the dissenters. Surely not. Teruel would never have allowed that, and Cevall said the issue had been taken care of. She'd never asked for clarification.

"If you prefer that qualifier." It was obvious Kanmar did not. "Three involved reported to me and I feel responsible for what they did. I should have put a stop to the talk when it was just chatter."

"If I'm not mistaken, they never actually did anything except talk, so you would have done even less than that." Unlike her uncle, who had actually acted on his fear.

"It was still treason, and I still failed to quash it."

"And you feel the need to make up for what they did."

That was a feeling she knew all too well. She would spend the rest of her life paying Asria back for what her uncle had done. For longer than the rest of her life, if she could legislate something. Maybe she could start with a memorial to those who had perished in the initial attack? She tucked that idea away for later. So much would have to happen before recompense was feasible, starting with the Haederans' removal from Asria.

"If you're worried about my motivations, I'd have volunteered anyway. I want them gone."

"Then it's good enough for me." She couldn't argue with that. That desire was all too familiar, and those words were exactly what she wanted to hear. She swallowed the last of her tea and yawned. "I do have one other question. You don't know Merritt, do you?"

Kanmar shrugged. "We served together on Emot, but that was a long time ago, and I didn't know him well. I haven't seen him in years."

"I see. I was just curious." Kanmar must be five years older than Merritt, and Emot would have been at least nine years ago. Too bad. She would have loved a fresh perspective on what Merritt had been like back then.

Kanmar grabbed her cup and cracked a smile before he turned to make two more cups of tea. "I have a few stories though, if you're interested in hearing them, ma'am," he said over his shoulder.

Avery covered her mouth with a hand to hide her grin.

"Oh, am I ever."

CHAPTER SEVEN

A week later, Avery still hadn't adapted to the ship's clock, even though March kept the ship on a twenty-five-hour Asrian day. The brief naps that allowed her to manage any kind of function during the day also prevented her from sleeping for more than two hours at a time at night. She would never get onto the ship's cycle if she continued that pattern, but at least it was temporary, wasn't it? Once they reached Ventana and there were natural lighting cues, her sleep would improve—but her wrecked circadian rhythm wasn't the only cause of her insomnia. It was also the inescapable anxiety on the ship.

She found herself on the bridge in the middle of the night after yet another aimless wander through the ship. At least it was more stimulating than sitting in an empty salon. The view out the front screen was black, and she found herself wishing they could slow down so she could see the stars. The view of the stars from her first flight in a spacecraft had dazzled her with its brilliance, though after twenty flights, it became all too familiar. Easily ignored.

She'd never take the view for granted again.

"Mind if I join you?" She slipped into the first officer's seat next to March and examined the controls. If he was anything like Kanmar, he'd hate the shadowing from his sovereign, but she was too desperate to be behind the stick of a spacecraft again to care much if she intimidated him.

"Only if you want to fly for a bit, Your Majesty. I could use the break."

Avery shot him a grateful but tired smile as he transferred authorization to the secondary panel in front of her. Flying something this large and advanced was more monitoring than flying, especially in the emptiness of deep space—there wasn't even the control stick she was used to in fighters. But it was better than the other on-board entertainment options. March gave her an overview of the spacecraft's navigation and controls, then leaned back in the pilot's seat as she took over what passed for flying.

"We'll have to slow down going by Ethryia," he said, leaning back and closing his eyes. "That solar flare they had last year is still spitting enough radiation across our route to make it hard on the hyperlight engines."

March's matter-of-factness belied his concern. Three Haederan-controlled transit routes lay just to the outside of the Ethryian system, and while Commonwealth intel suggested they were lightly patrolled, there was always the chance something would go wrong.

"Can we speed through there anyway?" she asked.

She wanted to see the stars of sublight travel, but not at the expense of their well-being. Maybe March was being too cautious about the solar flare, coddling the spaceship too much. Some pilots did that, though she never had. Coddling a fighter in a skirmish could get one killed. Quickly. And a flight being hard on the hyperlight engines was one thing, but running into a Haederan ship was quite another. They could always have the engines repaired on Ventana if needed.

"Technically we can keep past light speed, but if we burn up the hyperlight engines, we won't have enough fuel to make it to a friendly planet. We'll be an easy target."

Avery focused on an automated check of the environmental systems. She should have known better.

"Come on—where's your sense of adventure?" Contrary to his words, March sounded like he wanted some of her nonexistent bravery.

She feigned a laugh. "I think that ended when I grew up."

Or when the Haederans had attacked Asria. Or when she'd become queen. Or when she'd stolen that fighter off the Haederan cruiser. It was so hard to tell when her life had ceased to be fun, but her sense of adventure had been smashed.

"True for all of us, no?" He shrugged. "It'll be fine. Even if we run into a Haederan ship, they'll be too busy to deal with a small merchant craft. We're no threat to them. Now if you don't mind, Your Majesty, I'm going to get a little shut-eye."

"Go ahead." Avery nodded, concealing a genuine smile that time.

March headed to the small compartment just outside the bridge that she'd never have a hope of sleeping in. She shook off the claustrophobia that had threatened to overwhelm her when she'd first seen the pilot's sleeping berth—she was flying a spaceship, finally flying without someone watching over her shoulder.

For the first time in a year, it didn't matter what the Haederans had done to her.

* * *

Hours passed, and Avery was almost to the point of falling asleep as well. They were well into the lightly populated Ethryian system now, running on sublight engines only, and moving much too slowly for her comfort. Her fingers had lingered near the hyperlight engine start switches more than once, but March was right—it was too risky to run them that hard with the flare so close.

She flipped through the status of each system to keep herself awake, but yawned and rubbed her eyes anyway. Thankfully, the job was straightforward, even for a pilot who was half asleep. Monitoring a highly advanced ship in deep space was boring, but boring was better than the alternative, wasn't it? Boring was always better than the alternative.

Environmental systems. Check. The gravity generators were running a little low—March must have turned them down to save on power until they were past Ethryia. Avery left them alone. Strapped in as she was, she didn't notice a difference. The sleeping passengers wouldn't either.

Navigation. All green. She yawned again, depressed at the sight of the navigation display. Ventana was still three weeks away, the coordinates so distant they might as well be in a different galaxy.

Propulsion. The sublight engines were functioning normally. Her finger hovered over the hyperlight engine switch again, but she pulled it back.

Targeting system . . .

There was only one target on the screen. It was over a thousand kilometers in front of them and crossing right to left, which must be why the system hadn't automatically alerted her to another ship. She glared at the blip, annoyed beyond reason that this targeting system wasn't nearly as accurate or responsive as the military systems she was used to. It was most likely another merchant spacecraft crossing their route, but it was close enough to be concerning.

What if it was . . .

The manual targeting analysis beeped in panic, and Avery straightened, simultaneously hitting the button which would call March back to the bridge, a prayer not quite formulated in her mind. If the Holy One had been protecting her for the past year, He was not any longer.

All the empty space in the galaxy, and they were going to cross paths with a Haederan heavy cruiser.

* * *

March hadn't stopped swearing since he'd returned to his seat five minutes earlier. Avery sat next to him without speaking as he tried to determine route after futile route that would take them unnoticed past the Haederan ship, but there were no nearby planets large enough to conceal them, not even a local space anomaly spewing some kind of high intensity radiation that would hide their signature. Even the Ethryian solar flare that had kept them at sublight speed wouldn't be enough to hide them from the cruiser's advanced tracking systems.

He finally stopped swearing long enough to concentrate, tapping an impatient finger on the navigation panel and an impatient foot on the floor, and Avery read his frustration. If they turned around, or even stopped to let the cruiser pass by, the Haederans would be suspicious, but the ship had slowed enough that continuing on their present path would cause a collision or worse.

There was no doubt they had been spotted. March cut the hyperlight engines off from standby, and she knew he hoped that even that slight reduction of power would be enough to keep them from glowing as an obvious target on the Haederans' screens. But at this distance, even their sublight engines had to be putting off a signature bright enough they might as well have been within visual range.

Sure enough, as Kanmar entered the too-crowded bridge, rubbing interrupted sleep from his eyes, the first call came across the comm.

"Unidentified merchant vessel, you have entered a restricted route. Transmit your identification over this frequency and prepare to be boarded."

The voice was cold. Professional, but cold.

"Boarded?" Avery repeated. She lowered her head to the side console. The coolness of the metal calmed her stomach enough that she could look up again.

March ignored her question. "This is the Brisian merchant vessel *Zephyr*. Identifications being transmitted."

"You aren't even going to tell them this isn't a restricted route?" she asked.

"Argue with them, Your Majesty? You know the firepower that ship has. This is the best-case scenario in this situation." Kanmar worked the controls to transmit their false identities. "We cooperate, they board us, they search us, they find nothing, and they leave. They're looking for weapons, supplies that we might be smuggling to their occupied planets, not people." He glanced at Avery. "Certainly not you."

A fast-attack corvette appeared on the targeting screen and pulled away from the cruiser—the boarding party, no doubt. She couldn't watch the distance between the corvette and their ship close faster and faster. With one last look at the stars in the viewscreen, she ran her hands over her face and ducked off the bridge to find Hadley.

She hadn't yet made it to his quarters when the ship shook, and she had to cling to a handhold, normally only used if the gravity generators failed, for support. Was the cruiser firing on them? March had complied with all their orders, but they were the enemy and not to be trusted. Maybe it would be a direct hit the next time, and death would be quick and painless.

Her breath caught. Or maybe it was just a warning, though the practice of firing a warning shot in space was treacherous, to say the least. To the victim, of course, not the aggressor. The thin hull wouldn't respond well to any kind of projectile hitting it, and if the Haederans were off by so much as a fraction in their targeting calculations . . .

The ship shuddered again, and that time she could tell it was a tow beam.

The corvette is only a distraction.

She could barely catch her breath as she struggled back toward Hadley's quarters on legs that were suddenly weak. The Haederans didn't mean to board them at all but planned to drag them aboard the cruiser. For a more thorough search? Or did they know more about who was on board than Kanmar thought they would?

Hadley dashed out of his room at the second shake of the spaceship and dragged her back to the bridge, where she sat down hard in a vacant seat behind March. Kanmar was finally arguing with the cruiser when she returned.

"*Imperieuse*, we're not carrying enough fuel for that trip." Kanmar twisted toward her and shook his head. "They're claiming our armament makes it too dangerous to board us. I can't imagine why they would want us and our imaginary weapons aboard, but they're a little insistent. You felt the beam."

It was as if she could see it out there in space too: an unbreakable thread that coupled their small craft to the enemy ship, even though it was impossible to see with the naked eye.

Hadley looked out the side window. "We can't hide anyone on board," he said, glancing at her. "Their sensors will pick up an extra person in a heartbeat. Think we can get away from them?"

March shook his head. "Not with the hyperlight engines shut down. It would take another twenty minutes to get them spooled up, and they would see what we're doing as soon as I turn them to standby. Anyway, they've made enough threats of what they'll do if we don't comply with everything they say. The only thing we can do now is hope the original plan works."

He didn't need to mention what the tow beam would do to their ship if they tried to break away, and there was no question what the cruiser had threatened. The Haederans wouldn't think twice about destroying a small merchant ship which didn't act unquestionably in accordance with their demands.

"How long is this going to take?" Avery asked. Sitting on the edge of capture by a Haederan warship was more than she could bear. Best to move on with whatever was going to happen on board the enemy ship. The sooner they were towed in, the sooner . . . what? Catch and release, hopefully. The alternative didn't bear thinking about.

"At this speed?" In the navigation display's glow, Kanmar's face was pale. "It'll be hours before they tow us in."

At least that would give them time to clarify their cover

stories. That would take all of ten minutes—then there would be hours to sit and contemplate their fate.

Perfect.

Avery shrank into the seat and wished it was a portal to safety.

CHAPTER EIGHT

In slow motion, at least it seemed to Avery, the merchant ship floated to the docking bay floor of *Imperieuse* thirteen hours later, while she floated between terror and absurd relief. *Zephyr* was designed for travel at high speeds, and with the engines shut down and only marginal backup power on, its life support systems had begun to object three hours before. But surely the tightness in her chest was her imagination.

March hadn't dared start the engines back up, though. Not until things were critical, which Avery was grateful they had not become. Out the window, a warning light flashed on the bulkhead, and atmosphere filled around the ship. The light went solid green, and the tech in the gallery window waved off to his side. Summoning the boarding crew, no doubt.

"That's it then." March cut the rest of the power to the ship. He looked as sick as she felt. "Just sit tight for now."

She breathed shallowly and focused out the forward window on the green status light, unable to move.

"Merchant vessel *Zephyr*, you have sixty seconds to open your forward boarding door and exit the ship, hands in the air."

Avery flinched. Kanmar punched the back of the seat in front of him.

She stood and let out a breathless giggle. "What were you expecting, Colonel? A welcome party?"

Kanmar shook his head, probably internally cursing her inability to stay calm. Nervousness could be so humiliating.

"I'm out first," he replied. "You"—he looked at Hadley—"behind me. Your Majesty, stick as close behind him as you can. March, bring up the rear and stay close to her. Remember, the goal is to have them question us and let us go. That's all. Do not improvise. This is not an intelligence-gathering mission."

That last statement was directed at Hadley, who favored Kanmar with a sardonic two-fingered salute. Avery stumbled to the boarding door behind him, but panicked at the last second and turned back toward the center of the ship, bumping into March.

"I can't do this."

He looked blankly at her, and Hadley caught her by the arm.

"You've got about fifteen seconds before they come through that door with an arc cutter, so *move*."

She shook her head, certain it was only his support keeping her upright. Didn't he know what was going to happen to them?

"Look," he whispered, "this isn't so bad yet. All you have to do is act. You've done that before. Hell, I've seen you do it. And don't panic. You can do this."

"All right." Shivering, she nodded, not believing her own words. "All right."

Kanmar opened the door at the gesture, and she walked as slowly as possible down the ramp behind Hadley, hands on her head, staring at the backs of his knees. That seemed cowardly, so she shifted her view to the back of his neck and immediately wished she hadn't.

An entire squad waited for them on the deck of the hangar bay, with rifles—not stun rifles, but the deadly kind—at the ready. It was hard to breathe and look at them, so she looked back down at Hadley's boots until he stopped.

At least two pairs of hands searched her roughly as she stood there, staring at the deck. A pointless move, meant for intimidation only. Did the Haederans think the occupants of a private merchant ship would be so foolish as to bring weapons on board?

She risked glancing up once more just as a rifle hit the back of her legs, sending her sprawling to her knees between Hadley and March, who had been allowed to kneel on their own. All she wanted to do was rub her elbow where she'd hit it on the deck, but she didn't dare move. The deck was cold, and she cast a frantic look at Kanmar. *They're going to kill us*, she tried to project to him.

He ignored her unspoken plea and turned toward the officer in charge, an Imperial Haederan Navy lieutenant who didn't look like he cared how his newest catch was treated.

"Which one of you is the pilot?" the lieutenant asked.

"I am," March said evenly.

Avery concealed a gasp as the lieutenant pulled a stun pistol and shot him in the chest. March fell face-first to the deck, and she held her breath until his breathing became regular again. Was this a new security protocol no one had warned them about, or just paranoia?

"That leaves you in charge?" the lieutenant asked Kanmar.

"My sister and cousins." Some color had returned to Kanmar's face, and Avery envied his nerve. He nodded and jerked his head toward her and Hadley. "I transmitted our identification earlier."

The Haederan narrowed his eyes at Kanmar, as if suspecting a trap, then turned to a waiting sergeant. "Start the search of the ship and bring over the palm scanner."

Avery stared at the deck, unblinking, barely able to breathe. The Haederans were supposed to believe the identification Kanmar had sent just after being intercepted. They weren't supposed to make any effort to verify it. That assumption seemed like a bad one now. So did the entire mission. But there was still a chance—

Kusir.

Avery winced as someone pulled her arm backward in a way it didn't want to bend and pushed it against the handheld scanner. In pain and without thinking, she tried to pull it away, only to have a pistol pushed against her skull.

Two Haederans with rifles approached and she froze, unable to breathe, unable to think, unable to fight any longer. Because this was overkill for one person. They were taking this interception too seriously. They were supposed to have boarded the ship, searched it, and let them go.

Why hadn't they?

The lieutenant stared at her, a warning, his hand twitching on his gun. The techs twisted her wrist into an even more awkward position, and she yanked it back without thinking. The scanner clattered to the deck.

Hadley swore under his breath.

Before she could breathe, she was face down on the metal, the pistol against her head replaced by a boot. She closed her eyes, waiting. It was all over now. Once the security guard put his weight on her head . . .

"Just what did you think this would accomplish?" The lieutenant's breath was hot on her ear as he pushed his pistol under her chin. He laughed at her sob. "Hold still, or there won't be anything left of you to identify."

Kanmar swore that time, though not as quietly as Hadley.

"Jessa." The reminder was clear. "Jessa, don't fight them. Just do what they want."

I can't. I can't.

She gritted her teeth, motionless. He and Hadley didn't understand. How could they not see what was going to happen to them? Only the thought of Merritt that flashed into her mind . . . She had to survive, if only for his sake.

The tech twisted her hand behind her back again. "Good scan this time. Give it five minutes for confirmation."

A tear landed on the deck, flattening out immediately. He had to be lying. Their entire plan hinged on their cover identities, but there was no way of falsifying prints or retinal scans. It was all over.

The lieutenant pulled her back up on her knees. "Her first."

What?

They jerked her up and toward the side of the hangar bay, and she chanced one last look back. Hadley looked bored. She'd have been insulted by his detachment if she hadn't known him better. Kanmar looked murderous. March . . . She couldn't look at him, still sprawled face down on the deck.

They took her to a small room to the side of the hangar, staffed with only one security lieutenant behind a desk who would figure out their identities soon. The tech had said five minutes. Did it really matter, anyway? The Haederan ship had spent a lot of time chasing down what they were supposed to believe was a private transport, and a quiet, fearful place of her brain told her they already knew.

"Name?" the lieutenant asked.

Her mind went blank. She couldn't remember. Couldn't remember her cover name, couldn't remember their cover story, couldn't remember anything. The lieutenant tapped a finger on his desk, then raised his eyebrows at her. Impatient, this one was. Jessa the miner would be too afraid to anger him by stalling.

Jessa.

That was it.

"Jessa Vincan." The answer was a whisper.

"You a miner?"

Avery nodded. At least the Haederans had skimmed the false information Kanmar had transmitted. That was something.

He made some notes and looked up again. "Citizenship?"

"I'm—I'm Asrian."

It sounded like a confession. But more than that, it was the key, though it was a fragile one now. She had to keep him out of the Commonwealth searches for as long as she could. Maybe by the time they got around to running a full search, they'd have all been released.

And stars really do fall.

The lieutenant looked her up and down, then snorted. "I figured as much. At least you can't lie about that. How did you get off Asria?" He swiped a finger on the desk and frowned, no doubt accessing information they had assumed the Haederans would never have access to. "No ship leaving in the last month has filed a plan across this route."

Avery suppressed a deep exhale of relief. So that was the source of the suspicion. Easily explained.

"We've been off-world for over two years. I wasn't there when you invaded. We—my brother and cousins—we've been hopping from system to system since then . . ." She let her voice shake, and that wasn't difficult either. She was too worried about the others, especially March. "We were heading to the Parchent sector to find work. I told them cutting through here was a terrible idea, but they wouldn't listen. We did nothing wrong. We didn't know this was restricted space. It wasn't on any of the charts. We wouldn't have done it if we'd known, I swear to you."

Talk.

She had to keep talking, like they would never expect so-called spies to do.

"Cousins?" The lieutenant made a few aimless marks on his desk. "None of you look anything alike."

It sounded like an offhand comment, but she wasn't so sure it was. And to think they had thought it wouldn't matter they didn't look like family. She and Kanmar looked similar enough, but the Haederans were seeing through their story earlier than they'd predicted. This whole plan was useless.

Avery shrugged, then mumbled, like a frightened civilian would, "I don't know what to say about that, sir. We just want to be on our way. I don't care about the situation on Asria or what you're doing there. We don't plan on ever going back. We only care about making a living. I just want to work and stay out of the way. Are you going to keep us here? What about our ship? It's the only thing we have. We need our ship back."

He sighed and was about to write something else—likely a notation on how unbelievable her story was, but that he couldn't prove it wrong until their identities were confirmed—when the door behind her opened.

Perfect.

More witnesses to her poor acting. Why hadn't they grabbed Hadley first? Hadley was the best actor she'd ever met. Everyone believed every single word he said. Well, everyone except the Asrian Defense Forces, perhaps. Strange how everyone believed him when he lied and not when he told the truth.

She was puzzling over that inconsistency when the sound of slow clapping filled the room. Confused, she frowned in the lieutenant's direction, but his attention was directed over her head.

"That was one of the most entertaining stories I've heard in a long time. Don't care about the situation on Asria, do you? I'm not sure I believe that." The clapping stopped, and there was a laugh behind her. "But you're improving. I'm very impressed."

That laugh . . . that voice . . . she'd know them anywhere.

Chase.

Chase was aboard *Imperieuse* with her.

A sudden dizziness grabbed her as she whirled to face him. Questions echoed in her mind, but she couldn't form any with her lips. Why was he here? How had he found her so quickly? The lieutenant was saying something behind her; Chase was saying something to her. It was only his lips that were moving, though— his actual words were lost as the blood rushed from her head. She was floating, drifting through someone else's life. Because he couldn't be right here in the room with her. He just couldn't.

"Easy now." A hand grabbed her elbow, though it wasn't threatening. "Don't forget to breathe."

Reality slammed into her, as violently as a fighter entering hyperspace. The daily nightmares had been bad enough, but this . . . Chase right *here* . . . She hadn't known until he took hold of her arm that she was shaking, her legs barely keeping her upright.

"Let me go." Her command was thick with fear.

"And let you collapse on the deck? I don't think so." He looked at her with a peculiar mix of irritation and something else. Triumph, that had to be it. He'd won, and he knew it.

She shrugged off his unwanted assistance and turned back toward the lieutenant who had stumbled to his feet upon Chase's entrance and was watching their interaction with a sort of horrified fascination. She silently pleaded with him with wide eyes. For what, she didn't know. It wasn't as though he could order Chase out. Could he? What was Chase *doing* here?

"Sir, no one told me you were—" The lieutenant regained his composure but still sounded incredulous. "You know this woman, Colonel?"

"For some time now, but not as Jessa Vincan," Chase said wryly. His attention turned to Avery. "Why don't you tell him who you are? The charade's over. It was a good try, though."

The lieutenant narrowed his eyes at her, her lie exposed much faster than either of them thought it would be. Or maybe he was narrowing them at Chase, wondering how he knew a manual laborer. It was hard to tell which one of them he was more exasperated with her at that moment. Did she have a chance at convincing them of the original story? That was a ludicrous idea. Chase was right there, and he knew her personally—there was no chance any longer.

"It's a simple question, my lady."

Chase sounded impatient now. She hated him for it. It would be a simple matter for him to tell the lieutenant who she was, but no, that would be too easy for him.

She licked her lips, barely avoiding biting them.

Sorry, Hadley . . .

"My name is Avery Rendon. Of Asria." It sounded like yet another confession. If nothing else, it was a much-needed reminder.

You are Avery Carina Victoria Rendon, Her Majesty the Queen of Asria, and you cannot be this afraid in front of them.

Her blown cover was almost worth the look on the lieutenant's face. "Not . . ."

She nodded, and the last of her hope vanished at his immediate recognition of the name. The lieutenant shook his head and raised his eyes to the ceiling, like he wanted no part of the mess he had fallen into. Chase stepped around her and handed him a data chip, and there was relief on the lieutenant's face when he stuck it into the desk and read the contents.

"Not to worry," Chase said, "she's being transferred to our custody. If you don't have any other business with her, I'll take her off your hands right now."

Horrified and suddenly unfrozen, she turned to stare at him. He wore the amused expression that had always aggravated her on Asria. Like the whole thing was a joke to him. Probably it was.

"Don't look at me like that." The amusement turned to a boyish grin. "You're our guest for now."

"You mean hostage, I'm sure."

Right. Annoy him. That always helped things before.

The lieutenant, staring at her transfer order and looking eager to be rid of both of them as soon as possible, interrupted before Chase could claim otherwise. "Do you require additional security, sir?"

"Do I?" Chase eyed her, the grin gone. "If it helps you make your decision, I'm not going to take you anywhere near a hangar."

The words were innocuous, but the underlying warning was not. What did he think she could do? Fight him with her bare hands?

"I'll . . ." She hated herself for her acquiescence. As much as she denied it to Hadley, the psychologists, and herself, Chase had done something to her, just like he'd done something to Elex Feye. He'd taken away her will and terrified her into compliance. Fighting him now, whether physically, emotionally, or psychologically, was out of the question. Not while he still owned part of her mind. "I'll go with you."

"Good decision." He addressed the lieutenant. "The others are yours for now. I'll have their identifications for you shortly."

* * *

Chase gestured her toward a side door next to the desk, not the one they'd both entered through. Avery hesitated, for just a second, while she contemplated the odds of escape, or at least the odds of making it through the door in the back of the room. There was no chance of Hadley seeing what was going on if they didn't exit back through the hangar, and he needed to know where she'd disappeared to.

Slim chance.

Grudgingly, she followed Chase into what looked like a main corridor. She slowed her pace after their first turn and looked around at what would hopefully, if there was any fairness in life at all, be her only visit to a Haederan ship. Even new and amateur espionage skills died hard.

"If you're trying to make me angry, that's the way to do it." He grabbed her upper arm and pulled her along next to him, disrupting her analysis of what looked like signs to the engineering section. "So was that lie back there."

"Like you've never pretended to be someone you're not. Besides, people have always used covers while traveling, since before we even made it into space." The view turned to a bland passageway that might be found on any ship of any planet's armed forces, and she forced her attention back to him. "It's always been safer."

"That's not what I'm talking about. You don't think they'll find out you lied about your last name? You wouldn't have wanted to deal with the consequences of that untruth if I hadn't found you first."

At that, she shot him a frantic look. He sounded mildly angry, which didn't bother her at all, but he appeared slightly curious, which did, since a curious Chase was bad news for her.

And how had he known that she and Merritt—well, it didn't matter. There were a dozen ways he could have found out they were married, none that involved a Haederan source at Villiers, though there was no question there was one. And there was no point in lying about their marriage since he already knew he could use Merritt against her.

No.

Since he *had* used Merritt against her.

"I didn't lie about that," she said reluctantly. "Spouses of the royal family take our name. It's been that way for hundreds of years."

And you don't know as much about Asria as you think you do.

"I see." Chase didn't seem at all flustered by his mistake or his accusation. "And how is Lieutenant Colonel Rendon doing?"

She jerked her arm away. "I think you know how he's doing."

"I wasn't involved in anything that happened at Alcaris. I wouldn't have any idea."

Liar.

"Do you really expect me to believe that? He *saw* you there."

"Please. He doesn't know what he saw."

He turned down a narrow corridor, and her eyes landed on a set of Imperial Security guards next to a door halfway down. She slowed again, the fear building. She didn't have to imagine what was waiting for her inside—she dreamed about it every night.

"Let me go." Avery ground her feet into the deck. "Just—let me go."

Chase ignored her half-hearted protest. He pulled her along and inside, and she blinked, relief washing over her. They were standing in a stateroom. It wasn't large, but it wasn't the smallest she'd ever been in. The size of a mid-level officer's quarters, perhaps. It certainly was larger than a cell in the brig where she'd expected to find herself. A single bed, cot-sized, but still a proper bed, was against the far wall, and the room was large enough for a small sitting area just inside the door. The sofa and two chairs opposite a low table looked more comfortable than the bunk, and she wished she could collapse in one. That would have to wait until she was alone. There was no lock on the inside of the door, in fact, no handle at all. It might not be the brig, but it was a prison all the same. Surely Chase hadn't arranged this with a half-hour's notice.

Chase watched her take in the room, that repulsive grin back on his face. "You look surprised."

"It's not what I was expecting."

Especially from you.

"I borrowed it from the political officer. We normally use it for . . . others. Would you prefer the brig, my lady?"

Her chin went up. "Yes."

If that's where Hadley and Kanmar were, yes. March ought to be in the infirmary. She deserved no better than any of them, even if she would lose her mind.

"You're lying," Chase said from the doorway, blocking any escape she might have in mind. "But it might ease your conscience somewhat to know that if it were up to me, that's exactly where you'd be. It's certainly where you belong. But fortunately for you, it's not my decision, so until I hear otherwise, you're our guest."

Somehow, he managed to say *guest* without a hint of irony. He had a strange definition of it, and comfortable cabin or not, she didn't want to be on the wrong side of a locked door on a Haederan warship. Even with the guards outside, anyone could walk right in. She looked past Chase, up and down the passageway, then around the room, wishing there was somewhere she could hide.

"Guests aren't usually locked in their cabins." She wished her voice hadn't cracked on the word *cabin*, but he terrified her. The situation terrified her. This trip was not supposed to have ended this way.

"Is that so?" Chase gave her a slight smile as he backed into the corridor, hand on the doorframe. "I suppose we'll have to work on our hospitality." The smile faded and his eyes grew serious. "You don't need to worry, not with them out here. No one will bother you, I promise."

The door slid shut.

CHAPTER NINE

AVERY PUSHED HERSELF UP FROM HER HANDS AND KNEES AND GLARED at the bunk, even though it was nonsensical to blame an inanimate object for her predicament. There was no space under the bunk for a person to fit. The entire bed was solid, though topped with a standard shipboard sleep pad. Strange how there were so many similarities between Commonwealth and Haederan ships. But that only meant there was nowhere to hide, nor any kind of weapon she could improvise. Under the bed had been her last option—there was nowhere else in the cabin to hide. Even the door to the head didn't lock.

Sabotage? Maybe some sort of sabotage would allow her to escape . . . but no, that was foolish. Where would she go if she got out of the cabin? She couldn't force her way past the Imperial Security guards outside, and even if she managed, the entire ship was a maze. She would never even find her way back to the hangar where she'd left Hadley and the others, and escape on a stolen enemy fighter was a onetime, unrepeatable stroke of luck, there was no doubt of that.

Surrendering to the unrelenting fatigue, she collapsed on the bunk. Sleep wouldn't claim her, though. Not now. Chase had said he'd borrowed the cabin from *Imperieuse's* political officer—the room's use was obvious. How many Imperial Haederan Navy officers had lain on this very bed reflecting on their untimely end?

She pushed the idea away and thought of March. He'd hit the deck hard when that overly paranoid officer had stunned him, and she couldn't shake her worry of his condition. She had no right to ask more people to sacrifice themselves for her.

Then she thought of Merritt and how panicked he would be when she didn't arrive on Ventana, even though it would be weeks or months before they would expect a message from her. Would the Haederans let Villiers know her ship had been captured? Likely they would not, and it would cause an uproar on Asria when they learned she'd disappeared. Over and over and over, she replayed every little decision and move they could have made differently, but the plain gray ceiling could only hold her interest for so long. She was close to drifting off when there was a knock at the door.

Avery jumped to her feet, wide awake, her mind screaming caution. But anyone bent on trouble wouldn't have knocked, so it must be Chase . . . though he belonged in the trouble category as well. More than anyone else, really. He entered at what he doubtless considered her silent invitation, like she had a choice in the matter. His genteel host act—and it had to be an act—was rapidly wearing on her nerves.

"You said no one would bother me." Politeness to one's captor was overrated, she'd decided a long time ago. "You could have at least given me time to reply."

"You thought I was including myself? I thought a familiar face might make the situation easier."

No one could be this oblivious to reality. To *history*. It simply wasn't possible.

"You're the last person who could make this situation easier," she snapped at him to cover the shiver that ran through her.

More of a nightmare, maybe.

Chase ignored her comment. "And I thought we could talk awhile. Socially, that is." He grinned at his own joke, or maybe the horrified look on her face. Probably both. "There's food on the way, too."

Waves of nausea washed over her at the idea of food—besides, Chase must have a very short memory if he thought she'd talk to him about anything. She could do nothing but stare at him and wonder why he'd bothered knocking as he dropped into a chair by the door and propped his boots up on the table between them. He'd left the door all the way open—for her benefit, she understood.

How considerate of you, Colonel.

He looked at her expectantly and held out a hand to the opposite couch. Avery sat, reluctant, but too tired and sick to argue. Chase's feigned politeness made her even more dizzy.

"Where is my crew?" she asked. Best to control the conversation before Chase got it established. *Or at least try.* She wouldn't be able to outmaneuver him for long.

"Crew? Is that what you're calling them? You can drop that story now, you know." He recrossed his ankles, looking more comfortable than he had a right to be. "They're fine, though not as comfortable as you are, I'm sure."

"Even my pilot?"

"Lieutenant Colonel March was released from sick bay just before I came here. I checked on him myself. He's perfectly fine."

Lieutenant Colonel March. Why had they bothered with cover identities if the Haederans had only taken an hour to find out the truth? Perfectly fine had to be a stretch, but if Chase was telling even a half-truth, it was a relief. Each time she closed her eyes, her imagination vacillated between March lying on the deck of that hangar and herself in a small, bright room with Chase.

"I want to see them," she replied.

"I'm sorry, my lady, but that's out of the question."

Was he hiding them from her or her from them? Who knew with the Haederans, especially Chase? Probably the latter. If they could hold on to her in secret . . .

Avery waved off the thought before her imagination could go down that dangerous path.

"They're my people, and I'm responsible for their safety. I don't believe you, and I need to know they're all right."

"You don't trust me at all, do you?" Chase's amused expression was back. "All right. Since you put it that way, I'll see what I can do."

She was trying to figure out how to respond to that lie when a steward walked in with the promised food that she'd already decided not to touch, no matter how hungry she was. Chase poured a cup of tea and held it out. She shook her head, though the action came off as more of a shiver.

"Why not?" He took a sip of the cup he had just offered her, then set it on the table between them. "For dehydrated space food, this isn't bad."

"I'm not hungry." She folded her hands in her lap, upright and stiff.

"Yes, you are. You must be." He looked at her oddly, then his laughter filled the room, so loudly that the guard stuck his head inside. Chase waved him off. "You're afraid I'm going to drug you." He sounded all too pleased at her assumption.

Avery flushed at his reaction.

Chase pulled his boots off the table and leaned forward with a look she hadn't seen since he'd first broken his cover as an Imperial Haederan Army military police captain—absolute callousness, with an undercurrent of mocking glee. The remembrance, and the way he looked at her now, made her shake.

"If there was such a thing as truth serum, I wouldn't use it on you. Just think of all the fun we'd miss." He gestured toward the door, and by extension the rest of the ship. The enemy ship. "I wouldn't need it here anyway. Have you forgotten where you are?"

Avery held her breath. It was impossible to forget where she was, but she ignored his threat, at least visibly. Maybe he wouldn't see her knuckles turning white as she wound her fingers together in her lap.

"I know where I am," she said. "What I can't figure out is why you're here too. You've been following me, haven't you? What do you want?"

"You're full of questions today, aren't you?" Chase kicked his feet back up with an uneasy smile, like it was the first time a prisoner had dared interrogate *him*. "No, I haven't been following you. I didn't even know you managed to get off Asria again. I'm curious about how you accomplished that, by the way. It appears we have a slight lapse in security out there." He glanced out the door, looking uncomfortable for the first time. "I'm actually on my way back to Haedera."

Good.

"Not on a courier ship?"

"I am not so important as that, my lady. I was just catching a ride. You were an unexpected and pleasant bonus."

An unexpected bonus he'd jumped on all too quickly for her comfort. He may not have been expecting her, but he'd certainly reacted to the news she was on board.

"Why are you going home?" she asked. "Not too happy with how you handled things on Asria, are they?"

If there was any justice in the world, he was returning to Haedera to face repercussions for what his superiors must see as a failure. She'd all but escaped from right under his nose after all, taking some of the Haederans' most secret technology with her. Valuable technology the Commonwealth was well on their way to replicating for their own ships.

"I paid for that failure more dearly than you could ever understand. But that's not why I'm going back." Chase scratched at the underside of the ring on his hand with his thumb. "My wife is dying. I was headed home to say goodbye." He cleared his throat. "Unfortunately, your arrival has changed that plan."

Wife?

Her eyes widened. "You're—you're married?"

The question came out as a choked laugh. That was unbeliev-able. What kind of woman would be brave enough to talk to someone like him on the street, much less marry him? Did he report every one of her movements to Haederan security? Threaten her any time she made an inadvertent less-than-loyal comment? Or maybe—and this was a more sobering thought than anything else—she'd married him for some measure of protection from the Haederan secret police that permeated every aspect of their society.

"Most people give their sympathies."

Avery frowned at the hurt in his voice. Chase was usually all but impossible to read, but there was no mistaking the devasta-tion on his face now.

No.

The devastation he *allowed* to show on his face. A calculated decision on his part. To gain her sympathy? She wouldn't tell him how unlikely that would be.

"Stars, but you're serious," she replied, almost to herself. She dropped her eyes to the tea in between them. "I'm . . ."

"I believe *sorry* is the word you're searching for."

"I'm sorry."

For her. Not for him. Never for him.

"She's been ill a long time. It was expected."

"But you left her and came to Asria anyway."

Where he'd tormented her for months on end. He'd ruined her life, her future. He was the reason for her panic attacks, for her nightmares, the anxiety, the vision problems, and the headaches that flared up with no warning at all. No, she had no compassion for him.

"I had orders," he said. "Sometimes they aren't as easy to comply with as I would like. I take it you've never been in that position, or you'd understand."

Avery shook her head—in disbelief, not denial. Was he only talking about his wife? Was it possible it was an apology for the things he had done on Asria? To her?

Probably not, but it was an opening, at least.

"You saw Merritt at Alcaris. Didn't you?"

The briefest flicker of irritation passed over his face, visible only in the tightening of a single muscle in his jaw. Was he annoyed she'd brought up that specific topic again, or just angry she was trying to control the conversation, period?

"You don't know when to drop things, do you?" The irritation returned—and stayed that time. "Fine. Yes, I saw him."

In a flash she was certain of what had happened there, even though she couldn't explain why. It had to be the irritation still visible on Chase's face instead of the smugness he was so practiced at.

"It was you." Every muscle grew weak. "You had him transferred to the infirmary after you saw what kind of condition he was in. You had him sent to Emot, where he'd be relatively safe."

Chase's hostile silence was answer enough.

"Why?" she asked in a breathless rush. "What's your interest in him?"

Mercy? Compassion? Those couldn't exist on Haedera. They weren't words that came to mind when one thought of Chase.

But then, Chase had protected Merritt before, refusing to arrest him when Taln Perrin had ordered it. He'd gone so far as to warn Merritt about the Haederan military governor's directive.

Chase brushed the questions off with a wave. "I don't believe in mistreating prisoners for no reason at all. It's messy and exhausting and rarely leads to any kind of useful information. I certainly don't agree with murdering them just to prove a point to their superiors or family."

Avery's mouth fell open before she could stop it.

"No, you simply take your orders from your emperor without question, torture your prisoners for the most imaginative and slightest of reasons to compel false confessions from them, and then send them off for someone else to execute. Do you think that exonerates you? Just because you don't watch them take their last breath? Do you think that makes you any better than your men who actually do those things? Well, it doesn't, and you're not."

The accusations poured out in one breath, and she gasped for air as she finished. Curse these Haederan warships and their nominal pressurization.

Chase tilted his head to the side, trying to fight a smile. It wasn't the anger she'd expected. It wasn't the anger she'd hoped for.

"How long have you been wanting to say all that to me?" he asked mildly.

She crossed her arms.

"That's not how I operate, and I think you know it." His amusement fled, replaced by disdain she felt in her bones. "I disagreed with how things were handled after that admittedly misguided operation by your Defense Forces. Once I saw for myself what was happening at Alcaris, I did what I could about it. It was nothing." He hesitated. "Although I hear it made little difference for Colonel Rendon in the end, and I am sorry about that. I couldn't protect him any longer once I left the planet."

He certainly had a warped sense of . . . honor? Avery could only stare at him in disbelief, both at his explanation and his apology, and her hand flew instinctively to her left eye. The vision there had never quite returned to normal, and the rest of the physical marks the Haederan soldiers had left on her body during her captivity had taken months to fade. She turned the too-obvious gesture into a scratch, thankful Merritt had never seen the bruises.

Chase let out a low laugh. "I honestly hope you're not comparing the consequences of your reckless and illegal espionage to the outcome of a legitimate military operation."

"I find it hard to believe you know anything about legitimate military operations, Colonel." She snapped her mouth shut. There. If her prior accusation hadn't infuriated him, that would.

"Still so bitter." He cast her a sour smile, and she silently congratulated herself on eliciting emotion from him. "It may have been an unpleasant few months for you, but you were never in any real danger."

"Unpleasant?" she shouted at him before she could stop herself. "You call what you did to me *unpleasant?* Delusional doesn't begin to describe—"

"Don't bother arguing with me. Do you realize you could have been executed for what you did? For just being who you are? You're lucky to be alive right now, my lady. You can sit here and object all you want, but you were comparatively well-treated, and I think deep down you recognize it could have been much, much worse. You've seen the results of Perrin's personal revenge . . . needless and extreme. If you remember, I told you he was furious with you for your refusal to cooperate with us. That was not a lie in any sense of the word."

His changes in topic gave her whiplash, though it was no surprise Perrin was behind the Haederans' treatment of Merritt and the murders of the other prisoners. She'd known from the minute they'd met that the man hated her for the most tenuous of reasons and hated Merritt even more. But Chase was right, torturing Merritt because of her refusal to collaborate was extreme.

What *was* surprising was that Chase had told her. A slip? No, it was intentional, but she couldn't think of a single reason he'd want her to think less of Perrin than she already did.

"Then he's probably furious with you now too," she volunteered cautiously, tamping down her fury.

"Perhaps." Chase flicked an imaginary piece of lint from his leg and took another sip of tea.

He sounded like he didn't care one bit what Perrin thought about him, but what had Hadley once said about the Imperial Security Command's oversight?

Right.

That they had none.

No, they reported directly to the Haederan emperor, outside the normal military chain of command. It was frightening to sit here with someone who would violate a general's order—no, orders—then brush them off like it was something he did all day, every day, with no fear of the consequences. Maybe there were none; Chase didn't act like there had been. Sudden alarm bells rang in her head at his openness.

She ran a finger along the arm of her chair, purposefully avoiding his gaze. "Why are you telling me all this?"

"Hmm." Chase's cup hit the table with a clank. "Let's call it an information exchange."

She met his eyes. "But I haven't—"

—given you any information. The bells grew louder, desperately clanging a frenzied warning she should have listened to earlier. Some people never changed. She was cold, shivering. Then so hot.

He tilted his head at her again and smiled, just like he had when they'd first met.

"You will."

The room closed in around her. She was back in the Haederan prison in Cadena where she'd spent weeks being manipulated by Chase, believing Merritt was dead, desperately afraid she herself would never leave. Darkness . . . the small cell . . . the guards who never allowed her to sleep. The merciless hunger and exhaustion and beatings that had finally driven her to give Hadley up. And now Chase was going to do it again, and this time there was no way she'd survive.

She was only grateful she made it to the head before she threw up.

* * *

After Chase disappeared, Avery wasted no further energy worrying about his declaration. Her initial reaction was a case of overblown nerves. There wasn't much he could want from her anymore, not unless he was curious about the Commonwealth's flight training methods, which she was sure he was not.

No, she was only a political hostage now, and Chase was only trying to frighten her, something she'd long believed was more of an entertaining pastime for him than anything else. She would have to figure out a way to stop herself from reacting to his provocations. He'd leave her alone if she didn't give him the responses he wanted—that was almost certain.

Instead of dwelling on his comments, she stood in the center of her quarters and surveyed her new realm, trying to decide between a nap and a form of whatever limited sabotage she was capable of. She was debating the intelligence of starting a fire in a locked stateroom aboard a spaceship with limited means of evacuation when the door opened, saving her from what would have been a regrettable decision. Any sabotage would have to wait, because three additional Haederan Navy guards—armed with stun pistols—stood outside next to the usual two Imperial Security ones.

"You have a visitor."

One of the navy guards beckoned her out, and she followed without a word, too inquisitive about a visitor on a Haederan ship to question him. All five escorted her to an observation deck three levels up and took positions just inside the door. Her curiosity was quashed when the man in front of the floor-to-ceiling window, who had been staring at nothing but the empty blackness of hyperspace, turned. He wore green Haederan fatigues, stripped of rank, but the effect was still chilling on someone who had always filled a room with his presence, no matter what he was wearing.

Without warning she was ten years old again, a young girl standing awestruck before the king.

CHAPTER TEN

"Avery!"

Her uncle held out his hands in greeting, a broad grin across his face. Mouth open, she eyed him in shock, more surprised by his manner of welcome than his appearance on a Haederan ship. Did he mean for her to hug him? He looked mystified by her unwillingness and settled for a kiss on her cheek as she intentionally stared away from him, out the window into the void. She couldn't look at his clothing, not that uniform on the uncle she'd once idolized and adored. She certainly wouldn't hug him.

"You look better than I feared you would," he said after an affectionate squeeze on her upper arm. Some of his Asrian accent had faded, replaced by a not-quite Haederan inflection. "I was so concerned when I heard you'd been detained. They're treating you well? I requested you would be, but you never know how well the emperor's orders will be followed out here."

That explained Chase's guest comment and his over-the-top handling of her. She hadn't known her uncle would have so much influence with the Haederans, especially with someone like Chase. The very idea was frightening and disgusting.

"About as well as you would expect."

Victor sighed. "I should have expected you to be angry.

Somehow I'd hoped you wouldn't be." He held a hand out to the couch in front of the window. "Can we talk?"

"I don't suppose I have a choice." Avery glanced back at the guards. Maybe they would take the hint and remove her from this nightmare. They only stared back.

"They'll take you back to your quarters right now if you'd like." He smiled, for a moment looking so much like his younger brother that she wanted to cry. "But I've missed you. I want to catch up."

A feeling and a desire that were not in any way mutual, but she followed him to the sofa and stared into the blackness. No stars. No hope. They were moving faster than light, and Haedera was ever so much closer than before. She tried to calculate how close they had been before, how many days since their capture, and how much longer they had to go . . . but there was too much missing data to estimate their arrival in her head. The ship couldn't be too far away if her uncle had left Haedera to rendezvous with them.

Unless . . .

"How long have you been here?" Perhaps Victor had been aboard *Imperieuse* the entire time. Perhaps he was responsible for all of this.

"I docked this morning. I wanted to see you earlier, but I had some business to attend to first."

"What kind of business?"

"Just some meetings. Nothing that you need to worry about."

An easy suggestion coming from him. She was worried about everything these past few days. Like what Chase really wanted with her. Like how the others were doing. Like how the Haederans were treating them. Like what Victor was doing here.

But since he was here, sitting right in front of her, it was as good of a time as any to ask what she'd been asking the Holy One for over a year. If she didn't ask now, she'd lose her nerve.

"Why did you do it? Everything that happened? I need to know why before this goes any further."

Victor's forehead creased, like he was surprised she hadn't warmed up to him more before she started questioning. But despite the nervous gesture, he nodded.

"You may have heard there was a takeover brewing—"

"There was no coup!" She jumped to her feet and away from him. *Not this.* He had to have some other reasonable explanation for his actions. Victor didn't move, simply looked stunned.

"There would have never been a coup! You and I both know it never would have happened! Teruel made sure of that. Nothing would have ever happened to you, and you could have gone on arguing withdrawal from the Commonwealth to the senate until you died a peaceful death at a hundred and ten." In the corner of her vision, she watched the guards move in but ignored them. They could do whatever they wanted to her, as long as she got in some last few words. "Instead, you've destroyed us! You let them in and destroyed everything!"

Victor crossed an ankle over his knee and raised an eyebrow, probably surprised she was aware of his feelings about the Commonwealth.

"You've always been naïve," he said, leaning back. "Too trusting. And Merritt has biased you against what Teruel's people are capable of." He glanced at her left hand, and she hurriedly covered it with the other. "It's no wonder, since he probably had everything to do with it."

"Merritt had nothing to do with any of this." Teruel had made certain he'd stayed clean. He'd even sent Merritt off-world when the scandal had first broken. "Even you have to believe that."

Victor's gaze didn't leave her hand. "If that's what you want to believe, go ahead. I can't believe you're trusting enough to think Teruel's senior aide didn't know about the coup, but that's love for you. Anyway, it doesn't matter. The Haederans would have taken Asria with or without my help. This really did benefit us."

Was he mad, paranoid, or a little of both?

"How did this benefit us?"

"It's very simple. Would you rather have a Haederan military governor—with the current one being, as I understand it, not the easiest person to deal with—or an Asrian viceroy?"

Her stomach twisted. So General Cevall's theory, the one she'd questioned him about when she'd first arrived at Villiers months ago, was true. Her uncle had fled Asria, fearing a military coup. He'd then handed his own planet over to the enemy, who had promised to prop him back up as a puppet ruler. A brilliant strategy to rid himself of the military he was so convinced was about to overthrow him. She couldn't argue with someone that paranoid, that afraid of losing his position.

"We don't need either. Asria has a queen."

Victor narrowed his eyes at her. "I don't suppose it's occurred to you that you don't actually have a claim to the Asrian throne."

"A claim? I don't know what you're talking about. The senate would never elect someone outside of the Rendon family. Even you knew that."

Victor shook his head. "And you've forgotten Quen so soon?"

No one had forgotten Quen, least of all her.

"The senate can elect whoever they want," she replied. "They chose to not elect Quen. Legally. Everything that's happened since you left, every decision that's been made, it's been done legally. Everyone on Asria can follow the law except for you. I can't believe their decision surprises you."

"Just a little. I have to wonder what they were thinking, choosing you over him."

Did her uncle remember he hadn't seen her older brother in fifteen years? Or that the senate had spent years trying to track him down? What did Victor expect would happen? If things had gone differently, she'd have ruled as Quen's regent anyway. That situation would have been preferable for her—but since it hadn't happened that way, she'd accepted her fate as queen.

Asria was hers.

"You would have to ask Grant Baylen about their election choice, since you can't ask your brother." That accusation had probably pushed Victor too far, but she was beyond caring what he thought of her.

"I had nothing to do with Lucas's death. If the story I heard was accurate, he was shot while trying to escape house arrest at the Sabino estate. Maybe if he'd stayed put, done what they ordered . . ."

Avery backed against the window, a sudden pain in her chest. Her uncle had betrayed his own brother. Her relationship with her father had always been cool and detached, but they were still family. How could Victor dismiss him like that?

She pushed a hand against the viewing window, testing it. Maybe it would break and suck her out into space. Put her out of her misery. The thick glass stood firm, and the words flew out.

"You had everything to do with it! You set this up. You let them take Asria. You could have warned him what was coming, if you really loved him. If you really loved us! Instead, you might as well have put the gun to his head and pulled the trigger yourself!"

The guards finally pulled her a safe distance away from Victor. She tried to slip her arms away from the guards, but they held firm. She supposed she couldn't blame them for that.

Victor approached her anyway. "This is not the way I wanted this conversation to go."

And he had the nerve to call her naïve.

"How did you think it would go?"

He rubbed his forehead. "We're headed back to Asria now. I had expected . . . I had hoped . . . to have your public support when I take my new position there."

Avery glanced out the window. They were headed back to Asria? She'd be allowed to accompany him? Even after she'd embarrassed the Haederans by stealing their fighter and turning their technology over to the Commonwealth? Victor was wrong. The occupation government would never allow her back in Cadena.

Unless . . .

Unless the effect of her public support for the new Asrian—Haederan—*whatever*—viceroy would override whatever espionage she'd been involved with in the past. It wouldn't surprise her. Commonwealth spy turned collaborator? It would look good for the Haederans. Wonderfully effective propaganda. *Even she has seen the light.* And the fighter incident would surely have been hidden from most everyone anyway. It would make sense if only a half-dozen top Haederan leaders knew about their stolen technology.

Deep breath.

But she would never do what Victor was asking, not even for a chance to return to her own planet.

Never.

"No," she said. "I refuse. I will not publicly support you."

"That was a fast answer." Victor rubbed his hands over his face, sighed, and rubbed it again. "You don't want to think about it just a little? Take as much time as you need. I hope you'll reconsider. Please?"

She shook her head, even though his appeal had come out as a plea.

"That decision puts you in a rather poor position, Avery."

"I don't care. I don't care what you do to me."

His eyes welled up at her answer, and her fury exploded. She tried to pull her arms back from the guards again, wanting to throw Victor against the wall, to punch him, to hurt him somehow. How dare he be upset about this? This was his fault. His doing. He had no right to be concerned for her life. Because they would kill her for not agreeing to this, and he would be the one to order it.

"You needn't look so terrified." Victor raised his hands in surrender and looked toward the door to the observation deck, probably wishing someone would interrupt and do his thankless task for him. No one rescued him, and he stared at her a long time before he continued. "But if I were you, I wouldn't expect to see the outside of a prison cell for a very long time."

Avery looked out the window into the vastness of deep space before the claustrophobia could take its anticipatory hold on her. She would kill herself before she allowed herself to be locked up like an animal, but it would be her decision when. Anyway, Victor was lying. She wouldn't live to see another week. Not on a Haederan ship.

Breathe. Slowly.

"And I'm supposed to believe your *emperor*"—she tried to put a scathing slant on the word, but her voice shook—"will let me live?"

"Oh, yes." Victor's shoulders slumped; he looked relieved to deliver some good news at last. "It was his idea, in fact. Something about being able to control me more easily if I don't destroy my entire family."

He was wrong, though. He had already destroyed everyone.

CHAPTER ELEVEN

Avery pulled her sleeves down as far as they would go and gritted her teeth to keep them from chattering. The interview room—she didn't know why they bothered calling it that; euphemisms weren't culturally Haederan—was freezing, and the breeze from the pressurization vent was blowing straight onto her face, tormenting her almost as much as the man who sat across the small table. Any kindness Chase had deigned to show her had disappeared along with her uncle's protection.

"I've been wanting to see you like this ever since you ran into me on the street in Cadena." He regarded her red prisoner's uniform with unconcealed delight, and she dropped her gaze to her bare feet to avoid his mocking eyes. "I knew your uncle would come to his senses when he got here and actually talked to you—saw how stubborn you are. I tried to tell him you would never agree to support him openly, but he argued with me for days about it. He said you could be reasonable when actually presented with the options. Can you believe that? Reasonable." His arrogant smile turned innocent. "It's like he doesn't know you at all."

"If you're here only to gloat, just get it out of your system and go away."

She would have snarled at him if she'd been capable of it, but three days in the brig had shattered her, and the attempted sneer came off as a wearied and resigned request. The hours that passed in her cell, marked only by the delivery of sparse and tasteless prison rations, had been empty, with no hope in sight. Maybe that would change once they finally took her to Haedera, but it would be months before they reached it. She didn't hold out much hope that the hostile planet would be any better for her than the prison on the ship. How could it be?

She'd thought of calling for her uncle dozens of times, had thought of telling him she'd changed her mind and she'd be as vocal as he wanted in support of his position of viceroy, but something had stopped her every time. Principle? It must be, because it wasn't her own desire. Were her principles worth this kind of life? Was she just tormenting herself by taking this stand?

"I wouldn't think you have anything better to do right now than listen to me gloat." Chase interrupted her roiling thoughts. "My company has to be better than sitting alone in your cell staring at a blank wall." He watched her for a reaction, she gave him none, and he looked faintly disappointed. "But no, that's not the only reason I'm here."

He took a small tablet from his pocket and laid it in between them, but kept his hand on it, like he expected her to take it from him. "You didn't tell me two of your crew were Haederan officers."

"They aren't." He'd caught her off guard, and she regretted her statement as soon as she'd spoken. Where was he going with this?

Chase flipped the tablet over without looking at it and pushed it toward her. "My information says they joined in Cadena under the amnesty program just over two months ago. Unless you have information that proves otherwise, they most certainly are, and will be treated as such."

And will be treated as such?

She reached cautiously for the tablet, which contained the two photos from Kanmar's and March's Haederan in-processing at Cadena. Icy dread seeped into her joints, a cold that had nothing to do with the already-arctic interrogation room. She'd never wished more for a pair of shoes and a blanket. Or real clothes. Or Merritt's arms around her. Preferably all four.

He's just trying to rattle you. Don't let him get to you.

"So what?" she asked.

"That makes their status as prisoners of war inaccurate," Chase said. "I made sure that was corrected in our system earlier this morning. They will be transferred to Haedera for trial as soon as the courier ship reaches us."

Trial.

"They're Royal Asrian Defense Forces officers." Her vision grew blurred as numbness replaced the cold. "You know that."

Didn't he? Of course he did. Chase knew everything.

"To use your ineloquent phrase, so what? I'll admit it's not very good publicity for the amnesty program, but it was a terrible idea to begin with. Perhaps this will be the end of it."

The mocking gleam in his eyes was gone now, and she knew. Even Chase would not celebrate the outcome of this disaster.

"You'll execute them."

Her voice was dull. More of her own people would die because of her. Numbness replaced the cold. The words hadn't come from her, but from a hazy cloud outside of her.

"Yes." Chase stood and pushed a button by the door to call the guards in. To take her back to sit for the next few months and contemplate how many lives she'd ruined and destroyed. "I wanted to make sure you were aware of their fate. You deserve to know."

Back in her cell, she cried like she hadn't since learning of Merritt's death. When that proved sadly and predictably futile in changing the situation, she screamed at the camera to be allowed to talk to her uncle.

But no one listened.

* * *

Avery was surprised when her uncle arrived two mornings later, the morning part made evident by his clean civilian clothes, lack of fatigue lines around his eyes, and coffee in his hand. The smell of the coffee made her stomach churn, and judging by the look on his face, her appearance alarmed him. She'd been crying for two days over Chase's news about Kanmar and March, and what he'd left unsaid about Hadley. What did Victor expect her to look like? And when had her uncle begun to drink coffee, anyway? Most Asrians, unless they'd spent significant time off-world, drank tea.

On second thought, that explained it.

Victor took a sip of coffee before setting it on the floor of the cell. Avery's knee twitched as she fought to keep herself from kicking it over out of pure spite. The smell would stick around for hours if she spilled it, and that one thought forced her restraint.

"I didn't think you'd change your mind so quickly," he said.

Not this again.

"I didn't change my mind." Was everything going to be about him and his traitorous decision from now on? "I need to talk to you about something else."

"I thought I made it clear that we have nothing else to discuss. When and if you decide to be reasonable about this, let the guards know." He turned his back on her, stopping at the closed door.

"Just listen to me for five minutes. Please. This is important!"

Perhaps the guards had walked off, because the door remained closed, and Victor turned toward her again, face blank. Avery took that as an invitation and told him in halting, broken words about Kanmar and March, how they had ended up on board *Imperieuse* with her, and their inevitable death sentences.

"Please help them," she finished. "I've asked you for very little, but this—"

Victor shrugged off her plea like he hadn't heard her at all. "It's not my concern. I won't get involved in internal Haederan matters."

"Have you listened to a word I've said?" *Coward.* "They're not Haederan. They're Asrian. Your own people! If the Haederan emperor has appointed you viceroy—if you are headed back to Asria—then it is your concern!"

The sudden realization made her sick—Victor would never act to save the lives of any Defense Forces officers, especially Kanmar, who would struggle with the guilt of what his own people had done for the rest of his life. Had Victor—had Victor himself exposed them to the Haederans, for no reason other than spite?

"And you know what you need to do to earn my help."

She didn't need to ask. He wanted her to trade their lives for her support. Like it was a game. Like lives were something to be dealt with like currency, behind the scenes, with no input from the people who stood to lose the most.

Avery rubbed her face. This had to all be a vile joke. She couldn't do it, not even for them, the people that had sacrificed themselves for her safety. What kind of leader was she to ignore that kind of loyalty?

"I can't do that. You know I can't." She crumpled against the wall.

"Then I don't know what to tell you."

The guards must have returned from whatever unsanctioned break they'd been on, because the door slid open when Victor rapped his knuckles on it. He all but ran from the cell without giving her another look.

Avery stared unseeingly at the opposite wall. Kanmar and March were dead already, just for helping her. Kanmar's wife would never know what had happened to her husband. Had she known he was risking his life, as Merritt had known when she left Villiers, or would Kanmar simply disappear, never to be heard from again?

Boots echoed on the deck outside, and she turned just as the guard was closing the door behind Victor. A flash of inspiration shot through her, one last thing she could try.

"Please. Can I see Colonel Chase?" The door closed before the guard answered. "Tell him I need to see him!" she shouted at the camera.

It was a waste of breath. The guard had ignored her request, her last chance. Even if he hadn't, Chase would never listen to her. She'd just made a fool of herself. Avery dropped her head into her hands to stare at the cold floor.

Her uncle—no, she would never claim that man as family anymore—*Victor* had left his coffee on the floor in his haste to get away, and Avery picked it up. She had to hold her breath against the unfamiliar smell. It seemed like years since she'd enjoyed coffee . . . years since Merritt . . . years since happiness.

Heedless of what the smell would do to her, she threw the cup against the opposite wall, blank no more.

CHAPTER TWELVE

She woke in a cell.

Dark, small, and with the smell of her own sweat and fear surrounding her.

She was in Cadena, underground, so deep down that sunlight would never reach her again. Her mother was dead. Her father was dead. Merritt was dead. Drex was—well, if he wasn't dead already, he would be shortly, once the Haederans caught him sneaking information out of the city. Hadley and Feye had deserted her. That was what Chase had said about them, wasn't it? That they'd recruited her then deserted her to certain death, not caring how she would be tortured before her execution.

And now the Haederans were coming again. She felt it deep in her bones, like a living, coiling, breathing thing. First, they would beat her, just for sport, so badly she couldn't fight them off any longer. They'd laugh as she lay on the floor in agony, unable to comply with their demands to move. They'd tire of that eventually and shout at her to stand, kicking her in the ribs again when she couldn't.

Then they would take her to Chase.

He would sigh at her appearance. He'd shake his head as he made a cursory check for any severe injuries the guards had inflicted. He'd make little sympathetic comments about the bruises that covered her body being the result of her own pointless defiance. And then he would make her tell him all about Hadley, all about Drex, all about the verium—

Her scream cut through the stagnant quiet of the cell. She had to escape before she betrayed Hadley and Feye again. Before Chase forced her to say other things, worse things, more important things, things that would destroy the Commonwealth forever.

And it would be her fault.

Avery threw herself at the door and clawed at it, but met unyielding, solid resistance. A nail snapped across the tip of her middle finger, but she continued to force her hand into the small crack between the door and the wall with no success. The attempt was futile. Useless. It was a spaceship. The doors were sealed in case of a depressurization emergency—what had she expected?

A spaceship.

She wasn't in that cell in Cadena after all, but aboard *Imperieuse.*

The continual flashbacks were terrible, yes, but reality wasn't much better. With a sob, she slid down to her knees and wept, slamming her head against the door in time with her heartbeat. It didn't matter how much it hurt. The pain gave her something to focus on, something besides the terror—and the smell of Victor's coffee lingering in the cell.

"Move away from the door."

Avery jerked back and glanced up, palm on her forehead, a lump already forming. The voice over the intercom wasn't angry. It wasn't cold. It wasn't emotional at all. It just . . . it just was, and that was the most terrifying thing of all. With the last of her strength, she shoved herself back from the door to her knees. It was only a pace—maybe not even that. It had to be enough to avoid their retribution.

The door opened. She couldn't look up from the three sets of boots on the deck outside, too afraid of what they'd do to her for the scene she'd just caused. But they only lifted her onto the hard bed. The startling gentleness allowed her to look up, even though she couldn't move to wipe her face dry.

"He wants to talk to you." The young ensign who had been almost kind to her when they'd first brought her to the brig looked and sounded concerned as he ran his fingers across her forehead, checking for injuries. "Don't do that again."

It wasn't an order . . . more of a plea. Had she slipped so far past reality this time that even her enemy was worried about her? She followed his gaze as he walked out the door, having apparently assured himself she wasn't seriously injured by her foolishness.

Past—

Past Chase. He stood there, just outside, his face unreadable.

Shaking, Avery dropped to the floor and hunched in the far corner of the cell, tears streaming down her face. Didn't the brig crew know what he would do to her? Why hadn't they left her alone to relive her memories again and again and again?

Because you asked for him. Screamed for him.

For hours.

Chase murmured a few long sentences under his breath to the ensign, then stepped inside. Avery pressed herself harder against the wall, but he simply stood there, silent, until the ensign came back. He handed Chase a cup of something steaming, along with something else she couldn't identify from her position on the ground. Chase shoved that something else in his chest pocket, then stepped inside and lowered himself to the floor at the rear of the cell, against the wall opposite her. Slowly, like she was a skittish animal he might frighten away if he moved too quickly, he held the cup out to her.

"He even listened when I asked for it hot."

Avery stared blankly at him. At his cordial tone.

"It's tea," he added unnecessarily.

Tea.

How her soul cried out for something so average, so normal.

But she still had some sanity left, even though the door was closing, trapping her in here with Chase. She wasn't stupid enough or damaged enough or delirious enough to take anything he offered.

"You drugged it," she whispered.

"Oh, give it a rest." By the deep breath he took and held, he was suppressing a frustrated sigh. "I already told you I don't need to drug you. I never have before." Without breaking eye contact, he took a sip, then held it out to her again. "There."

Avery reached out, but her hand was trembling too violently. She shook her head and wound her arms around herself. Chase scooted forward to set the cup in front of her, then moved back against his wall.

"When you're ready." He gave her a slow smile. "Can't promise it'll taste as good cold as it does now, though."

She stared at it, then him. "What do you want?"

"You asked to see me. I'm here."

She had.

But now she couldn't do it. She would have to leave Kanmar and March to their deaths, because she couldn't move past what Chase had done to her enough to ask for his help. Not now.

She began to shake again. "I didn't mean it. Please go away."

"I thought you'd been holding yourself together a little too well the past few days." He crossed his legs and leaned against the wall, drawing lazy circles on the floor with a finger. His gaze grew more intense; his head tilted at a familiar angle. After so many weeks, she knew that look, knew what was coming. "I suppose it was only a matter of time until this happened. How long have you been like this?"

Oh, here were the questions.

She stiffened, staring him straight in the eyes. Those Voirian-blue eyes that disgusted her, because they reminded her of Hadley. Of the Haederans' occupation of Voirs long before any of them had even been born.

You know exactly how long I've been like this. And you know exactly why.

He didn't wait for her to answer. "And in over a year, they haven't helped you?"

So he knew. He knew, and his disapproval sent a hot flash of rage through her soul. Even worse than his apparent mind reading, infuriating on the best of days, was the blame he was assigning to Asrian personnel at Villiers for neglecting to 'fix' her.

Instead of himself.

The real reason.

"I'm good at hiding it," she said.

Except from Merritt. Merritt knew how bad off she was. Merritt had held her every night in their quarters in Villiers while she cried. Merritt still wanted her, as broken as she was, and she hated herself for it. He'd gone through far worse, he must have, yet he held her together when she was falling apart. She didn't know how he did it, didn't know how she'd ever be able to repay him for just being there. For treating her like his Avery and not some broken mess of a queen.

"I'm surprised you're able to."

No apology, no guilt, just a simple statement. Maybe Chase had seen the psychological consequences of his work before—no doubt he had—and her response didn't surprise him. Maybe he didn't care.

"It seems you're surprised by quite a few things I'm able to do." She tried to summon a scowl, but the headache that had flared from hitting her head on the door . . . With the panic gone, now it hurt.

The words were harsh, maybe. Had she pushed him too far? It didn't matter—the last of her terror melted in the triumph that flashed through her entire body at the memory of launching that Haederan fighter off the cruiser. She reached for the cup, and her hands shook a little less that time. Like they were reaching for the stick of a fighter.

"That's true." Chase's forehead creased. He stared at her, then at his hands, then back at her. "The other day, you asked me why I did what I did for Colonel Rendon."

Avery sucked in a breath. She couldn't nod, couldn't even breathe, in case he realized what he was saying and changed his mind. She only stared back.

"I heard from a fairly reliable source," he began, "that several Defense Forces prisoners were being held at Alcaris—in a separate building from the rest—in explicit violation of an agreement the Haederan Army had made with the Commonwealth after the massacre there. When I questioned Perrin about it, he denied it. But before he threw me out of his office, he blamed Imperial Security—after all, he claimed, forced disappearances and unrecorded prisoners were our technique."

His cheeks grew red. "Except I knew everything we were and weren't doing in Cadena and I knew we weren't involved in anything like that at Alcaris. I became curious."

Nosy. You mean you became nosy.

But whatever the reason, Chase's concern for Merritt felt good. Almost as good as the tea tasted.

"I got my hands on the list of casualties from that night," he went on. "It wasn't hard to cross-check the names of the survivors with their current locations. Most were still being held at Alcaris, but two of the group were listed as having been transferred to Emot. When I checked with the camp commander there, he said they'd never arrived. He'd questioned the army in Cadena about his missing prisoners, of course, and they'd told him that both had been killed trying to escape on Asria. It was beyond obvious. Perrin didn't even bother to hide what he was doing.

"So, I went to see Colonel Rendon, who was very much alive, though I suspect he may have wished otherwise at that point. I didn't know how bad it was until I laid eyes on him, only that Perrin had a special interest in him. And I had a good excuse. I thought I'd be able to find out from him where you'd gone. About any friends that may have helped you. Something, anything, to get myself out of the mess I was in after losing you."

He tilted his head sideways. "Do you want to hear details?"

Avery held the tea against her chin and breathed deeply before taking another sip. It was impossible to identify the ingredients. Lavender? A strange thing to find aboard a warship. It had to have come from someone's private stash.

"Yes," she answered. Merritt hadn't told her details. He wouldn't tell anyone the details. His injuries told most of the story, but not all.

"I don't think he recognized me, which wasn't surprising." Chase indicated his Imperial Security Command uniform with an offhand wave. The uniform Merritt had never seen him wear until then. "Plus, he had a fever—probably an infection from that broken leg. He couldn't move, could barely raise his head when I walked in."

He cleared his throat. "It was obvious someone didn't want him flying again. His ankles were broken. One of his knees was shattered. They'd had quite a bit of fun with a knife and his chest. I'd already seen the unofficial record of the other things they'd done to him—activities which hadn't left such obvious physical marks. I can't believe they wrote that kind of thing down. It's a wonder they didn't take pictures."

Avery gripped the cup harder. "Don't tell me you have ethical standards when it comes to torture, Colonel." The intended sarcasm came out as a coarse whisper.

Oh, Merritt. It's no wonder you wouldn't talk about it.

"I never touched you like that," Chase replied quietly. "And I ordered those soldiers not to. They wanted to, you know—but they didn't dare defy me. Everyone has their limits, and that's one of mine." His lip twitched at her horrified expression, like he'd thought better of giving more details about Merritt's experience, no matter what she'd agreed to hear. "In any case, it was obvious he needed medical care—care I permitted you, I might add."

Her side twinged as she slouched there against the bulkhead. Those broken ribs, an early gift from the Haederan guards, acted up more and more these days, just as she was forgetting the agony of trying to breathe as her own body betrayed her. How much of their torture had been frustration at the restriction Chase had placed upon them?

She discarded that idea almost immediately—Chase had wanted her broken, after all. He'd let them do what they wanted to her, within reason, of course, so he'd be the one safe person she had to cling to. It was the only reason he'd allowed the medic to attend to her when her injuries prevented her from doing anything but crying and shaking on the floor. He'd wanted her gratitude, her appreciation, her trust. It was all so obvious now.

She blew out a deep breath and focused on how the splintered lavender swirled in the cup, grateful Chase hadn't lingered on that last part of his narrative. She would have taken a dozen broken ribs over what they'd done to Merritt.

"He needed surgery," Chase went on, "and so I intervened. Made up a story, said Imperial Security had an interest in him. The details of that interest were classified, of course, well above their level, although they all suspected it had something to do with you. I told them we'd be fetching him for interrogation once he was lucid enough for a chat. Surprisingly, no one argued with me." He shot her a dark smile at his own sarcasm. "I gave orders to have him sent to the infirmary the next day, all the while praying he'd live through the night."

Avery took another swallow of tea, just to wet her mouth enough she could speak. "Why not right away?" she whispered. Not that it mattered now. Merritt had survived, and that miracle was because of Chase's interference.

"I didn't want him to connect me and his transfer—just in case he was more coherent than I thought. And I couldn't be accused of compassion. I had a part to play, and for Perrin not to find out what I really wanted with Colonel Rendon, I needed to play it well."

"For some reason, I don't believe 'heartless Imperial Security Command officer' is an act with you," she said ungratefully. Chase had no conscience. Helping Merritt was just another game to him. A way to demonstrate his power over the Haederan Army.

A way to keep himself entertained while he did his time on a backwater Commonwealth planet.

Or was it something else?

"Perhaps not." The borderline smirk that had appeared at her accusation turned to concern. "How is he now? Really."

"He—he was fine when I left. He might even walk again one day."

She pulled her lips back in a false smile. Fine besides the nightmares, though not as frequent as hers, that he hid from her. Even Merritt's nightmares were quiet and contained, and he'd brushed her off when she'd confronted him over them. *Just a bad dream. I'm going for a walk, love,* he'd said the first time he'd woken up next to her bathed in sweat.

"Thank you for what you did for him," she continued. "But none of what you've told me explains why."

"I felt like doing it." Chase lifted a shoulder. "So I did."

"Then why can't you help me?" It came out as a plea, though more for a confession of his true motives than for help. If she didn't know him better, she'd have taken him at his word. But there was more to it, and *I'm not going to tell you* was the unspoken truth. Then, even quieter, "Why won't you?"

Chase settled back against the wall and checked the time. "You know what you need to do. Either you go back to Asria with your uncle or we continue on to Haedera. It's your choice." He ran a hand over his face and yawned. "You should consider yourself honored to be given one."

"That's not a choice! It's—" It was impossible, that's what it was. He couldn't expect her to decide like that. He might as well be asking which foot she wanted cut off. "I—"

Chase's features swirled until those hated blue eyes disappeared, and she squeezed her eyes shut against the dizziness. Haedera, Asria, Victor, Chase . . . she didn't care any longer. She only wanted Chase to go away . . . just wanted . . .

Sleep.

"I just want to sleep right now."

Yes. Sleep was all she wanted that very second, whether or not it was in the brig. Her eyes were so heavy. She couldn't open them, couldn't stay upright one more minute, couldn't—

Chase chuckled, and in that second, she hated the sound more than she hated him. "It's about time."

He didn't sound surprised. Why didn't he sound surprised?

He stood, and before she could fight back—before she could make her traitorous and uncooperative body move away from him—he'd lifted her onto the bed and rolled her on her side. She tried to move her arm, tried to smack at him, but he pinned her firmly in place until she stopped, exhausted. A sharp prick pierced her upper arm, and before the darkness claimed her, she swore she heard the sigh he'd been holding in.

CHAPTER THIRTEEN

Avery's eyes flicked up toward the camera on the ceiling of the interview room once more. Across from her, Chase's patience appeared to be evaporating by the minute, but she'd wanted to talk to him alone. Not him and whoever else out there felt like listening to their conversation. Not this time. This time everything that needed to be said needed to be between the two of them and no one else.

Chase raised his eyebrows in impatience as she met his gaze once more.

"If you're going to stare at the ceiling for another half hour," he said, tapping a finger on the table between them, "I have other things to do."

"You drugged me," she answered. "You lied to me, got me to trust you, and then you drugged me."

It wasn't what she'd meant to say, but the accusation poured out anyway. At least the fury that had consumed her when she'd awoken that morning had died down somewhat. Time and prayer had a tendency to help with that. Even better, the full night of sleep had helped her anxiety—but she would never thank Chase for that. Or even admit it to him.

"And you'd been screaming your head off for hours." The

tapping stopped. "They were tired of listening to it, and I can't blame them. When was the last time you slept through the night?"

"I don't know, but it doesn't matter. You had no right—"

"You are a prisoner. I have every right to handle you as I see fit." His voice had chilled. "Now, you asked for me. What do you want?"

Unconsciously, she looked up again. She was out of time. If she delayed again, Chase would walk away. She had to ask now. Had to beg. But not in front of *them*.

Chase sighed and addressed the offending camera. "Turn it off."

The small green light on the camera remained lit, but the door behind him opened less than a minute later.

"I can't do that, sir." The lieutenant commander in charge of the brig looked like he wanted to be somewhere else. Anywhere else. Or perhaps telling anyone but Chase they couldn't have the camera turned off.

"Why not?"

Such a simple question, yet so fraught with menace. The officer might not be able to read the tone in Chase's voice, but Avery could. Easily. He was on dangerous ground and didn't even seem to realize the extent of his misstep.

"I can't leave you in here with an unsecured prisoner, sir." He sounded mystified by Chase's blasé suggestion as he narrowed his eyes at Avery. "It's a security issue."

She suppressed an ill-timed laugh, her anger vanishing like it hadn't ever existed. What did he think she could do? Chase was almost twice her size, and she didn't want to imagine the repercussions if she attacked him.

"Then chain her to the table, I don't care, but if that camera is not off in the next ten seconds, I'm holding you personally responsible. You're not cleared for this conversation and neither is anyone else out there."

The officer gave Avery one last nervous look and bobbed his head upward. The light went off, and he headed for the doorway, clearly intent on escaping Chase as quickly as possible. Then, as though he had second thoughts, he stepped back inside, pulled her to her feet, and jerked her hands behind her back.

"What are you—" She tried to spin toward him, but he pushed her forward again. "You can't—"

Chase bit his lip, his eyes dancing, and her fury at his expression distracted her from the rest of her protest. Metal was around her wrists and the officer disappeared out the door before she could blink.

"Take these off me, Colonel." She twisted around for Chase to see. "Now."

Chase leaned back in his chair and regarded her with a look she recognized and didn't like. "I can't do that. You heard the commander—you might overpower me and escape through this locked door." He pressed his fist to his mouth and coughed down a laugh. "I'd love to see you try, but it appears he doesn't, and it's his brig. Sorry."

"Don't even pretend." The venom in her tone was not, apparently, enough to drop him dead where he sat. "You're not sorry."

He laughed again, not bothering to hide it that time. "Not even a little," he said with a grin as she glared at him and dropped back into her chair. "So, you wanted the camera off, and it's off. Let's talk."

She swallowed and looked back at the camera, but the light was indeed off.

"You know what I want."

"Yes." Chase smiled, still pleasant. "I do know what you want. And what *I* want is to hear you ask me for it."

"I need your help." Avery picked at a fingernail to stall her request. It wasn't as though she was destroying a perfect manicure.

"With?"

"Kanmar and March." She swallowed again. How she hated him. She would have killed him for his pretended ignorance if she'd had half the chance. "I know the Haederan Navy has a case against them. But they aren't Haederan officers, they never intended on being such, and you know it." Kanmar would be furious with her for broadcasting that information, but the Haederans knew it already. The time for pretending, the time for cover stories, was long gone.

"Hmm. You're saying they joined under false pretenses, intending on sabotaging our efforts on Asria from the beginning?"

Avery's eyes went wide, and the sinking feeling in her stomach, a constant companion over the past few weeks, became a rock. She'd made things worse. It was obvious where he was going with that question.

"We might be interested in them ourselves, if that's the case," Chase continued, almost to himself.

"No!" She couldn't have just destined them to whatever Imperial Security would do to them.

"No?"

His eyes were still innocent and wide, and something about his demeanor gave her hope. That was it—if Chase truly had any professional interest in Kanmar and March, they would have been in Imperial Security Command custody the second they'd landed on board *Imperieuse*. He wouldn't have agreed to speak with her to begin with. The very fact he was sitting in front of her now —*laughing* at her, no less—meant he had already decided to help. He was only waiting for her to humiliate herself to his satisfaction.

She closed her eyes and took a deep breath.

"I am asking you. If you want me to beg you, I will beg, but these are my people, and I will not leave them to this fate without doing everything in my power to help them. I'm not asking you to have them released, only that they be treated like the other Defense Forces personnel that are still being held on Asria. Please have their status changed back."

"I think you overestimate my influence." Chase leaned back in his chair and checked his chronometer. She knew that indifferent look now—a cover for his keen interest.

"I don't—" It was probably the first time in his career he'd suggested that to anyone. How painful had it been for him to imply that his influence was not, in fact, as extensive as he usually claimed? It wasn't true though, there was no question about that. Especially after what he'd done for Merritt. "I don't think I do."

"Hmm." His apathy changed to thoughtfulness. "Why would I do this for you?"

"I don't know," Avery admitted quietly. Why indeed? Chase had no reason to help her, even less reason to help two men he didn't know. Empty, she looked at the floor. Kanmar and March would die now, and it would be her fault. "Because I suppose that even after everything that's happened, I still prayed you might have some kind of soul."

And that was the absolute truth, right there.

He stared at her for a long time, his face utterly devoid of emotion, then drummed his fingers on the table.

"Yes. I think I'll do it—on one condition."

His attention wandered around the room, and she wanted to scream at him to get on with it, but that was Chase. He would draw out whatever he had to say just to torment her. And if he knew she was impatient, he'd make her wait ten times longer.

"Your life for theirs," he said at last.

"My—"

He couldn't mean . . .

Could he?

"The emperor will want someone's blood over this. Yours or theirs. It won't matter to him. It certainly doesn't matter to me." Chase shrugged and leaned sideways in his chair. "The offer's only on the table for the next thirty seconds though, so I'd decide quickly if I were you."

That same familiar numbness settled around her, cool and protective this time. Had she meant what she'd told Chase? She hadn't meant she would sacrifice her *life* for them. Her father had given his life for Asria, and look what he'd gotten in return. Nothing. Nothing for himself and nothing for Asria.

Still . . .

I will not leave them to this fate without doing everything in my power to help them.

"Yes," she replied.

"Yes?"

Chase drew back, looking more surprised than she'd ever seen him. No, not surprised, exactly—perplexed. Clearly it wasn't the answer he'd expected. Did he think so little of her?

"Yes. I agree to your condition. My life for theirs."

The silence that followed her statement weighed more than a planet. Chase's uproarious laughter broke it, and she jumped at the sound, her eyes wide.

"You didn't really believe I was serious, did you?" he asked. "What kind of control would you be over the viceroy if you were dead? Stars above, I wish you could see the look on your face right now, my lady."

"I—"

Speech evaded her. He'd been *toying* with her?

"I'll help them, and you don't even have to die for me to do it. I was serious about a condition, though. And that condition is . . . you owe me. At some point in the future, you will owe me something that I will determine when the time comes."

He would give her an advance on a favor? There was no way Chase would trust her like that. Not for an indeterminate period.

"And if I don't follow through?" she asked.

His prior amusement vanished. "I think by now you know me well enough to realize that you do not want to cross me in that manner. And you will keep in mind that if I do this for you, I can undo it just as easily—for as long as the two of them remain in Haederan custody. That could be months. Years. Do not test me on this. Do you understand?"

"I understand." She nodded her wordless and resigned agreement.

He left with a curt nod of his own, but not another word, and she waited for the guards to return her to her cell.

No one came though, and with her hands behind her back, she was becoming more and more uncomfortable every minute. Her legs were stiff, and the camera was still off, so she stood and circled the small room over and over. Walking kept her warm, at least. Had they forgotten about her? Would they hear her if she knocked on the door?

What must have been over an hour turned into several, and a guard finally came in to release her hands, but left her there alone. The camera turned back on and she put her head down on the table.

It didn't help. She was about to lie down on the floor to stop the room from spinning when Chase returned. Silently, he led her to an open holding area on the other side of the brig, and her breath caught at the sight of Kanmar and March sitting there. Instead of the red clothes she wore, they were dressed in the Defense Forces uniforms they'd hidden on board *Zephyr*.

Both flew to their feet when they recognized her, to the alarm of the guards at the doorway.

"What the hell is going on, Your Majesty?" Kanmar stared at her, dazed despite the anger in his voice. "They wouldn't let us see you—I thought the worst. Are you—did they—"

"I'm fine." A lie, but he didn't need to know the whole truth. This was about the two of them now, not her. "I was more worried about you."

He took a breath. "One minute they're telling us we're on our way to Haedera to face charges of treason and sabotage—as *Haederans*, and the next they're handing us our uniforms and telling us we're on the next courier ship out to Emot." Kanmar sounded furious, but there was hope in his eyes.

The Haederan prisoner of war camp on Emot.

"I made a deal." Avery leaned against the wall, her whole body weak with relief.

"With him?" March jerked his chin at Chase, who stood at her side, hands on his hips. "Do you know what he is?"

"I know who he is." A mechanical laugh emerged. She knew

Chase better than March did, that was for certain. "Are you questioning my decision, Colonel?"

Because you probably should.

"No, Your Majesty." Perhaps remembering who he was talking to, or maybe just relieved an execution didn't appear to be in his near future, March took a step back, and looked at Kanmar. "We can't leave her here."

"You can and you will." After what she'd just done, they were going to argue with her? They needed to take the favor and run before it was rescinded. "I didn't do this so you could debate with me about it."

They exchanged a glance with each other, ignoring her sharp expression. Before they could argue with her further, a space operations officer ducked inside, wearing the same uniform Kanmar had been when they'd left Asria. Avery jumped at his appearance, all argument forgotten.

"We're ready to go, sir," he said to Chase.

So soon? She turned to ask Chase, but the guards were already escorting Kanmar and March out.

"Colonel Kanmar, wait." There was one last thing, even though asking made their departure all too real. "If you see Merritt before I do, tell him . . ."

Her eyes grew wet. Embarrassed, she wiped them, praying no one had noticed her emotion. Kanmar nodded his understanding, and they disappeared past her. To relative safety, she hoped. Once they were out of sight, she focused on Chase.

"Why are they leaving now?" she asked. "We're already headed to Asria. Why a courier ship?"

He shrugged. "I didn't want anyone changing their minds at the last minute. There was a ship on board, and I appropriated it. I thought you'd be pleased."

Chase had taken this more seriously than she'd ever expected he would. The relief made her sick to her stomach, and placing a hand over it didn't help one bit. Made it worse, in fact. How strange. Shouldn't she feel elated instead of ill? Something was wrong. Something was horribly wrong.

That was it—Chase expected her to believe he couldn't order a courier ship to get himself back to Haedera, but that he could arrange one for two Asrian prisoners?

He'd lied.

"You orchestrated this whole thing, didn't you?" It was the only explanation for his lie, and she'd bought into his scheme without question. Would she ever learn? "To buy my cooperation."

He laughed. "You give me too much credit. It's a good idea—I wish I'd known how soft-hearted you are—but no. I don't have much use for you anymore, not after you stole that fighter. That case was over when it became apparent we couldn't close the leak. But who could resist that plea of yours?"

His laugh was too genuine for someone who was lying. Chase was a good actor, but he hadn't bothered this time, which meant she had not been manipulated. And that showing a bit of gratitude was the least she could do, no matter how difficult.

"Thank—"

The dizziness returned, so severe the entire room spun, and before she could reach out to grab on to something, anything, even Chase's arm, she collapsed to the floor.

CHAPTER FOURTEEN

Light.

Even through her closed eyelids, it glowed. It was brighter than her cell, so much brighter than when she woke up every morning. Opening her eyes would solve that mystery, but Avery squeezed them even tighter as nausea washed over her.

"I know you're not asleep anymore," came the familiar Haederan voice.

Against her will, her eyes flickered open.

Chase stood by the door of the infirmary room, a sharp look on his face, completely at odds with his laughter of a few minutes —or had it been hours?—before.

Avery looked away from him to the needle in her hand. They must have knocked her out after she'd fallen to the ground and . . . and done what else to her? Truth serums might be a myth, but she didn't trust the mythology enough to leave unknown drugs pouring into her system and pulled the needle out before he could stop her. It hit the floor with a ping, and she waited for him to hold her down so the medical personnel could replace it.

He didn't bat an eye at her action, and at his lack of response, embarrassment replaced the fear. This was no interrogation—he only glared at her.

"You're in a lot of trouble," he said.

"I know that."

Her mouth felt like someone had stuffed it with fabric. Did he think he was telling her something she didn't already know? She'd been in a lot of trouble since their ship had been intercepted. No, that wasn't right. She'd been in a lot of trouble since his people had attacked her planet. Being in trouble was nothing new.

"I actually don't think you know the half of it." He settled into the chair next to her, arms crossed, and stared like he'd never seen her before. "Or do you?"

"How . . . how long have I been like this?" His icy tone didn't make her want to answer honestly. Then again, nothing about Chase made her want to answer his questions honestly.

"Four hours."

Avery narrowed her eyes at him. "Four hours! Why was I unconscious for four hours?" Panic flared. Panic and rage. She must have hit her head on something when she'd fallen in the holding cell. There wasn't much of a headache, but she reached up and felt all around her scalp anyway. No bump. No bloody gash. "What did you do to me? You don't need to drug me each time I'm the least bit inconvenient to you!"

"The chief medical officer gave you something to help you sleep. I had nothing to do with it, but I'd consider it a gift if I were you. You need the rest, and you aren't getting it on your own. How are you feeling now?"

How was she feeling? Idiotic question.

"How do you think I'm feeling?" she asked. Besides bitter, exhausted, and full of rage, which were probably not the answers he was after.

"I imagine you don't feel very well."

That was the understatement of the century.

"You wouldn't either, if . . ." *If you'd been locked in a cage for weeks with no freedom in sight.*

"Believe me, I have no idea what it's like to feel like you do." A strange expression flashed across his face. Wistfulness? "I think my wife probably does, though."

Avery hand flew to her mouth before she could stop it. Was she *dying*? It couldn't be that bad. The nausea was terrible, but surely—surely dying must feel worse than this. She would know if she was that bad off. Wouldn't she?

The fear caught in her throat.

Unless he was implying a more mundane explanation for her symptoms—but no, that wasn't possible. That couldn't be possible. She was only reading into his comment, an offhand remark that could mean almost anything. Because of all the worst potential complications, what he had just suggested would vault her current situation straight over bad, past worse, and into catastrophic territory.

Nausea welled up again at her comprehension, and that time, even on an empty stomach, she couldn't stop it. When she finally looked up after retching for what seemed like hours, gasping for air, her chest aching, eyes red and watering, Chase was still watching her dispassionately from his chair, his arms still crossed.

Then she was sure.

"Eleven weeks." His voice wasn't just cold now, but frigid.

No.

Avery wiped her face as cold prickles spread across her body. It had to be a mistake. It was only the stress of being imprisoned on an imperial warship, destined for Haedera. That was all. The situation was enough to make any sane person ill. Chase was rarely wrong, but he had to be wrong about this. Or maybe even—

"You're lying," she said.

"What possible reason do I have for lying about this? It's not as though it's a lie I could pull off for very long. And it doesn't matter anyway, because you already know I'm telling the truth."

She did now. The lightheadedness and fatigue that had persisted for weeks. She'd thought it was stress. Stress and fear and homesickness and wanting Merritt. How the smell of the coffee Victor had brought in to her cell had made her ill enough to throw it at the wall. She'd fallen in love with coffee the first time she'd tasted it on Ventana, and it hadn't made any sense. Six months ago, she would have drunk it no matter who had left it there. The prickles turned to blades of ice, slicing through her skin.

"It's a boy, by the way." His voice warmed just a fraction. "You really didn't suspect, did you?"

"Not until five minutes ago." There were too many emotions at once to comprehend. If she had, she never would have left Villiers, no matter how much Baylen begged her to go. "Can you —will you get word to Merritt?"

"You know I can't do that."

"Can't or won't?"

"Do you really think that matters at this point?" He leaned toward her, seemingly incredulous. "How could you be so reckless?"

"I'd think you of all people would be thrilled about it." He dared call her reckless? She would have to be flippant about it now—the only way she could hide her fear. "You now have one more way to threaten and coerce me."

"You have no idea how I feel—" Chase cut himself off as the door opened and the chief medical officer walked in. "

"Am I interrupting anything?" he asked Chase. "I can come back later."

"No."

"You told her?"

"Yes."

The doctor turned his attention to Avery, apparently tired of Chase's one-word answers. She understood the feeling all too well. "How do you feel?"

They all needed to stop asking questions they knew the answer to.

"Better than I did," she admitted. That was honest, at least. A few hours of sleep in a room bigger than a closet had worked miracles, even though Chase's news had had the opposite effect.

"Still nauseated?"

She nodded. It was impossible to believe women had ever dealt with this—for over a hundred years, Asrian women had received implants which prevented it. Who knew if the Haederans had any similar technology, or if it was available for . . . prisoners.

The word made her even sicker.

"That's curable, if you're agreeable to the cure." In less than a second, the doctor stopped her from imagining her immediate bleak future. "It's—well, you probably use the same sort of implant on Asria." She nodded again in relief, and he glanced at Chase. "Gareth?"

"Fine by me."

The doctor stepped out, and Avery narrowly stopped herself from making a comment about needing his permission for medical treatment. Confronting him over that would do more harm than good.

"Gareth?" she asked instead. The idea of anyone being on a first name basis with Chase was incomprehensible. "Don't tell me there's someone brave enough to call you that."

"We've known each other twenty years." He looked at the door, then back at her. "He's trustworthy."

Trustworthy.

"Who else knows about this?" she asked.

The nausea returned. Not Victor. *Please not Victor.* He would find out eventually, though; there would be no way she could hide this from him. It would be in the ship's computer system by now if anyone cared to look.

"Just the three of us. Ian sent everyone else out before he drew your blood. It's in your file—which isn't as private as you would think or hope, by the way—as dehydration. Which I suppose it was, ultimately. I would appreciate it if you would keep it just as quiet as we have."

And his niece passing out from dehydration was something Victor wouldn't even blink at. A baby, though . . . Victor might not be threatened by her, but an heir? Someone else the senate could sink their claws into? Their newest figurehead? That would change things. He could never find out. Not unless she had Asria back.

"And I suppose you're adding this to your list of things I owe you for."

She twisted her fingers around the edge of the sheet and swallowed hard. At the rate she was accumulating favors from Chase, she would be in debt to him well into the next decade. It was a sobering thought.

"No." Chase shook his head. "This one's on me."

"Why would you do that?"

"I suppose," he said without meeting her eyes, as he pulled his sleeves down. "I ended up liking you more than I should."

With that perplexing statement, he stood and disappeared.

Avery could never be sure when a large ship was decelerating out of hyperspace—the pilots couldn't slow it down as rapidly as a fighter, after all—but a faint lurch told her the large Haederan cruiser had just done so. A new pilot, perhaps, or one who didn't care about his passengers' comfort. Or maybe it was simply a new form of motion sickness.

Whatever the reason, a surge of anticipation flowed through her and tried to twist its way to happiness—and then stopped. She would not be departing the ship for the surface once they reached Asrian orbit. They were only dropping Victor off. Then they would take her to Haedera like they planned, ever since she had the misfortune of running into them on the way to Ventana.

At least the others were safe. Kanmar and March would arrive on Emot soon, and Chase had told her yesterday that Hadley would be sent down to Alcaris. She hated that the Haederans were using the former Defense Forces headquarters as a prison, and Hadley . . . well, he would never want to set foot on Asria again once this was all over.

She wiped the tears away before they could take hold. They were within the Asrian system even now, and she wouldn't see her home. Because no matter what assurances Victor had made, no matter how kind Chase had been the past few weeks, she still wasn't sure she would live to see . . . well, anything. Not Merritt, not her child, not Asria again. Not a free and independent Asria.

But Chase arrived an hour after breakfast, holding the clothes she'd been wearing when her ship had been intercepted. He looked her up and down and frowned at the prison uniform she wore, like it had been her decision to wear it, then handed her clothes over.

"I want to show you something," he said. "Get changed. I'll be back in five minutes."

She dumped the hated red clothing on the floor of her cell and threw on her own clothes before he could change his mind. Her gut told her he didn't intend to take her off the ship, and that was disappointing. She'd hoped against hope that she would end up on Asria again, but it was the observation deck Chase had in mind, the same one where she'd met Victor.

But Victor wasn't there this time, and instead of the empty shadow of hyperspace, Asria hung in the window, the star just peeking over the horizon. The planet was more beautiful than she remembered, and it was hard to keep the tears at bay as she watched it slowly move beneath them, scattering the star's rays. She had known it was out there, but seeing it made it too real.

"What—why?" she whispered.

"I thought you might like to say goodbye." Chase settled into a chair by the door and nodded at her. "Take all the time you want."

Goodbye.

Avery turned back toward the window and brushed the tears away, but they wouldn't stop this time. They were sailing over Cadena now, so fast the city was disappearing past the window. It was hard to recognize Asria's capital from orbit; the lights that normally sparkled gold in the dark of night were a deep black speckled with white instead. The Haederan curfew and their nightly shutdown of the main power grids were still in place.

She sank onto the sofa and watched as the shadow of Cadena marched onward, and the dark of the mountains took its place. Nothing she'd done in the past year had made one difference. Her parents were dead, Drex was dead, her planet was held by the enemy, and no help had come to them. There was nothing left.

But that wasn't true, was it?

No, it was the greatest of lies. Even now, there were blessings to celebrate. Merritt was alive. He had survived more than she would ever be able to, and he was alive. And now their son, too. She had to live, if only for them.

And the mountains below—the entire planet—called to her. It was home. It was better than going to Haedera, better than the unknown of being a prisoner on that hostile world. If she could just get back down to Asria, she could disappear. Find Merritt and disappear. Somewhere safe, him and the baby and her. They'd wait out this occupation, and then she'd make them all pay.

It would be easy.

She spun around toward Chase before she could think better of her decision. "Is my uncle still on board?"

"It's not even dawn in Cadena. I assume he is." He leaned forward in his chair and scrunched his forehead. "You haven't changed your mind, have you?"

As if on cue, Cadena flew under them again, glittering a little more brightly this time around.

"I think—I think I have."

And he must have known she would have if he brought her here. Had he planned it? Hardly. He could never have been certain what she would have decided, and he had no motivation for wanting her to return to Asria. Over and over, he had made it clear he believed she belonged . . . well, not as the ruler of a free Asria, that was for sure. The look on his face confirmed his displeasure with her decision—or maybe just the fact someone with more power than him had given her the ability to make it.

"Then I'll have him informed," he replied.

"I'm going to get Asria back, you know." Avery stiffened. "Neither you nor he nor your empire will win this in the end."

Chase stood and motioned toward the door. "I have no doubt you will try, Your Majesty."

CHAPTER FIFTEEN

THE CAR MADE ITS WAY ACROSS THE ANCIENT STONE BRIDGE TO THE palace, and for a moment Avery was ten years younger and headed home after a weekend at Sabino. She had worried for months that the Haederans would have chopped the trees down, but they were still there, though nearly leafless in early autumn. It had had come early to Cadena this year, but the palace that peeked through the trees looked exactly the same as it always had. Her skin prickled in unexpected warmth despite the weather. Home was still home, no matter what treasonous uncle laid claim to it now.

The warmth turned to ice as the thinning trees gave way to the grand courtyard, and in the palace's side garden a large Haederan flag waved in the breeze—an affront on so many levels. The royal family had never even flown the Asrian flag, except on the uniforms of the few who had served in the Defense Forces. For hundreds of years, the Rendon family had considered it a redundant declaration of loyalty, and Victor Rendon in particular had disparaged the showiness of it.

A tasteless display of fleeting allegiance, he'd always claimed.

Avery had always assumed he was referencing their greater allegiance to the Holy One, but now . . . She suppressed a sigh as the wind whipped the flag toward her. Yes, any flag would have been bad enough, but the one flying above the palace now, with crossed swords in front of some sort of mythical Haederan beast, was unacceptable.

It would have to come down.

And you're as delusional as Victor.

She brought a finger to her mouth, then stuck her hand in her pocket before she could chew on her nail. Tearing the flag down would be all but impossible with the security that surrounded the palace. To be sure, the Haederans had been all over Cadena since the invasion, but not like this. The guards who milled about the drive and the ones in position on the roof appeared more serious than she'd ever seen them, and she couldn't help but grin. They were worried about something, and worried Haederans were something she could never see enough of.

And, perhaps, something she could create more of. There was no way she could run them off Asria—not alone—but she could make their lives miserable, no matter what she'd promised Victor. It was something to look forward to, no matter how much dread had shadowed her since departing *Imperieuse*.

Her smile faded when the car stopped, and an Imperial Security Command captain opened her door and introduced himself as Brennin Kern. Close to her age, fit, and upper-class Haederan, there was no question he'd been ordered to the palace by Chase. His uniform was a surprise, and unnerving enough on its own, but it was his eyes—eyes that had seen things—that bothered her. She looked away from them before she lost her nerve.

"Not even bothering to hide it, are you?" she asked his boots.

Kern only mumbled in reply, and her dream of fleeing the palace and finding her way back to Villiers evaporated as he followed her inside, obviously intent on shadowing her the entire way to her rooms.

"I can find my own way, you know." She narrowed her eyes at him. "This is my home."

"Is that what you think it is?"

She ground her teeth together in frustration. Even though his Haederan accent grated on her, he sounded cultured, and she already hated him for it, perhaps more than for the uniform he wore. How long had he been here? A year and then some, doubtless. Probably one of the officers Chase had had following her around before.

"What else would it be?" she asked.

"Most would call it a prison." He raised his eyebrows innocently. "You didn't really think we'd leave you to your own devices in Cadena, did you, my lady?"

We've learned was his unsaid warning, despite the unexpected courtesy.

"Fine. Then take me to my rooms and leave me alone. It's been a long trip."

"No, no." The slightest bit of amusement flashed across his face, then was gone. "Not your rooms. The guest suite."

"Which guest suite?" There were several in the palace. "And why?"

"Upstairs. One that's more . . ." He shrugged as they walked through the door. "Secure."

Avery had no answer to that. Quietly, she followed him through the familiar corridors that brought back so many memories. The guest suite in question on the third floor was one that hadn't been used more than a handful of times since her father's branch of the Rendon family had permanently moved to Cadena. Overlooked and practically neglected when her grandfather had renovated the rest of the palace decades prior, it smelled of chemicals and dust.

She sneezed as she examined it, grateful for the excuse to look away from Kern. Contrary to her spacious set of rooms two floors higher, this single bedroom was a closet. A large bed with a velvet settee at the foot sat against the far wall, respectably appointed, but it only made the small room even smaller. No network access here; the unmodernized room was probably one of the few in the palace without it, and

Kern's choice of accommodations suddenly made a bit more sense.

Static fields had been added to the window that boasted the Cadena skyline and the mountains in the distance; there was no way out through that. She'd loved the panorama as a child, but now . . . Ignorance truly had been bliss. To add to that insult, the network portal, necessary in this older wing of the palace, was missing, which meant she would be blind and deaf to the happenings around her. A small round dining table, made of antique wood like the rest of the furniture in the palace, sat in front of the bed. Only one chair sat next to it.

It would be a lonely existence, then.

Not that she'd ever had many visitors at the palace, not even Merritt, who'd always avoided the place unless he had no other choice. And there was an ancient fireplace that a servant might be talked into lighting. A cozy winter night in front of a roaring fire . . . Yes, captive or not, this current arrangement was better than the brig aboard *Imperieuse* where she'd spent too many days.

Kern remained in the hall outside, watching her with his arms crossed in his best attempt at intimidation. Avery was suddenly grateful for the single chair—it meant she wouldn't have to socialize with her new shadow.

"You'll stay here unless your uncle or I say otherwise," he said. "No wandering the palace. One of the servants will bring your meals and anything else you need. You can lock the door from the inside, but be aware I can override it if necessary."

Disheartened by that restriction, Avery opened the small wardrobe, set against the wall instead of a closet. Two dresses, four pairs of pants, and three shirts hung inside; a small stack lingerie lay on a shelf beneath them. She let her fingers run through the fabric that wouldn't even fit for much longer.

"Where are the rest of my things?" she asked. Nine pieces of clothing. Victor had to be kidding.

"Destroyed last year, I think. It looks like you have enough to live on, though." Kern checked his chronometer. "Oh, and before I forget, you've already been granted a brief reprieve. Your uncle requests your presence in an hour for dinner. I'll come collect you ten minutes prior. Dress nicely."

She gathered just enough courage to shut the door in his face.

* * *

For several hours Avery considered feigning illness to avoid dinner with Victor, but that needed to be kept as a last-ditch option for another time. She wouldn't be able to avoid him forever, anyway. The silk sapphire dress she pulled out of the wardrobe fit a little too snugly, and she tossed it to the floor. Just as she'd feared, nothing in her tiny wardrobe would hide her condition for very long.

She chewed on a nail as she imagined her uncle's reaction if she were to arrive at dinner in the same clothes she'd been wearing since Chase had handed them back, way up in orbit. Kern's instruction to *dress nicely* had to have come from Victor, and it wasn't worth the argument. Not yet. She picked up the dress, shook it out, and tried it on again. It didn't look as bad now as it would in another month, and in a stroke of luck, it was one she'd liked. It was the same dress she'd worn when she saw Merritt for the first time after returning permanently to Asria, and that was as good as a slap in Victor's face, even if he couldn't possibly know the symbolism behind it.

It turned out her uncle preferred to take all his meals in the formal dining room now. Yet another strange transformation in the Rendon family, if only a small one. It had always been Victor's idea to have family dinners in the small dining room off the kitchen. The food just tasted fresher there, he'd always claimed. Where she ate never made much difference, but as she stood in the entrance to the dining room, Kern having trailed her the entire way downstairs, she would have rather been anywhere else.

This is not your home either, Victor.

"Avery." Victor stood when she entered, a glass of wine in his hand. "I'm glad to see you've started listening to my wishes."

That kind of hello after weeks apart didn't bode well for her. It certainly wasn't the warm greeting he had given her aboard *Imperieuse.*

"Anything to get out of my new quarters." She tried and failed to keep the bitterness out of her voice. "And I don't see that a meal with you is anything I should avoid—is it?"

"Maybe not. Would you care for a drink? There's another guest joining us, but it looks like he's running a little late."

Implant or not, her stomach rolled at the thought of alcohol.

"No, thank you. And who?" After so many years, she could dine with Victor, but small talk with a stranger was another matter entirely. One she wasn't sure she would ever be up to.

Victor smiled. "It's a surprise." Footsteps drummed across the marble outside, and he looked past her at the source. "Ah, Governor. I'm glad you could make it."

Governor?

Her knees grew weak as Taln Perrin crossed the hallway behind her. He smiled at her, his arrogance undiminished by the fact she'd stolen the technology that had allowed him to take Asria in the first place. Did he know Chase had told her he was responsible for what had happened to Merritt?

She looked at Victor, and he raised a hand in invitation. "If you can't be polite and welcome our guest . . ."

Avery gritted her teeth. She couldn't play this game for long. Even spending the next twenty years in that brig aboard *Imperieuse* would be better than having dinner with Perrin, and Victor must know that—just like Perrin must realize that the last time he'd seen her had been in the library of this very building when he'd ordered her and Grant Baylen's arrests.

"General." She inclined her head just a fraction, hoping it was enough for Victor. "I hope you're having a pleasant evening."

Perrin opened his mouth in response, and Victor, perhaps wondering how long it would be before she said something he would regret, interrupted to wave them over to the table. Avery sat without a word, pleased the servants appeared unhappy with the current situation. It seemed Victor wasn't nearly as popular among the few Asrians she'd encountered as he probably imagined he would be. Certainly not among the palace employees, all of whom knew the fate of King Lucas and her mother.

"I have to say, I was quite surprised to hear you were headed back here." Perrin took a sip of some foul Haederan liquor. No Asrian wine for him. "I'm even more surprised the powers that be allowed it after what happened on the *Aurora*. If it had been my decision . . . well." His chin rose. "You certainly wouldn't be here now."

Aurora.

Her smile across the table at Perrin was finally unforced. That would be the name of the cruiser she'd stolen the fighter from—Perrin had never been well-versed in keeping his mouth shut. It was a wonder he was a general, but maybe that was why he had been stashed on Asria as a military governor. Perhaps even the Haederans wanted to keep him from making mistakes.

"Then I think we're all glad it wasn't your decision," she replied, reaching for her glass of water.

Right. That was an improvement.

Perrin shot her a dark look, then turned his attention back to Victor. "I'm glad you're back, Victor. I heard your return had been delayed and prayed I'd been mishearing things."

"You're that eager to leave Asria?" Victor asked.

"It's been a long year." Perrin looked at Avery. "And some months. Retirement is calling, and I can guarantee you that I won't be enjoying it on this planet."

"Leaving us so soon, General? I'm sorry to learn our hospitality hasn't been sufficient."

Kusir, would she ever learn to shut up? The unbidden Voirian curse reminded her of Hadley, and her eyes dropped to her lap. She was saved from Perrin's cutting response by dinner, and the conversation dwindled to nothing as she focused on the first course. Though simple, it was the best food she'd had in months —certainly since she'd left Villiers.

Head down, thoughts focused on Merritt, it took a minute for her to realize Perrin was talking to her again.

"I'm sorry?" she asked.

"I said, I hear congratulations are in order."

The blood drained from her face, and she lay the fork down by her plate before her hand started shaking, along with the rest of her. How had Perrin found out about the baby? Chase had said no one knew. That everything had been kept quiet. If anyone knew about keeping things quiet, it was him.

"I—thank you."

"I was astonished to learn that Merritt Parker was alive after what happened at Alcaris last year." Perrin took another sip of his drink. "But you know how information can be twisted around when it comes to things like that. I was even more surprised to learn that you'd still have him after how broken they say he is. But there's no accounting for taste, I suppose . . . or love. You knew about this, Victor?" he continued, like she wasn't sitting right across from him.

Victor glared at her, but Perrin's lie had rendered her speechless. "Not until I saw her on the *Imperieuse*, although I've suspected it for quite some time. They've been off and on for . . . what has it been, Avery, a decade now?" He shrugged. "Poor decisions then, poor decisions now. She'll come to her senses."

Avery stood and brushed a small crumb from her skirt. Dinner with the two of them—being in the same *room* as the two of them —was intolerable.

"I'm sorry, but I'm not feeling very well. Please excuse me." She nodded at Perrin, hoping the gesture would placate Victor enough to not make a scene over her exit.

It didn't work. She was halfway to the lift, Kern nowhere to be seen, when Victor called her name. He'd actually followed her out? That wasn't a good sign—oh, she would hear it from him now. She whirled around, too angered by Perrin's games to care that she'd already violated Kern's rules.

"I got dressed," she snapped at him. "I went to dinner. I played along with him and listened to his despicable words. That man hates me, but that probably doesn't come as a surprise to you, does it? You set this up for no other reason but to humiliate and hurt me. Do you even know—"

—what he did to Merritt?

"Yes, you went to dinner," Victor conceded with a nod. "And believe it or not, I do appreciate the effort, though I'd have liked it if you could have been a little more polite to the governor. He still has a great deal of influence on Asria, especially in Cadena. Even more in this palace."

Be polite to the man who'd tortured her husband, then played dumb about it just to garner a reaction from her? Victor had no idea how hard it had been to not wrap her hands around Perrin's throat.

"I tried." That much was true. She couldn't help it if she wasn't capable of making enough of an effort. "I really did."

"You're going to have to try harder, especially at the ball. If you couldn't handle this, what makes you think you'll be able to hold up the rest of your end of our agreement?"

"Ball?" Victor couldn't seriously be considering throwing his annual birthday ball. Not now. Not when Asria was like this. "But you're not . . . I mean . . ."

"The king of Asria anymore?" He gave a short laugh. "No. But it is the end of the traditional harvest season, if a little late, and things are becoming somewhat normal on Asria again. I believe a celebration would do us all a bit of good, and I also believe it would be a wonderful opportunity for you to prove your word to me."

Avery swallowed. He wanted her to appear at a dance full of Haederans and act like a collaborator. Well, what had she expected when she agreed to support him? This would be the most public support of all.

"I'm not sure the Haederans would like to socialize with me," she admitted.

"If you'd start acting more like my niece and less like a Commonwealth officer, they'd be fine with it."

"I have nothing formal to wear." *I don't have* anything *to wear, Victor.* The excuse of any woman trying to avoid a celebration, and in her case, all too true. *"Especially to an event like that."*

Victor sighed. "I'll have credit issued first thing tomorrow. Go shop. In fact, talk to my secretary in the morning. She'll need help planning the ball, and you'd be the best person for that. But next time I host a dinner, especially for a Haederan official, I expect a better presence from you. Don't make me remind you again."

Avery nodded.

"And one more thing—I want that ring off your hand."

He stalked off before she could argue.

CHAPTER SIXTEEN

K ERN HADN'T STOPPED TAPPING A BORED FOOT ON THE FLOOR OF THE tenth-story conference room since they'd arrived at the senate building a half hour ago, and Avery wasn't sure she could handle another five minutes of the irritating noise—nor his satisfied glances at her. Her only consolation was that the four Haederan Army soldiers who had trailed them all morning had remained on the aeroflyer pad on the top of the building, supposedly to guard the vehicle. It was obvious that their withdrawal was intentional, though, an opportunity to avoid Kern.

If only she had that option.

"Don't you think this surveillance is overkill?" she asked. They'd taken an aeroflyer for what was only a fifteen-minute trip by foot—though Kern had claimed it was because of the weather —and now he was sitting too close to her for her comfort. Where did he think she was going to disappear to?

"Well, let's see." He stopped tapping his foot to count off her sins on his fingers. "The last time you were left unsupervised, you found yourself a new job, smuggled I don't even know how much classified data out of Cadena, escaped the city altogether, and ulti-mately stole—" He looked around. "Something. So no, I don't think this extremely minor supervision is overkill. You're lucky to be allowed out of the palace at all."

Avery didn't bother arguing that she hadn't smuggled *that* much information off Asria. And there was no point in arguing the truth, not really. Kern could believe whatever he wanted, even though it would have been more useful for her purposes if he thought she was incompetent.

She rolled her eyes toward the window and tried not to wonder why Perrin had called her here so quickly. Understanding his motives was a losing battle, but she didn't have to wait long. Perrin arrived thirty seconds later and shot Kern a sharp glance.

"Out."

Kern's eyes narrowed at the order, but he muttered a courtesy under his breath and left before Perrin said anything else. Perrin's stare shifted to her and turned predatory. Reptilian, almost.

"I told you if I had my way, you wouldn't have set foot on this planet again," he said by way of greeting.

"Am I here so you can overrule the viceroy's wishes?" Apparently they weren't going to exchange any pleasantries, and if that was Perrin's plan, he needed to get on with it.

Perrin sank into the chair beside her and flung a piece of paper haphazardly on the table. "Not yet. Maybe later, if you cease to be of any use to me." He jerked his chin at the paper.

She drew it toward her with a tentative finger and scanned the words, deep lines growing on her forehead. It was a letter, a request from the local governor in Tarragona. Kanmar's home.

"They're requesting a Haederan investigation into the mining operation there." She looked up at Perrin in confusion. "The prefecture government had sent the same request last year, and you said no."

"I've decided to allow it this time. You'll go out there and convince them nothing is wrong, that our erlite mining is merely a standard commercial operation. Persuade them that there's no need to worry, and that they can stop this incessant questioning. I've grown quite weary of it."

"Me?"

"You agreed to support the viceroy in his duties. Right now, I can't think of a better way to show your loyalty to him than to speak to the prefecture governor on our behalf, can you?"

Our behalf.

Avery ran her finger along the edge of the paper. Supporting her uncle was supposed to include nothing more than further awkward dinners. Even Victor's ball, uncomfortable as it would be, would be nothing like acting on behalf of the Haederan emperor in Tarragona.

"Of course . . ." Perrin shrugged. "If you'd rather not comply, we can consider your agreement with His Excellency void right now. If that's the case, I'm sure Captain Kern would be happy to escort you somewhere a little more secure until other arrangements for your custody can be made."

"What if I'm not successful?"

The eyes grew colder. "You'll have to make sure you are."

"All right." She forced herself to stay still. Gaze on the floor, she blinked twice and steeled herself. "I'll go."

"Good. The shuttle leaves from Luron in four hours. You'd best pack quickly." Perrin stood, and she held her breath as he circled behind her. His hands hit the table, and she jumped as he leaned over next to her. "If you breathe one word about the verium to anyone—in Tarragona or anywhere else—your game is up. You'll do as I say, and nothing more. Dismissed."

Dismissed?

Who did he think he was?

She stalked into the corridor without a response and headed for the stairs instead of the lift. Before she knew what she was doing, she was dashing down instead of up to the aeroflyer pad. Kern darted after her, hollering for her to stop the entire time.

"Productive visit?" he asked, when he finally caught her five floors down. "You're going the wrong way, you know."

"You and I are going to Tarragona on a propaganda visit, it seems," she said over her shoulder. Perrin and his threats had made this unfriendly Imperial Security officer seem a better companion for the moment, and she was angry about that as well. "I hope you like long shuttle rides and provincial Asrian food. And I'm walking back to the palace. I don't care what you think or how cold it is."

Kern protested the rest of the way down, but she didn't care. She was halfway across the lobby when he finally grabbed her by the wrist.

"I don't know what you think you're doing, but I'm not going to chase you around the city. If you can't live with the limitations your uncle has placed on you, I'll have no choice but to consider your agreement with him broken and move you elsewhere."

It was almost word for word what Perrin had threatened. Had Kern given Perrin the idea, or the other way around? Maybe it didn't matter, but if they were in agreement, things wouldn't be easy for her.

"Fine. Then may we please stop by the senate temple first, Captain Kern? In case you hadn't figured it out yet, I'm having a bit of a bad day, and I'd like to pray a bit."

Prayer might not solve anything today, but if nothing else, it would earn her a walk through the senate gardens. Kern and his thin Haederan blood would survive, for it wasn't that cold, not yet. He would be in for a rude awakening when winter set in for good.

"All you had to do was ask." Kern matched her tone and added a soulless smile as he waved the door open. "After you, my lady."

Avery paused in the doorway to get control of her rage as a man pushed his way inside, knocking her against the large glass door. It was one ultimate insult on a morning where everything else had gone wrong.

"Watch where you're going," she snarled at him.

Kern smothered a laugh at her rudeness.

"My apologies, madam."

Zenos Hadley's eyes showed no recognition as he passed by into the bustling lobby of the senate building—but Kern's widened in what could only be dismay.

CHAPTER SEVENTEEN

<hr>

THE AEROFLYER SLOWLY DESCENDED ONTO THE PALACE'S ROOFTOP pad, but Avery barely noticed. If what Chase had told her aboard *Imperieuse* was true, Hadley had been sent to the Haederan prison at Alcaris. What was he doing walking around free in the middle of Cadena—sauntering into the senate building, no less? Hadley was good, even rescue-from-prison good, but he wasn't escape-from-prison-on-his-own good.

And Kern. Just the thought of his reaction to Hadley's entrance sent a hot flash of fear through her. It was obvious Kern had recognized him—which wasn't surprising if he knew about the *Aurora* incident—but he hadn't made even the slightest move to intercept him. Had he been too surprised as well?

Likely not. After all, it wasn't as though Kern couldn't leave her standing there in what might as well have been the middle of the street in order to apprehend an escaped prisoner of war. He would report the sighting as soon as he could, however, and Hadley would be on the run. Hopefully, he'd be able to simply vanish. Asria wasn't the largest planet, but it was still a planet— easy to disappear for a while.

Avery rubbed the bridge of her nose in frustration as the aeroflyer settled onto the rooftop. But if he *had* escaped, what was he doing in the senate building? The only plausible explanation was that he'd known *she* would be there and had been attempting to contact her—but there was no way he could have known her schedule.

Kern was lost in conversation with the pilot, so she slipped out of the flyer and into the lift tube before he could follow. The glass-walled cylinder drifted down, and she pulled Merritt's ring off and kissed it before stuffing it into her pocket.

Her hand smashed into a light item that hadn't been there that morning. Cautiously, after an unnecessary look around the small, empty tube, she drew out a slip of paper.

Ran late. Sorry. Will try again.

Avery shoved the note back in her pocket and stared unseeing at the lift tube door as her heart pounded. It was just like Hadley to show up in the middle of an occupied city where he was a wanted man like it was a completely trivial act.

Trivial, that was, as long as he was cautious of Kern.

* * *

It turned out it wasn't Kern she needed to be cautious of, but Chase, who was standing just outside the door to the lift tube when she exited. Seeing him in the palace should have been more of a surprise, but there wasn't much he could do to surprise her any longer. With an almost-theatric sigh, she stepped around him and turned toward the private residence, knowing—well, hoping —he wouldn't dare follow her inside.

"Ignoring me isn't a very gracious hello after so long." To her dismay, he pursued her down the sun-drenched hall. "Where are you going in such a hurry?"

She was supposed to be gracious to him now?

"I'm going home," she replied. And the quicker she returned to her room, the better. Hadley's note needed to be disposed of somehow.

"That's too bad. I'd heard you were headed to Tarragona. I thought I might join you."

"Join me?" That froze her, and her forehead creased in honest confusion as she turned to face him. He couldn't believe she was thoughtless enough to go with him anywhere voluntarily, could he? The idea of spending half a day on a shuttle with Kern was bad enough.

"Well, why not?"

Her gaze flickered from the crossed swords on his collar, to the hidden note in her pocket, to the plush ivory carpet, then finally back to his earnest face.

So many reasons.

"The aeroflyer only holds two." *And you won't be one of them.* "If you want to go to Tarragona with us, you'll have to find your own way to the shuttle base."

She slipped between the two Haederan soldiers at the doors, the guards meant to keep her in and any danger to the viceroy out. Their very presence made her jaw tighten. Victor didn't deserve their protection. He didn't deserve anyone's protection. Not even the passive fortification of the ornate wooden doors lined with bulletproof fabric.

"If I wanted more than a pleasant trip out of town, you would know it," Chase called after her. "To start with, I wouldn't be alone. I certainly wouldn't be politely inviting myself along."

Her chest grew tight. Would they not just open the door and let her in?

"Reminding me of what you're capable of isn't the way to earn my trust, Colonel." Her voice was so quiet she wasn't sure he could hear her. "Much as you might believe otherwise."

"I'm not asking you to trust me. I'd question your sanity if you did." He chuckled, just a little. "I'm merely asking you to switch your travel plans around a little."

She spun toward him. "What's in it for you?"

"Do you think you're the only one who hates being stuck in

Cadena? I'd love to see more of Asria. You're not bad company either, if you'd stop snarling at me for five minutes."

"I'm not—" She inhaled as her arms relaxed at her sides. "I'm not snarling."

"You are. You're always snarling at me. But I suppose I can overlook that right now." He grinned at her. "Any other objections, my lady? Because I have an answer for every one of them."

A snort would be even more unladylike than the snarl, so she merely shook her head.

"Good—then we have an aeroflyer to catch. Go pack. I'll wait."

* * *

Even with Chase at her side, Avery found it hard to hold in the excitement as they took the lift back up. The aeroflyer she and Kern had returned in was still parked on the roof, and a cold gust spun around it, whipping her hair and clothing in circles. She put a hand to her pocket as they approached and the breeze grew stronger. It wouldn't take much for Hadley's note to fly out.

The note.

She bit the inside of her cheek. How could she have been so careless? She'd had half an hour to dispose of it, but between fretting over Perrin's warning and Chase's invitation, it had slipped her mind. No matter. This was fixable. She'd find *something* to do with it, even if she had to eat it.

"What's in your pocket?"

Avery jumped at the question. Chase had dropped her bag just short of the aeroflyer hatch and was eying her with the dangerous interest she knew so well.

"Nothing."

"It doesn't look like nothing." His gaze fell deliberately to her side.

"It's my ring." She glanced at the flyer behind Chase's head, decided that was too guilty, and looked him in the eye. "Victor doesn't like me wearing it, so I don't when I'm at the palace. I took it off earlier, and now I'm going to put it on as soon as I get in the flyer."

Her rambling explanation might as well have been a confession. Would she ever learn to keep her mouth shut around him?

"It's Victor now, is it? Such a casual manner with which to address the viceroy." He moved closer, so close she could smell something like aftershave. "Just the ring?"

Avery nodded, once, her entire body tense.

"Then you won't mind if I take a look."

"I—" He couldn't be serious. "Yes, I mind."

Avery took a backward step toward the lift tube door. Surely she could make it downstairs to an incinerator. But—she stiffened—not if she bumped into Kern.

"None of that, now." He twisted her arm behind her back, trapping her.

She rotated toward him but couldn't escape his grip. Slamming her foot across his instep wouldn't help either, not with those boots of his, but she tried anyway. Kern dug his fingers into her wrist, then seized her other arm, twisting that one behind her too.

"Stop it." She tried to turn her head backward to whisper at him. "You're hurting me." Scaring her was more accurate, but maybe it was enough for him to let her go.

"Stop fighting me, and it won't hurt," Kern said without pity. "Just let him search you, and I'll let you go."

"I'd be a fool to get in this flyer with you without doing it, anyway, wouldn't I?" Chase crossed his arms, all joking gone. "Hold her still, Captain."

Face red—though whether it was from rage or fear or shame, or just that damn autumn wind that never stopped—Avery held her breath. This wasn't about security at all, as he claimed—it wasn't as though Kern had worried about the same earlier. This was about humiliating her, about making her remember her place, about reminding her who he was and who she was not.

"Cry all you want," he said in a calm voice, moving toward her. "As long as you stop fighting. This will go faster if you do, and then we can all get on with it."

She hadn't been close to crying, but that tone—how she hated it. His attempt at control was so obvious now. Well, this time she wouldn't fall for it, and anger was the best antidote to his mind games.

"Do you think I care about making your life easier?" she spat at him. "The three of us can stand up here until the stars fall from the sky for all I care."

Behind her, Kern laughed. Chase ignored them both, just swept his hands down her sides and into her pockets. He palmed the ring and held the note up between his thumb and forefinger, eyebrows raised in complete seriousness.

Kern released her and grabbed the note from over her shoulder. Chase's gesture must have been directed at him, for he darted out the door without looking back. Avery held out her hand, and Chase slapped the ring into her palm.

"Get in."

"I—" He couldn't possibly think she would be foolish enough to go anywhere with him now. "I don't think this is a good idea."

"You don't listen to anything anyone says, do you?" He pushed her firmly toward the hatch, and she climbed inside, wishing she was anywhere else. "Get in the flyer."

"The note was from Merritt," she said, settling into the seat. There wasn't any way he could know otherwise, was there? The wording had been vague—intentionally, if she knew Hadley at all. "It was sent to me, and it was personal."

Chase swung into the seat opposite her, tossed her bag at his feet, and closed the door over them in one effortless movement, ignoring her claim. "Ready?"

No.

"But General Perrin specifically said I wasn't to leave Captain Kern's sight."

And if Perrin had a problem with it, she could say goodbye to the little freedom she'd gained from Victor. This whole thing was a bad idea. She needed out of the flyer, needed to get back home before anyone noticed she was missing.

Needed away from Chase.

"I don't report to him." He took one last look out the window as she moved to unclasp her harness, then knocked over his head on the wall behind him. A second later, the aeroflyer lifted off, trapping her inside.

"Yes, but . . ."

She settled back in her seat and folded her hands. Everyone on Asria reported to Perrin. Even Chase, as disinclined as he was to accept that kind of authority.

"I serve the emperor, not Taln Perrin." His hand moved, perhaps inadvertently, toward his collar. "And you are still in Imperial Security Command custody, more specifically mine. The general can disapprove of my decision all he wants, but his orders regarding you are less absolute than he would like to believe. Kern will catch up at the shuttleport."

The ship banked away from the palace, and Avery's stomach flipped. Was it the sudden turn or Chase's intentional reminder that she was still a prisoner? A well-treated one now, there was no denying that, but a prisoner nonetheless.

Chase ignored her distress and pulled a tablet from his pocket. She leaned against the window as they veered onto the higher-altitude aero street for ships leaving town. It was a better view than anything she'd had in a long time, and she suppressed a sigh of wistful homesickness. Sooner than she wanted, they were past midtown Cadena, sailing through the valleys between the mountain ranges.

She'd flown through here in the early days of her relationship with Merritt—that intoxicating time before they'd spent her first year at the academy on Ventana ignoring each other's existence. One afternoon, despite her protests that they were too far from civilization, he'd landed his flyer in a small valley at the base of a waterfall. As they explored it, the ever-present bottle of wine chilling in the pool at the base of the cascade, she had been convinced they were the first people to ever set foot there. At least, that was how it'd felt to her silly, innocent heart.

She squinted out the window as the flyer banked again, wishing she could find the valley again. Maybe it was up that small canyon on their starboard side, where the leaves were still red. The ravine didn't look all that familiar, but then, it had been almost ten years since Merritt had taken her there. They were still too far away to tell. Maybe she could talk Chase into a short flight up the canyon, just to see if she recognized—

"You still hate me, don't you?"

Avery forced her attention inside. Chase had set his tablet down and was watching her intently. How long had he been staring at her? And what kind of question was that?

"Yes." But hadn't she prayed to be released from the anger that ate at her? "No. I don't know."

"You don't seem very sure. Which is it?"

"Yes. I still hate you." He was leading her into conversation again, even though she didn't want to say a word to him. How did he do that? "I do."

"Hmm." Chase folded his arms and examined her while she tried not to squirm under his scrutiny. "I don't think you do. I think you want to, but you don't, and I think that just kills you."

"Do I really need to give you an exhaustive list of good reasons I have to hate you?" Avery exhaled and shifted back into the center of her seat to eye him warily. He really was as oblivious as she'd believed when they'd first met. "Starting with who you are and what you've done on Asria, including to me personally?"

He laughed and stretched an arm over the back of his seat. "You're still hung up on that? I'd have thought a year and then some would have given you a bit of perspective. I already told you how lucky you were. What happened was nothing personal."

Heat brushed over her, anger and terror at once. The Haederans had held her for months in a tiny cell, starving her, beating her, threatening her, all on Chase's orders, and he was saying it wasn't *personal*? If only she could dismiss it as easily as he did.

"Yes, I am still hung up on *that*, although *that* doesn't even begin to cover what happened to me because of you. A year is not nearly enough time to forget that kind of—"

"That kind of what?" His forehead creased—in delight or confusion, she couldn't tell. "Deceit? Yes, I can imagine learning that your enemy was actually your enemy must have been quite distressing for you."

"Don't mock me, Colonel."

"Don't make it so easy, my lady."

He thought this was *funny*?

Avery looked away in disgust, but she wasn't quick enough to avoid the laughter in his eyes. She clasped her hand over her mouth, but it was too late for that, too. An unwilling laugh escaped, and there was nothing she could do to keep it from showing on her face.

"I suppose the answer to my original question is no, then," Chase said.

"It may be difficult to hate you," she replied, "but your egotistical satisfaction is something completely different." She glanced out the window, and her laughter vanished like it had never existed at all.

They were headed in the opposite direction of the Luron shuttleport.

* * *

They landed in a rolling field east of Sabino, still green in the early fall. In the distance the Pelanco Mountains and memories of Merritt beckoned, but Chase guided her away from the peaks and toward a large rock under a tree a half kilometer away from the aeroflyer. The ship was hardly visible beyond the crest of one of the taller hills, and Avery quashed a sudden fear he'd brought her here to kill her. A silly thought. He wouldn't have needed to bring her all this way to do that. No one would have prevented him from shooting her in the middle of Cadena itself.

The rock turned out to be a pile of stones from the nearby creek, and Chase halted her in front of it with a gentle touch on her elbow. Leaves fluttered in the autumn breeze above, and there was a softness to the air she hadn't felt since she'd last seen Merritt. Softness and something darker, an odd combination she didn't understand at first.

"What is—"

The breeze stopped; the world skidded to a halt. And the hope. The hope she hadn't realized she'd been clinging to for the past year floated away like dried autumn leaves in Cadena, leaving her empty. Death drifted all around them here, but it was not hers, for there was only one grave Chase would deem important enough to show her. And if he knew where her parents were buried, that meant the Imperial Security Command—the Haederan Empire's experts in everything extrajudicial—had been involved in their deaths. And that meant they hadn't been shot escaping house arrest in Sabino like General Cevall had told her, like she'd believed all this time.

The Haederans had brought them here to execute them.

Her legs went weak, like she and Chase had just walked ten kilometers uphill instead of just a short distance down the rolling slope. All she wanted to do was sink to her knees, but Chase's sudden grip under her arm kept her upright. Somewhere in the haze, she recognized it as help, but his intentions didn't matter. At his touch, her throat tightened so much she could barely swallow. Her heartbeat thrashed in her ears. The breeze picked up again, raw on her exposed skin, a copy of the terror her parents must have felt when they realized why they'd been brought to this remote meadow.

She took a deep breath and focused on Chase's face, letting his uniform fade away into a green blur in her mind. The fear faded away too, as a quiet comprehension took its place. No matter the circumstances, her mother and father wouldn't have been this afraid. Like Merritt, they knew what came next.

"Your uncle talked the emperor into ordering it," he murmured. "I'm so sorry."

"But why?" Avery could only stare at the rocks as he held her up. "My father signed the surrender agreement, no questions asked. He left Cadena when the occupation government ordered him to. He never fought you. He wasn't political. He was fiercely Asrian, yes, and loyal, but he—he wasn't a threat to my uncle or your occupation. And why only them? Why not me too?"

All questions Chase couldn't possibly have answers to. All questions she wouldn't trust his answers to.

"You'd have to ask your uncle about that. Not that I'd suggest you do so." He blew out a deep breath. "I imagine he felt you would be easier to control. Less of a symbol of Asria than your father. Or maybe he's just sentimental in his own way."

"How long have you known about this?" She stepped away from him, trying to calm herself. The fragile lace of trust that had appeared in the aeroflyer frayed, even though he owed her no explanation. It was war, and she was the enemy.

"Only a week or so. It took a lot of digging and more than a few threats to figure out what happened to them. The information was well-protected." At her skeptical expression, he added, a touch defensively, "I swear to you, whatever terrible things you have ever believed about me, I wasn't involved in this. This is not something I've ever been involved in. I never met your father, nor visited Sabino. And I—I had other priorities back then. Priorities that kept me in Cadena."

You, Avery understood. She searched his face for any kind of deception, but there was none, only a profound depth of sympathy and compassion.

He has a conscience after all.

"Can I—"

She snapped her mouth shut before she could ask the foolish question. He would never give her privacy with her grief. The most she could ask would be for him to stand over her and pretend to ignore her tears while she prayed and screamed and cried out to the Holy One about the injustice.

Chase pulled a brick of incense and a lighter from his pocket and handed them over. "I'll be on the flyer. I'm trusting you to come back when you're ready. Please don't make me regret that." He kissed his fingers and pressed them to his forehead, and, with a short wave at her, headed up the hill.

CHAPTER EIGHTEEN

THE SIDE TRIP TO HER PARENTS' GRAVE HAD CLEARLY DELAYED THEM more than Kern had wanted, and Avery forced herself to ignore his disapproving look as he sat beside her at the circular table in the Tarragona prefecture hall. Technically, it wasn't hard to focus on something else, since the picture window across from them overlooked some of the most beautiful country outside the capital region. Rolling hills and karst outcroppings filled the view, much older and just as beautiful as the high mountains outside Cadena.

She could have stared out that window all day if it weren't for the furious prefecture governor in front of it.

"And if that's not bad enough," the man went on, louder than before, like he'd noticed her daydreaming and didn't approve, "they've conscripted our own people to work down there." His face grew crimson. "It wasn't enough for them to destroy our land. Now they're going to use us as slaves too?"

"When did this begin?" Avery cast an annoyed glance at Kern over the new information.

"Two days ago. The army went door to door through the village, pulling out every man over the age of fifteen, except for the prefecture council. Over six hundred people!" His face grew redder. "My son is down there now, Your—" He caught himself just in time, spurred on by Kern clearing his throat.

Yes, yes. You and your empire refuse to accept that I'm the duly elected queen of Asria, and you personally can't stand the fact most Asrians consider me their sovereign. You've made your point, Captain.

"I'm sorry, Captain Kern. It's Lady Avery, of course." The governor took a deep breath. "Please forgive me."

Somehow, she avoided a laugh. "It's—"

Chase silently entered the conference room to sit next to Kern, and her courage slipped away as he made eye contact. No matter how kind he had been the day before, he and Kern were here for one reason only. Well, Kern was here for one reason only, and that was to enforce Perrin's wishes. But what about Chase? Was he here simply to annoy her?

Focus.

"It's only erlite mining, sir." The lie was hollow. Perrin might believe otherwise, but he wouldn't be able to hide his verium operations forever. "To supply their fleet. I dislike it as much as you do, but the security you speak of is standard procedure to prevent theft." A low rumble sounded across the hills outside, and she swallowed, looking for storm clouds. It was the automatic movement of a pilot, even one who hadn't flown in a year. There wasn't a cloud in sight, and she focused on him once more. "However, I will discuss the conscripted workers with Governor Perrin."

Who would say exactly the same thing he had before, with an added admonition about her failure to quash the upheaval at Tarragona.

"But I must request that you cease your interference with the Haederans' work here." She took a sip of water as another rumble shook the building. "I cannot promise the next encounter with the Haederan Army will end as peaceably as they have in the past."

In fact, I know it won't.

The governor stared at her, his lips pressed together in a thin line, then glanced at Chase and Kern. When Chase leaned over to whisper at Kern, his expression softened somewhat, like he'd finally realized she had absolutely nothing to do with any of this. He pushed himself up from his chair and nodded at her, then vanished without further argument.

The job was done, though if permanently or well enough to suit Perrin was anyone's guess. Avery wandered out of the prefecture hall with one last jealous look at the view, Chase and Kern behind her, then stopped in front of the flyer they'd requisitioned from the Haederan commander at Tarragona.

"I want to see the mine," she said. What she really wanted was a small sightseeing tour and to delay their return to the Haederan garrison at Tarragona, but Chase and Kern didn't need to know her true intent. "So I can report back to Perrin as accurately as possible."

"No." Kern's response was immediate. "Absolutely not."

What did it matter to him anyway?

"It won't take long," she replied, "and we're late as it is."

That wasn't a lie. Thanks to Chase's side trip, as much as she'd appreciated it, they were behind schedule. So behind schedule they were to spend another night at the garrison, and she didn't want to spend more time there than absolutely necessary.

The night before had been bad enough. She'd lain awake on a military-issue cot for hours, unable to sleep with the sound of Haederan troops right outside her room. Even the locked door couldn't assuage her anxiety—it had reminded her too much of the prison in Cadena, too much of the invasion, too much of *Imperieuse*.

At her argument, Chase leaned against the flyer and crossed his arms. It must have been an unspoken order, because Kern sighed.

"A quick stop," he said. "You won't talk to anyone. Then we head directly back to the garrison, since we won't make it back to Cadena tonight." His lip twisted, and it was clear it was the agrarian nature of Tarragona that bothered him. *To civilization, and soon*, he must be thinking.

But staying away from civilization a little longer was fine with her.

* * *

The flyer descended through the verdant ravine, all but skirting lower-hanging foliage. The pilot must have been having the time of his life with this rough terrain, but Avery wished he would stay a little farther from the canyon walls. Even though they'd slowed —probably so he could react to upsloping terrain quickly enough with a fast course reversal—she didn't like to rely on a stranger's decision-making ability. Especially a Haederan's. She turned from the window and glanced across the flyer, wishing she could telegraph her unease to the pilot.

Her eyes grew wide.

Two Imperial Security Command officers sat on the opposite bench, unarmed, murmuring with each other. Chase, yes, she recognized him immediately, and he was looking at her with his familiar curiosity, but next to him was—

Avery blinked.

Captain Linden?

She couldn't move, couldn't breathe. The shuttle lifted off Asria into space, taking her farther and farther from the safety of Villiers. Feye was dead back at Alcaris, and her hands shook, cuffed behind her back. It was cold in space, so cold, and she couldn't stop shivering. Why couldn't she breathe? Her chest was so tight. Painful. She had to get away, if she could just take a breath. Had to—

Linden cocked his head at her.

"What's wrong with you?" he asked, curling his lip.

Avery gasped. She shook her head and rubbed her wrists, trying to get the feeling back in her fingers.

But her hands were free. It was Kern sitting across from her, Kern who had spoken. Not Linden, the Imperial Security officer who'd detained her at Alcaris. They were racing through the canyons near Tarragona, on Asria, not in space at all, and while she wasn't *free*, she wasn't destined for Haedera, either.

She repeated the details over and over to herself, but the litany wouldn't clear the past that wrapped around her, choking her. Blood pounded in her ears while Chase squinted at her, not curious now, but bewildered. And . . . and then alarmed? Before she could object, he'd unlatched himself and moved from Kern's side to the end seat on her side. She didn't want him closer, but the simple visual change was enough. *Too embarrassed to look at either of them*, she focused out the nearest window.

Deep breath.

Hold it.

Breath out.

She repeated the process over and over, wishing she was alone in her humiliation.

Chase broke the silence as her heart slowed. "It's pretty out there." It was probably the most complimentary thing he'd ever said about Asria. "I didn't realize it would be so green."

Kern grunted in reply. "Pretty if you enjoy being smashed against a limestone wall, sir." He glanced at Avery, and a smile flashed behind his hardened eyes. "Which I personally would not."

It's all right. It's all right. It's all right.

They don't mean to harm you. Not now.

Chase laughed, clearly for her benefit. "I highly doubt he's going to smash into—"

The flyer lurched into a steep bank, and despite the harness, she clutched the handhold next to her, a Voirian curse on her lips. She could have flown these canyons in her sleep without needing to perform such an aggressive maneuver, so what—

Chase glanced outside, then at her, and pushed the comm button next to him. There was no answer from the pilot, and he pressed it again. The flyer leveled off and sped up before a response came.

"Sorry, sir." The intercom crackled. "Mine's a crater. We're headed back to the garrison."

A crater?

He went silent then, and she was falling, though the aeroflyer was climbing now. She cast a confused look at Chase, and he shook his head.

"Let him fly."

Her breath came in quick gasps again. Surely there was some mistake. Mine collapses didn't happen on Asria, not anymore. The safety devices under the surface were too advanced, the protocols strictly adhered to.

But Tarragona was a Haederan mine.

A Haederan mine using Asrian forced labor.

Expendable.

Maybe they didn't care.

Of course they don't care.

Chase frowned at her and pushed the intercom button again. "Any other information?"

The reply was immediate that time. "Garrison says it looks like some kind of thermonuclear detonation, sir. It was deep, but we're not taking any chances. We're two minutes out, and the shuttle's waiting for you there. You're cleared back to Cadena."

Not even an accident, then. Her eyes were blurry, but it wasn't from tears. The universe had gone hazy, like she was underwater, as the flyer descended, slowly this time. They landed on a pad inside a row of electrified fencing, and she sat, unable to move. Numb. Green uniforms swirled outside the window, but she couldn't focus on any of them. The door to the flyer opened, and someone undid her harness and pulled her out.

Get inside, just in case . . .

Should be safe here . . . we think the detonation was too deep underground for any fallout.

The surrounding voices blended together into muted noise. Avery let Kern pull her along the breezeway toward the larger shuttle site, not caring that the early evening air was growing cold, that the shuttle pilots were too spent for the ten-hour flight home, or that Kern was leaving bruises on her arm in his own haste for a haven. They slipped between the buildings in the cool breeze, past a group of men standing on the patio. They were talking and laughing among themselves, and for a horrifying second, her mind cleared, freezing her into place.

They weren't dressed in green like Chase and Kern. Like the other men at the garrison. Like the soldiers who patrolled Cadena. Like every other Haederan in uniform on Asria.

They were wearing blue.

Royal Asrian Defense Forces blue.

A weak noise emerged from her mouth. There was no rank, no insignia, but she'd recognize the uniform anywhere. In her left ear, there was a profanity she could barely understand through an exaggerated Haederan accent. Confusion swirled around her again, stealing the momentary clarity. Chase didn't swear. Never had.

"Get her on the shuttle. I'll find the pilots," he said. "And whatever you do, don't let her leave."

Kern tugged her through a door on the far side of the breezeway and she twisted back to see the group of blue-clad men again. Chase blocked her view. It seemed an eternity before they reached the shuttle and Kern followed her on board.

"Stay here." Chase slammed the hatch shut.

Avery fell onto the sofa just inside the door, a hand over her mouth. She wouldn't cry. Wouldn't. There had to be some explanation for this. It had to be a mistake. Because over six hundred Asrians couldn't be dead in less than a second. It just wasn't possible.

Denial was so easy.

* * *

It was half an hour before Chase and the two pilots climbed aboard and the shuttle lifted off toward Cadena in the darkness. He sat next to her and ran his hands over his face.

"I'm sorry."

"Leave me alone." Avery stood and collapsed in a single chair on the other side of the shuttle. It was the wrong decision, because the pain on his face was obvious from across the aisle. He had no right to be upset about this. None.

"You need to hear this, and you probably need to hear it before we land in Cadena." He took a deep breath. "The ones who did this were Asrian."

No. It was supposed to look like they were Asrian. It had been a setup. Even through her pain, that much was clear. The delay. The grave. She and Chase and Kern weren't supposed to have been at the garrison at all. They should have been on their way back to Cadena. She wasn't supposed to have seen what she'd seen there.

"They weren't Asrian!" she screamed at him. "You saw them at the garrison. I know you did!"

His ears turned red, but he continued like she hadn't spoken.

"Asrian insurgents placed the device. Intel says they blew up the caverns to ensure no more verium could be mined there." His voice hardened. "They knew their own people were being used as conscripted labor and took the mine out anyway. Over verium—made useless by you. They'll claim it was erlite, of course. The Haederan personnel you saw outside were returning from a search and rescue mission. They were forced back by the radiation before they even got close."

"Wearing Defense Forces uniforms? You can't possibly think I'm that naïve!"

No, he was only trying to guilt her, trying to blame her, trying to distract her, and she wouldn't fall for it. She wasn't some kind of animal to be comforted with a stroke on the head before slaughter.

"I think you're in shock and confused, and you have every right to be."

Her hands balled into fists, and she pressed them into her forehead, not caring if she left marks. The pressure didn't take her mind off anything. She screamed into her hands, not caring what anyone thought, because the pain . . . the pain was deeper than anything she'd felt before, even on the night of the invasion. More had died that night and the days that followed than at Tarragona, but somehow it wasn't like *this*. Now they were hers to watch over, and she'd failed them in the worst way possible.

She sobbed over the realization as the shuttle climbed higher and higher. When she finally looked up, eyes scratchy and swollen, Chase was holding a cup of tea in front of her, but she shook her head.

"Leave me alone. I just want to go to sleep."

"It's the middle of the day in Cadena, and you haven't been long enough to be off that time. I know you're not tired. And by the way you're shaking, you need to drink something, not sleep."

Avery gritted her teeth. "I don't need to do anything you tell me to do."

Chase stiffened and drew in a slow breath. "You are perilously close to treason, my lady, if not over the line already. You forget who you're speaking to."

"Hardly." Her voice cracked. She could never forget who held Asria's future in their hands. It was a miracle she hadn't pushed Chase too far long before now. "I know exactly who I'm speaking to. I know exactly who did this." She summoned up all her courage, despite that feared uniform he wore. "And don't even think for a second that you aren't complicit in this. It might as well have been *you*!"

Chase stared down at her, fury and compassion warring on his face, but she didn't blink. He would have to strike her first, and even that might not be enough. It was a long time with only a quiet, deferential murmur from Kern as company. Then, compassion prevailed, and he set the cup next to her seat.

"All right, then." He gave her one last look, like he wanted to say something else, sighed. "We'll be in the back."

Avery curled up in the seat and closed her eyes as he and Kern passed by. As long as they left her alone. As long as the ten hours passed quickly. It would be easier to pretend everything was fine if she was home. Hushed voices trickled forward, but she ignored them. She *had* lied to Chase . . . between the time difference and the devastation she'd just witnessed, she wasn't tired at all.

Just stunned. And overwhelmed. And angry.

Perrin would pay for this.

They all would.

CHAPTER NINETEEN

PERRIN HAD BEEN STARING OUT THE WINDOW AT ALCARIS IN THE distance for almost ten minutes now, but Avery's feet and hips had been aching since she'd walked in. Why didn't they tell women about these aches and pains that made life miserable? She wouldn't sit down next to Kern though, no matter how badly she hurt. She'd never make herself appear smaller in front of Perrin. So she stood there in his office, arms crossed, rocking back and forth from the balls of her feet to her heels and shifting from side to side.

She would stand here for as long as it took.

"And just what do you think you saw at Tarragona?" Perrin finally asked, turning toward them.

"I saw them at the Haederan garrison, General." Avery clenched her hands into fists so tightly her knuckles ached. It would take longer than three days to destroy those memories. "Haederan troops wearing Royal Asrian Defense Forces' uniforms. I want to know who's responsible for this. I want to know who ordered it. You? Or someone else?"

It was a rhetorical question. No one but Perrin could have ordered this. Mass, public murder wasn't an Imperial Security method, and the Haederan Army soldiers only cared about forcing enough Asrian compliance to make their own lives on this backwater planet easier. The only question was *why* he had done it.

And she had to admit she had no idea. It was a heinous act, even for him.

Perrin's gaze flashed to Kern, and she wished there was less confidence in his expression. To her surprise, she even wished Chase was there, but he'd departed for Haedera the day before.

Your family is your enemy and your enemy is . . . your friend?

"She was distraught, sir." Kern straightened in his chair, then stood, unusually meek and respectful for an Imperial Security Command officer, Avery thought with no small amount of scorn. "She saw the rescue team upon our return to the garrison and thinks—well, it's obvious what she thinks. And it's understandable why she'd prefer to believe that." He met Avery's eyes, a cold emptiness in his. "But clearly, she is mistaken."

They were closing ranks. Haederans were Haederans, no matter what.

"Then you need to convince her she is mistaken, Captain." Perrin spoke like she wasn't standing right there between him and Kern. "I don't care how. Do whatever you need to do."

She stiffened at his threat.

"And until you get your prisoner under control," he went on, "I want her confined to the palace. I won't have her spreading rumors about this all around Cadena."

How dare he. He couldn't possibly—

Spreading rumors?

She fought a smile. Perrin would hate himself for giving her the idea. How long would it have taken her to figure it out if he hadn't mentioned it? She wouldn't spread rumors. She'd spread the *truth*. Somehow, she would let everyone on Asria know what had happened.

"Of course, sir."

"There's really no argument here," Perrin said. "We have the security footage. We have the interrogation tapes."

"What?" Her heart skipped a beat. Security footage made sense—why else had they been wearing Asrian uniforms?—but the Haederans had a prisoner?

"You didn't tell her?" Perrin asked Kern. His lips thinned as he turned back to Avery. "They captured one of those rebels while you were on your way back here. We're just about to broadcast his confession. I think we should watch it together." He smiled at her. "Just in case you have questions."

"You faked that, too," she snapped, forcing down a scream. Perrin had thought of everything to cover his tracks. There was no doubt the confession had been recorded at the Haederan base at Alcaris—then the not-so-guilty party shipped back to his home world, lest he be recognized on Asria.

But why? Was he that concerned about her cooperation? Did he really think she'd believe Asrians were responsible for this?

"I don't have to fake anything." Perrin laughed. "They're not the first insurgency we've dealt with on this planet. And this? I don't think your rebel groups will enjoy much support from your people after the truth comes out. Six hundred and twenty-seven men gone just like that, killed by their own people. You Asrians can't claim a moral high ground any longer."

Avery took a step toward him, heat in her cheeks.

"Let's go," Kern hissed. She ignored him and took another step toward Perrin.

"She's not going anywhere." Perrin narrowed his eyes at Kern. "But you are. Coffee. Now."

"Sir, I don't—"

"Now, Captain."

Kern blinked—then retreated.

Perrin turned his attention to her. "Sit."

Half of her wanted to bolt after Kern and never come back, half was too curious to move. If she was to do anything about

Perrin's lie, she needed to know exactly what he was proclaiming as the truth. She dropped into the chair in front of Perrin's desk. Perrin waved his hand at the viewscreen on the far wall, bringing up nothing but a blank screen with the Haederan seal.

"A little early." He snuck a look at the empty cup on his desk. "But that means we can talk a bit first."

Avery raised her eyebrows in invitation. Whatever Perrin wanted to say, he'd wanted to say it away from Kern. That didn't bode well for her.

"I will end you." He smiled down at her, like they were speaking of the first day of spring in Cadena after a long winter. "If you tell anyone what you think happened at Tarragona, I will kill you. If you mention the verium, I will kill you. If you tell Captain Kern about this conversation, I will kill you."

"Even you aren't rash enough to try, General."

Her steady voice surprised her. Or maybe it didn't. Perrin was afraid of his emperor. He was afraid of what little power she still had on Asria. Of what she'd *done*. Of the support she appeared to have from Imperial Security.

"Rash? No. But accidents happen, my lady." He let his empty cup dangle toward her. "You just saw how easily I got rid of the only protection you have."

Avery stiffened her neck, refusing to look out the door toward wherever Kern had disappeared.

"His Imperial Majesty might even be persuaded that you're a liability to him. That this agreement of yours is a sham. That's if anyone listens to your claims to begin with. You're just as broken as that husband of yours, and no one will believe a word you say. You talk, and you're taking an enormous risk for nothing." He shook his head. "Lots of things can still go very wrong for you."

Her face burned. He couldn't insult Merritt like that. Not after what he'd done to him. But Kern returned just before she stood, saving her from a rash decision. He slammed the coffee on Perrin's desk, splashing some onto a nearby tablet, then flopped into the chair next to her. Perrin drew back a little at his casualness, like he was about to say something, then turned away, as if he'd finally realized pushing Kern too far might be detrimental to his lifespan. The viewscreen flashed on, catching her attention.

She knew immediately that she shouldn't have stayed.

The small room on the screen was dim. Concrete walls, steel floor. The only light was directed toward the man sitting in a chair in the center—all the better for the cameras to record, she knew. Shifting shadows suggested at least two other people, but they were staying clear of the camera. She didn't need to see them to know who they were. Or who they were supposed to be, at least.

Avery chanced a look at Kern for the only reassurance that existed in this nightmare, but his uniform was too vivid a reminder of her own time in that small room. She looked back at the man—the *Haederan soldier*—in the chair.

He looked Asrian, or Asrian enough, but that wasn't surprising since Haederans were a thousand times more varied in physical characteristics than her own people. It wouldn't have been too difficult to find a dark-eyed, dark-haired one wandering around Cadena. How much had they paid him for this? Or had he complied with these vile orders out of loyalty? Because he was afraid of saying no?

That had to be it. Haederans didn't question their emperor.

She couldn't take her eyes off him. He was dressed in the same blue uniform she'd seen at Tarragona—though it was dirty now, torn in multiple places. His head was lowered, hair shorn. His shaking hands were handcuffed in front of him and held a dimly glowing tablet in his lap.

He's Haederan.

You know he's Haederan.

It's a false confession.

This is nothing like what Chase did to you.

Nothing like what he forced you to say.

Perrin's theater was still close enough to the truth to make her sick.

"Go ahead." The voice from the shadows was quiet, calm, and undeniably Haederan.

Avery put a hand on her mouth as a chill ran through her body. She glanced out the window, out at the deep blue sky and a flock of birds flying past, just to anchor herself back to reality. That quiet serenity—how many times had Chase spoken to her just like that in a room like this? It usually followed one beating or another . . . he liked to play the compassionate one. The one kind person she had to depend on.

Sure enough, when the man raised his head to answer, she saw his face hadn't been spared. They'd worked him over early, possibly even before the explosion, for the bruises that covered his face were dark—all the better for the cameras for the record. Perrin had planned this well, down to the last detail. Haederan soldier or not, her jaw tightened in sympathy.

"My name is Major Bernat Castell, Royal Asrian Defense Forces."

Naturally, he sounded Asrian, from the east if she had to guess, with a fake Asrian name. It wasn't as though it was difficult to mimic accents. Hadley might be especially good at it, but it wouldn't be difficult to find a Haederan who—

"Three days ago, while in possession of illegally obtained intelligence, I and twelve others from my former unit infiltrated the Haederan erlite mine at Tarragona. Our mission was to destroy the mine to prevent erlite from being mined there." He looked straight ahead, his expression flat, then back at the tablet. "We can no longer allow them to use our abundant natural resources to supply their fl—fl—"

He looked up, eyes widening toward the shadows. He groped for the tablet, but it slid off his lap to the floor.

Avery held her breath.

This part wasn't planned.

He flinched at something she couldn't see, and she matched it, knowing what was coming. It didn't stop her from crying out when the pistol hit his nose and he fell to the floor.

Kern cleared his throat. "I think that's enough for now."

"I don't know. She looks rather fascinated by the proceedings to me." Perrin chuckled and took another sip of coffee. "I think we should watch the rest."

"You've made your point, General. She's been suitably terrorized." Kern looked at her, his face unreadable—but Avery was sure the fear on hers was evident. "Let's go, my lady."

Kern stood, and she pried her hands away from her mouth and follow him to the door, head high. He motioned her into the hall, then stopped in the doorway to gaze at the viewscreen, his head cocked and eyes narrowed in silent, appraising disapproval.

"I don't know, sir." He lifted a shoulder. "It'll do for the average Asrian, but if you were going for accuracy . . . all you had to do was ask."

He slammed the door shut behind them as the past and present swirled together into a colorless fog. The voice from the screen droned on quietly, but Avery couldn't make out any words through the closed door.

But Perrin's laughter was still audible.

* * *

The palace servants had also gathered to watch the televised confession that afternoon. It must be the talk of Asria right now. Locked in the guest suite on the second floor, Avery only knew because dinner was delivered an hour later than normal, profuse apologies accompanying it. It didn't matter. She wasn't hungry.

She stood in front of the meal the servant had placed on the lonely table—cold bass from the coast with a side of garlic rice. It was one of Victor's favorites, which meant he was enjoying his dinner tonight. Celebrating something? It was such an inappropriate meal for such a dark day. She was glad he hadn't invited her downstairs . . . it would be a long time before she could play his game again.

Her calves ached, her entire body dehydrated from the afternoon she'd spent crying, so she stood on her toes, stretching her sore muscles. A memory flashed through her, as vivid as the one of Tarragona, but infinitely more pleasant. Eight years old, she'd curtseyed in front of the king, the uncle she barely knew anymore, before beginning a flawless performance of one of the more modern Asrian dances. Even her mother, who'd never been vocal about Avery's skill at anything, had applauded her.

It felt like someone else's life.

Before she knew it, she was humming the tune of an Asrian folk song under her breath. It wasn't something she'd ever danced to before, but the combination of her first love and musical devotion to Asria warmed her.

With one hand on the table, she stretched a leg out. The movement made her strong, powerful. As powerful as Perrin, just . . . just differently. Slightly off balance, she brought her toes up to her opposite knee and her arms over her head.

There. That wasn't so hard. Perhaps—

A cough broke her concentration, and she stumbled onto her raised ankle. Victor stood in the doorway, and she flushed in embarrassment.

Or was it anger?

"I didn't hear you come in," she said.

"I wanted to see how you were doing." He held a tablet out. "And give you this."

Avery limped toward him to take it—just her luck, she'd fallen harder than she'd thought—and her brow creased.

"Dresses?" She swiped through the pictures. They were beautiful, much more beautiful than anything she'd worn in a long time, but the idea of wearing any of them to a ball filled with Haederans sickened her. "You're still holding the ball? After what happened?"

Victor's face was a rock, absolutely devoid of emotion. "Why not? It'll show those rebels that Asria will go on under Haederan control, and nothing they do will change that. No matter how many of their own people they murder."

"But it wasn't—"

She set the tablet down and closed her eyes. Seeing the devastation at the mine in her imagination didn't help. And it didn't matter if Victor truly believed the official story. He would stick to the Haederans' narrative, just as Chase and Kern had.

"Taln said you were convinced it was a Haederan false flag operation. He said he tried to talk you out of it, but that you were just as stubborn as ever. I'd hoped he was just being Taln." Victor sighed. "I don't know why you have to argue with facts. I don't know why you have to press him like you did."

Because I saw them. I saw them, and so did two Imperial Security Command officers who looked just as horrified as I.

"I'm not arguing." Avery rolled her ankle in circles, but it protested the movement. "I mean, I won't any longer."

"I'm glad." His expression softened. "Look, I know things haven't been easy for you lately. But I do hope you'll have some fun at the ball. They aren't all that bad once you get to know them."

Delusional.

"I'll keep that in mind." She collapsed on the chair, hoping it was enough of a hint. "But I need to get some sleep tonight."

"All right. Goodnight."

He looked around awkwardly, then nodded his leave. An elderly servant arrived less than ten minutes later to collect her dishes. She had been a recent addition to the palace just before the invasion and had left shortly after. Victor must be in desperate straits to call back former employees.

"The viceroy won't be happy that you haven't eaten, my lady." The servant shot a displeased glance at the almost untouched dishes.

"He was just here. And I've eaten enough." Avery grimaced as she ran a finger across the side of her ankle. "But I could use some ice and dermtape if you can scrounge it up from the clinic."

"Certainly, Your Majesty."

Avery shook her head. "I know you all have orders not to call me that—Marguerite, yes?"

"You remember." Marguerite's dark eyes sparkled. "But it is your title, is it not?"

Was it? It was so hard to remember who she was sometimes. Avery nodded reluctant agreement, and Marguerite pressed her lips together in understanding.

"Do you need anything else tonight, Your Majesty?" she asked.

The question was lightning through her soul, physically painful and hopeful at the same time. She answered before the sudden bravery fled.

"I need a flag. An Asrian one."

* * *

The dermtape worked its magic in less than ten minutes, so standing was painless, though her ankle was quite stiff. The flag Marguerite had wound around her chest scratched at Avery's skin under her shirt, but it wasn't an unwelcome feeling, exactly.

"Are you sure about this?" she asked Marguerite. People who helped her ended up dead. Drex. Even Elex Feye. "I'm certain you've seen my shadow."

Of course, Kern was probably off sleeping wherever it was he spent his nights, but he wasn't the only Haederan prowling about the palace—just the one Marguerite needed to be the most concerned about.

"I'm sure, Your Majesty." Marguerite winked at her. "That young boy doesn't frighten me, no matter what uniform he's wearing."

"Right." Avery laughed quietly. Kern was thirty if he was a day. "Then let's do it."

Marguerite knocked on the door and the Haederan Army guard ducked his head inside. "She twisted her ankle," she told him. "Dermtape didn't take care of it, so it probably needs the ultrarestore machine. Can you help me get her downstairs for the medic to look at it?"

The soldier glanced between them. "Let me see it first."

Avery cringed as he knelt in front of her, but his touch was gentle and her ankle still swollen enough to pass as injured. She closed her eyes, hoping to hide the guilt there.

"Looks sprained," he said. "Can you walk?"

Avery shook her head, cringing even more at the idea of him coming even closer, but there was a part to play now. She let him support her under the arm and help her downstairs to the small infirmary. The palace medic was on duty but asleep upstairs, so she leaned back in a chair to wait for him. Marguerite had disappeared as soon as they'd left Avery's room. The corporal looked bored; Avery's racing heart slowed. She ran through her plan in her head over and over, and each time she did, she breathed a little easier.

"What the hell happened?"

Avery jerked upright at Kern's voice. Did the man ever sleep?

"I was dancing. I just fell badly. It's nothing."

She swallowed the lie. This had been a terrible idea. The guard might have fallen for her lie, but Kern never would.

"Dancing?" He narrowed his eyes at her.

Yes, actually. I was dancing, and it felt good.

She was trying to put more words together when Marguerite rushed in, pale.

"Captain!" The affected relief in her voice was impeccable. "There's a group of men skulking around the east service entrance. Dressed in black—come quickly!"

Kern's gaze twitched from Avery to Marguerite to the corporal. He jerked his head at the corporal, and the two of them ran from the room. Marguerite followed them at a distance, and Avery laid her head back against the wall.

She was alone.

And free.

* * *

It was too bad she couldn't make it away from the palace and into Cadena where she could disappear, but the sentries patrolling the walls prevented that. No matter. She'd made it to the side garden with the help of the evening power shutdown, and her lips moved into a smile of their own accord as she stared up at the Haederan flag. One touch of the button on the pole brought it down, and she piled the dark navy and gold fabric into a ball and tossed it into the shrubs nearby.

The Haederans could figure out who had done it if they bothered to investigate, but it was the last thing she was worried about. If they were so concerned, they'd harass palace personnel about the matter, and she would end up confessing to protect them anyway.

Victor would rage for a long while and say, *you agreed to cooperate with them. With me. And you know how I feel about those flags, Avery.* She snickered at the image.

Kern would roll his eyes before making some idle threat. The worst that would happen after that would be yet another reprimand from Perrin. In any case, it wasn't something she'd lose sleep over tonight. The increased morale tomorrow morning—of most of the palace, at least—would be worth it. The decreased spirits of Victor and the Haederans would be worth even more.

It took more time than she'd wanted to unwrap the Asrian flag from her chest and run it up the pole, and as she pulled her shirt back down, voices sounded nearby. She knelt down next to the bushes, pressing her body far enough into them to leave scratches. Marguerite had sent Kern and the others toward the opposite side of the palace, but now the Haederans were resuming their regular patrols. She'd been just two minutes too slow swapping the flags out.

She swore to herself. Kern would be furious about her late-night walk, but she would be able to convince him that had been all it was. Until tomorrow morning, at least, and after a good night's sleep, she could deal with if he discovered her trick. Or so she prayed.

With one last jealous look at the shelter of the shrubs behind her, she stood on her still-stiff ankle to meet her fate—only to throw up in the bushes.

CHAPTER TWENTY

AVERY STILL WASN'T SURE HOW SHE'D MADE IT BACK INTO THE PALACE undetected the night before. She was even less certain why she had woken up to the Asrian flag folded by her pillow, the twin asteras staring her in the face. An obvious warning, but from whom? The Haederans should have wanted to make an example out of her. Or had Marguerite reconsidered and returned it before anyone had noticed? If she had, she should have hidden it somewhere besides the top of her bed. What if Kern had seen it?

But Kern hadn't said a word about it when he'd knocked on her door earlier, which meant he didn't know she'd swapped the flags out. No, what he had said that morning was, *I want you to show me around Cadena today. I'm tired of getting lost in this wretched city.*

This was what her life had been reduced to—a tour guide. For a Haederan. An Imperial Security Command officer. One who had sacrificed her to Perrin to prove his own loyalty, no less.

Today, though, she'd use the freedom to her advantage.

"Don't you own a map?" she asked as she and Kern walked down the street that ran from the palace to the back side of the senate temple.

Or half a brain?

Cadena's roads were curvy, but she'd always insisted to Merritt that made them easier to navigate. Grid systems like those used in Ventanan cities were her downfall, each street looking just like all the others. In any case, spending more time with him than necessary wasn't at the top of her list of things to do. Worse, the uneven road was hard on her healing ankle, but Kern hadn't taken no for an answer that morning.

"I thought you'd want to spend some time out in the city." He shrugged, stepping over a hole in the rough pavement. "And you must enjoy showing off your planet."

"To you?" she asked. "Not really."

She stopped in front of one of the traditional Asrian restaurants, one with flats on the second and third levels. Moss and ferns sprouted from the damp concrete sidewalk on the shaded side of the street, and she inhaled the earthy scent. Yes, this looked like the right spot.

Deep breath.

"Especially because you lied to him," she went on.

"Excuse me?" Kern's eyebrows rose.

Avery squared her feet to stay steady on the rough cobblestones. Like Chase, it was obvious he wasn't used to impertinence, and she took a protective step away from him, down onto the worn street. That regrettable move made him taller and even more threatening.

"You lied to Perrin about what you saw at Tarragona. Why?" The answer to that question was obvious, but besides stalling, she wanted to hear his explanation. She *deserved* to hear him try to explain.

"You had a panic attack in the flyer on the way to the mine . . . a flashback, Colonel Chase said. To what? I don't know or care." Kern turned his back to her and continued toward the temple, only to realize she wasn't following. He checked his chronometer and sighed in exaggerated annoyance. "You looked like death—or that you'd seen death. You weren't in any shape to determine what you saw back at the garrison, or how accurate your memories are, and believe me, I'm sorry for what you went through there." That insincere apology completed, he held his hands up in impatience. "Can we keep moving? There's a market near the temple I want to see."

Kern was curious about an Asrian market? Now she'd heard everything.

Avery stood firm and glanced up at the windows above the restaurant. There was no movement inside. What if the Haederans had found Wynne? There were rumors they were rounding up former Defense Forces personnel again.

"Then why did you and Colonel Chase look like you'd seen death as well?" she asked. "Or didn't you recognize the look on his face?"

Kern actually huffed at that. "I know him well enough. And contrary to what you seem to believe, I don't relish the idea of murder. Even of Asrians."

Right

"It's just a necessary part of your job, is that it?" She raised her voice, half for effect, half because he'd truly made her angry with that ridiculous claim. A door slammed above them, but she didn't look up. "Just business, right? Do you think it exonerates you if you don't *enjoy* it?"

Kern's mouth fell open. "If you know what's good for you, you'll stop now."

Ah, there was the expected threat. It was mild, though—she could keep pushing a little more. Victor's protection was finally proving useful.

"Excuse me. Is he bothering you, ma'am?"

At least, Avery let herself look up. The slim, dark-haired woman coming down the stairs on the outside of the building was comfortingly and achingly familiar. Dark hair like Avery's came to her shoulders in waves, and that piercing gaze that had once been such a liability couldn't have been more welcome. If Kern had been a little less Haederan, he might have realized that slim figure came not from self-induced starvation like half the socialites in Cadena, but from her work.

Wynne.

Wynne stopped short. Her eyes flashed from Avery to Kern—or more accurately, to his uniform—and then back again, elegant eyebrows raised in interest.

"No. He's not bothering me." Avery turned her expression blank, all recognition forced to the distant corners of her mind. As hard as it was to turn away from Wynne, she faced Kern again. "You and I both know it was Haederan troops who blew up that mine. You can't keep it hidden forever. I won't *let* you."

He clenched his jaw and caught her by the elbow. "Let's go."

"Madam!" Wynne pursed her lips. "Do I need to contact the police?"

"I am the police," Kern all but growled at her. "And this is a private discussion you would do well to forget you ever heard."

Wynne's eyes focused on Avery, the lightest touch of askance there. She could only imagine the conflict going on in Wynne's mind: walk away like any sane person would, or rescue her former charge from a man feared only slightly more on Asria than his home planet.

"It's personal," she stammered, wishing more than anything she could let Wynne at Kern, but violence couldn't be part of this plan. Not yet. "Everything's fine."

"Personal?" Feigned revulsion flashed across Wynne's face, and Avery fought a smile. "Then go be *personal* somewhere else."

With that, Wynne stormed back up the stairs to her flat. Kern let go of Avery's elbow, and she followed him around the next curve at a faster pace than her aching ankle allowed. He looked around, then slammed her into the wall as Wynne's flat disappeared around the corner.

"Do you know her?" he asked, his gaze darting behind him.

"Know her? I don't know what you mean."

His fist hit the brick wall next to her head. She flinched and closed her eyes. Kern wouldn't hit her, would he?

He might. He must hate having his hands tied by the emperor's edict.

"It's a simple question." He took a step toward her, so close she didn't dare inhale. "Do you know that woman? Do not forget that after we return to the palace, I can figure out who she is in less than five minutes. It would be better for both of you if you told me the truth right here, right now."

The same threat from Chase might have worried her, but it didn't matter what Kern did. He wouldn't stop whatever cultural mission he appeared to be on to report Wynne. Avery only prayed she managed to tell someone before he did.

"Of course I don't know her." She struggled to bring a condescending tone to the surface, all too conscious of Kern's arm next to her throat. "This isn't the kind of neighborhood I frequent." She let out a shrill laugh, the nerves overcoming her courage.

"Is something funny to you?"

"Didn't you notice? She thought—she thought we were together."

There.

That would throw him off for a while.

"Not if you were the last woman in the galaxy." Kern didn't find it nearly as funny as she pretended to. "Let's go."

He didn't say another word as they approached the market square, already bustling with customers. It wasn't a place she normally patronized—large crowds like this sent her into a kind of slight paralysis—but it was good to see some parts of Asria continue unmolested by the Haederans. Gold and blue tents swayed in the gentle breeze, covering wares all the way from costly southern-hemisphere ceramics to the local freshwater eel from the high-mountain lakes. And so many Asrians . . . more than she'd seen since before the invasion. So many of her people were spread about the booths and tables, like life for them was normal. Laughter, such an exotic sound to her lately, rang through the plaza, interspersed with that familiar accent she'd never appreciated. And the children who ran around the booths, begging for candy—

Well, it was a glimpse into her past life—and her future one.

The familiar sight was enough to make her cry, and Kern looked at her in annoyance as he moved from stall to stall, examining the merchandise. For someone who didn't like Asria, he was strangely interested in its more cultural aspects. She hung back a few paces, both embarrassed by her tears and fascinated by his curiosity.

They stopped by a dozen stalls, and most of the sellers nodded wordless greetings to Kern, though some of them engaged him in meaningless conversation. Was it self-preservation, or too-ready acceptance of Haederan rule? Whatever the reason, it was discouraging.

"Listen up!" The Haederan voice cut through the morning chatter of the market as a squad of Haederan Army soldiers shuffled through the crowd. "Market's closed for the next week. Pack up your things, everyone," the lieutenant in front hollered.

Kern dropped a handwoven silk scarf back on the table and swore under his breath as the sellers packed up. Avery looked questioningly at him. They'd all seemed to comply without too much fuss.

He shrugged. "They do stuff like this every once in a while. Keeps you people from getting too comfortable. But they just came through yesterday, and I didn't expect—" He swore again as the lieutenant approached through the throng of people.

"Sorry, sir," the lieutenant said. "That includes you." His gaze swung to Avery, then to the slower of the patrons making their way back onto the street. His lip curled. "Get out of here. Now. Are all you Asrians deaf or something?"

"She's with me" —Kern plopped a coin on the table and shoved the scarf into a pocket—"and we're not leaving."

The lieutenant processed that statement for a full minute, probably assuming the same thing Avery had implied to Wynne earlier.

"Sir, I don't want to make a scene," he finally said. "Please leave." He rubbed his forehead, his mind clearly spinning as he tried to figure out how to deal with Kern. "You can come back next week and eat more eel on a stick with your girl."

Avery's skin crawled. Somehow it was different to hear someone else imply it.

Kern narrowed his eyes. "Lieutenant, just what do you think —" His mouth snapped shut, and he turned to Avery. "Never mind. I don't have patience to deal with this today. We'll come back some other time."

She tilted her head in amused surprise. Kern could have easily ignored the lieutenant's order . . . could have arrested him just for confronting him and ruining his day. She let out a silent laugh, and Kern turned those narrowed eyes at her.

Then she saw it.

Hadley was making his way down the stairs on the opposite side of the plaza near the temple. She hadn't known it was possible to recognize the back of someone's head at this distance, but it couldn't be anyone else. His gait was too recognizable after days hiking through the Pelancos with him. She opened her mouth to shout his name, then remembered Kern at her side.

Think fast.

"Captain, can we head that way? Back through the temple toward the senate building? These crowds . . . I really hate these crowds."

If only she could bump into Hadley again. Hadley would send her another message. He might even find a way to wrestle her away from Kern. They could disappear, like she'd wanted to when she'd first arrived back on Asria. Kern might have made a grave error taking her out in public like this.

Surprisingly enough, he nodded. Maybe he liked the horde flowing in the opposite direction as little as she did. Once they passed through the temple into the senate complex, there wouldn't be nearly as many people. She didn't want to risk him seeing Hadley, but it was a risk she'd have to take.

A risk Hadley would take.

The lieutenant shouted after them. Merely leaving wasn't good enough, it seemed—he wanted them to leave *his* way. Kern ignored him. Hadley's head bobbed over the top of the crowd, then was gone.

Avery quickened her step, wishing Kern would hurry along.

"What's the rush?" he asked.

"The crowds remind me of . . . things." They actually reminded her of nothing except her youth in Cadena, but Kern wouldn't know that. He thought she was addled enough as it was. "I just want to get out of here." She altered their course a little toward where Hadley had disappeared, but there were too many people.

Hadley was gone.

CHAPTER TWENTY-ONE

AVERY RAN A FINGER ACROSS THE DELICATE FABRIC OF THE DRESS THAT had been delivered earlier that day. Victor had vetoed the cerulean blue she'd requested of the palace dressmaker—no surprise there —but the backup fabric she'd chosen was almost as beautiful. More purple than maroon, it fell in layers of chiffon to her ankles. The skirt was studded with translucent crystals, just like the night skies over the Pelancos. The delicate lace that edged the neckline and upper arms was itchy with smaller silver crystals and tonal embroidery, but the effect was more than she could have asked for.

True, it pushed the edge of the budget Victor had allocated for it, but she had no compunction any longer about spending his money. If he was going to force her to mingle with the most important Haederans on Asria, she would look good while she did it. His money was Rendon family money that belonged to her anyway.

She ran her hand across her not-quite-flat stomach and let her thoughts languish in the past just a little while longer. The last ball she'd attended at the palace had been before she'd left for Ventana and the academy. She'd never had a break long enough to allow for the twelve-week round-trip between Ventana and Asria, and Merritt had been too busy with the Defense Forces to visit her. So that last time, they'd danced at Victor's birthday ball like the night would never end. It had, to her chagrin, and she'd said goodbye to Merritt for the next three years.

What a waste of time apart that had been.

Because now, instead of Merritt, it was Kern who stood in front of her in a formal black Haederan uniform with his arms folded, giving her Victor's threat by proxy—though Kern appeared to be slightly fuzzy on the details of the consequences if she remained in her room. Victor himself probably was as well.

Kern cleared his throat, drawing her attention back to him. "You're making my job difficult."

"Believe it or not—" His grumble forced her to her feet, bare feet and all. "I don't really care how difficult your job is."

"You should." His complaining undertone ceased. "You know it's a waste of time to fight this."

"Hardly." She fell to her settee once more, just to anger him. Just to stall.

Well, and to put her shoes on.

"Put on the damn shoes and let's go." He must have picked up on her last intention, because he grabbed the gold heels from the floor and let them dangle in front of her. "And be quick about it."

Perhaps because of his profanity, his Haederan accent grated on her more than usual, and she did what he ordered simply to shut him up. Still, the shoes went on slowly, and she stood even more slowly. There was only so much she could take.

"Happy now?" she asked.

"Thank you." He sighed dramatically, then held out his arm in what had to be a false display of chivalry.

You've got to be kidding me.

At her silence, he jerked his hand back as though she'd hit him, but she didn't care. Victor hadn't left her any choice but to attend, but she would never act as though the Haederans belonged in that ballroom downstairs—or that Kern was anything but the enemy.

She took her time walking down the breezeway, even with him tagging along at a respectful distance behind her. No matter how cold it had been, the autumn flowers were still in bloom, and the scent swept over her, bringing peace along with it. *So familiar*. She could have stood outside for hours indulging in the scent and the sight of Cadena's few visible stars, but too soon they were standing in the ballroom's doorway.

The sight made her take a step back.

As familiar and strange as the event had seemed from her quarters, seeing it in person was worse. She'd played in this room as a child, and though it lost some of its sparkle as she grew up, it was still beautiful. The marble floor, quarried from the southern reaches of the high Gallis Mountains, contained flecks of gold she'd spent hours trying to pick out. Her mother hadn't told her until years later that it wasn't really gold, and Avery hadn't believed her.

The chandeliers predated the Asrian Civil War, back when they'd used candles to light the entire palace. They were electric now, except for the remembrance ceremony every year when the palace staff spent a week removing the bulbs and replacing them with candles. It was a solemn and holy event that she hadn't appreciated until she was older. There was no chance Victor would continue the tradition now, and her shoulders sagged. It had meant so much to her.

But even that wasn't the worst part.

No, the worst part was that Kern's black dress uniform appeared to be specific to Imperial Security, and the regular Haederan soldiers wore navy ones that almost mirrored the Defense Forces uniforms she was so used to seeing in this very room every year for the king's birthday, and she forced herself to back the bewilderment until her mind settled firmly in the present.

But if there was any question of when she existed and who

filled the ballroom, it was answered when Kern deposited her at Victor's side and walked off, grabbing a drink off a servant's tray as he went. She watched him go, inordinately jealous of his freedom.

"I'm glad you could make it." A slight smile of approval appeared on Victor's face, but vanished when he noticed her hand.

Avery's jaw tightened. The ring. How had she forgotten the ring?

"Excuse us, please." Victor took her by the arm and led her a safe distance away from his Haederan guests. "I told you I didn't want to see that on your hand ever again."

"It's a habit." As much as she wanted to argue, Victor would never forgive her for creating a scene at his ball. She'd have to be subtle. "I'll go take it off," she said, knowing he'd never let her slip away for even the short walk back to her room. He'd have to let her blunder go, or risk her escaping and never coming back.

Instead of agreeing, Victor's eyes narrowed. He glanced back at the small group that was waiting for their return, then held out his hand. "Hand it over."

"You'll never see it again after this." If she gave him the ring, she'd never get it back. "I promise. I'm sorry. But please let me keep it tonight, Uncle Victor."

There. The ring for some family love. That hadn't been so hard —if he bought it.

Victor gave her a look that said she'd pay for her disobedience later, but escorted her back toward Perrin and two other officers she didn't recognize. From the expressions on their faces, she was alone in that regard.

Wonderful.

Her reputation had preceded her, although whether that was a good or bad thing was anyone's guess. She switched her untouched drink to the opposite hand and shook hands with an approaching woman whose name she forgot as soon as it was spoken. The wife of . . . well, someone high in the Imperial Haederan Navy. How nice that they were bringing their families to live on the planet they detested. Things were better in Cadena.

The woman must not have known who Avery was, for she chattered on about the winter weather in Cadena, the fashions in the tonier sections of the city, and the lack of Haederan food in the local restaurants.

Behind a faux smile, Avery wanted to scream. What had she expected? Didn't she realize she was halfway across the quadrant from Haedera? Her husband claimed her as she was developing a response to the food complaint, and his facial expression said that while his wife might not know who Avery was, he did.

That left her with Victor, Perrin, and a Haederan admiral she'd never met. He seemed all too pleased that Avery was back in Cadena, and she didn't have to guess why. It had become a game for her.

Do you know I stole a Haederan fighter?

Do you?

Or maybe you?

You don't know, that's for sure.

This admiral knew what she'd done; there was no question about it. Maybe he'd even been aboard *Aurora*. He asked question after question about her flying background, which she answered the best she could—until he asked if she had any experience with Haederan space fighters.

Got you.

She smiled demurely over her glass. "Admiral, I'm afraid my only space training has been in Commonwealth ships, and only trainers at that."

He raised bushy gray eyebrows in her direction, seemingly perplexed at her outright lie. Victor and Perrin turned sullen looks on her, but she didn't care what they thought. After all her dread, this wasn't so bad. In fact, it was one of the most enjoyable experiences of the past year. Hadley was right, she could act.

Hadley.

Her smile slipped. Had she listened to her uncle's inner circle's inane prattling long enough that she could walk away and hide in a corner?

A servant floated by with another tray of drinks, and Avery grabbed another one, then wandered toward an empty window in an alcove all the way across the room. It wasn't as though any of the Haederans would follow her. Except maybe the admiral's wife who had already talked her half to death, but right now she was all the way across the room, having cornered what looked like a former Asrian senator's wife. She would find out who that senator was later—after she got Hadley out of her mind, and her head back in the social game.

"Lady Avery?"

Avery turned to smile at the senator's wife, who'd crept up next to her while she'd been daydreaming about escape. Lindsa Mateu . . . *that's right.* Senator Mateu had always been friendly toward the Rendons, but that history carried no weight since the invasion. And what a perfect stroke of luck—Lindsa had always been quite the social climber.

"Lindsa." Avery plastered the phony smile back on her face. Small talk first, then she'd drop the idea in Lindsa's mind. Unless Lindsa's gossiping tendencies had changed, it wouldn't take long before the story spread all over Cadena. "It's so nice to see you again. It's been what? Four years at least?"

"At least that," Lindsa said. "And you've turned out wonderfully. It's so nice to see you here, after . . ."

After the Haederans invaded our planet, murdered my parents, and tortured me for months? Yes. Very nice.

"It's been a long year," Avery replied. Lindsa couldn't possibly know about all that. "But Victor has been gracious enough to allow me to live here."

"You must hear amazing stories from the Haederans, living in the palace. It's been fascinating talking to them tonight."

A Haederan admirer, then. She wouldn't forget that. Still, she couldn't have asked for a better opening.

"All sorts of stories." Avery widened her eyes in innocent shock and interest. "Did you hear the rumor that it was actually Haederan troops who blew up the mine in Tarragona?" She glanced across the room to make sure Victor was still far, far away, and her stomach dropped. *Kusir*, Perrin was headed her way.

"But they had surveillance footage showing otherwise." Lindsa ran a finger through her dark curls. "Everyone saw it. I don't know how anyone can support the freedom movement now."

Perrin was just steps away now. Why was Lindsa speaking so loudly? She had to change the subject, and quickly.

"Well, it was just a rumor." Avery shrugged. "I couldn't really say if it was true or not."

Too late.

"Excuse me, Madam Mateu." Perrin took Lindsa by the arm and led her a few paces off. "I'm afraid that Lady Avery . . ."

She could only hear snatches of their conversation after that.

Very troubled . . . hears and sees things that aren't there . . . a result of some unpleasantness last year . . .

Humiliated at his accusations, Avery turned away from them, but not quickly enough to miss Lindsa's sad glance at her as she drifted back to her husband. The pity in her eyes was almost worse than Perrin's accusations.

Because she wasn't insane. Was she? Hadn't she seen those soldiers at Tarragona dressed in blue? The memory was so fuzzy now.

"I warned you," Perrin said from behind her. "But now I see that warning was unnecessary. No one believes you, just as I knew they wouldn't. I have to say, convincing everyone you've lost your mind is easier than coming up with a good explanation for your death. Though I wouldn't press me much further, if I were you." He swirled the toxic liquid in his glass. "Now that that's taken care of . . . are you not enjoying the party?"

Avery closed her eyes for a fraction of a second, then turned toward him. Like bad luck dictated, she had to be wrong about one of the Haederans following her away from Victor, and of course it would have to be Perrin. Maybe Victor had sent him over to bring her back. Couldn't they just leave her alone for five minutes? Did Perrin think she was going to break out the window?

"Enjoying it? Not really. There are too many Haederans in this ballroom."

And on Asria.

"That's funny." Perrin's speech was slurred. "I think there are too many Asrians here. And I wouldn't say the one standing in front of me is holding up her end of her bargain with His Excellency very well. I don't relish the idea of telling him about your less-than-cheery attitude tonight."

"I'm here, aren't I?"

She only had to fake enjoyment and her support of Victor and his position. She didn't have to enjoy it. Even Perrin must understand that.

"You are. And you're acting like you'd rather be anywhere else."

"Maybe I would." Avery ran a finger along the edge of her glass. What would happen if she threw wine all over Perrin and that despicable uniform? She set it on the window ledge before she could succumb to the temptation. "I don't know why that surprises you."

In the window reflection, his eyes narrowed. "I told you if it were my decision, you wouldn't be back on Asria at all. They'd love to get their hands on you on Haedera. Watch yourself, or I'll make sure—"

"Excuse me, Governor."

The new voice cut Perrin off before he could finish whatever idle or not-so-idle threat he'd planned, and she turned to see Chase standing at Perrin's side.

Kusir.

He was supposed to have left Asria. Gone. Back to Haedera, or at least on his way by now. He wasn't supposed to be at Victor's ball.

Avery took a deep breath.

Perrin might have had her cornered before, but now she was trapped.

CHAPTER TWENTY-TWO

Perrin's eyebrows rose at Chase's appearance.

"Colonel. This is unexpected. I hadn't thought you'd be here tonight, what with—" He glanced at Avery. "I'm sorry, how rude of me to skip introductions like that. I don't suppose you've met Colonel Chase of the Imperial Security Command." The corner of his mouth slid upward, then turned into a full grin as she raised her eyebrows at him. "But what am I saying? I arranged your introduction last summer, didn't I? You must know him quite well after your time together, I'd imagine. Or more precisely, he must know you quite well."

Well.

Perrin was a fountain of all sorts of intriguing information. It appeared she could stop blaming Feye for handing her over to Chase. Forgiveness came easier with that knowledge. Perrin, on the other hand . . .

Chase tolerantly ignored Perrin's last comment, something he appeared to be well-practiced at. "I had a change in plans." He edged next to her, and she sidestepped away from him. "I hate to interrupt, but I have some business to discuss with her. It won't take long, then you can have her back. Sir."

"Whatever you have to discuss with her must be more important than our conversation. We were just finishing up anyway." With one last meaningful look at Avery, Perrin strode off. "Enjoy," he called over his shoulder.

Chase didn't spare him a glance as he left. "You look lovely," he said with a smile. He lifted his glass in a toast, took a sip, and set it on the window ledge next to hers. "That's not so bad either, as Asrian wine goes. I could get used to living here, I think."

Avery narrowed her eyes at the glass, obviously filled with wine from the Rendon estate at Sabino, then at Chase. He'd over-acted his politeness, there was no doubt he had another motive besides an altruistic rescue from Perrin. Before she could stop herself, her gaze swept over his black uniform and landed on the Imperial Security Command insignia on his collar.

Just call him on it.

"And you look threatening."

"That is the idea." Chase laughed. "It certainly works wonders on you."

Avery clenched her teeth. It wasn't the reaction she'd been aiming for.

"I trust you're feeling better?" he went on. "I heard you've been ill since we returned from Tarragona."

"Of course I've been sick." She lowered her voice, not even knowing why she was whispering. Every single person in this ballroom needed to hear what she was about to say. "Perrin murdered them. How do you expect me to feel?"

"You're still carrying on with that delusion?" Chase glanced around at the revelers with a straight face. "Do you feel this is an appropriate place for those kinds of accusations?"

Her hand twitched. What would happen if she struck him, right here in front of everyone?

"Do you feel as though you have any right to lecture me about what's appropriate and what's not?" She used the offending hand to tuck a stray piece of hair behind her ear and forced herself to change the subject. Arguing with Chase was hopeless. "I—I thought you'd left Asria."

And for some reason, I was disappointed by that.

"I did, but I didn't get far." He adjusted his collar and glanced back toward the crowd. "There's no longer an immediate need for me to return to Haedera, so I was ordered back to the surface."

What did that—oh. Avery mustered every bit of kindness she could. It took a while, and more than a few deep breaths.

"I'm sorry."

"Thank you. She was special." His sorrow vanished between two of her heartbeats and Gareth Chase the grieving widower became Colonel Chase the Imperial Security Command officer again. He held out his arm. "Dance with me."

Avery had never understood how the hairs on the back of someone's neck could stand up, but she was certain hers had just done so. She took a step away from Chase, but he matched it, pushing her up against the window. When she put her hand back to steady herself, her contentious ring clinked against the glasses, but she grabbed it behind her back before the wine spilled.

"Dance with you?" she echoed. "I don't—I don't think so."

"It was not a request." Chase's words were curt. "Your other option is I arrest you right here in front of your uncle and everyone else, and I am almost positive you would prefer option number one."

Her heart thumped. No, this had not been a kind rescue from Perrin. Why hadn't she walked away when she still had the chance?

"You have no reason to do that," she said.

Or every reason, depending on how much he knew about what she'd been doing.

Chase ignored her subdued objection, and she didn't trust him to not follow through with option number two, so with an automatic look of longing at their abandoned glasses, she took his extended arm. His uniform sleeve was scratchy on her bare forearm, and she tripped over her own feet as Chase led her back to the crowd of Haederan revelers she'd wanted to avoid.

"I don't—" She wrested her loose shoe back on with the opposite foot. They were playing Haederan music now, and the guests were performing a dance she'd never seen. It looked easy enough to learn, but maybe pretended ignorance was a way out of her predicament. "I don't know this dance."

"I imagine you learned to dance as a child." There was no pity in his words. "Since you grew up in such a place. Brennin says you're quite good at it."

She couldn't even nod. All she could manage was a wide-eyed stare at him. Did he know she'd faked her injury? Was he drunk? Surely not—drinking that much would be counterproductive to his carefully controlled façade. This was the Chase she'd feared ever since that night in the cell deep underneath Cadena, the man who still haunted her nightmares, kind favors or not.

"I thought so. Then I'm sure you can figure it out. You're not getting out of this."

Well, she'd survived much worse than a dance with Chase and would survive this too—depending on what else he wanted, for there was no question a dance wasn't the only thing. She watched his steps, memorizing and translating them to her part, and the concentration diluted some of her fear. It was good to focus on something benign that took this much attentiveness. It was good to focus on something that wouldn't get her killed if she made a misstep. Despite her partner, it was enjoyable, and she silently congratulated herself on her skill. Once upon a time, she *had* loved to dance, and while Merritt was a good technical partner, he had never really—

"I knew you weren't a slow learner." Chase pulled her closer and whispered into her ear as she struggled to pull away. "That's why for the life of me I can't understand how you haven't learned to back off and mind your own business yet." His voice grew lower. "I know what you've been up to, and if you know what's good for you, you'll stop now."

Holy One, help me.

How in all the galaxy had he found out she'd talked to Wynne? Or was this about the flag?

Kern. It had to be Kern. He wasn't as incompetent and unobservant as he'd led her to believe. She'd underestimated him, and he'd probably wanted her to do so all along. He'd been testing her, had given her just enough freedom that she'd hang herself. And she had. He would pay for his subterfuge later. Somehow, she'd make him pay. But right now . . .

Count his steps. Focus. Answer him.

"I'm not up to anything. How could I be, locked in a single room with Kern following me everywhere I go?" She had to appeal to his sense of secrecy, then maybe he would let her go. "And people—people are going to stare if you don't let go of me."

Chase's grip on her tightened from dance partner to something else, and she fought back a whimper as his fingers dug in the back of her shoulder.

"Don't play dumb. You're not nearly as good at it as you think you are. And don't lie to me. I don't want to have to remind you how I feel about that."

What did he want her to say? It wasn't as though she could admit she'd stopped in front of Wynne's flat on purpose, that she'd choreographed her argument with Kern. Avery tried to concentrate on her feet, but the fear that swirled around her made that impossible.

"This silence sounds like a confession to me." His voice grew even softer in her ear, and she had to fight to hear it over the music and chatter that surrounded them. "I think we need to go somewhere else and talk about all of this. Probably at length, if experience is any indication. You can be so . . . stubborn. What do you think? I hope you don't have any important plans for the next few weeks."

"Please stop." A quiet sob finally broke through at his ominous suggestion. She looked up at him and gave him the slightest shake of her head, hoping no one else could see the hot tears that had formed in her eyes.

"Quit crying if you don't want everyone to stare." A surge of irritation cut through his threat. "I won't drag you out of here right now, but consider this your last warning to stay out of things that don't involve you." He released her and stalked through the main ballroom doors, leaving her shaken, pale, and desperately wanting to murder Kern.

* * *

Instead of a murder she'd never get away with, Avery settled for a long respite on a bench in the small garden outside the ballroom. She drained two glasses of a lemon tonic—one sent by her uncle, the servant told her—as she deliberated. It was the traditional Asrian drink for after-dinner scheming, and Victor's tacit approval of her break from the ball reassured her.

No, Chase's threat had no merit. He'd wasted his time tonight, even though he must have secretly loved the whole thing. No one would ever believe her stories about Tarragona because Perrin was clearly adept at convincing people she was insane, and the flag? That might as well have been a practical joke. Harmless to the Haederan occupation in the grand scheme of things.

Hadley, on the other hand . . . She needed to see him, and it was apparent he wanted to talk to her. But they hadn't communicated beyond the note he had slipped in her pocket when he'd bumped into her at the senate building, and Chase and Kern had no idea who the note was from. So that meant Chase's comment about what she'd been up to was regarding her run-in with Wynne and the flag, not Hadley. Had Kern even told him that Hadley was free and roaming the streets of Cadena?

Maybe. Maybe not. She would have to take the chance.

Chase would never know.

CHAPTER TWENTY-THREE

The morning after Victor's galas were always difficult for most guests, but the sensation that washed over her when she got out of bed the next morning was beyond that. Avery hadn't overindulged in anything the night before—too much Chase, perhaps—but felt like she'd drunk a liter of Sabino's best, although she hadn't touched wine, already too sick to risk even a sip. When Kern knocked on the door to gather her for breakfast with Victor, she'd just finished throwing up for the second time since waking.

She'd spent hours lying awake the night before, dreading that very outcome, and now the woman in the mirror looked sick, thin, and pale, with dark circles under even darker green eyes. And her hair—well, there was nothing to be done about the curls, so carefully done up the night before, now limply hanging to her shoulders.

"Tell Victor I won't be able to make breakfast this morning," she called through the door as loudly as her protesting body would allow.

It must not have been loud enough, since Kern knocked again. She rinsed her mouth with water, dredged up a robe, and opened the door to face him. If he took one look at her, there'd be no way he could accuse her of lying.

"You're sick again?" Just as she'd expected, he drew back and wrinkled his nose, no doubt hoping he hadn't eaten the same thing. "What did you eat last night?"

"Probably the same thing you did."

Avery waved a hand at him and collapsed in a chair. It wasn't as though the food had been that varied at Victor's ball. How many other guests were this sick? If Victor had half a brain, he'd already be working damage control over this incident. Before the rumors started. Kern himself was probably living on borrowed time. She was suddenly appreciative of the nausea—it overshadowed her glee at the image of him sick in his bed.

"I hope not. But no one else in the palace is sick, so I think I'm safe." Kern wrinkled his nose again, and that time she couldn't hide a smile, no matter how awful she felt. "You know, ever since you showed up here, you've been acting like my sister." He looked around and lowered his voice. "Before the implant."

Chase had told him?

She shook her head, a reflexive action, discouraged that Kern had noticed how sick she'd been since her return to Cadena. She'd done a good job of hiding it, even though she'd lost more weight than she could afford. But why was she this sick, anyway? Bad Haederan technology, it must be. Were Asrian implants this ineffective? There was no one she could ask about it, but it seemed a sick prank to play on women.

She put her head in her hands. Maybe it wasn't that the implant was ineffective—maybe it wasn't an anti-nausea implant at all. Maybe it was a tracking device. Maybe that was how Kern had reported all her movements to Chase. She should have known better than to trust a Haederan doctor. Or worse, Chase.

Her stomach rolled again.

"I've heard they don't always work." She tried to sound casually curious. It was unlikely, but perhaps Kern would let something slip. Something to guide her in the right direction. *Poor technology or a tracking chip.* It had to be one or the other.

He scoffed. "They work perfectly. But not on food poisoning. I'd watch what you eat a little more carefully." He gave her a strange look, then bolted.

* * *

They work perfectly.

Kern was gone—to convince Victor she was truly ill and not defying him, she hoped—but his claim circled around and around in her head. He'd been certain, both of his sister's experience and his own declaration. But then, if it wasn't a medical implant, he had every reason to lie. It wouldn't surprise her.

They work perfectly.

If it worked perfectly, why was she so sick? They'd injected her with a tracking chip, then. The Imperial Security Command used them on some prisoners, but Chase had never so much as threatened her with it. Something like a tracking chip—he wouldn't hide that from her. No, he'd tell her exactly what he was doing to her, just to revel in her response. In her anger. In her fear.

Besides, after the doctor had pressed the injector against her upper arm and inserted the implant, she'd felt like herself again for the next few weeks. Even in the brig aboard *Imperieuse*, with anxiety clawing at her insides, she hadn't felt like this. Which probably—*almost surely*—meant her paranoia about him injecting her with a tracking or listening device was just that. Because it had done just what he and Chase claimed it would.

It had made her better.

Temporarily, at least.

Until she'd returned to Asria.

To Cadena.

To her uncle's home.

They work perfectly.

She had felt fine in Tarragona. She'd eaten the tasteless Haederan food they'd served her at the military garrison, and after the queasiness that had hit her the week before, it had tasted like the finest cuisine she'd ever eaten. It had been two days of physical, if not emotional, bliss. Even on a mission from Perrin. Even knowing hundreds of Asrians had died just over the hill. Even as she'd sobbed and screamed at Chase the entire way back to the capital. The emotions, some of the strongest she'd ever experienced, had left her with nothing more than a pounding headache.

They work perfectly.

Was Victor—

Could he be poisoning her? After last night, it was the only explanation. Most nights, unless he requested her company, she ate alone in her room. It would be simple enough for Victor to contaminate her food in the kitchen. It would be even easier for him to stop a servant on their way up with her food.

She should have known something was wrong at the ball, when the servant had brought out a drink especially for her in the garden. After how he'd acted over the past few weeks—after how he had acted earlier that same evening—he should have stormed out there himself and dragged her back in. He'd sent her a drink instead, probably the drink responsible for this latest bout of sickness, and she'd attributed noble motives to the gesture. She was suspicious of everyone else these days, why hadn't she been more suspicious of her uncle? Her uncle who'd already proven he couldn't be trusted.

Holy One, how could You let this happen?

She flopped on the bed and stared at the ceiling, her palm over her stomach.

Victor knew.

He knew, and he was poisoning her with something that mimicked the nausea of pregnancy. She could have gone weeks— months, if she lived that long—thinking it was a normal symptom, only she was immune to that symptom thanks to Chase and *Imperieuse's* chief medical officer.

It would have been a perfect plan, otherwise. She would have slowly wasted away, assuming it was a natural occurrence, until it was too late. Victor stood to gain everything the Rendon family still controlled financially, plus untold sympathy, if his niece died . . . especially of pregnancy complications. And he would never have to worry about her taking her rightful place as queen of Asria if the Haederans were ever ousted.

Perfect.

But even though she knew what he was doing to her now, there was nothing she could do to stop him.

CHAPTER TWENTY-FOUR

ALL THE LIGHTS IN HER ROOM FLASHED ON, AND THE RESULTING flash was so bright it woke Avery from a dreamless sleep. She covered her eyes and flung her hand uselessly through the air to turn them off again, but they remained lit. When her vision finally adjusted to the illumination, Kern and three other Imperial Security Command personnel stood at the side of the bed, all fully dressed and armed. She tried to wave at the light again, this time to dim it, but Kern blocked the sensor with his hand.

"What do you think you're doing in here?" she demanded.

Her mouth went dry as the last bit of drowsiness crumbled. A middle-of-the-night visit by Haedera's secret police. This was the way it was on Haedera when they came for you. She'd known intellectually how it happened, but it was something one couldn't really understand until they experienced it. Not fear like this.

"Isn't it obvious? You're under arrest."

Kern must have thought he was humorous in his declaration, and she breathed a silent prayer that someone would walk by to stop him, but there was no one. No one would be in this area of the palace in the middle of the night—even the servants were asleep. Who would challenge him anyway?

"For—for what?" She hadn't done anything. Nothing Kern

knew about, anyway. Even if he'd somehow learned about the flag, this was overkill. He was supposed to have reprimanded her, that was *all*. Not this. Never this.

Wynne.

Avery's heart—and Chase's warning—beat in her ears. This was about Wynne. Kern had found her, he had figured out who she really was—

"They always ask that," Kern said to the lieutenant next to him. He tossed her the same clothes she'd worn the day before. "Treason, what else? Get up and get dressed, or I'll do it for you."

"Can I have five minutes?"

Shaking, she climbed out of bed, holding the clothes in front of her like a shield. She could scarcely move, every limb heavy and shaking. Getting dressed would be a challenge.

"You've got two."

They disappeared out the door, and Avery threw the rumpled clothes on, then dug through the wardrobe, searching for something warmer to wear. Cadena could be cold in late autumn, especially in the middle of the night, and she was already shivering—though she wasn't convinced it was the weather.

Treason.

She would disappear tonight, just like so many others the Haederans took from their homes. Just like last time, only this time there would be no Hadley to rescue her. Unless—but no, the window was secured, and there was no way out through those static generators. As she examined the chance of escape through it anyway, loud voices rebounded outside and the door swung back open.

Kern, the three other Haederans, and her uncle stood outside, watching her scrutinize the window. She dashed back to the small bathroom and vomited, trying to ignore the dizziness that had stalked her for the past week.

They would kill her. Her and the baby. She would never see him take his first breath or smell his hair or hold him against her. He'd never run through the vines at Sabino or play hide-and-seek in the palace. Merritt would never even know he had a child. Would the Haederans delay her execution long enough—

She vomited again at the thought.

"Are you quite finished?"

With her ears ringing the way they were, Kern's question was barely audible as he bent over her. His icy tone was clear enough though, and she could only shake her head, unable and unwilling to push herself up from her knees. She sat back on her heels instead and tried to focus.

"Too bad," he replied to her silence. "Time's up."

He jerked her hands behind her, and cold metal on her wrists cut through the hot flashes. She tried to flatten herself to the floor, but there was a prick on her upper arm, followed by a sharp burn which spread downward, refusing to retreat.

She froze. This was for real. She let Kern and the lieutenant lift her up, terrified they'd throw her to the ground if she resisted.

Does it really matter now?

"I don't believe this." Victor caught her eye as they dragged her into the hall. "What have you been doing? We had an agreement that you would cooperate with them. I can't save you from everything." He turned his attention to Kern. "You can't take her!"

Didn't he realize she was dead either way? He should thank Kern for taking care of his problem for him.

"Your Excellency, you need to step aside. If you don't get out of my way, I will be well within my authority to arrest you as well."

It sounded like his tolerance for Victor was wearing thin. About time.

"Uncle Victor, it's a . . ."

Why had she called him uncle? What had she meant to say? *Mistake?* A curtain fell over her, and confusion moved in like a black hole. She tried to back away from it, but it came at her faster and faster. Her last rational thought was of Merritt.

* * *

Whatever Kern had drugged her with, it'd made her entire body so heavy that they'd had to haul her from the palace. Avery had done little walking herself, had sat without resisting through the aeroflyer flight, staring vacantly out the window as they landed at what looked like the former Defense Forces headquarters at Alcaris.

Where Merritt had been held for months.

Where Perrin had ordered his torture.

The dizziness and nausea returned in full force at that realization, and she knew she would never make it to wherever they were taking her without becoming sick. But somehow, despite the heaviness of her limbs that had slowed their walk to a crawl, she did. Kern pushed her onto a cot inside a small cell, but instead of locking her in, he handed off his pistol to the lieutenant and slammed the door shut from the inside. Avery stared at him with glassy eyes as he sat her upright and removed the handcuffs.

"I didn't do anything." It seemed important to defend her innocence, however questionable it was. "Where am I? What—what's going on?" Was it starting already? This wasn't a Gareth Chase interrogation technique, there was no question about that.

But it might be Kern's . . .

"Imperial Security building at Alcaris." Kern looked at the ceiling and ran a hand through his hair. "I can't answer the rest right now." He flopped on his back on the hard bench opposite her and closed his eyes.

Avery gathered enough strength to move her eyes around. Rough white walls, cold gray floor, one window—covered in impenetrable glass, painted black, of course—and a sealed door. That sealed door took her breath away, and she gagged at the familiar feeling of being crushed under a ton of steel. She tried to put a hand over her mouth, it flopped uselessly back into her lap.

"If you're going to throw up again," Kern said, eyes still

squeezed shut, "I'd appreciate it if you didn't do it on the floor. It'll pass soon."

"How do you know?"

"So many questions from someone who was just yanked from her bed." He sat up, looking more exhausted and irritated than he had a right to. "I knew I should have given you another dose. He warned me you'd be a pain in the—"

The door opened, cutting him off.

"Thank you, Captain. I'll call you when I need you again." Chase stood in the doorway, and Kern darted by him without giving her another look.

Being taken from the palace was bad enough, but it wasn't nearly as bad as seeing Chase *here*. She still couldn't move more than a twitch, and couldn't defend herself at all—Kern had been her last defense.

"You really are predictable." Chase laughed softly as he shut the door behind him. "Calm down. I'm not going to hurt you."

She couldn't do anything but close her eyes. "You had me arrested, drugged, and brought here in the middle of the night, and I'm supposed to believe that?"

"I can see how that might be concerning, yes."

"You can see how it might be *concerning*?" She studied his face, looking for the joke, but Chase appeared completely serious. "Either tell me what's going on—what I'm supposed to have done —or leave." After a moment's hesitation, she added, with a little more defiance, "You can take the rest of your people with you."

Chase sat down on the cot Kern had vacated. "Believe it or not, the last thing you want right now is for me to leave." At her scowl, he held his hands out in a plea. "Look, it's already wearing off. He didn't want you to struggle and hurt yourself. It's protocol for noncompliant prisoners during transfer, and I warned him about you." Despite the late hour and his prior somberness, his eyes sparkled. "You should thank him. I would have rather watched you fight."

She didn't doubt that. "What do you want, Colonel? I assume

there's a reason we're not having this conversation at a decent hour in the palace."

"It was a necessary ruse," Chase conceded. He leaned against the wall and regarded her thoughtfully. "You know your uncle is trying to kill you."

Her stomach flipped. Hearing it stated so bluntly, from someone who terrified her on the best of days, was more than she could stand in the middle of the night, and her eyes welled up. Furious at her lack of control, she rubbed them until they hurt.

"I know he is."

He narrowed his eyes. "And you were going to . . . what, just let him do it?"

"I only figured it out a few days ago. And in case you hadn't noticed, I'm fairly limited as far as options go." Fury replaced her fear. She wiped the last of the tears away. The slight movement took all the strength she had. "I don't know why this involves you, anyway. I'm fairly certain you would be happy to have me dead."

"I need you alive, short term. Perhaps even long term. And I have to admit, your failure to simply fall into my short-term plan is rather surprising." He glanced at his chronometer, then at the door. "Maybe everything you accomplished last year was luck on your part and not some dormant espionage skills I thought I could use."

"It may come as a surprise to you, but I don't have the patience for these games right now. In case it's not obvious, this *ruse* of yours has taken a few years off my life."

"You'll survive." Chase lifted one shoulder in an *it wasn't my idea* motion. "Someone wants to meet with you," he said. "Which means I need you to meet with him, and you haven't made it easy for either of us."

Hadley.

Kern's strange actions over the past weeks hadn't been so she'd hang herself, no, not even close. The note Hadley had slipped her—Kern had disposed of it for her. It had been a favor, a protective act even. Not a threat. He'd given her every opportunity to meet up with an escaped prisoner. A Commonwealth operative.

Why?

"It looks like you've figured it out."

"I've figured out who." It was too hard to believe. Hadley was conspiring with the Haederans? No, not just the Haederans, the Imperial Security Command. It was a fascinating and unexpected turn of events. "But he's not—you didn't—"

Turn him like you did Elex Feye.

Chase snorted. "No. Everyone's making their own decisions here."

"Then I don't understand the why part."

"That's something he'll have to tell you himself." His gaze hardened. "And after he does, you will do nothing except sit quietly at the palace and respond to Perrin's requests. I didn't bring you back to Asria so you could put yourself on his hit list. You need to back off, lie low, and sit tight until I tell you otherwise. You will not tear down another Haederan flag that Kern needs to replace before it's discovered, you will not antagonize the governor, you will not hire an assassin to murder your uncle, you will not spy on our troops in the palace, and you will not spread the truth about what happened at Tarragona. To anyone."

"Why not?" Avery gritted her teeth. "You and I both know he needs to pay for what he did."

Chase waved his hand, seemingly recovered from his horror of the explosion. "If you think that's the most important thing happening on this planet right now," he said, "you're sadly mistaken. And since I know you don't think I'm serious about you staying quiet, I'll tell you this—Wynne Ferran is here with us now. I don't think you want to add to that tally, so I'd keep what you know a secret."

"You *arrested* Wynne?"

"She was in my way," he said calmly. "You put her in my

way, my lady. If you keep going the way you've been going, you'll be accepting full responsibility for anything else that happens."

"Where is she?"

"Relax. She's here at Alcaris and being treated well for now. We'll send her home as soon as I can be certain she won't talk."

Chase's threats were losing a little of their sting, and against her better judgment, Avery believed him. It didn't seem like Wynne was in any imminent danger, but something else he had said—

She pinched the bridge of her nose in frustration. It was too late, her emotions too muddled for clear thinking.

I didn't bring you back here?

She swore under her breath as his meaning hit, painfully. The observation deck aboard *Imperieuse.* How had she fallen for it? Chase hadn't brought her there to be kind at all. He hadn't brought her there to say goodbye to her planet, to her life. He'd *wanted* her to decide to return to Asria.

I have no doubt you will try, Your Majesty . . .

That title had only crossed his lips once.

"You." An angry voice flew out of her, one she'd never heard from herself. "You've been manipulating me this whole time. I don't know what your goal is in all of this, but I am not your puppet."

"On the contrary. You're a perfect one." Chase mimicked the strings of a marionette with both hands and a grin that made her forget she'd ever been afraid of him. "I'm only surprised it took you so long to figure it out."

"How would I have figured it out? You've kept me in the dark from the beginning."

His grin didn't fade. "You would have, if you'd bothered to ask me who Perrin's second favorite prisoner at Alcaris was. I suppose I can't blame you for not being more curious, though. You were a little . . ." He snickered. "Upset and intoxicated."

"Fine." The nerve of the man, throwing her misplaced trust in him back at her. "Who was Perrin's 'second favorite prisoner?'" she ground out in a low, furious tone.

He shrugged. "Lieutenant Colonel Stev Kanmar."

Her eyes widened.

Kanmar had set her up. Delivered her to Chase like a package, one with a pretty bow on it. It was no wonder Chase had reacted to her appearance aboard *Imperieuse* so quickly. It was no wonder he hadn't been surprised to see her. She would never let Kanmar get away with it, wherever he was now.

Probably Haedera.

Heedless of the consequences, she flew at Chase, anger overriding the sweltering fear that had threatened to consume her since she'd awoken that night. Kern had been right—he should have given her another dose.

Chase jumped to his feet. He grabbed her wrist with one hand before she could strike out at him and pushed her face-first against the wall. She thrashed against him until his arm pressed firmly against the back of her neck.

"Did you really think that was a good idea?" His voice was sharp and low behind her as he dodged a blow from her foot. "I need you to stop fighting and listen to me very carefully. I need you to trust me. I have no plans to harm you and I expect the same consideration in return. Is that perfectly clear?"

What a stupid question.

He twisted her arm further behind her and she yelped. "Do you understand?"

His voice was calmer that time, and her muscles relaxed despite the pain building in her shoulder.

"Yes," she bit out.

"Good. Now sit."

Obediently, as logic and more than a little self-preservation took over, she dropped onto the cot, a hand protectively over her stomach. It was only her face that hurt though, and she reached a hand to her cheek where the wall had scratched it.

"Don't be so melodramatic. You're not even showing." Chase

eyed the scrape on her face with frank approval. "You needed to look like it was a rough night anyway." He cleared his throat and reached for his pocket. "Maybe the rest of your stay in handcuffs would leave marks enough to—"

"No!"

He shrugged again, and she hated herself for letting her anxiety show. "If you insist. But Kern is outside with the antidote right now, which I swear I will withhold for another month if you try anything like that again."

Avery curled her lip at him.

He laughed out loud. "You didn't honestly think I was just catching a ride on *Imperieuse*, did you? I needed you back on Asria. Oh, I knew you'd make your way back here eventually, sentimental as you've become, but I didn't have time for you to make the trip to Ventana and back. I saved Kanmar from Perrin the same as I did for Colonel Rendon, and he owed me. He was grateful for my help, and when I told him he'd be doing it for Asria . . ." He spread his hands. "I didn't coerce him. Just asked if he'd be willing to help me. To help you. For some reason, he was desperate to do anything for his queen."

Of course he'd been willing. Anything to make up for what his men had done to her uncle.

Chase's smile faded away. "So, I orchestrated a little jailbreak. Sent him home to Tarragona, manipulated some paperwork, gave him a clean record, and had him join the Haederan Navy under the amnesty program. It wasn't as though I had to hide him in plain sight like that for long—just long enough to make sure he was in charge of your flight off Asria. And don't give me that look," he said, as she screwed her face up in disgust. "Even you aren't naïve enough to think Imperial Security doesn't have a source at Villiers."

She didn't take the bait. There was really no suitable response to *that*.

"But then he had a change of heart. He told me he wasn't leaving Asria if it meant leaving his family defenseless, that he wouldn't leave them open to retaliation by escaping and infuriating Perrin. The fool kept talking about turning himself back in to protect them, so I promised I'd watch over them the best I could. My trip to Tarragona was partly to keep an eye on you, but mostly to check on them. I never expected—"

Dread circled about her, stealing most of the air in the cell. Whatever Chase had to say, she already knew it would be horrifying.

"Never expected what?" she asked.

He blew out a deep breath. "I failed him, and his three sons were killed in the mine."

Oh, Holy One.

"Does he know?" she whispered. "Someone needs to tell him."

Chase nodded. It shouldn't have been possible for him to look any sadder, any more regretful, but there it was, plain on his face.

"I wasn't honest with you before. My wife died last year, after you escaped and I was recalled to Haedera. When I left Asria after the explosion, I wasn't headed home—I went to visit the prison camp on Emot. I hated leaving you to deal with Perrin on your own, but I needed to tell Colonel Kanmar in person what had happened to his family. I owed him that much." He exhaled. "And now I owe you an apology for what Perrin did to you while I was away. When Brennin told me he made you watch that recording . . . it was inappropriate and cruel, and I'm sorry."

She gave him a slight nod, acknowledgement for the apology. For his pain. But she couldn't think about what Perrin had made her witness, not here.

"And Colonel March?"

"Wrong place at the wrong time. Maybe one day you can tell him the entire story."

"Why did Perrin have such a problem with Kanmar?"

Chase shrugged. "It was personal. Pointless, really. Just after the annexation, Perrin observed a few of the Defense Forces officers' interviews. Kanmar—" He laughed, a little of the sadness gone. "He spat at Perrin's feet. Apparently, the general has been nursing a bit of a grudge since then. Not enough to go after him, mind you, but he was thrilled when Kanmar was captured that night. Two of his least favorite Asrians, walking right into a trap he'd set. He made both him and Colonel Rendon witness the executions."

"I'm surprised Perrin cared that much about such a small insult," she said.

"Are you? I think you know him better than that." He raised his eyebrows, then sighed. "I was testing you aboard *Imperieuse*. I had to know that you would trust me enough to hear me out when the time came—until then, I doubted you would, and you had every reason not to. And I needed to know if you were willing to sacrifice everything for Asria. Of course," he said, gesturing to her stomach, "that was before I learned of that. Now . . ."

He stood and knocked on the door. Kern entered, a small case in his hand. Despite what Chase had implied it was, anxiety flared.

"What was Victor giving me?" she asked. If she didn't keep talking, she'd have another panic attack. Visions of clawing the walls so hard her nails broke slipped through her mind.

Chase hesitated. "Fehyde."

"What's that?"

"It's . . ." He scratched his forehead, then pressed his eyes closed with his fingers, like her question had physically pained him. "It's made from the sap of the medilla cactus. Very common on Haedera. And deadly, with long-term ingestion."

Avery frowned. "And you just happen to have the antidote?"

He and Kern exchanged looks. Neither one of them answered, and the sickening truth struck her. It had become too easy to forget who they really were.

"You use this on your own people, don't you?"

More silence.

Disgusted, she let Kern inject her and wiped the small spot of leftover blood away.

Deep breath.

Hold it.

Breathe out.

"Feel better?" Kern asked.

"No." She didn't feel as close to death as she had, but that was all in her head. "Should I?"

"You will. In the next ten minutes, I'd say." He sounded confident. "But I've only got enough to get you through the next month, so be careful what you eat and drink when you're at the palace."

"Then what?" A month would be enough time for Victor to figure something else out.

"We'll see," Chase said.

Promises, promises.

"And now?"

"You spend the night here. Maybe a few nights. Appearances, you know." Chase smiled, more relaxed than he'd been since he'd entered. Her obvious distress had to be entertaining for him. "Kern will stay with you in case the viceroy gets suspicious. He shouldn't be able to argue his way in here, but stranger things have happened."

They were so concerned about Victor that they felt the need to continue this charade? She wished she was anywhere else, even within Victor's striking distance, but Chase was probably right.

"Unless," he continued, "you'd rather have other company. It's up to you."

A few nights trapped here with Kern was the very definition of hell. She found herself nodding.

CHAPTER TWENTY-FIVE

Pacing was easier than sitting, but even pacing was wearing her down. The adrenaline was gone, Kern's drugs out of her system, and the night had left her drained. Sleep wouldn't come though, not now. Not with Chase watching her. Not since he'd decided it would be another three days before he'd release her. It was hard to decide what was worse—the idea her uncle was that determined to kill her, or the prospect of spending three days in an Imperial Security Command prison.

There wasn't much to do to kill time. She prayed, avoiding Chase's stare as she walked from the door to the window and back again. She prayed for protection, for wisdom, and most of all, that the Holy One would speed up time.

But time slowed instead. The black window was opaque, to be sure, and no cues came from outside, but the lights in the cell, dim when she'd arrived, finally brightened. It was day then, and the simple fact that her jailers were allowing her to know the time reassured her. This was protection, just as Chase had claimed.

Avery finally turned toward him. He looked bored by what was essentially guard duty, but she knew him well enough to know he was not.

"How did you know?" she asked.

Chase looked up from his intense study of his hands. "How did I know what?"

"About me." She'd meant to ask how he'd known Victor was trying to kill her. Why had her mind twisted it to something else? No matter, she wouldn't lose this opportunity. "What I was doing, I mean. Last year. Did General Perrin really tell you, like he said at the ball?"

Something dark crossed his face. "Why does it matter who told me?"

Avery sat and pulled a thin blanket around her. The Imperial Security guards had delivered it along with breakfast, but it did little to ease the chill that had settled into the cell.

"It just does. To me."

And to Zenos Hadley.

Chase sighed and rocked back against the wall on the cot opposite her, hands clasped on one knee. He studied her for a moment, like he was debating whether to tell her the truth.

"When your uncle arrived on Haedera," he began, "he informed the emperor that you were a former Commonwealth officer and suggested you weren't to be trusted if the invasion was successful. I was sent to Asria with the fleet to wait and investigate if necessary. It wasn't long until Perrin called me to the surface. You were asking questions he didn't believe you had any personal interest in. You probably didn't know back then that paranoia is a Haederan trait. One many of us are quite proud of."

He chanced a small smile, but she didn't return it.

The verium. It had to be her nosiness about the verium mining. She should have known better than to press Perrin like she had back then, but Chase was right—she hadn't known mistrust was so imbedded in their culture. But what else should she have expected from a planet where everyone accepted the constant surveillance like she accepted the sun coming up each morning? She would probably be the same way if she'd grown up on Haedera.

"So yes, Perrin was telling the truth at the ball, although it was only a guess on his part. He had no idea what you were up to, just that you were up to something. Neither did I, not at first, even though I should have known from the very beginning. Our asset—"

Avery's abrupt inhalation silenced him. Feye hadn't been an asset. Traitor or not, he'd been a person, not someone for Chase to use and discard.

"We didn't find him until later, if that's what you're wondering. Not until after Zenos Hadley broke you out of there. He didn't give you up, not until the very end."

Yes. That was what she'd been wondering for months. Feye had maintained in his last message to her that he'd never told Chase about her, but she hadn't quite believed his insistence. But what reason had he had to lie? Compassion seeped through the chinks in her anger, and this time she didn't force it away.

"Anyway, it was easy enough to follow you and find out what you were doing after Perrin tipped us off. The army may not have known what you were up to, but you didn't really hide your tracks from me very well. Once I told them to back off and give you some freedom, it was even easier. Though finding out who exactly you were working for and how much you'd learned took—"

"I remember."

Her response was sharper than she intended. Those weeks deep underground in Cadena with Chase would haunt her forever, and it was a wonder she'd remained this composed, here in this cell with her tormenter turned temporary protector. The nightmares . . .

She brushed them off. They would be back as soon as she fell asleep, and it was one reason she was keeping herself up. There was no point in reliving them earlier than absolutely necessary. No point in humiliating herself in front of Chase.

"I know you do."

Chase looked more uncomfortable than she'd ever seen him, but she wasn't about to ease his discomfort. He could feel guilty about what he had done for the rest of his life as far as she was concerned. The guiltier, the better.

"The Commonwealth believes you used Major Feye's sister as leverage against him," she said. "Did you?"

"Yes."

Back to the one-word answers again, though this time an odd glimmer of defiance sparked across his face.

"And?"

"And what?"

"Is she alive?"

"She is, and considering the alternative, not altogether displeased with the turn her life has taken."

"What turn is that?"

"She is living on an undisclosed planet with her daughter. Hers and Rhys Linden's. He is not alive." Chase offered that news with the emotion of a rock.

Half shocking, half predictable, but the shocking part was none of her business.

"I didn't—I didn't suppose he was."

She had the uneasy feeling she was partially responsible for his death. She'd always hated Linden, a man she'd only known a few hours, just because he was Haederan. Just because he worked for Chase. Just because Feye had betrayed her to him. But she hadn't had another choice, had she? If she hadn't escaped Linden, Chase would have learned everything she knew about the verium. She would be a prisoner on Haedera right now, broken, crushed, a shadow of her real self. If she wasn't dead already.

No, she couldn't second-guess her split-second decision to steal the fighter now. She hadn't known Linden would be executed for his failure, not then. And she'd done her duty. She'd escaped.

The assertion didn't help her guilt.

"I said you would never understand how much I paid for my failure, but now . . . I think you might understand now." Chase stood and pretended to look out the black window. "The emperor told me all would be forgiven on my part if I took care of Linden for letting you get away. I refused. I should have never left him alone with you, and I accepted—I still accept—full responsibility for that decision. He didn't deserve death. I argued that in writing the entire way back to Haedera and then to the emperor's face once I arrived. His Majesty didn't care about any of my arguments. He shot Linden himself, and then as punishment for my insubordination . . ."

His lilt grew thick as he leaned his forehead against the window.

"He executed my ten-year-old son. Cut his throat right in front of me. I screamed at him to let me take Marc's place, but they pulled me away from my own child as he knelt sobbing in front of that throne. I'll never forget the way he looked at me at the last second . . . at the one person who was supposed to protect him and failed. I'll never forget—you can't imagine the blood, Your Majesty. I pray you'll never know."

Avery could only stare at his back, a hand over her mouth. Even more surprising were the tears for someone she hated, and she didn't care if Chase turned and saw them. It was no wonder he had manipulated her medical records. Guilt, indeed.

"And you would still serve a man like that?" she whispered.

"Until his death or mine." The words were crisp, but Chase didn't turn around. His hand disappeared in front of his face instead. "Next question."

"Next—next question?"

"I know you have more. You might as well ask them all while I'm in a giving mood."

"I—" She had so many other questions, but it was clear he was finished with the subject of Linden and his son. "What's Kern's problem with me?"

He chuckled, though it didn't sound happy. "He's got someone back home. From what little he's told me, she's not all that serious about him, and I suspect he doubts she'll be around when he gets back. And like any good Haederan, he doesn't like

Asria, or any other Commonwealth planet. Don't take it personally."

Kern was in love? It was impossible to picture. The poor woman, even if she was Haederan.

"Then why is he here?" she asked. Chase shook his head, and she sighed at his denial of a question she really wanted answered. "Then what about this one? How bad are things in Cadena now? Truly?" She was no longer naïve enough to believe everything was fine just because the Haederans were allowing temple markets. They hadn't loosened their grip, even if it appeared so on the surface.

"I won't answer that one either."

"I want to know. I deserve to know."

Avery stood to pace again and stopped next to him to pick at the black paint on the window. It didn't budge under her nail.

"I don't know why you'd do that to yourself," he replied.

She crossed her arms and glared at him.

"All right," he said, taking a step toward her. "You want to hear how things are going on Asria? The things no one else is telling you? Do you want to hear the army has arrested all the former Defense Forces people they could find after that stunt they pulled with you last month? Major Ferran is lucky we got to her first—she's off their list now. Do you want to hear that the reason Cadena has been so peaceful over the past six months, peaceful enough for some to bring their families over, is because your people who refuse to cooperate are being slowly moved to camps on Emot?"

Avery backed away from him, but the wall stopped her. Chase stopped so close she couldn't focus on his face and took a breath.

"Or that my people have been working around the clock doing things I *know* you don't want to hear about? Or that rumor has it that Perrin has found a way to destroy the Defense Forces base at Villiers? Or that just last week, we executed fifteen rebels for a planned attack on the governor's flat? Is that what you want to hear?"

"They aren't rebels. Don't call them that. They're Asrian."

It was a weak declaration. Chase was right, she hadn't wanted to hear any of that—but what she wanted had stopped mattering when her father had been murdered by the Haederans and the senate had elected her queen.

"Semantics, Your Majesty. But not a surprising belief from someone who seems to have forgotten she is only a prisoner." He produced a bottle of water from below the cot and took a long sip. "Now get some sleep. You're going to need it."

CHAPTER TWENTY-SIX

How she'd missed these little garden shrines scattered around the senate complex. Surrounded by weeping maples, this particular one was more peaceful than life had a right to be right now, three days after her staged arrest. The trees blocked most of the sound from the streets on the opposite side of the temple, hiding her and Kern from curious witnesses and making it easier to focus on more sacred things. How had she ever argued with Drex about the Holy One's presence? It was tangible in the artificial clearing. They'd been sitting here for hours, long enough for both her and Kern to pray—separately—at the tiny altar at the other end of the garden. Over two hours later, she still wondered about the contents of his conversation.

"How much longer are we going to sit here?" she asked, picking at a shard of wood on the leg of the bench.

"Until he shows," Kern replied from his position on a boulder diagonal from her. He folded his arms. "No reason to orchestrate a clandestine meeting between you two now that Colonel Chase has told you everything."

"But how do you know he'll—"

She flinched as someone cleared their throat behind her. Kern ducked outside the stand of trees, and Hadley slid neatly into the space next to her on the bench, grinning. She didn't return it. Was she supposed to be relieved or absolutely terrified to see him?

"I'm here," she said. "You're here. That one out there has apparently been trying to set this up for quite a while. Now talk."

"You don't waste any time, Your Majesty." Hadley's eyes crinkled. "You don't have to be so demanding. Really. We have plenty of time to talk."

"I don't think that's the best thing to call me right now," she said. "If for no other reason than Captain Kern will probably duck in and correct you."

"You don't think?" Hadley looked around. "I don't think anyone can hear us in here, but if you insist, we can skip that title for now. How does Captain Rendon sound instead?"

Even worse.

Avery put her head in her hands. "General Torin was supposed to rescind my commission, not promote me. I hope he doesn't think that gives him any kind of sway over me, because I have more important matters to deal with. I'm not even sure it's legal for a monarch of a Commonwealth planet." Even an occupied one. She looked up. "Hold on. That means you've spoken with them. And that means they're close enough for fast comms."

"Ah—yes. Yes, I have. You didn't think I've been wandering around the city taking leisurely lunches every day, did you? Or attending balls." He winked.

"Hadley."

"I bet you looked great. Maybe next time you'll save a dance for me."

"Hadley." She gritted her teeth that time and looked pointedly in the direction Kern had disappeared to. "It's wonderful to see you, alive and well especially, but what do you *want*? Why have you been following me around? They told me you were sent to Alcaris. Surely you didn't escape!"

"Even after I broke you out of jail, you continue to underestimate me? What will it take for you to learn what I'm really capable of?" Hadley scratched his head. "Fine. Not too long after I arrived back on Asria, they decided to transfer me."

She stifled a gasp. "To where?"

He waved a hand at her. "Relax. It was a setup." He laughed. "Although you should have seen the looks on the faces of the Haederan Army guards when your Imperial Security Command friends showed up for me. They thought I was done for, and I believe they felt a little sorry for me. Maybe they were worried they'd miss my charming wit. Not enough to argue over my transfer, naturally."

"Naturally." Avery flushed at his joking accusation. "But they're not my friends."

Hadley grinned. "Your friends were careless about it from the minute they arrived. They made a lot of mistakes, and it was easy to get away. Once I got into town, it was even easier to disappear. You were a little harder to find, even with help. It wasn't as though I could show up on the steps of the palace and knock on the front door."

"Someone I know arranged for the transfer to be sloppy, didn't he?"

"You're catching on." Hadley looked around once more. "I can't tell you anything else, not here. You'll find out eventually, one way or the other."

"Fine." It wasn't, and she was desperate to know what Chase needed from Hadley. Neither of them would ever tell her though, not until it suited their purposes. "What do you want with me this time?"

Hadley grinned. "I told him I wasn't doing what he wanted until I made sure you were all right. I'd assumed they'd taken you to Haedera, so it was quite the relief to see you alive and well in Cadena."

"Alive, but not quite so well." Avery tapped a finger on her lips, dismissing her comment. Hadley had to assume she was talking about the overall situation. He had enough to do, it seemed, and he didn't need him to save her from Victor. Victor was her problem and her problem alone. "All of this stealth, just for that?"

"Just for that. I had to make sure you were safe before I agreed to anything. But since you're here, I should probably also tell you to keep an open mind when things start happening." Hadley looked up at the setting sun. "I have to go now. Stay safe."

He stood, kissed her hand, and vanished.

* * *

It was a silent walk back to the palace, but at least it *was* a walk, unlike the drugged manner in which she'd been taken away a few nights ago. The evening was mild, Hadley was safe, and Kern had been blissfully quiet since they'd left the shrine. He hadn't even commented on Hadley's use of her title—and she had to admit, it was nice to hear someone besides Chase use it.

Something was grating on her though, like a forgotten word on the tip of her tongue that she couldn't manage to spit out. Like something dark was simmering just under the surface, waiting for the right time to boil over. She worked her way backward from her talk with Hadley, the hours spent sitting in the shrine with Kern, Chase's disturbing revelation about his son, Victor's attempt on her life, all the way to her arrest at the palace. There was enough over the past few days to make any sane person uncomfortable.

That had to be it. It was just stress. Her life was a mess right now, and it wasn't as though things had been pleasant since she'd returned from Tarrag—

The quiet street twisted around her.

"It was a test," she said to herself as her stomach rolled along with cobblestones. Antidote or not, she was going to throw up right there on the sidewalk. She turned to Kern. "It was a test," she repeated. "Wasn't it?"

"What was a test?" Annoyance cut into his tone, like he'd been enjoying their silent walk just as much as she had.

Perrin killed them. For no reason. All those innocent people.

"The explosion at Tarragona." She covered her mouth, desperately afraid she'd be sick. "Perrin was testing explosives to be used at Villiers."

"I don't know what you're talking about." To Kern's credit, his confusion appeared genuine.

"You already know it wasn't Asrians who did this. And you know that even though it's almost useless to the Haederan Empire now, Perrin would never destroy his precious verium mine unless he had a good reason. Villiers is his good reason." She gasped for air, the realization coming at her like a train. "He can't stand that the Defense Forces has been spitting in his face for the past year. He can't stand that the Asrian government has thumbed its nose at him in spite of the fact your emperor has placed him in control of Asria."

"And you're telling me all this why?" Kern looked bored as they turned the corner.

"I have to warn them." She couldn't lose Merritt again. She couldn't stand by and witness that much death—but Perrin would make her witness it. "Please. It'll be a massacre otherwise."

"Not going to happen." He sped up, his boots echoing in the still night.

"If you don't help me—" Did she dare threaten him? She'd done rasher things, more frightening things. Kern's help might be her only chance. "I'll tell Perrin where your true loyalty lies."

"Yes, with His Imperial Majesty." Kern made a noise somewhere between a laugh and a snort. "I'm sure the general will be shocked to hear that of an Imperial Security officer. Simply horrified."

Oh, this was such a chance, but if she was correct . . .

"I'm not talking about your emperor." She swallowed. "I'm talking about Gareth Chase."

The boots stopped.

"You don't know anything."

It wasn't a clean denial, and then she knew.

"I know you've gone to great lengths to set up a meeting with Hadley—a meeting Colonel Chase wanted. I know no one higher than him authorized that little operation of yours. I know you hate Asria. I know you can't stand being my keeper. I know with one call you could be off what you see as this backwater little rock, back to doing whatever heinous things you prefer to be doing on Haedera, but you aren't. And I know—I know that Colonel Chase all but told me Perrin's plan for Villiers three nights ago."

Chase had implied it, but he'd glossed right over it. Still, how had she missed what he'd said? He'd never have wanted to let something this important, this secret, this damaging slip, but he had.

. . . rumor has it Perrin has finally found a way to destroy the Defense Forces base at Villiers . . .

"And I think he knew I'd figure it out and do something about it," she said, her breath short. Chase, for a reason she couldn't begin to guess, wanted Villiers safe.

Kern's eyes were steel. "What do you want from me?"

"I need you to help me get to Villiers." She inhaled, saving the clean night air. Chase might want Villiers safe, but she *needed* Merritt and their son safe. "But we won't be going alone."

CHAPTER TWENTY-SEVEN

AVERY LEFT KERN IN A REMOTE PALACE GARDEN AND BRUSHED OFF the questions from the Haederan sentries. No one else questioned her as she headed to Victor's night office in the main wing, praying he was there—this plan wouldn't work if he was working late in the senate building, where he spent most of his days. The three guards milling about in front of the door suggested he was not. Victor had some of the same guards he'd used before the invasion, and she hated the fact they were loyal to him over their own planet. She especially hated the young one who was standing in front of the office door now, and she memorized his face in case he survived to see the end of this. His betrayal would not go unre-membered.

"I need to see him," she said to him. "This instant."

"You'll have to make an appointment." The young guard's face betrayed a certain smugness at her current position in the palace. "It's late, and His Excellency is busy right now."

"I doubt he's that busy. Get out of my way." Avery shoved past him to the door, meeting little resistance. If this was all the protection Victor had, he needed much better.

To her surprise, Victor *was* busy—or at least in a meeting with Perrin. She stopped mid-stride in the doorway as soon as she saw the general, thankful she hadn't stumbled in shock. Confronting him hadn't been a part of her original plan, but until Kern could take care of him, she would have to manage.

Victor's eyebrows rose as she stepped through the door. "May I help you?"

"I'm sorry for the interruption, Uncle Victor, but it's urgent I speak with you."

Perrin jumped to his feet from a lounge chair beside Victor's desk. "How the hell did you get back here?"

"You mean why is Imperial Security not still holding me at Alcaris?" Avery smiled at him. "They made a mistake. Got some bad information. You know how it goes."

"A mistake?" Perrin's eyes creased, becoming near slits. "They're not in the habit of arresting people by mistake. They're certainly not in the habit of releasing their prisoners after three days." His gaze landed on the scrape on her cheek, and she was suddenly grateful she'd infuriated Chase enough to earn it. "Or at all, as I'm sure you're aware. You must be very lucky."

"I suppose I am. You'd have to talk to Captain Kern about that."

"I will. And then I'm reassigning him. I can't have him seizing people from the palace in the middle of the night like he did. This isn't Haedera, and it reflects rather poorly on Victor and your agreement with him, don't you think?"

Could he *have* Kern reassigned? Perrin might like to order him around, but Imperial Security was well outside his authority.

Avery's gaze fell to his sidearm. Perrin rarely went around Cadena armed. No, he couldn't have Kern reassigned—but he could have him killed. Or take care of the problem himself, if he was desperate. It wasn't as though there were many Haederans on Asria who would challenge him.

"I thought my orders were clear." Victor turned his scowl from her and her obviously concocted story to the guard behind her. "We were not to be interrupted."

"They were clear." Avery cut in before the guard—or Perrin—

could reply. "But I have some news for you, and it can't wait." She smiled at him this time, reveling in Perrin's glare. This would infuriate him as well, especially after what he'd done to Merritt. And it felt wonderful to share the news with someone, even the man who was trying to kill her. "You're going to have a grandnephew."

"Is that so?" Victor took the not-quite-news-to-him more calmly than she ever thought he would. He really thought he had it all figured out, didn't he? Still, his mind had to be racing, trying to decide how he'd continue to poison her once nausea was off the list of known symptoms. "Congratulations. May the Holy One's hand be over him always."

The prayer sounded like a challenge instead of the traditional Asrian blessing that it was, and her gut twisted at the threat. Perrin's comm beeped, and he stepped out with the guard trailing him with only a sneer in her direction, much to her relief. Probably to his own as well— until he found out it was a false request from Kern.

"Thank you," she said to Victor, giddy that the first step of the plan had already gone well. "But you knew all about it already, didn't you?"

"I've suspected it for a few weeks, but I wasn't entirely sure, and you weren't talking." Victor fiddled with a tablet, then pointedly set it aside and folded his hands on his desk. "I assumed you would tell me when the time was right. It's wonderful news. Does Merritt know?"

She couldn't hide a laugh at his feigned concern. "It's such wonderful news that you poisoned me to get rid of us both, is that right?"

Victor turned deathly pale and struggled to catch his breath. "I never—"

"A Haederan-made toxin, no less. I wonder where you could have gotten that? Not on Asria, that's for sure. It causes nausea, but you already knew that too. You thought you were so clever, and really, you were. The only problem is, I was one step ahead of you the whole time. You'd have been better off just shooting me." She was grateful his hands were in sight after she delivered that needling suggestion.

"What are you talking about?"

"I knew about the baby before we departed *Imperieuse*." She managed to keep her voice steady. "The Haederans gave me an implant on the ship."

"You—" Understanding dawned somewhere in Victor's paleness. "They won't get away with this."

"Who won't get away with what?" He was delusional, just like she'd suspected since this whole mess had begun. "The Imperial Haederan Navy will not discipline a medical officer for giving appropriate treatment to a prisoner. Especially when the only reason to withhold it was so she wouldn't figure out she was being murdered. That doctor did nothing wrong, and even your influence won't be enough to have him punished."

Victor stared at her without seeing, and she plowed onward.

"So, I have a deal to make with you. You tried to kill the queen of Asria. Attempted murder, treason, it doesn't matter what you want to call it. That's life in prison. Except thanks to you, we're not really the Asria we used to be, are we? Which means the old restrictions on capital punishment don't hold true right now. And since you've destroyed our legal system as well . . ."

Victor's paleness changed to a sickly gray sheen. "You wouldn't kill me. You don't even have the guts to have someone else do it. You wouldn't get away with it, anyway. Not here. Not now."

"Do you want to test me on that?" she asked. "Quite a few people in Cadena don't like you so much anymore. Loyal Asrians, and maybe even some Haederans. You think they approve of their emperor putting an Asrian in charge of their conquered lands?"

"Then what deal are you proposing?" Victor sounded so serious that there must have already been a foiled assassination attempt or two. If there'd been attempts on Perrin's life, surely Victor had been a target as well.

"It's easy. The easiest deal you've ever made." It would even be easier than the deal he'd made with the Haederans, the one that had given them his homeland. The deal that had killed Drex, her parents, and almost Merritt as well. "You come with me, and I'll make sure you're safe. I'll make sure you aren't executed for the things you've done. I let you live, and you let my child and me live."

"Come with you where? Let me live how?"

"Villiers." Her heart finally settled into a normal rhythm. "The senate is dying to try you for treason." She fervently wished Perrin could sit right next to Victor to answer for his crimes. Unfortunately, he'd be safe on Haedera by the time that happened, enjoying his retirement.

Victor chuckled then, and a bit of his color returned. "You don't honestly expect me to go with you, do you?"

"Well, no. I didn't actually expect you would go willingly." She pulled Kern's backup stun pistol from her pocket and aimed it at Victor's chest. "That's why I have this."

He stood, hands in the air, still smiling. "You'll never be able to drag me out of—"

"Viceroy!" Perrin dashed back in alone, his eyes bulging, gasping for breath. "You're going to want to head to Alcaris immediately. A group of Commonwealth ships just engaged our fleet outside of Emot."

He froze when he saw Avery's weapon.

She turned the stun pistol on them both.

CHAPTER TWENTY-EIGHT

Avery hated to be grateful to Kern for anything, but she wouldn't have been able to roll Perrin behind Victor's desk on her own. That task completed, the two of them stared at Victor's motionless body.

"This was a bad idea." Kern prodded him with a boot. "We'll never get him out of here without someone noticing. And there's a storm moving in. Snow, they're saying."

"No one will question you." Avery rose from her kneeling position next to Victor. Traitor or not, she had to make sure he was still breathing. "By the time anyone asks the right questions of the right people, we'll have disappeared."

I hope.

Kern sighed. "It'll have to work." He hefted Victor up over his shoulder. "I can get him out of here myself. Go ahead of me and clear the way the best you can. Side servant's entrance, the one right next to the garden under your room. There's a car waiting."

"A car." Avery looked at him with disdain. "We can't drive through Cadena in a car. What about the flyer?"

"Army personnel wouldn't give me the flyer. Said Imperial Security had revoked my authorization. Why did you think it took me so long to get back here?"

"Perrin can't do that, can he?"

A chill ran through her. Kern's sigh of resignation made a little more sense now.

"No. But he can make it look as though someone else did." He looked apprehensive for the first time. "That's not even the bad news. If he's decided to chance the repercussions over falsifying that kind of order, there isn't much else he won't do. You didn't tell me he had it out for you so badly."

"And the Commonwealth Navy?"

"You only wish. I had to get him out of there somehow."

Her stomach sank. She'd been so hopeful Perrin's outburst had been the truth. She ducked out the door and down the hallway. Kern had taken care of Victor's guards—she wouldn't ask how— and this part of the palace was silent. The lights were off this late in the evening, and the moon barely shone through the stained-glass windows. Maybe she and Kern would make it out of the palace undetected after all. She could feel her way around the entire palace in the dark, even with her eyes closed. She hoped Kern was having as easy of a time as she turned the corner into the hallway that led to the kitchens.

His footsteps were behind her, and the presence of another person—even if he was Haederan—calmed her enough to shake off the similarity between this darkness and the darkness the night the Haederans had invaded. It helped that the moonlight sparkled down through the abundant skylights, illuminating this part of the palace so much she could see Kern's shadow slowly keeping pace behind her. With the freshly subdued Victor in the back seat of the car—Avery didn't ask where Kern had obtained it—they slipped silently into the almost-empty street.

"I have a question." She sank against the seat, into the shadows. "Why did you agree to help me so easily?"

"I didn't think I had." He didn't look at her, focused on the dark, damp street instead.

"You did." She laughed quietly. "Although I have to say, I'm fairly surprised one of Colonel Chase's subordinates would do something like this for him."

Kern shot her a sharp look.

"I'm not as oblivious or damaged as you seem to think, Captain. He's up to something, he's swept you up in it, and you're completely amenable to his plans. I can't imagine why you'd go along with something that skirts treason." At least the Haederan definition of it, which was rather wide indeed. "Why?"

"Maybe you hadn't noticed, but he outranks me. I'm just following orders."

Avery raised her eyebrows at him. "I'm not that naïve, either. If that was truly the case, you'd just as soon turn him in as do what he says."

Kern sighed and propped his elbow up on the door. "He saved my life, all right? And I haven't done a great job of repaying that favor. A rather poor one, in fact."

"Poor how?" It wasn't as though someone like Chase needed many favors. Did he even accept them?

"You're not the only one who's had it rough lately. I stood by and watched something terrible happen to him—to his family. Let's just say I was surprised I woke up the next morning. I'm even more surprised he still trusts me."

"His son." A chill settled over her soul. "You—you saw it."

"I didn't just see it," he mumbled. The car slowed, and Kern's gaze became even more distant than before. "I—"

Against her will, images flooded her imagination, as vivid as though she'd been there herself. She had no idea what the Haederan throne looked like—likely no one in the Commonwealth did —but her mind filled in the gaps.

A weeping boy. Chase, paler than she'd ever seen him. Kern and other faceless Imperial Security officers holding him back. It had been bad enough to hear the story from Chase, but knowing Kern was about to give even more details . . .

She wouldn't have been able to live. How had Chase?

Kern became even quieter. "The emperor told us Colonel

Chase was on his way back to Asria. He asked us to pick his son up and bring him to the palace to let him say goodbye. I should have known right then . . ."

She wanted to tell him to stop, that she knew the rest, didn't want to hear the rest, but she couldn't make her lips move.

"Marc didn't question it when we arrived for him. Didn't fight us. Didn't seem afraid. I remember wondering if he really didn't know what his father did for a living, even though we all knew he must. Or maybe Colonel Chase had kept that part of his life. Still, that boy trusted us, though the Holy One knows why. When we arrived at the palace, he was so excited to be there, so excited to see his father—he skipped down that hallway to the throne room right in front of me."

Chase's son was probably the only person to approach the Haederan emperor like *that*.

"And then, when we got inside, Colonel Chase was there. When he saw his son, he—I'd never seen him look like that. I'd never seen him actually shake. You know how controlled he always is. Hell, before then, I hadn't known he had a heart. And before the emperor pulled that knife, even before he ordered that child to kneel in front of him, I knew what we had done."

Kern took a deep breath.

"He fought us. Elbowed me in the ribs. I was damn lucky he didn't break something—as it was, I had a bruise for a month. But we did exactly what His Majesty ordered. What he had ordered of us. We held him there and forced him to watch while his life was destroyed." His voice actually cracked. "And then we watched as he held him . . . as he rocked back and forth in front of the throne for hours, covered in blood."

Avery could barely breathe. She tried to blink away the image of Chase holding his son's body, but it hung there in front of her, worse than she could have ever imagined.

"And he threatened you over it."

"He didn't need to threaten me." Kern snorted, his usual inso-lent demeanor back. "You know that's not his style. He asked if I would take part in something His Majesty didn't know about—couldn't know about—and I said yes. I didn't even need to ask what it was. I'd do almost anything for him to make up for what I didn't do before."

He met her eyes, just long enough for her to see the guilt and pain there, then looked away.

"I know what you think about Haedera, especially Imperial Security. I know you think we're violent barbarians, and I know you think I'm a monster, but that—I was never involved in anything like that before. Until I watched His Majesty kill a child and did nothing about it. I couldn't have prevented it, but I should have tried anyway. You want to talk about monsters? That man was—is," he quickly corrected himself "—the monster."

Was?

With all his time on Asria, Kern was forgetting what it was like to be Haederan. It was no wonder he wanted to get home, back to the woman waiting on him, back to the status quo, back to his real life. Ignoring the existence of his emperor was a sure way to get himself killed. She turned to make sure Victor was still knocked out, the pity she felt for Kern—and Chase—too uncomfortable to focus on.

Kern hit the brakes, and she flew forward, barely catching herself before her head hit the dashboard of the car.

"What are you doing?"

"Checkpoint." His face was grim.

"Can't you talk your way through?" Her heart began to race. The fact he'd stopped like that meant he didn't think he could. "It's an army one, isn't it? Won't they let you by?"

"It's not a permanent one, and if I'm not mistaken, it was just set up tonight. I don't know what they're looking for, and I can't take the chance it's you." He glanced into the dark back seat at their unconscious captive. "Or him."

"Or you."

"Yeah." Kern sighed again, and this time it sounded like fear more than anything else.

There was one place that was safe—and probably empty now, thanks to Chase. She didn't know how to break a lock, but there was no doubt Kern could do it in under five seconds, and that was if Imperial Security hadn't left the door unlocked to begin with. Did she dare offer? They didn't have much of a choice.

"I know somewhere we can go."

* * *

It was dark under the staircase in the alley next to Wynne's flat, but Avery sat frozen in place. Kern had dragged Victor from the car in the back side of the alley without anyone noticing, but neither of them were eager to leave the safety of the shadows.

"Wait here." He checked his chronometer again, then fiddled with his pistol. "I'll go up."

"No, wait." Avery pulled him back down by his sleeve as he moved to stand. "Let me do it."

"If anyone sees you, they might recognize you." Kern looked irritated for the first time that evening. "Whereas if they see me knocking on her door, they'll be too afraid to interfere. Hell, they won't look out their windows for another three hours."

Avery checked Victor's pulse, delaying her acknowledgement Kern was right. "Fifteen minutes. If you're not back . . ."

"I'll be back."

She collapsed back into the shadows and tried not to shiver in the steadily dropping temperature, but true to his word, he was back in less than five.

"Here you go," he said, handing her a pistol. "Good news— she's home."

"What?" Chase had suggested they wouldn't hold Wynne very long, but she hadn't dared believe it was the truth. "How?"

"Don't know." He shrugged. "The bad news is that I don't think she believed me when I said you were down here, and I doubt she handed over her only weapon. Now you can go first.

I'm not keen on her blowing my head off when I go back up there."

Avery shoved Wynne's pistol in her pocket and slunk across the alley to the stairs. Kern followed, slower under Victor's weight. The door was still unlocked, and she nuzzled it open, hoping she wouldn't be greeted by a barrage of gunfire.

But Wynne was standing right in the center of her living room and looked . . . well, terrified was an understatement. The terror turned to anger when she recognized Avery, then back to fear when she saw Victor, tossed over Kern's shoulder. Her mouth opened, but Avery cut her off before she could speak.

"Wynne, we needed somewhere to go. I'm sorry we're here, I'm sorry we've put you in more danger, and I'm sorry—" How could she phrase this? Even Wynne, fearless as she was, must have been terrified when the Imperial Security Command had come knocking on her door in the middle of the night. "I'm sorry they arrested you because of some foolish idea I had."

"Never mind that." Wynne exhaled. "But what do you mean by bringing him here?" Kern, not Victor, judging by her scathing tone. Although it was hard to tell. After all, Wynne had been furious so long ago when Avery had told her she wanted to overthrow the Haederans alone. Risk wasn't her specialty.

But loyalty was.

"I didn't have a choice. I couldn't drag Victor here on my own."

"You shouldn't be dragging him anywhere! Especially with him." Wynne sighed. "You trust this man? This Haederan?"

"No." Avery glanced at Kern, who'd dumped Victor on the floor and was checking out the windows, pretending to ignore their conversation. "I don't trust him one bit."

Kern snickered at the window.

"I see. And what's your plan for—ah—"

"Victor?"

Wynne narrowed her eyes at the form of address, too distant

for Avery and too informal for her. "For the viceroy, Your Majesty."

"I hadn't thought that far ahead."

"Of course you hadn't," Wynne snapped at her. "You never think. You just act."

If Wynne only knew how much thinking and planning and strategizing this had taken. She'd wanted Victor to pay for his sins for months.

"Wynne, look. Just sit down and listen, please."

Wynne sat uncomfortably on a chair after shooting Kern's back another scathing look.

"It's a long story," Avery began. "And I know you think I'm naïve and a child, but—he's helping me. And he was helping you too, really." She recounted what Chase had told her. "You must know the arrests have started again. The Haederan Army wasn't going to leave you alone much longer."

And that was her fault as well. Everything was her fault.

"She was low on the list, though why they weren't more suspicious of the queen's former bodyguard is beyond me." Kern shook his head, clearly appalled by the army's decision. "No matter now. They won't bother her now as long as she keeps her head down. Defense Forces personnel of special security interest are our responsibility," he confirmed.

"Then I suppose he can stay for a while. I don't like it, but . . ." Wynne nodded at him, most of her hostility gone. If she was this forgiving, Chase hadn't lied—they really hadn't bothered her too much. She picked up the cup of tea from beside her and stared at it, then at Avery. "I just have one question. You're not really with him, are you?"

Avery laughed. "Not if he was the last man in the galaxy."

A small smile crossed Kern's face.

Wynne laughed back. "Good. Then I have a surprise for you in the bedroom."

CHAPTER TWENTY-NINE

AVERY KNOCKED FOUR TIMES ON THE DOOR PER WYNNE'S instructions, then slowly pushed it open. The bedroom was dark; not even moonlight shone through the blackout curtains. She didn't dare get closer to the closet if Merritt was armed as Wynne had said. She stopped in the doorway instead, prepared to duck back outside if the worst happened.

"Merritt," she whispered. "It's me."

Her voice might as well have lit up the room. The light that flashed on from the opposite side of the room certainly did. Before she could step inside, Merritt was up and across the room. She threw her arms around his neck and buried her face in his shoulder, trying to hold back tears. He tried to lift her face to his, doubtless intending to kiss her, but she clung so tightly to him that he let go.

"Just let me hold on to you for a second. Please." Her fingers drifted down his jawline. "I need to know you're really here."

"I'm really here," he said into her ear.

He smiled, and even in the shadows she could see the smile in his eyes as well. He was so solid beneath her hands, and his scent, the lightest smell of sandalwood soap, was painfully familiar.

She drew in a shaky breath and looked up to the familiar outline of his face. "But how—"

Merritt shook his head. "One kiss and I'll tell you everything."

"Deal."

She closed her eyes, and if she hadn't been convinced before that he was standing in front of her, she was now. Merritt's hand was behind her head, his lips were pushing into hers, and he was pulling her closer until she was wrapped in him, safe from the entire world.

Safe.

Chilled for the first time since she'd left the shadows of the alleyway, she pulled away.

"Mer, are you safe here?"

"Safe enough." Merritt's gaze fell to the pistol and the stun pistol holstered at his waist. "As things get these days, I suppose."

"But that won't get you out of here if the Haederans see you."

"Then they won't see me," Merritt said in amusement. "They didn't see Wynne sneak me up here, did they? They didn't catch me the entire way from Villiers, either."

"Teruel let you go?" Her eyes widened. Merritt hadn't snuck out, had he? Like she had with Elex Feye not so long ago?

"Well, I don't think he thought he could keep me there once we got word you were back on Asria. Do I get to hear that entire story now?"

She didn't want to talk about that, but Merritt deserved to know what she was doing on Asria, sheltered by the uncle she hated, so she started with the flight to Ventana, the stop at Brisia, their inception by the Haederan cruiser. She left out the part about Kanmar and March—there was no point in worrying Merritt with their story now, especially if they were safe on Emot.

"And then," she finished, "*he* offered me security on Asria if I agreed to support him." She couldn't even say the name of the man lying unconscious in Wynne's living room.

"And you agreed."

"I had a reason." There was no condemnation in Merritt's voice, but she felt a powerful compulsion to justify her decision to him anyway. "This war won't last forever. It can't possibly. The only other choice was letting them take me to Haedera, and I couldn't do that. I had to get back here, even if it cost me everything. Because—"

She took a deep breath and laid her head on his shoulder again.

"Because you're going to have a son," she said, her tears wetting his shirt. "And I will do anything and everything I can to protect him."

She stared up at him, her heart pounding. Merritt blinked, and it was the only response she could distinguish in the dim light. Why wasn't he saying anything? Was he angry? What was he *thinking*?

"I can't believe how much I love you." He reached out a hand and placed it gently on her stomach. "I can't believe how lucky I am."

"I didn't want to tell you like this. Mer, I'm so sorry about everything."

"Sorry? Love, this isn't something to be sorry for. Not in the slightest. This is something to celebrate, and we will. Soon. I promise."

"I made a terrible decision," she admitted. "I shouldn't have agreed to what Victor wanted."

"You did what you thought you had to do with the information and options you had at the time. I can't believe allowing yourself to be taken to Haedera as a prisoner would have been the right decision." He ran his fingers down her cheek, and she shivered. "Agreeing to his demands wasn't the wrong thing to do. Do you know how I know?"

"How?" If he kept being so reasonable, she was going to cry even harder.

"Because we're together now."

"Not for long." Avery glanced around the dark room. "We

can't stay here much longer. They have to be closing in on us by now. And Perrin—he won't rest until he finds me."

"It's the safest place right now. I thought I'd have to break into the palace to find you—you really saved me some trouble."

"Merritt, I don't want you to risk this for me."

"Perhaps you're forgetting the roles society has placed upon us, Your Majesty." Merritt grinned. "Not," he added, "that I wouldn't do this for you, whoever you were. If I don't risk my life for you, what's left?"

She gripped his hand tighter. His love had always been too humbling.

"But you look absolutely shattered." He brushed a loose strand of hair from her face. "Look, we can't go anywhere tonight. I was only hiding out here until I could get closer to the palace tomorrow morning, but now that you're here, sleep. You get some rest, and tomorrow morning we'll decide our next move, whether that's heading to Villiers or somewhere else."

She nodded and let Merritt lead her to the bed. Heading out to Villiers that very second sounded better to her, but Merritt was right. She could barely move, and Perrin would be sure to spot their small group moving through the empty capital in the dark.

The last thing she remembered was her head in his lap and his hand wound through her hair.

* * *

Whispers drifted into her dreams. They wanted something from her, wanted her to wake, wanted her to do things, wanted her to make decisions, wanted her to leave this warm cocoon and head again into that raw, cold world. And she couldn't, she just couldn't. Not now.

"She needs to see this, sir. Now." Wynne's voice was quiet but insistent.

The next thing she knew, Merritt was shaking her gently. "I think you'll want to see this, love."

"What time is it?" She rubbed her eyes. "Can coffee be involved?"

"Already brewed."

He smiled, pulled her out of bed by the hand, and led her to Wynne's small living room. It was cramped with the four of them, and Avery eyed the front door as she sat. She didn't ask Kern what he'd done with Victor, but judging by the foot he'd thrown casually across his opposite knee, there was nothing to worry about on that front.

"All right," she said as Merritt set the steaming up beside her. "What's so exciting this early in the morning?"

Wynne handed her a small tablet and hit the power button.

"I'm sorry it's recorded," she said. "From yesterday morning. I usually check more frequently than this, but . . ." She glanced around the room at the motley group. "There was a little too much excitement last night for me to remember."

Even at Villiers, Avery hadn't ever seen what the Haederans referred to as propaganda broadcasts, the transmissions from Asrian resistance bases they'd been trying to stamp out for the past year. But here it was, a woman wearing the uniform of a Defense Forces major, sitting in front of an Asrian flag.

"An unknown source provided these photos," she was saying, "corroborating the high-level report that it was Haederan special operations troops, not Asrian resistance members, who were responsible for the carnage at Tarragona."

The coffee forgotten, Avery leaned forward, hands on her mouth, as photos scrolled across the screen. There wasn't anything else to say. She was clearly the high-level source, but photos? She hadn't taken photos. But there they were on the screen, six men in sanitized Defense Forces uniforms standing there in the garrison courtyard in Tarragona. They were all dark-haired, to be sure, but in these pictures, they didn't look remotely Asrian.

"You did it. You proved Perrin was behind the explosion."

There was grudging admiration in Kern's voice as he drained his third cup of coffee since she'd awaken.

"I only told Wynne what had happened. I didn't take pictures of them!" She looked at Kern in horror. The pictures were clearer than anything she could have wished for. Certainly less foggy than her memories of that night had become. "And neither did you. We were together the entire time at the garrison."

"No, I didn't." His admiration faded, replaced by something as close to fear as he'd probably ever experienced. "And no one else in Imperial Security would have taken and released them to an Asrian resistance media source. No one," he repeated. "Do you understand that?"

"Wynne." Her jaw was tight at what Kern hadn't said as she stood and paced in front of Merritt's chair. "Did you tell them about this before or after—"

"Imperial Security arrested me?" Wynne shot an acidic smile at Kern. "Before. I couldn't tell my contact how I knew, though, and I don't think anyone believed me. That's why it took so long to get this released."

"Excuse me." Kern stepped into the kitchen with Merritt behind him. Muffled words echoed, some between the two of them, some on a comm. "Bad news," he said when he came back. The circles under his eyes had grown darker in the past minute and a half. "There's a detain-on-sight order for you. Perrin is —angry."

Well, that was to be expected.

"So we sit here," Avery said. "We'll be safe for a while."

"Well, there's a problem with that." Kern hesitated. "Somehow he had found out that Major Ferran was released from Imperial Security custody. They'll be looking here next."

Merritt blew out a deep breath. "Then we're getting out of here. Now."

"And going where, Colonel?" Kern's sneer showed through his fatigue. "Lots of people are looking for you as well. If you're the only help she has, the two of you won't get far."

"I'll get her to safety." Merritt looked him up and down slowly. Trust him to be the one to treat an Imperial Security Command officer with borderline contempt. "Don't worry about that."

"We need to split up. You get to Villiers," Avery said to Wynne. Kern couldn't know the resolute tone in Merritt's voice, but she did, and there would be no arguing with him now. "Take Victor. He needs to answer for what he's done, and I'll just hold you back." She turned her attention to Kern. "Look, Captain, I won't ask you to do anything you'll regret, but you're neck-deep in this already. Will you help her?"

"You're actually asking me to go to Villiers." Kern sounded afraid Wynne would drag him there along with Victor no matter how much he protested. Or maybe he was just resigned to his immediate future, suddenly out of his control. "You know what'll happen to me there."

The flat fell silent, except for the soft murmurs on the tablet. Wynne pushed the power button to silence it and stared uncomfortably at Kern. At the crossed swords on his collar. Had she remembered he was Haederan? The enemy?

"You'll be treated fairly," Avery said. It was the truth. It *had* to be the truth. "You have my word on that. Wynne?"

"I'll do everything I can." She pursed her lips. "Whether or not they listen to me is a different story."

Kern muttered something that sounded like agreement, set his coffee cup on the windowsill, and nodded at Wynne.

"Then let's get the former viceroy out of here, ma'am."

Avery and Merritt gave them a ten-minute head start. Just sitting there seemed a waste of precious time alone, but they could only stare at each other, frozen on Wynne's sofa. Was he as afraid as she was? She squeezed his hand, wishing there was another option. Some other choice besides walking out into certain danger.

Only the hope that Wynne and Kern would make it to Villiers with Victor kept her from falling apart.

No. It was Merritt's steady breathing next to her that kept her sane. Only his faith that they'd be safe as well.

Wynne had turned the lights and heat off, hoping the Haederans would assume the flat had been unoccupied for some time, and the frosty night air was leaking in. Avery shivered, though whether that was fear or the weather, she never would have been able to decide.

"All right." Merritt wrapped an arm around her, and his warmth gradually eased the shivering. "Let's go."

Avery didn't argue, couldn't bear to sit there one more second. Whatever was going to happen needed to happen, and it needed to happen quickly. There wasn't any point in putting it off, and so hand in hand, they tiptoed down the stairs. The winter air hit her, fully waking her and dissolving any residual warmth. Between the curfew and the coming storm, the alley was quiet and cold, the main street silent.

It was a deceptive calm. Even though Kern and Wynne had moved away from the flat unnoticed, the Haederans would close in on this part of town before long. The car Merritt had brought over the mountains was another five kilometers away, and Avery had little hope they'd find it without being spotted. She stuck to the shadows next to the building, a hand on the rough brick wall to keep her balance. There was no snow accumulating on the leaves that blew through the narrow way, but the ground was slick enough to be dangerous.

They hadn't gone two blocks when the humming began. It might mean nothing—curfew violations were frequent, especially in the more crowded sections of Cadena—but it might mean everything.

Her heart threatened to stop when she recognized the tune.

A Haederan folk song.

But the lack of stealth meant he was a routine sentry, a regular Haederan Army police officer—like she'd thought Chase had been—not the soldiers sent to find her. That was something, at least. Still, if they turned around now, if they ran, he would be suspicious.

"Kiss me," Merritt said under his breath. "Quickly."

He shoved her against the wall, his arm across her forehead, and pressed chilly lips to hers. There was no intimacy there, no love, just brutally efficient strength. The aloofness and the feel of the icy wall against her back made her struggle for just an instant, made her put her hands on his chest and try to push him away. He pushed her back against the wall even harder and squeezed her hand, as if to say *sorry about that*.

The unsaid apology was enough. She relaxed against the brick, praying that Merritt hadn't acted too slowly and that the darkness hid her features. Maybe this Haederan soldier wouldn't hassle a couple of young lovers. Maybe he'd issue a stern warning and move on—or escort them home at the very worst. Maybe he wouldn't notice Merritt was carrying not one, but two pistols.

Maybe.

She closed her eyes as the humming came closer, then stopped.

"You know you're out past curfew, sir." The soldier sounded young and intimidated. "By several hours, in fact. Got an explanation?"

Merritt parted her lips with his tongue and kissed her deeper, ignoring the question, then pried himself away and laughed.

"Come on, Corporal," he said, affecting a deeper Asrian accent than usual. "Her parents don't like me. I bet you know what that's like. Can't you cut a guy some slack?"

"And an alley in the middle of a snowstorm is the best you can do?" The corporal snorted amusement and pity. "You there—" He jerked his chin at her. "Come out of those shadows. Let me see you, too."

Merritt's eyes fell on hers, and her stomach dropped at the fear there. His hand slid from her chest to the pistol at his side, but she rejected his idea with her eyes—with the army closing in on them, a shot would be heard. Instead, she rested her head against him in reluctant compliance to the corporal's order, half-visible, but still shrouded in darkness.

Just like a young woman ashamed of being caught would do.

The Haederan laughed again. "Nabbed yourself one of those socialite girls, did you? It's no wonder her parents don't like you." He hesitated. "Look, just get inside. I don't care where you go, but I'll be back this way in half an hour. You two better be gone by that time. I don't want to arrest either of you, and you don't want that either."

His humming resumed, then grew quieter as he moved down the street. Avery breathed again into Merritt's chest, his heartbeat steadying her own and his body warming her soul.

Until the corporal swore out loud.

CHAPTER THIRTY

IN THE SILENCE OF THE NIGHT, THE SOLDIER'S SHOUTS ECHOED SO
loudly Avery could barely hear Merritt's footsteps behind her.
And the snow. Of course the snow Kern had predicted had started
and had started in earnest. It rarely happened so early in Cadena,
but it was falling around them now in clusters like stars, already
sticking to the north side of the street. Even so, Merritt's steps
were louder than they should have been. Her calves had started to
cramp ten minutes before, and she stopped to massage her right
leg. It was the wrong decision. Her breath had been short before,
but the break made starting again impossible.

"Merritt," she said, gasping for air. "I can't breathe. I need—I
need to take a break."

To his credit, he didn't question, just shouldered his way
through one of the less sturdy doors lining the alley.

"Inside."

What looked to be a warehouse was dark and smelled like
fuel, but it was safe, at least for now. They picked their way
through the empty building. An interior room—with a small
skylight that provided just enough moonlight to see—looked
good enough. Merritt locked the door from the inside, and Avery
sank down against the wall.

"What if we don't make it out of here?" she asked.

Merritt knelt next to her and massaged her calves. In the moon, his fear was visible. "We'll make it out."

"But what if we don't?"

He scooted up to her and pulled her close. "We always have before. Right?"

She sighed. "Right."

Even after that night Perrin had told her Merritt had been killed, they'd both survived, had both made it out of certain death. And now he sounded so sure things would work out the same way. That meant they might have a chance, no matter how slim the chance had been just five minutes before. How did he always sound so confident, so sure, when she was thirty seconds away from falling apart?

"But would you—would you mind if I prayed anyway?" he asked.

"I think we could use His help right now."

Merritt squeezed her hand and closed his eyes. A second later, voices rang through the building, and he swore and pulled her to her feet.

"We need to split up," she whispered. Even as she said the words, she stepped closer to him.

"Absolutely not." He didn't hesitate. Gripped her hand harder, in fact.

"Look, if one of us gets away, we can get help. Because if Kern and Wynne don't make it to Villiers, there's no way anyone will know we're in trouble, and it'll be hours before Kern and Wynne arrive there, anyway."

Even on the best of days, it wouldn't have been easy. Roadblocks, checkpoints, and now the snow. The mountains between Cadena and Villiers might be relatively low in elevation, but they'd become impassible if this weather kept up.

Merritt bit his lip, considering her argument. "Meet you in the city garden? Say by dawn? There's that small pavilion on the east side."

"Yes. All right."

Avery nodded and stepped toward the door. They'd picnicked there, so long ago, and she could find the place frozen and blind with fear. The Haederans wouldn't be looking for them in the middle of a park in a snowstorm.

"Wait." He grabbed her wrist and pulled her back toward him. "I love you, Avery."

She blinked back tears. "I love you too. And I'll see you soon."

Merritt squeezed her hand and was gone.

* * *

Her footsteps were silent on the cluttered floor of the warehouse right up until she tripped over another piece of scrap metal. Did she simply remain still and hope the Haederans didn't search this part of the building? She squeezed her eyes shut in a soundless prayer, a call for wisdom, then opened them to see searchlights flashing in the distance.

Around a corner, down a hall, it didn't matter where the Haederans were. They'd find her eventually. Probably sooner. She pressed herself against the wall and moved south, hoping the debris which littered the floor of the warehouse would be less piled up in that direction. If she could only find an exit to the back alley, she'd be able to disappear.

There—her fingers felt the doorframe, then the solidness of the heavy door.

And icy wind hit her face as she cracked it open and peered outside. Even with the snow, it was as shadowy in the alley as she'd expected, with only the sound of a small animal scurrying about. As carefully as she could manage, she shut the door, thankful the snow made her every move quieter than usual.

It was almost closed when her wrist went weak. The door lurched from her hand and slammed shut. She cursed under her breath, but there was no one here in the alley. If she ran, she could be gone before the Haederans located the source of the sound—

"There!"

His shout echoed in the alley. She spun in the other direction, abruptly and uselessly aware of how sodden her shoes had become. Her eyes focused on the three soldiers headed up from the south, then on two more coming from the opposite direction. Panicked, she grabbed hold of the door handle to cut back through the warehouse, but it had auto-locked from the inside.

Of course.

She pushed back the memory of her near-escape from the Haederan prison in Cadena that had left her with permanent scars. She'd been so close that time too, but that door had been locked as well. And that night they'd hurt her, really hurt her, for the first time, before bringing her to Chase, who'd—

She wouldn't think of what he'd done to her. Not now. Because the Haederans wouldn't harm her tonight. She was watched from on high. By the Haederan emperor himself. Victor had implied as much.

The chill of the evening sank deep inside of her—or was it the weather?

Because Victor wasn't around to protect her any longer. She'd made sure of that. And shooting Perrin, even with a stun pistol, had surely used all up all Haederans' mercy toward her. Their emperor was on Haedera, and Perrin was in Cadena, furious with her. Too furious to care whose orders he disobeyed.

With that realization, the memory of that night in the prison washed over her. The soldiers grabbed her as she fought to unlock the door, their ungloved hands like ice. She withdrew into herself, the only safe place, unable to fight. Their hands were all over her, searching her, then her feet were leading her through the snow of their own accord. She certainly wasn't ordering them to move.

But burning through the fog there was one bright spot, one small thing she could cling to, and it kept her from falling apart. If the Haederan Army had her now, that meant there were fewer of them searching for Merritt. He had gotten away, he had to have gotten away. And when she didn't show up in the garden in the morning, he'd do something. He'd promised everything would be all right.

"Got him on the other side of the building." The lieutenant's comm crackled at his side as they shoved her into a waiting car. "Meet you at Alcaris."

* * *

An hour later, Avery's head smacked against the side of the car as they pulled her back out, and she bit back a gasp. Behind her and the three soldiers who'd driven her in circles through the icy streets, a flight of Haederan interceptors screamed into the sky, and for a moment, the pain in her ears overshadowed the pain of their rough handling. She was grateful when they escorted her into the nearest building; the heavy doors blocked most of the jet noise that was making her nascent headache worse. But when she reoriented herself—

A kitchen.

The barracks kitchen?

"What is this?" Explanations swirled in her brain, but she couldn't pin down a rational one. "Where are you taking me?"

"Governor wants to see you," the lieutenant said.

"He wants to see me here?"

Even though she tensed every muscle she could, she couldn't stop shivering. This wasn't good. This wasn't good at all. Perrin had brought her somewhere she wouldn't be noticed. Somewhere where no one could interrupt whatever plans he had for her—and Merritt? The kitchen was devoid of any suggestion food might have been prepared there recently, and like the rest of the city, bitter cold.

She clenched her fists at her sides as they led her into the walk-in freezer. Merritt was there, seated in a chair with his arms crossed, plus Perrin and four other Haederan soldiers. Perrin had a deep red mark on his cheek where his head had met the floor in Victor's study. The headache he had must be bad enough, but he'd look worse tomorrow. She should have shot him twice. Merritt's face was a mask of granitelike fury which turned to horror when she entered. He jumped to his feet and tried to move toward her through the group of Haederans.

"Sit," Perrin said, stabbing a finger at him.

Three of the soldiers pulled their pistols. The fourth, a major she recognized from Perrin's office, put a hand on Merritt's arm and directed him back to the chair. Not caring what any of them thought or did about it, she ran to him, but he was silent as she embraced him. What had transpired before her arrival? Something terrible—why else had they spent so much time driving her around?

"Sir." The lieutenant who'd escorted her in looked uncomfortable at the scene. "There's an Imperial Security hold order on her." He swallowed. "Shouldn't we—"

"Shouldn't we what?" Perrin asked, aggravated.

"Hand her over to them, sir," the lieutenant suggested doubtfully.

"That was issued when she returned to Asria." Perrin waved a hand, and her stomach sank at his dismissiveness, even with Merritt next to her. "It's administrative. Nothing to worry about."

"Yes, sir. But what about Colonel Park—"

"Get out!" Perrin hollered at him.

The lieutenant scampered out the door—hopefully to alert someone, anyone, of what was going on.

She shook her head. What a foolish hope. The man might disagree with whatever Perrin had planned, but he'd never say a word, especially to the Imperial Security Command.

"Anyone else have a problem with this?" Perrin asked the soldiers, a hand on his forehead. Yes, that post-stun headache was firmly in place, and it couldn't have happened to a worthier person. The room was silent in response; not even the whirr of the refrigeration fan was audible, and he turned to Avery. "Did you really think you'd get away with it?"

Avery shook her head without knowing why. She'd done so

many things she'd thought she would get away with. Shooting Perrin was only one of them.

"No. But he had nothing to do with any of this. Let him go."

"Avery . . ." Merritt's voice was low, warning, but he didn't touch her.

"I don't care if he was involved or not," Perrin said.

"Why? What's your problem with him?"

Beside her, Merritt sucked in a deep breath. Was he that afraid of Perrin? Was she the only one in the room not afraid of him? Would no one else stand up and challenge him?

"Besides the fact you care about him?" Perrin turned pale, so quickly she wouldn't have noticed if she hadn't been staring at him, then red again. His hand flickered to his forehead, then back down before he could rub it again. "The Asrian bastard killed my son."

"He did what?" She raised her eyebrows at Merritt.

Something you want to tell me, Mer?

"The general seems to believe I shot down his son the night of the invasion." Merritt finally looked at Perrin. "Incredible, I know."

"That's ridiculous." Her gaze alternated between the two of them. She hadn't even known Perrin had a son. "Even if your son was—even if he was shot down that night, you can't possibly know who—"

"Colonel Parker was flying a Nightflare during the offensive, was he not?"

Colonel Rendon.

"So were hundreds of others," Merritt said steadily.

More like thousands.

Avery opened her mouth, then closed it. And Perrin couldn't possibly know which Nightflare had shot down his son's ship. Could he?

"I watched his ship explode. I felt him die." Perrin clenched his fists. "And you were the only one who called in a kill from that sector at the time. You were the only one who made a report about that kill when you all retreated to the surface. You think your Defense Forces destroyed *all* the mission reports that night before we made it to the surface?"

Beside her, Merritt's entire body stiffened. Judging by Perrin's sneer, she wasn't the only one who noticed the movement.

"One of the first things I had my techs do when we took Alcaris," Perrin went on, "was to go through the remains of the mission files from the invasion. We pieced them all back together. It was you." That last was accompanied by a hiss and a stab of his finger toward Merritt.

There it was. Perrin didn't hate Merritt because of what he meant to her. No, it was something far more personal, something he'd never forgive. Something she couldn't argue with—but would anyway.

"They wouldn't have been firing on your ships in the first place if you hadn't attacked us." She raised her voice as she stepped away from Merritt. "And you can't possibly call what the Defense Forces did an *attack*. You invaded our home! Even you aren't shortsighted enough to ignore that truth."

"You could have surrendered as soon as the fleet entered your system. We gave you that chance, but you fought instead. It's you who's responsible for those deaths, and he will pay for them."

Perrin snapped his fingers at the soldiers surrounding them.

Before Avery could take another breath, before she could argue that she'd had no say in the Defense Force's decision to fight—not that she'd have made a different one—they pulled her away from Merritt. She kicked so hard her feet lifted off the ground, but it didn't make a difference.

"Avery, don't."

Merritt had never used that harsh tone with her before. It made her stop faster than anything the Haederans could have done to her.

Merritt is afraid for me.

Perrin swung twice at him as they held her back. She didn't hear the impacts—only her own screams.

CHAPTER THIRTY-ONE

MERRITT FELL TO HIS KNEES FROM THE BLOW TO HIS STOMACH, AND Avery reached for him, knowing she'd never make it the five steps between them. The soldiers pulled her right back, gripping her tighter as she struggled. Her heart pounded against her chest, but she ignored it, because what was the point any longer?

"Let him go." She'd say it over and over again until Perrin listened to her. "Let him go."

"You are not in charge here, and you have defied me for the last time." Perrin raised his eyebrows, his upper lip twisting into a snarl. "From the first day, you've been nothing but a nuisance, and now you're a threat. I won't tolerate it any longer. If this was Haedera, you'd be dead already. Thanks to His Majesty, I can't touch you, but I don't really need to, do I? Not with the one you love the most right here." His eyes dropped from hers, landing lower. "Although . . . maybe I'm wrong about exactly where."

He shook his hand out and wriggled his fingers around. If only he'd broken a few on Merritt's jaw. Then, like he'd read her mind, like he knew the worst thing he could do, he reached out and brushed those unfortunately not-broken fingers against her stomach.

She hadn't felt sick all night, not until now. Her stomach

twisted in a light, feathery movement, and she couldn't hold back the tears any longer. Her son was finally moving within her. Didn't he know what was happening? That she and Merritt couldn't protect him?

Perrin turned to lift Merritt's head by the chin. "I think I'll let you pick which one of them you lose. You can live out your life on Haedera wondering where it all went wrong. Until the emperor decides you've suffered long enough, that is. Maybe he'll have pity on you and make it quick."

Her eyes swept from Perrin's bitter smile to the blood dripping from Merritt's mouth. The tears fell harder, erasing both men. It was an impossible choice, yet she knew he was serious.

"Avery." Merritt shook his head. "Don't listen to him. This isn't a choice you have to make."

"She will make it," Perrin said. "In the next thirty seconds, or she will lose both."

"It's not your choice," Merritt insisted. "He won't harm you— or my child."

Somehow, she bit back the cry that was forcing itself up.

Because Merritt had already decided for her.

But she couldn't let him—she couldn't. Why wouldn't time stop? Why couldn't she have just one more day, just one more hour, just one more minute before this insanity took their lives? Why had she insisted she and Merritt split up earlier that night? They might have had a chance if they'd stuck with Wynne and Kern. Especially Wynne. Her former bodyguard would be devastated when she learned of this.

Why had she destroyed her own life?

You didn't destroy anything. Perrin is doing this to you, to Merritt, to your son, to Asria. This isn't your fault.

Her own argument fell on deaf ears, but she nodded agreement to Merritt's choice.

"Good," Perrin said. "Not that I'm surprised. And now that he's made that decision for you—where is he?"

"Where—" Her head spun. She couldn't have answered

Perrin's question if she'd wanted to. Didn't even know how to answer it. "Where is who?"

Perrin's fist met Merritt's jaw. The crack of bone on bone echoed somehow beneath her screams, but Merritt merely gritted his teeth together harder.

"Captain Brennin Kern. The Haederan traitor you convinced to kidnap your uncle." Perrin chuckled as he shook his hand out again. "I wonder how you could have convinced him. Maybe you aren't as faithful to Colonel Parker as he thinks you are. It wouldn't surprise me. You've been separated for so long that you must have finally realized how ruined he is."

"I don't—I don't know what you're talking about." Her chest tightened. It wasn't enough for him to hurt Merritt. It wasn't enough to kill him right in front of her. Perrin meant to destroy him emotionally first. "Merritt, I never—"

She snapped her mouth shut. Why was she playing Perrin's game? She wouldn't deny something she hadn't done. Merritt knew the truth.

"My lady." Coffee and the faintest hint of liquor swirled around her as he stepped closer. "You'd best not play games with me. If you don't tell me where they went, I'm certain you'll tell Gareth Chase, and I'll be more understanding than he will be. You wouldn't want me to call him in, would you?"

"I—"

"You've got fifteen minutes to decide who you'd rather talk to," Perrin added.

"Fifteen minutes?" Her breaths became quick gasps. Chase was here? Well, he had to spend his nights somewhere. Alcaris made as much sense as anywhere else. "He's here?"

"Somewhere." Perrin smiled, evidently mistaking her relief for fear. "I'm sure you'd rather tell me where Captain Kern took the viceroy before he makes his way to this building."

Fifteen minutes.

She just had to hold out fifteen minutes. Perrin might find Chase's skills useful, but he was afraid of him, and Chase had nothing but disdain for the general. He would help. He would do something. Even he wouldn't allow this brutality.

Especially him.

"Major," Perrin said to the soldier behind her. "Find Colonel Chase. He should be in the Imperial Security building. If he's not there, try their barracks. Wake him up if you have to."

"Yes, sir."

The major scampered past Avery with a smirk, and waiting for his return was the longest fifteen minutes of her life. Merritt stood, unsteadily but unchallenged by the Haederans, questioning her with his eyes, but she shook her head. If it was answers he was after, she didn't have those. Reassurance? She didn't have that for him either.

Especially not when the Haederan nearest him, noticing Merritt's glance at the chair, kicked it away. Merritt put a hand on the wall instead. Perrin, perhaps realizing his punching bag was recovering too quickly, struck him on the cheek with the back of his hand. Merritt slipped down the wall without a sound, and one of the soldiers kicked him in the ribs.

"Stop." Her protest was weak. "You have to stop."

"You were looking for me, General?" The familiar voice made her jump. "Strange place for an evening meeting."

Avery couldn't turn around, too afraid her relief would show. She closed her eyes instead and willed her betraying smile away.

"One of your officers abducted the viceroy tonight—after your prisoner shot me." Perrin pointed at the mark on his face which was becoming darker by the minute. "She's responsible. She knows where they went. I want you to find out, and quickly."

"One of my officers?" Chase asked with mild surprise. "I find that hard to believe . . ."

Avery stared at him. He'd trailed off because he was coming up with a story. Something he could say to protect Kern, and by extension, her.

Make something up. You're good at that, Colonel.

". . . but I wouldn't be surprised if she made it appear that way. She's been deceitful and unmanageable from the moment I met her." His eyes were cold. "You didn't really think she'd settled down and accepted this occupation, did you, General?"

Avery's entire body went numb.

"Well, find out," Perrin repeated, his voice dripping skepticism and impatience. "I don't feel like standing around here all night."

It was strange how one could feel evil, even without seeing it. It circled around her, in front of her, taking up the entire room. When she opened her eyes to the sensation, Chase stood there, less than a pace away, staring at her with sickening confidence. She'd seen that look before, long ago when he'd first confronted her in his office about her work for the Commonwealth. She hadn't known then how bad things were about to get—hadn't known the things he'd do to her.

She knew now.

But now he was acting.

He had to be acting.

But what if he wasn't?

Chase was Haederan. An Imperial Security Command officer, the cruelest of them all. He had no loyalty to her, no love for Asria, and nothing but contempt for the Commonwealth. He'd brutalized her and destroyed her life. No matter how much he'd denied it, he'd probably had everything to do with her parents' deaths. He'd likely ordered their executions himself. After all, her uncle was the perfect one to accuse. Chase had been kind to her occasionally, yes, but he was capricious. Always had been.

Only capricious wasn't the right word, because nothing he did was random. Every decision he made, everything he'd done for her or refused her had a reason behind it. *I can't question the prisoner if she's screaming in pain,* she'd once overheard him say to the medic in the prison in Cadena. Helping her had been a means to an end. Maybe every kindness over the past months had been to gain her trust, to keep her off guard for just this kind of situation.

The tears she'd shed while watching Perrin hurt Merritt had dried, but her left eye grew blurry, as it always did when she was tired or stressed. Her cheek stung, like it remembered the force of Chase's hand against it, remembered every beating by the guards. The beatings he'd allowed.

No, not allowed.

Encouraged.

Ordered.

The corners of Chase's eyes crinkled. "Remember that long conversation I promised you at the viceroy's party?" he asked. "It seems we're going to have it after all." He let the smile he'd been holding in escape. "I can't wait. But let's find somewhere a little more private to have it, shall we?"

Oh, yes. Trusting him had been a *terrible* mistake.

"No. You can't." Avery took a step back, forgetting the Haederan soldiers behind her. She stumbled over their feet, barely staying on hers. Chase took her by the arm and twisted her toward the door, away from Merritt. "I won't leave him!"

"He stays here," Perrin told the soldiers standing next to Merritt, as if there was any question as to whose orders they'd follow.

"Wait." Chase jerked her to a stop and turned to look at Merritt with disdain. "She's right."

Avery began to shiver.

"I want them both," he said, not bothering to look at her. She wanted to scream at Chase to leave him alone, but her voice had fled her, along with any courage she'd been clinging to. "You know," he went on, "I've always wondered what would have happened if I'd used him to get to you. Would you have broken sooner? I thought I'd never know the answer, but it seems I have a second chance to find out."

Perrin shrugged his frustrated and impatient consent and nodded at the soldiers behind Merritt to pull him up. Chase tightened his grip as she tried to step toward him.

"I want him back alive," Perrin cut in.

"You needn't worry about that," Chase said. That familiar

disdain swept from Merritt to Perrin. "Some of us know what finesse is."

"I don't have time for your subtlety, Colonel. I said alive, not unharmed."

Chase's jaw tightened. "If it's information you want, you'll let me do my job. If you simply want to keep beating him, then by all means—continue as you were before. Sir."

Perrin's face turned red at the accusation and Chase's undisguised scorn. "Then do your job. And do it quickly."

* * *

They tossed her and Merritt in a holding cell in the Imperial Security building that had been her protection just days earlier. Literally threw in Merritt's case, though Avery wasn't sure how much of that was intentional and how much of it was his unsteadiness on his feet. She helped him lie down on the metal bench, and he closed his eyes. She wanted to talk to him, to see how badly he was injured, to discuss how they'd find a way out, but the two Haederan soldiers who'd brought them there were standing right outside the bars. She ran her fingers through his hair instead, thankful the cell didn't have a solid door. That would have been the end of everything.

Besides their breathing and the occasional cough of the sergeant outside, the cell and hallway were silent, like a tomb. She'd expected it to begin immediately, per Perrin's impatient orders, but a long wait made more sense. Chase was giving her time to think about what was going to happen. Time to anticipate. Time to worry. Time to remember just how easily he could make her say anything he wanted. He'd done it before, hadn't he?

And now he had Merritt.

He'd said he wondered if he should have used Merritt last year. If he'd known Merritt had been alive, would he have? Really? Probably not. The whole thing was a game to him. She'd challenged him, and he'd welcomed the challenge. Like his disdain for nonexistent truth serum, using Merritt would have been too easy—a waste of his skills.

Even so, she had to wonder what she would have done if Chase *had* forced her to choose between Merritt and Asria. The obvious answer, the one Merritt and the senate and the Commonwealth would have expected her to make, was Asria, of course. Intellectually, it was easy. But deep in her gut . . . was it that easy of a decision? The question was too painful to contemplate—and it bordered on treason. What kind of leader was she?

She flung that thought away. It was over and done with. Chase hadn't used Merritt against her, and she hadn't betrayed Asria to save him. Hypothetical situations weren't helping anyone. She had to focus on the present. She had to break the silence, had to get the two Haederans on her side before Chase came back for her and Merritt.

"He's an escaped prisoner, you know."

The corporal jumped at her voice. Merritt opened his eyes, then narrowed them at her.

"He belongs in the prison camp on Emot," she said. "And you know it. You don't want to be involved in what Perrin intends for him. I know you don't. You don't want to be caught up in his personal revenge."

The young corporal's childlike eyes grew hazy at that. Anxious. She could almost hear the disquieted wheels turn in his head.

Good. He was the one to focus on.

"You can't kill him, Corporal," she went on. "Do you want to answer for that if the Commonwealth ever finds out what you've done here?"

Not that they ever would, but he didn't know that. If anyone was going to help her, it would be this young soldier who was looking more and more skeptical by the second.

"I guess he'll be shot trying to escape," the sergeant said, giving the corporal a look of annoyance and slamming her hope to bits. "Now shut up. You'll have plenty of time to talk later."

Avery sat back, her mind spinning. There was a remote chance —but no. She and Merritt could never take all three of them at once, and that wasn't even considering whoever else was in the building. Hopeless. There was only one way this would end.

But it would end with her and Merritt together.

Chase's boots sounded in the hallway a half hour later as she reclined against the wall with her eyes closed. It was sooner than she'd expected. Sooner than she'd wanted, definitely, but Perrin had made his timeframe clear.

He looked from Merritt to her then back again and nodded at the soldiers. "Interview room two. And watch her. She doesn't have much to lose."

So, Perrin hadn't been exaggerating—he did plan to send her to Haedera after killing Merritt. After the trouble she'd caused over the past few days, she should have expected it. Once Perrin's story reached him, the Haederan emperor would want to witness her execution himself. She wouldn't live long after she arrived there—not that she would want to. Not without Merritt.

"Out." The sergeant pressed a button to open the bars and gestured at them with his pistol. "Now."

"I can't walk."

Merritt sounded frail. Sick. It wasn't like him to admit to weakness, especially in front of *them,* and Avery shot a frightened glance at him. He shook his head wildly, his eyes latching on to hers.

There was no fear there.

He's not as injured as he's letting on.

"I'm going to help him." She held her hands up, palms toward the soldiers, trying to assure them that was all she meant to do. "Merritt, it's going to be all right."

The sergeant snorted his disagreement as she helped Merritt out of the cell. Chase was down the hall, preoccupied with the keypad to an interrogation room. He keyed in his code—once, twice, three times, shaking his head at the pad as he did so—then pressed his fingers against it.

Her heart pounded as she watched. Once the security system verified his fingerprints, they were out of time. But her eyes met Merritt's again, and this time there wasn't just a lack of fear.

There was hope. Confidence.

Avery squeezed his hand, and they both lunged.

CHAPTER THIRTY-TWO

The sergeant went down under Merritt's weight like a feather, and Avery flung herself at the corporal. Mouth open, he glanced from her to the sergeant, already lying on the ground. His hesitation was a terminal mistake, for Merritt's first shot hit him in the back. Chase turned at the sound, hand on his stun pistol, but she'd already taken the corporal's gun. Her warning shot hit the door next to Chase's head, and he held his hands out to the sides.

"Toss that to Merritt," she ordered. "Now."

He complied with a condescending smile, even with two guns pointed at him. It was amazing. Did the man ever let go of his arrogance?

"It won't fire for him," Chase said as Merritt grabbed the stun pistol and shoved it in his pocket. "Or you."

Avery sighed inwardly and raised the corporal's gun to his head. Kern's had, but it would be just like to Chase to have a pistol with a fingerprint interlock.

"This one probably will," she replied.

"You don't want to do that." Hands in the air, Chase suddenly sounded very serious.

"No, I really think she wants to do that," Merritt replied, steadying himself against the wall.

"Open that cell back up and drag them inside," she said. "Or I'll shoot you too." She backed against the wall, relieved when Chase immediately complied with that instruction as well. It might only be seconds until one or both soldiers woke up.

"Now what?" Chase asked.

Yes, now what?

It wasn't as though she had a plan. She hadn't known she and Merritt had had enough of a chance to make a plan.

"Merritt?"

"How many people are in this building?" Merritt asked.

"You two have no idea what you're doing, do you?" Chase's arrogant grin was back. "Did you really hope you'd accomplish something like this? Just the two of you, no backup, no strategy—"

Avery wanted to shoot him, just to rid him of that smile.

"How many?" she repeated.

"No one else. It's been evacuated."

Evacuated?

"Why?" She sniffed the air. No fire. Not even the least bit of smoke. Were the Haederans afraid of a bit of snow? That was possible, but unlikely—they'd been in Cadena for a winter already. A small snowstorm wasn't anything new.

Chase just watched her, silent. She wanted to lock him in with the soldiers, but he could simply reach through the bars and unlock the cell with a handprint. Why hadn't the Haederans ever anticipated locking up their own people? Did they only do that on Haedera?

She suppressed a hysterical laugh at the inconsistency. "Handcuffs. Toss them over."

Doubt flickered in Chase's eyes for the first time. "You aren't really going to . . ."

"Yes, I am really going to, and if you don't want to be unconscious when I do it, you'd best stop arguing and be quiet. Toss them over right now."

The metal hit the floor with a clang that must have echoed throughout the entire building. No matter what Chase claimed, he had every reason to lie about the building being empty—and he'd just made a lot of noise.

"Merritt, can you?" she asked, dangling the handcuffs toward him.

Merritt chuckled. "As long as you're ready to shoot him if he tries anything."

"Believe me, I'm ready."

Chase glared at her, and Merritt laughed. "I thought you might be. Turn around, Colonel."

"This is ridiculous." Chase faced the wall and shot her a glare over his shoulder as Merritt applied the cuffs. "What do you think you're doing?"

"What does it look like I'm doing? Merritt and I are getting out of here, and you're going to help us." Avery tapped the pistol against her thigh. "I'm just not quite sure yet how you're going to do that."

He turned to stare blankly at her and Merritt, then burst into laughter.

"I know you've been through a lot, Your Majesty, but I didn't know you were this paranoid. If I didn't know better, I'd say you were part Haederan." He chuckled. "You're wrong though—I'm not going to help you."

He took a step toward her.

Merritt pushed him back a pace.

Avery raised the pistol, level with his head.

"I already have," Chase said.

The pistol dropped, even though she struggled to keep it level.

"What are you talking about?" Her voice shook.

"My lady, you've known for days I'm on your side." All the mockery was gone from his voice. "I got you away from Perrin, let you sit here for much longer than any of us could afford just so

Colonel Rendon could recover, gave you time to take out those soldiers—I can't believe they didn't notice the looks you two were giving each other. I even locked them up for you—and this is what I get?" He shook his hands behind his back. "I didn't expect to be restrained as a thank-you for rescuing you. Or threatened with my own weapon."

"Avery?" Merritt sounded as unsure as she felt. "What's he talking about? What does he mean that he's on your side?"

Oh, no.

Could she have been this wrong about being wrong?

Not capricious, no . . .

"I—" She couldn't answer Merritt's question because she didn't know the answer. She was weak all over, barely able to keep a grip on the gun. "But you—you said—"

"That I was bringing you here to find out where you sent Brennin and your uncle? Did you expect me to tell the governor I was going to walk you two out of their freezer and release you?"

She couldn't cry. She couldn't, even though it was all she wanted to do. The overwhelming relief that washed over her came from somewhere deep down, an instinctive place she couldn't argue with. Chase had helped Merritt. He'd saved her from Victor. He was working with Hadley, and next to Merritt, there was no one she trusted more.

"You terrified me at the ball."

"Not nearly enough, it seems."

"You told me you'd wanted to see me in prison from the moment we met."

Chase shifted and glanced down.

"I did say that, didn't I." His lip twitched. "I had to—how did you phrase it? I had to 'get it out of my system.'" He chuckled, but it didn't sound normal. "You are the enemy, after all. And terrible at reading people," he added, not unkindly.

"That's not fair. It's your job." She smiled, more out of giddy relief than anything else. "Merritt, let him go."

"He could be lying," Merritt countered.

She eyed Chase carefully, but he'd plastered a look of innocence across his face. He was right—she was terrible at reading people. Just like Merritt had always insisted.

Still . . .

"I don't think he is." She took a deep breath. "Merritt—you know he was the one who ordered your transfer to Emot."

"I find that hard to believe." Merritt narrowed his eyes, but understanding dawned in his features. Understanding and pain. Remembrance of things he never wanted to remember. "Why?" he asked Chase.

"You were dying. Why would I stand by and let that happen? Whatever you may think of me, know this—I have never treated a prisoner like Perrin treated you. I find it personally reprehensible."

Merritt's lips thinned as he glanced at her. "That's debatable. But it's also not what I mean. I'm sure you don't take a special interest in every prisoner wronged by the Haederan Army."

"Maybe I do." Chase tried to shrug, but with his hands restrained, the movement was an almost imperceptible twitch.

"We don't have time for this." Avery massaged her temple with her free hand, then reached for Merritt's pistol. "We can debate his intentions later. Just let him go."

"Wait." Chase smiled at her, like they were the only ones there. "I want you to undo them."

"Why?" she asked sharply. "We don't have time for your games."

His smile didn't fade. "Because you don't want to, and I want to see the look on your face when you do it."

Avery clenched her fingers until her knuckles hurt, then handed her pistol to Merritt. No matter what he'd done for her and Merritt, Chase would never change. Ever.

"Where's the key?" she demanded.

"Top right chest pocket." He grinned down at her, oblivious to Merritt's stun pistol pointed at his head.

It was almost impossible to dig through his pocket without

slapping the grin off his face. She removed the handcuffs slower than necessary, then slammed them and the key against his chest. Chase shoved them back in his pocket with one last smirk at her and gestured toward the door.

"Now what's your plan?" Merritt asked.

"I'm going to drive you out the same way you came in."

"And no one's going to stop you?" she asked. Chase was beginning to sound as naïve as she felt.

"How long have you known me, Your Majesty?" He laughed and exchanged a look with Merritt, one she didn't like. "There's no one on Asria with the authority to do so. Besides, they're all a little busy right now."

Avery didn't ask, just followed Chase outside and around the corner to an unmarked Imperial Security transport. Merritt followed, ostensibly to protect her, but it was clear the physical activity had taken a toll. She helped him into the back, and he leaned his head against the side and closed his eyes. It was a thankfully short—and unchallenged—drive away from Alcaris, where Chase stopped on one of the darker streets just outside the base and stepped out.

A chill ran down her spine as she slid across into the driver's seat.

"We'll never get out of the city," she said to Chase. "The checkpoints—"

"You'll get out," he said. "Easily. That revolt you wanted to start? Thanks to you, the city may as well be burning, Your Majesty. It makes the protest the night we met look like a child waving a toy flag around."

"I never wanted—" It was a pointless objection. Avery pressed her lips together, but even that couldn't hide the smile. "You're wrong."

"Like I told you at the ball, you're terrible at playing dumb. I can't believe Perrin's fallen for it all this time." Chase shook his head in mock disapproval, but the laughter in his eyes was pride. "It's the only reason you would have risked Kern's wrath to speak to Major Ferran like you did. And once you get out of town, none of this will matter. You'll be the least of the Haederan Army's worries in—" He checked his chronometer. "I'd say another hour, at the latest. Brennin didn't tell you?"

"Tell me what?"

"Avery." Merritt smiled from the back seat as she turned. "You must have figured it out by now."

Her hand went to her throat.

Of course.

Was she the last to know everything? It explained everything, especially Merritt's timing.

"Kern said it was a trick," she whispered to him, barely believing her own words. "To get Perrin out of my uncle's office. The Commonwealth—they're really on their way here?"

"I'm surprised Perrin could keep his mouth shut about it in that freezer. He must have wanted to keep every shred of hope from you. They've already engaged our fleet on the far side— didn't you hear the interceptors leaving?" Only the fatigue in his eyes hinted at his emotions over the imminent end of his empire's occupation. "Half your fighters just appeared out of nowhere. Like magic. Our navy can't figure how they slipped through our sensors . . . the reports are saying it's almost like the Commonwealth copied our stealth technology."

"Imagine that," Avery said, barely able to keep her voice steady.

"Yes." He gave her a small smile. "Imagine that. Now get out of here. I have two lost prisoners to track down and an interrogation to conduct once I find them."

"Colonel, wait," she said as he turned to go. Her whole body was shaking, but she had to know before the chance was lost forever. "Why did you take those photos at Tarragona? Why did you—"

Chase looked at the ground and sighed, then back to her. "Because as much as I've been trying to keep you out of trouble since you got back here, I knew I wouldn't be able to manage it for long. Once it became clear you weren't going to drop what happened at Tarragona, once Brennin informed me you'd told Major Ferran, once I found out she was so well-connected with multiple resistance groups . . . well, you didn't leave me much of a choice. Whatever was going to happen needed to play out with all the information."

He looked up and down the street and shivered, the snow falling faster and faster around him. "And I couldn't let Perrin get away with what he'd done. Even if the Commonwealth's attack fails tonight, everyone will know the truth."

Snow wafted into the car, settling on her eyelashes as she ran through a dozen different responses. The cold didn't clear her racing mind—or maybe words just weren't adequate for what he'd done.

"It'll never be enough, but thank you," she finally said. "For everything."

Chase gave her a quick salute and walked off into the darkness.

* * *

Merritt had fallen silent hours ago, after patching himself up the best he could with the med kit under the seat, and his soft breathing hinted of a shallow sleep. Avery was quiet too, unwilling to let herself become distracted while driving the dark mountain roads—free of snow now, but still slick. It would only take one wrong move to slide off the ice, and she focused all her attention in front of her.

Until the first streak in the dark sky caught her attention, gold and sparkling among the clouds. The flashes continued as they climbed farther into the mountains, too bright and low to be anything but a space battle, and her breathing became shallow. She'd had no reason to doubt Chase, but *seeing* it happen after so long was something completely different.

"Merritt, are you awake?" She pointed, even though he couldn't see the gesture in the dark. "Look up in the sky."

"I see it," he whispered. "It started twenty minutes ago."

She knew he wished he was up there too, but that desire was lost to her now. Those dreams were lost to her forever, it seemed. Safe. She just wanted to be safe, her and Merritt and the baby.

And so they were silent the rest of the way to Villiers as the flashes continued above them.

CHAPTER THIRTY-THREE

Avery knew it would be impossible to ever forget the look on General Teruel's face when she and Merritt arrived at Villiers. Even with her presence, the security personnel in the airlock had refused them entry until the general had come up to see the situation for himself. He'd immediately escorted her and Merritt downstairs to the detention area.

"It's about time you made it back to explain this, Merritt. I didn't expect a kidnapping when I allowed you out of here." Teruel stared at his former king. Victor was slumped on the floor of a holding cell, asleep. "It, uh, it looks like a trial will be in Mr. Rendon's future after all."

"I'm afraid I can't take credit for this, sir." Merritt grinned in response, amazingly recovered from his ordeal, though Avery was certain the bruises would be even more painful the next day. "It was hardly my idea, but I couldn't say no to her . . . request."

"You couldn't say no to the queen, or to your wife?" Teruel rubbed his forehead, hard. It was likely no one in Villiers had had much sleep in the past few hours. "Never mind—don't answer that. Your Majesty, you might as well meet us in the command center so we can get you up to speed on what's going on up there." He looked back at Merritt and shook his head. "You too.

Congratulations on a successful mission, but we're going to talk about all this when things settle down. In private."

With that, he disappeared into the lift tube, probably to pour himself a stiff drink.

Merritt turned his grin to her. "He'll get over it. In fact, I doubt he'll even remember any of the negatives to what we did when this is all over."

"You hope." She squeezed his hand and laughed. "I'm glad I don't work for him."

She moved to Kern, sitting morosely in the next cell over. His jacket was gone, the laces from his boots confiscated, but it didn't look like they'd harmed him. Wynne, sitting cross-legged next to two guards outside his cell, had a lot to do with that. Still, he looked like he wished someone would give him a sharp knife so he could end his part in this drama. He looked up when her shadow appeared in front of him, but didn't say a word.

Neither did she, for a long time. Then, finally, "Thank you." She had to pull the words out of herself, but she owed him. "I told you I won't forget what you did, and I won't. I'll see that you're released—and repatriated, if that's what you want—as soon as possible."

"You know I can't go back there now."

"Then maybe we can work something out." She didn't have any idea what she could work out with a Haederan officer, but Kern had done nothing terrible on Asria, not really. Maybe not even on Haedera . . . she really had no idea. But the Defense Forces had no real reason to hold him after this all ended. "I'll come see you again when I can. Wynne, stay with him?"

A little of his gloomy exterior faded, and that at least was worth the gamble. With one last threatening glance at the guards, she let Merritt lead her into the next lift tube.

* * *

She caught up with Teruel not in the command center, but in the canteen, pouring himself a cup of coffee. However much he'd had lately, it didn't appear to be helping, and she hated to be the bearer of more bad news. He ran his hands over his eyes as she entered, probably realizing his coffee break was about to be cut short, and held the cup out to her.

Avery shook her head at the deferential offer. "You look like you need it more than I do, sir."

"Especially after what you're about to tell me, if I'm not mistaken."

"How did you—"

"Years of experience." His eyes darted toward the chair beside him, then back at her, as if he hoped she hadn't seen yet another sign of fatigue.

She gestured for him to sit. What use was formal etiquette now? "General Perrin intends to destroy Villiers," she said. "He ordered the destruction of Tarragona himself as a test."

Teruel narrowed his eyes. "Our intel hasn't suggested anything like that. The opposite, in fact—the information that came in tonight suggested Tarragona was the work of disgruntled Haederan Army troops who believe we're not being treated harshly enough. It's definitely a better account than my people being responsible." He rubbed his neck. It hadn't occurred to Avery how personally devastating Perrin's lie would have been for Teruel. "How do you know this?"

"I—" Teruel might pass out if she told him about Chase. "I have a reliable Haederan source."

"How reliable?"

"Beyond reproach."

"Why am I not surprised?" He sighed. "Timeframe?"

"I don't know." Her stomach flipped. How she wished she did. "But I'm concerned Perrin will push his timeline up if he suspects the battle is almost over. Part of this is revenge, and I don't believe he'll just let it go."

"Did this reliable Haederan source indicate how soon evacuation might be required?"

"I really couldn't say." She shook her head once more. "I'm so sorry for the limited information."

"Then I'll discuss this with the team within the next hour. We'll work on finding somewhere safe to send you."

"I'm staying."

"Your Majesty—"

"I'm staying." It wasn't as though there was anywhere safe for her on Asria anymore. Not with Perrin hunting for her. If she died in Villiers, well . . . "And you won't convince me otherwise."

"Understood, Your Majesty." Teruel stood to pour himself another cup of coffee—and pulled a flask from his pocket this time.

* * *

Avery had never been to the command center at Villiers, mostly because the Defense Forces hadn't had access to any worthwhile information over the past year. There'd been a skeleton crew monitoring local transmissions, but they might as well have been incommunicado as far as space was concerned—the Haederans had done too much damage to their satellites and most other transmitting stations, and the ones they hadn't destroyed, they'd controlled since the invasion. One officer at a time had stood continuous watch in the cavernous room at the lowest level of the base, but it was a formality.

Now, with Commonwealth ships able to relay constant data to the surface, the room was once again the nerve center it had been laid out to be. The curved viewscreens that took up three walls were filled with a layout of the Asrian system and beyond, showing the location of each friendly and enemy ship. Personnel hurried from station to station with data too critical to be transmitted any other way.

Avery wandered the room, taking in the status. Merritt flitted from post to post, studiously avoiding Teruel, though she was certain he would report everything he was seeing back to him at some point. There were murmurs back and forth between stations, but the vast majority of the communications took place on headsets—the better for the strategists to concentrate.

Of course, there wasn't much strategy needed today. It was a waiting game now, and her heart skipped a beat each time another Haederan interceptor vanished from the screen. Each red ship was replaced by two more, and with one Commonwealth ship destroyed for each Haederan ship gone, it seemed hopeless. It wasn't the salvation they'd all prayed for over the past year. Besides, it was too difficult to watch death in real time, even the deaths of her enemies. Had Perrin stood on a command ship that first night and watched his son's fighter explode?

She found Teruel in a quiet corner retrieving more coffee from an aide. The general swiveled at her appearance, his eyes bloodshot and drooping.

"I hate to be the one to tell you, Your Majesty," he said, "but it's not going well for the Commonwealth."

She knew that from watching the screens. From the Commonwealth fighters that disappeared and weren't replaced. From the soft conversations that grew quieter and quieter every minute. From the concerned look Merritt had shot her across the room a half hour before. Rumors of mass evacuations were already spreading outside the command center. Villiers, their one safe place on Asria, destroyed soon by Perrin's wrath.

This wasn't how the Commonwealth's arrival was supposed to go. Even Chase had assumed it would be a one-sided battle, that his fleet would be run out of the system before daybreak. He'd said so. Not in so many words, but he'd looked more conflicted than she'd ever seen. How could they both have been so wrong?

"How much longer do you think they can hold out?" she asked.

"Maybe a day." Teruel shook his head. "If they're lucky."

A day.

Her legs turned to rubber. A day until the Commonwealth was run off—or worse, destroyed—and her planet firmly in the hands of the enemy again.

"And then?"

"If *we're* lucky, the Commonwealth retreats, maybe all the way back to Ventana, and we go back to how we were before. If not . . ."

Avery rubbed her eyes. If not, reprisals, executions—and Perrin's plan to destroy Villiers would come to pass.

"I understand," she said. "I think I need to get a little sleep before that happens."

In truth, she was almost dead on her feet, and with Teruel's update . . . well, she needed a good cry. There wasn't any need for her in the command center, anyway. Not now. They'd call her back to sign the surrender. To be taken into custody by the Haederans. She couldn't bear to think about what would happen after that. Right now, she'd just savor her last few hours of freedom.

Of life.

"Your old quarters are empty. But please, let me have someone escort you."

Haederan paranoia was apparently contagious, but Avery was too tired to argue with him. She leaned against the wall while Teruel disappeared to find a security officer who wasn't in the detention area gawking at Victor.

Victor.

Her limbs grew heavy. Her uncle, who had doubtless woken up by this time, and . . . well, she'd stop by and see him later, when she wasn't so fatigued and terrified. When she figured out what she'd say to him. Something harsh. Something hateful.

But if you hate him for what he's done, you're no better than Perrin.

She couldn't revel in what had happened to him, no. Reveling in his failure wouldn't be gracious, and he was still family, after all. A Rendon. The Holy One's child. Once upon a time, even she had loved him.

Murmurs, quiet at first, then louder than anything she'd heard in the command center that day, cut through the hushed silence and her own churning thoughts. Teruel dashed back toward her, and her legs went weak. This was it, what she had feared.

The chatter grew louder as he motioned her to the nearest station without a word. She perched on an extra chair, unable to hold herself up.

"Put them on speaker," Teruel ordered the operator. He leaned closer to the microphone. "Go ahead."

She shook her head, pretending the gesture would stop the horror that was coming. She wasn't ready. They weren't ready. There had to be more time. Just five more minutes of hope before life ended for good.

The faraway beam message crackled as she tried to temper her panic, then steadied.

"Villiers, this is the Commonwealth battle cruiser *Talon*. The Haederan Navy has requested a cease-fire."

* * *

It had taken Teruel the better part of fifteen minutes to get the command center calmed down, after which he'd shuttled Avery and a half-dozen senior officers to a meeting room off to the side of the command center. Behind him, a smaller screen showed the status—still thousands of Haederan and Commonwealth fighters hovering in Asrian space, yes, but they weren't disappearing off the screen any longer. Merritt stood across the room with a tablet in hand, barely able to keep his eyes off her or the grin off his face.

"I don't trust them." Contrary to the temporary peace in space and the celebratory mood in the command center, Teruel looked grave as he addressed the group. "They've sustained minimal damage to their ships, and their surface defenses are intact. I won't say it's a trap, but there's something strange about this."

"Maybe they're tired of fighting," one officer put in.

"The Haederans?" another one argued. "Not likely."

It deteriorated into an argument within thirty seconds, but Avery stood against the wall, silent. Teruel was right—there was something strange about a request for a cease-fire this early in a planetary battle. Had it even been a full day since Perrin had raised the alarm about the Commonwealth entering the system?

Strange.

But strange described the happenings every day on Asria since she'd returned, from Victor's deliberate attempt to murder her, to Chase's borderline-treasonous behavior, to Hadley following her around Cadena, to Kern's—

Kern.

Her eyes widened in realization. Kern hadn't been afraid Wynne would drag him to Villiers at all. He had *wanted* her to. He'd been afraid she *wouldn't*.

"General," she said. "We need to talk to your prisoner. Now."

* * *

For someone who'd just been released from a detention cell, Kern didn't look the least bit grateful. But then, Avery supposed she wouldn't be grateful either, if that temporary freedom came with handcuffs and a group of enemy guards. They deposited Kern in the conference room, and Teruel fixed him with a stare he was probably used to using on unenthusiastic subordinates.

Kern glared back, more annoyed than compliant. It made sense. After working for Chase, there was no possible way Teruel could intimidate him.

"Why is your fleet willing to suspend hostilities after less than a day of fighting?" Teruel asked.

"So soon?" Kern should have looked surprised at the question, but somehow didn't.

"Yes, Captain. 'So soon.' You can see why that's a disquieting turn of events, one we don't quite trust. I think you know what's going on. What are they up to?"

Kern looked at her.

Avery raised her eyebrows at him.

Just talk.

He sighed, his only support having turned on him. "What ship did the request come from?"

"What does it matter which ship requested it?" Teruel narrowed his eyes.

"It matters." Kern didn't look willing to say another word.

Teruel looked at one of the other officers and raised a hand in invitation.

The officer cleared his throat and glanced at his tablet. "Ah, that would be *Ardent*, sir. One of their destroyers. Suspicious as hell that they've taken on absolutely no damage, by the way."

"Then you can consider that request just what it is, General." Right in front of them, Kern sank back into his chair. No . . . not sank. He deflated completely. "This will all be over soon."

Teruel narrowed his eyes. "Care to explain further?"

"I can't, General. Not right now." Kern looked at Avery. "I'm sorry, but someone else will have to do the explaining, Your Majesty."

"Then this someone else needs to show up and explain." Avery gestured at Teruel to hold off more questions. "Where is he?" The last she had seen him, he'd been sauntering off into the dark Cadena streets, probably trying to think of a story to keep Perrin happy.

Please, Holy One, let him be safe.

She blinked. Had she just prayed for Chase's safety?

"I don't know where he is. Somewhere in Cadena, or at least he's supposed to be. I don't know." Kern sat back. The look on his face would have been accompanied by a sullen crossing of his arms if they hadn't been cuffed behind him. "But he's with a friend of yours, and that's all I'm going to say."

Hadley was keeping Chase safe from Perrin?

Avery couldn't help the smile that escaped as she glanced around at the seven sets of eyes staring questioningly at her.

Teruel frowned, but it would take long to explain the entire story, and the Commonwealth was waiting for a reply.

This was it. What they'd all prayed about for so long.

"General, we're going to have to discuss this in much more detail later, but for now—tell the Haederans they have their cease-fire."

CHAPTER THIRTY-FOUR

IT WAS THE STRANGEST COLLECTION OF PEOPLE SHE'D EVER BEEN A part of, this delegation of Commonwealth, Asrian, and Haederan officials congregating to determine if the cease-fire requested by *Ardent* would be extended. In the main senate chamber, where she'd first met Perrin so long ago, Avery sat between Grant Baylen and Admiral Mann, commander of the Commonwealth Navy's Seventh Fleet—the woman who would have been her superior in another life. How things changed.

Perrin cast a glare across the table in her direction, and she wasn't sure if he'd even noticed who was sitting on either side of her, so intent was he on trying to kill her with his eyes. It was difficult to keep from smiling at him, but she managed, just barely. He would never forget she'd shot him, would never forget she and Merritt had thwarted his plans for them both.

"This ludicrous and unsanctioned cease-fire ends in six hours, and I will not authorize an extension." Perrin pounded his fist on the table. "Regardless of whatever coward of a destroyer captain made the initial call, this decision is solely mine to make, and I'm rejecting it. I suggest each one of you be off the surface before the clock runs out. If you know what's good for you, you'll be out of the system, although you don't have much time at this late hour." His glare at Avery grew darker. "That includes you and Colonel Parker. My tolerance for your games has ended."

Avery tried to choke down her sympathy for the Imperial Haederan Navy captain who'd requested the cease-fire. If the temporary peace ended and Perrin had any say in what happened to him, he wouldn't live long. Neither would anyone else, since Perrin clearly intended to make sure this thing dragged out as long as possible. The Haederans would never mutiny against him. Under his orders, they would fight until they had no ships, no interceptors, and no troops left. Was it only his pride at stake by this point? It wasn't as though he wanted Asria for himself. Victor might, but the former viceroy wasn't going anywhere just yet. Anywhere except prison, if she and the senate had anything to do with it.

"No one else wants to see these hostilities continue, General." Admiral Mann leaned forward in her chair, hands folded on the table in front of her. Avery couldn't help a stab of envy at how clean her nails were. "Your own people don't appear to want it. We can keep going the way things are, but it's best for all concerned if we end this quickly and peacefully, right now."

Perrin's face grew red.

Mann held out a hand in appeal. "But as you said, it's your decision."

The long pause that threatened to stretch on for minutes. Avery was certain everyone could hear her heart beating. Or maybe they couldn't, because Perrin's enraged thinking was almost as loud.

"Actually, ma'am, it's not his decision anymore."

She swiveled at Chase's appearance through the main doors. Perrin shot to his feet, even more livid at having been interrupted in his rebuke of the Commonwealth's wishes.

"It isn't your decision, Colonel," he snarled at Chase. He jabbed a finger at Avery. "Are you responsible for this outrage? She should be dead right now. Traitor. Coward."

It wasn't clear if he was speaking of her or Chase. Either way, it was an impressive accusation.

"You're right. It's not my decision." Chase smiled at him, and she was glad it wasn't directed at her. Not a smile like that. Even in the darkest days of her imprisonment, Chase had never looked at her with such coldness. "I'm just the loyal messenger this time."

There must have been an underlying meaning in Chase's words and mocking tone which no one but Perrin understood, because he sat heavily, as pale as the marble floor.

"There's no way he agreed to this," he said under his breath. "It's not possible. His plans were so direct, so specific—he's wanted this forever."

"He didn't. His eldest son and successor did." Chase ignored his sputtering and turned to address Mann and Baylen, his eyes skimming over Avery like she didn't exist. "His Imperial Majesty wishes to inform you that he desires and approves a two-day extension to the cease-fire and requests you further discuss this matter with him directly." His gaze moved to Avery, a familiar expression settling there—but one she hadn't seen in a very long time. The one that meant he was laughing at her on the inside but trying desperately to hide it. "After he speaks with the queen. Alone."

Oh.

She swallowed, everything coming together at once.

The Haederan emperor, the man once so feared across the quadrant, the man who'd orchestrated the attack on her planet and a dozen others, the man responsible for the death of millions . . .

He was dead.

* * *

The six-person flyer landed in the tall grass in the field outside Cadena without even a thump. The snow which had blanketed the city two days before was gone, and a balmy autumn was once again firmly in place. Avery stepped out into the sun and shaded her eyes with a palm, Chase and two Commonwealth security officials behind her. The two Haederans who'd met the flyer briefly but efficiently searched her for weapons. Across the meadow, three Defense Forces officers were doing the same to a middle-aged man standing in front of a larger orbital shuttle. The Haederans nodded at her, and she picked her way across the meadow, through the leftover puddles, toward the emperor.

He wasn't what she'd expected, even though what she'd expected was fuzzy. Instead, it was a mop of brown hair, half-gray and longer than appropriate—a deliberate insult to his militaristic homeland, she suspected. The trimmed beard and expensive dark suit that put Grant Baylen to shame sealed that hunch.

He gave her a slight nod and held out his hand. "Owin. It's a pleasure to meet you, my lady."

"Likewise." She hesitated a moment before taking it. "I'm surprised to see you and not your father." There was nothing left but brutal honesty. There was more of it coming, anyway.

"My father died six months ago." He didn't bat an eye at her frankness. "Murdered, unfortunately."

Avery took a step back. "That—that was not in any of the reports I've seen."

Not that she'd seen much of anything in the past few months. Surely she'd have heard something at Villiers, though. Had Teruel hidden it from her? Had Chase? He must have. What was he playing at now?

"No." Owin smiled. "Even on Haedera, it's been a closely guarded secret. For my safety."

"I see."

"You must understand—"

The smile became lopsided. He cut himself off and began to walk along the shore of the river. Avery followed next to him, the irony of a warm autumn walk with the Haederan emperor shadowing her.

"There are certain factions on Haedera that will never be happy until we've taken the entire quadrant," he went on. "More than the entire quadrant, I sometimes suspect. It's what my father wanted, and it's what they expect from me as well. His death has been kept quiet from all but a few people, so I could do what I felt needed to be done. That secret ended this morning when my succession was announced on Haedera."

"And what did you feel needed to be done?"

"This goes no farther than the two of us." The emperor exhaled. "Thaopra and Hanides were not liberated by the Commonwealth. Not exactly, anyway. Yes, there was a battle for each planet, but they were both skirmishes. In short: we let them go. Your fleet couldn't have put up a proper fight if they'd wanted to."

If he was telling the truth, then the Commonwealth was in as bad of a condition as the rumors said. But did it matter? Two friendly, innocent planets liberated—however it had happened, it was good news.

"And Asria?" It was hard to hide her disdain for his phraseology. "Are we being 'let go?'"

His lips curved; his eyes did not.

"Asria has been a little more complicated. I had to make sure the Commonwealth knew there was no need for prolonged violence in the skies here without allowing most of my own forces to know the same. It's my understanding you know the operative who was able to get that information to them."

Hadley.

Hadley would have been able to contact the Commonwealth after they arrived in the Asrian system. And Chase had been the one to talk him into doing it, though how Chase had convinced Hadley to do anything . . .

Owin's lips thinned. "But this is only a cease-fire for now, my lady. Not a surrender. It will never be a surrender, even if it means this fight continues for the next thousand years." His eyes hardened as they met hers. "We will never give Asria up. You're hardly an uninhabited planet like most of the others. Not one that I can justify losing permanently. That kind of leniency would be too much of a risk to my authority. To my life."

The warm meadow suddenly chilled.

"Then what are you doing here?"

He stopped and faced her. "Call it an armistice, if you don't want peace with us. Call it what you will. But I'm going to give you a choice. I will leave you alone to rule Asria—with a provisional senate, if you're so inclined. In return, you'll allow the holdover of a small number of Haederan troops on Asria—nothing you haven't allowed of the Commonwealth. You'll agree to diplomatic relations between our two planets, regardless of any prior agreements with the Commonwealth. Last, you'll allow specific economic activities of ours to continue here."

The verium mining. Would they ever give that up? *Your verium doesn't matter anymore,* she wanted to scream at him. Surely he knew that.

"That's not freedom."

"It's more freedom than you have now."

"We could continue to fight." Her spine stiffened. It was the easy decision. One both the senate and Commonwealth would expect her to make. There was still a bit of Commonwealth officer left in her, after all. "That option still exists."

"You could." The emperor picked up a rock and skipped it into the river. "But we both know the Commonwealth is fatigued. Your own forces are in even more disarray. You may have taken down some of our remote ground sensors, but you can't organize any kind of significant orbital offense. In over a year, you haven't even been able to establish a significant resistance movement. That revolt the other night? The one I'm told you had a hand in? It's already been quashed, both in Cadena and Tarragona."

Her eyes went wide. There'd been an uprising in Tarragona as well? In her most fantastic dreams, she hadn't thought it would spread there. And what other cities that Owin didn't know about? Failed uprising or not, the seeds of rebellion had been laid.

"You know what you're up against, my lady." Owin's expression hardened. Clearly, he'd taken her reaction for disappointment. "Do you want to take that chance?"

Yes.

She did. She wanted them to pay for what they had done, down to the last man.

"I don't see a downside to this agreement." He skipped another rock. "For anyone."

"Especially you."

He lowered his head briefly in acknowledgement, and she watched him toss another half-dozen rocks in silence. At least he was honest about the fact his proposal had major upsides for him as well.

Holy One, what would you have me do?

It would be so easy to say no.

So easy to send this Haederan back to whatever ship he'd come from.

So easy to keep fighting.

So easy to make the Haederans pay for what they had done.

To avenge those who had died during the invasion and at Tarragona. All those regular citizens who'd met their end at the hands of the Imperial Security Command. Even—she'd almost forgotten his name, but his face was seared into her mind—even Jon Gavni, executed by Perrin so early on, just to make a point to her. Wasn't revenge what she'd wanted since the invasion? Didn't the lives of all those people matter? Could she live with herself if the Haederans didn't atone for what they'd done?

Revenge comes from the Most High, not you. Even with what Victor did to Asria and to you. One day you'll see.

Drex might be gone, but his words would always be with her. And the Commonwealth had suffered losses. She had watched those white dots disappear off the viewscreens at Villiers, each one signifying the death of one or two Commonwealth pilots. The battle over Asria hadn't yet begun, not really. The Defense Forces couldn't mount an effective offense, just as the emperor said. His military was also tired, and it was always possible the Commonwealth could perform a miracle, but it would be fighting over nothing. Death for no reason.

And there had been too much death already.

Avery picked up one of the gray rocks by the river's edge, worn smooth by its journey down from the Gallis Mountains. The stone was weathered and eroded and worn in the most violent of ways, but still beautiful. Still—still useful, in some ways. Owin skipped another rock, silent, as she ran a finger along the edge of hers.

"Taln Perrin must answer for what he's done here," she said to him. "The Asrian way—I will not accept his execution as punishment. That is nonnegotiable. And the Commonwealth may have other ideas for Asria. They may not agree to an armistice."

She skipped her rock into the river. It would be Admiral Mann's decision in the end. Wouldn't it?

It's yours, Your Majesty. Yours and Baylen's, and he's just as tired of war as you are. He'll understand if you make the call now.

"We can discuss his fate later. As for the Commonwealth, they will not continue to fight over a planet that doesn't want continued war," Owin said.

It wasn't what she wanted to hear about Perrin, but she'd wear Owin down on that one eventually.

"While I am not opposed to diplomatic relations"— she picked up another rock—"Asria has agreements and treaties in place that prevent such a relationship."

"That is your problem to work out with them. Although I am certain," he said, brushing dirt from his hands, "that those agreements and treaties can be amended. I hear you're rather persuasive when you want to be."

Avery gave him a slight smile. "I'm less certain of what they will allow, but prior to the senate being reinstated, I will bring the issue to their attention." A shiver started on her scalp and worked its way downward. "That is, if the Haederan Empire will guarantee my safety from Haederan interests in transit to Ventana."

Owin chuckled. "You didn't find your stay aboard the *Imperieuse* to your liking? I would imagine not—Lord Chase said you were rather displeased with the whole affair. We can make sure that doesn't happen again, of course. I can even provide you with an escort, if you'd prefer."

Lord Chase?

Her mouth opened, then shut. She glanced back at the Asrian aeroflyer, where Chase looked to be in deep conversation with one of the Commonwealth officers who'd accompanied them. She wrinkled her nose at him, wishing he could read her displeasure from across the meadow, then turned her confused gaze back to Owin.

Owin laughed out loud that time. "I'm sorry. Gareth hates the title, but his distaste makes it all the more fun to use. He considers it a boyhood taunt, even though his title wasn't given until his marriage. More than that, he feels it restricts some of his more clandestine domestic work. He and my father had a dreadful row over it years ago." He lifted his shoulders. "No matter. He's much more useful to us off-world anyway, as I know you're well aware."

Her blank stare was making her look like an imbecile, and there was nothing she could do to break it except scowl at Chase's back again.

"Ah." Owin laughed again, louder that time. "He didn't tell you any of it. Typical—Gareth's always been the secretive one." He motioned her forward, and they resumed their walk up the river. "He grew up in my father's court as a favor to his parents. They hoped to make an easy life for him through his mother's family connections, but he went his own way instead. I'm not sure why we were surprised when he chose Imperial Security. But make no mistake—his career was built entirely on his own merit. I'm sorry your paths crossed like they did, but to hear him tell it, you've given him almost as much hell as he's given you."

"That certainly explains his personality."

"The anti-authority complex?" Owin asked. She bit her lip at the ruthless accuracy, and he grinned. "You'd think so, but no. That's just Gareth. Always has been." He shook his head, and his smile slipped. "From the start, we've been more like brothers instead of distant cousins. For my sister, it eventually became even closer."

Chase was married to the emperor's daughter? Surprising news, yes, but somehow the revelation didn't strike her as strange as it should have.

Why?

"I was sorry to hear about her," she said automatically. Carina's etiquette lessons were finally paying off. "It was a great loss for you and him."

The sudden realization slammed into her.

Merritt.

That was the real reason Chase had been so protective of him. The reason he'd saved Merritt's life more than once. It hadn't been a game after all. Not a display of his power, not boredom, not anything malicious. Chase was tied unwillingly to circumstance and his planet's royal family, just like Merritt was now. How much of Merritt did Chase see in himself?

"She's somewhere the pain can't touch her any longer." He shrugged. "And we've all lost people, no?"

"We have." No sooner had she replied than the full meaning of Chase's identity hit her like lightning, tearing into her heart. It'd been horrifying enough before, but now—her hand met her mouth as a vile feeling welled up in her chest. "Your father murdered his own grandson," she blurted without thinking.

"I know." Something, not quite sadness, touched his eyes. "I think Gareth will forgive him—though I have no idea how."

Avery had scarcely opened her mouth to reply when a shout cut across the meadow. She flinched at the sound, but Owin didn't move, his eyes focused on two men in civilian clothes heading across the meadow. His personal security, it had to be, because Chase was behind them. She took a step away from the emperor, memories of the invasion all too clear, but they stopped in front of Owin and nodded respectfully at her.

"Sire," the heavy one in the darker suit said. "I'm sorry to interrupt, but he—" He gave a quick glance over his shoulder at Chase. "He thought you'd want to know immediately." He swallowed. "General Perrin is dead, sire."

Avery moved forward a pace. Surely not—surely it must be a mistake.

"There was a disturbance outside one of the senate aeroflyer sites," Chase said, stepping around the guard. "The general was attempting to take his personal aeroflyer. Security personnel confronted him and reminded him he was not to leave Cadena while negotiations were ongoing. There was a scuffle, and when they tried to relieve him of his weapon, he turned it on himself. I'm sorry, sire."

Avery caught her reflection in a small puddle. Her expression hadn't changed. How was it possible to feel relief and sorrow at once?

"That's a convenient story, Gareth." Owin's expression had turned stony. "When may I expect the army's report to be available?"

"You can't. It was Imperial Security who confronted him, sir."

Chase met her eyes, but she couldn't read his expression. Guilt? A confession? An apology? She couldn't tell—and he never would. There was silence, except the howl of the wind and the water washing upon the shore.

"That doesn't answer my question, Colonel." Owin's voice was hard. "Did someone allow him to do this?"

Chase cleared his throat. "I wasn't there, sire. I'm afraid I don't have details, but you'll have our full report tomorrow."

"I look forward to reading it." Owin sighed. "What's done is done. May the Holy One have mercy on him." He looked at Avery. "Well. What do you say we head back now and work out the details of the armistice with the others?"

She nodded. "That sounds perfect."

CHAPTER THIRTY-FIVE

No matter what kind of fuss the palace security people had put up when they'd moved in, Merritt's small row house was the perfect place to hole up while repairs to the palace were completed. Sabino was out of the question and would be for some time, and Avery had vetoed all suggestions for a temporary home on a Defense Forces base. But the drafty old house allowed her, Merritt, Wynne, and a few servants to live in relative comfort, and that was just fine with her.

"I'm not getting off this chair for the rest of the night." She kicked her feet up on a stool and scowled at them. "I don't think I could, even if I wanted to."

"I'm sure you could." Merritt grinned. "You look wonderful."

"You're supposed to say that because you're my husband."

"I'm saying it because it's the truth and because I love you." He perched on the arm of the sofa and ran a hand through her hair. "And you know, all's not lost. There are always things we can do even if you refuse to get up." His mouth met her earlobe. "Like this . . ." A hand moved lower. "Or maybe this . . ."

Wynne tapped a light hand on the doorframe. "I'm sorry, Your Majesty, but Colonel Chase is downstairs. He says it's urgent, and that you'd want to see him immediately."

"He's alone?" she asked sharply. Alone, he was still unwelcome, but not as unwelcome as he'd be with a group of his officers. No matter how much they'd helped, she'd never forget waking up to see Kern in her room.

"Of course he's alone." Wynne looked vaguely offended. "He wouldn't have been allowed through the outer perimeter if he wasn't. I can ask him to leave, if you'd like."

Yes, I'd like. But Chase would only turn up again and again until he got whatever he wanted from her.

"No, that's all right. I'm sorry. Tell him I'll be down shortly." She looked at Merritt, then pushed herself off the chair, even though she wanted to plant herself in the velvet and never leave. "I'd love to keep him waiting for at least an hour, but the sooner I get this over with, the better."

"Want company?" he asked.

"Yes." Avery laughed shakily from the top of the stairs as she slipped on a pair of shoes. "But what I *don't* want is for him to see I'm still terrified of him. You can come rescue me soon." She hobbled downstairs to greet Chase, who was waiting just inside the front door, flanked by two palace guards.

"Congratulations," he said, by way of hello.

"It's a little early for congratulations, but thank you."

"You're quite welcome." He held out a small box. "For you."

Avery took it with tentative hands. "Did they look inside this?"

Chase laughed. "It's only a baby gift, Your Majesty, but yes. If it makes you feel any better, it and I were thoroughly searched."

"Then thank you for this too." Her feet and hips were already aching—and if her ears weren't mistaken, Merritt was running a bath upstairs. "Wynne told me you have news?"

"Yes. I thought you'd be interested to know that I have a new position."

He was looking forward to telling her his news; the taunting glint in his eyes gave him away. Avery tilted her head, gripping the box as hard as she could. What had Hadley said about Chase's next assignment, so long ago?

"Head of your Interstellar Counterintelligence Division, if I'm not mistaken," she replied. "I hope you'll be wildly unsuccessful."

That felt good, if not regal or grateful. But Chase was still Chase, and she was nowhere near forgetting.

"Thank you." He looked faintly shocked by that knowledge, or maybe her brashness. "I think. But your information is quite dated." His frown turned into the smile she dreaded, the smile that meant he was about to surprise her with something she would hate. "I turned that down in favor of one that makes better use of my skills. It's temporary, of course, but I think you'll find it interesting."

Avery waited for specifics, but he didn't continue.

Fine. I'll play your game.

"Then I hope it's something that requires you to be on the next courier ship off Asria. Tomorrow morning, perhaps?" *I could help you pack.*

Merritt's steps sounded behind her, and the tension in her shoulders eased as he appeared next to her.

"You would love that, wouldn't you? No, I'm sorry to disappoint, but it looks like I'll be remaining in Cadena for a while." Chase smiled again. "I'm the new cultural attaché at the Haederan embassy on Asria." He held up a hand before she could say a word. "I know, I know. The position itself is a slight demotion, I'll admit, but it should prove—educational."

Beside her, Merritt coughed down a laugh, or maybe a snort. It was hard to tell through the haze of shock. The only thing she could tell was the blood had drained from her face and Chase was laughing.

Laughing at her.

"Cultural—what—you—you know nothing about Asria!"

Her mouth kept moving, but no sound came out, and she finally closed it. It couldn't be true. Someone had *permitted* this?

Someone was *allowing* him to stay on the planet? He should have been long gone. She should have known . . .

Chase stopped laughing just long enough to reply. "That reaction," he said, "made it worth delivering the news in person."

"I'll fight this. You can expect a protest to be filed with your ambassador first thing tomorrow."

His smile didn't fade at her threat. "You won't do that," he said. "Do you remember that favor I did for you? The one I said you would owe me for? I'm sure you remember it well—I certainly do. I think it's time I collect the payment for it. And all you have to do is . . . nothing." He watched in amusement as she stood wordless, a flush spreading across her cheeks. "Well, I won't take up any more of your time tonight, Your Majesty. I hope you have a wonderful evening." He gave Merritt a polite nod. "Colonel."

The guards followed him out, and Avery stared at the closed door until Merritt's arm wound around her waist. She turned her stare to him, wide-eyed.

"Can you believe the nerve of that man? He may as well have shown up and introduced himself as Haedera's head spy on Asria."

Merritt managed to control his voice, but his eyes still laughed. "But that would break his cover, and then you would be within your rights to ask him to leave the planet."

"You're laughing at me."

"Never." He pulled her closer, and she had to lean back to look at him. "You know he's only trying to frighten you. Or something."

"Well, he succeeded. He's going to be living in Cadena!" It was a nightmare come true. "I don't suppose there's anything I can do about it."

"Probably not. You can file an objection with the Haederan ambassador, but what did he mean about a favor?"

"There are some things you don't want to know." She covered her eyes with a hand. Chase had finally done it, though this wasn't even close to the kind of favor she'd been worried about. "Let's just say he let me off easy, if my endorsement of his new job is all he wants."

Merritt frowned at her less-than-forthcoming explanation. "What did he mean about a favor, Avery?" he repeated.

She looked at the box in her hands, then up at Merritt and swallowed. "I promised him a favor in return for . . . lives."

Please don't ask me for details.

Merritt stared at her, seeming to debate with himself.

"Then I'm proud of you," he finally said. "I know he's impossible to deal with and brings back all sorts of memories, but he'll have to go home eventually. And for whatever it's worth, you know we're doing the same thing on Haedera. So's the Commonwealth. We know it, they know it, and the Haederans know it. It's just another spy game, love—something I think you may know a thing or two about."

"Merritt."

He pressed a finger against her lips. "And I hate to say it, but . . ."

"We're better off with him than someone else?"

"The enemy you know."

"You have to be all logical."

"Logical, that's me. Let's go back upstairs," he said, and kissed her forehead. She closed her eyes, and the kiss moved lower. "You owe me a dance."

EPILOGUE

At first glance, it seemed an odd monument, this white obelisk in the middle of nowhere. But it was said to be where some of the first Haederan bombs had fallen to the Asrian surface another lifetime ago. Time stole so much—but it also gave so much.

Merritt circled the pillar with a discriminating eye. Flowers surrounded it, placed there by mourners, of course, since not much grew in this windswept valley east of the Gallis Mountains. He picked up a few wild cylva blooms which had been scattered by the ceaseless wind, then sat on one of the stone benches, his own bundle across his lap. The implants in his legs hadn't taken kindly to the long flight from Cadena, nor to their current arid surroundings.

But he *had* flown here, making the flight the doctors had insisted he'd never be able to make, and that new ability meant solitude. Time alone with his thoughts.

"I wish this hadn't been necessary," he said out loud, knowing how foolish the wish was. Time flowed on, and you couldn't slow it or stop it. Avery had said the same thing just a few weeks ago when they'd visited her parents' grave outside Sabino.

But the time for mourning was almost over, wasn't it? So much death, so much pain, and yet there was so much hope. He saw it in Lucas's deep blue eyes and Avery's brilliant smile and in the small ways his planet healed each day. Time flowed on, and for now, it brought joy.

"Mama!"

The shrill yell of a toddler cut through his thoughts. A small child, around a year old, was just cresting the top of the hill, her mother behind her. She fell to the ground when she noticed him and began to cry, reaching up for him.

"Grace, leave the nice man alone." The woman picked her up and rocked her on her hip, but the crying didn't cease.

"Do you mind if I try?" Merritt asked. He hadn't realized how hard it would be to be away from Lucas for just a few hours.

"I don't want to impose." The woman looked at him warily, but relief at his offer seemed to overwhelm the suspicion. "She gets like this sometimes."

"It's no problem." He knew the relief of handing a screaming child off to someone else. "My wife had our first last week. A boy."

He smiled in remembrance. He'd wanted a daughter, but he'd fallen completely and utterly in love with his son. An everyday miracle, everyone kept telling him, but somehow it was different when it was your own.

She handed the child over. The tears stopped immediately, and the girl patted his cheeks and laughed.

Merritt laughed back. "See? There's nothing to cry about. The sun is shining, your mama loves you, and you've learned early how to wrap men around your finger."

"Thank you." The woman sat too, but kept her distance. Did she know who he was? No, she wasn't Asrian, and the baby looked even more foreign. Almost . . . unless he was mistaken, she looked almost Haederan. The upper-class kind that was hard to find on Asria anymore. There had to be a story there, but he'd never ask.

She noticed his interest in her daughter and took the baby

from him with a frown. The child gurgled with happiness, her prior outburst forgotten.

"I heard a Haederan paid for the monument," she said casually, her arms tightening around the child. "Can you believe that?"

Oh, yes, he believed the rumor—because he was one of the very few who knew it was the truth. It had been his idea, a use for the money the Asrian government had given him as compensation for his time as a Haederan prisoner. It was laughable really, since as he'd pointed out to Avery, the Asrian government had been supporting him since he'd entered the Defense Forces and would support him for the rest of his life as prince consort anyway. If the Defense Forces medical board decided he could keep flying, they'd be supporting him double. He didn't need the money, and what better use for it than a memorial?

But on the day he was to have made the first payment, Avery's accountant had called. *Someone else has already paid in full,* she'd said. Merritt had pushed her for a long time before she'd admitted a Haederan officer had shown up the day before with a valid credit chip for the entire amount. He'd been Imperial Security, she'd said, and even though the war had officially ended, she'd been too frightened of him to ask questions. Certainly she hadn't told him no when he'd insisted. After hearing that story, Merritt hadn't needed to ask questions of his own. He'd immediately tracked down the offending party at the Haederan embassy.

Chase had barely denied what he'd done.

Avery would be . . . well, furious would be an understatement if she ever found out. He had the nagging feeling he should tell her, but some things were better left alone, weren't they? And if Chase felt guilty enough about what he'd done to spend this kind of money on a monument to Asrians, he wasn't going to be the one to turn it into an interstellar diplomatic issue.

"I keep hearing that rumor too," he said with a laugh. It *was* kind of funny, if you tried not to think about the not-so-generous things Chase had done. "But I have it on good authority that the queen's husband paid for it himself."

At least the queen's husband had had every intention of paying for it himself before a meddlesome Haederan got involved, and he would stick to that story until the day he died.

"I figured it was just a story. It didn't sound like something a Haederan would do." She turned pensive and stared off past the obelisk at the mountains in the distance. Merritt had the uncomfortable sense she was looking into the past. "But they're not all bad, you know."

He looked down at the girl, who was on her hands and knees drawing circles in the dirt with that intent look only a child could have.

"What happened to him?" he asked, taking a guess.

Her eyes widened, like he'd accused her of something worse than treason, then she shrugged. "It's a long story. Him, her, being here on Asria. All of it." For a moment he was afraid she was going to cry, but she smiled. "But if I could love him, then maybe . . ." She shrugged again and tried to smile. "I don't know."

Could love him? The girl's father was yet another casualty of this war, then.

"Then maybe we can all move past this eventually." Sensing she wanted privacy with those thoughts, he stood. "I need to get back home. I hope you find what you're looking for here."

"Your Highness?"

Merritt sighed to himself, resigned, then plastered on a fake smile, the one Avery always laughed at. Anonymity truly was just a dream now, if even this off-worlder knew who he was.

"Congratulations on the baby." The woman glanced at her own with adoration. "Maybe they'll do everything better than we did."

"I hope so." Merritt gave the child one last wave as he headed back to the flyer.

Holy One, I hope so.

ACKNOWLEDGMENTS

Unbroken Fire is the book that almost didn't happen, a thousand times over. Thanks to Beth, Kate, Meghan, Hope, Amber, and Christi . . . it did.

ABOUT THE AUTHOR

Anne Wheeler grew up with her nose in a book but earned two degrees in aviation before it occurred to her she was allowed to write her own. When not working, moving, or writing her next novel, she can be found planning her next escape to the desert—camera gear included. She currently lives in Georgia with her husband, son, and herd of cats.

For more information:
www.anne-wheeler.com

ALSO BY ANNE WHEELER

'Last Mission'

The Brightest Void
Vortex

Crownkeeper

Crownkeeper Novellas
Treason's Crown
War's Crown
Queen's Crown

Shadows of War
Asrian Skies
Unbroken Fire
Shattered Honor
Faded Embers

The Star Realm Saga
The Stars Wait Not
A House of Nebulas

www.ingramcontent.com/pod-product-compliance
Lightning Source LLC
Chambersburg PA
CBHW021809110726
47902CB00006B/1707